THE RESOLUTE MATE

KIRA NIGHTINGALE

ÉDITIONS SPOTTISWOODE

DEDICATION AND TRIGGER WARNINGS

Dedication

This book is dedicated to my awesome readers who cheered me on and celebrated each and every milestone with me. To my amazing family who supported my long working hours, made me tea and brought me cookies – you guys are the best! And to my parents—thank you for agreeing to never read my books :)

Trigger Warnings

This book contains some adult themes and lots of spice. There are characters dealing with grief in this story as well as references to domestic violence.

Published by Éditions Spottiswoode

First edition 2024

ISBN (ebook): 978-1-7382838-7-3

ISBN (paperback): 978-1-7382838-6-6

CONTENTS

Chapter One

MAI

"He's late," Ryan growled, his deep voice barely above a whisper.

I drummed my fingers on the worn wooden table, my gaze darting between Ryan and the entrance of Bottley Bar. It felt good to be back here, despite the reason why. My best friend, Sofia, had made this place into a safe haven for Shifters and humans alike. It was a space where people could socialize, share gossip, and connect with friends. I'd already overheard a group of four Shifters arrange to take some meals to Mrs. Adlow, a human who, according to their worried voices, had fallen while gardening and broken her arm. Under Oliver, the old Alpha, Shifters and humans never mixed. It was good to know that when my brother, Jem, took over, he changed that.

I glanced around at the rest of the Bar. Being a coffee shop during the day and a bar in the evening, the furniture had to fit both clienteles. Not easy to pull off, but Sofia had done it with style. The mismatched armchairs and loveseats, upholstered in warm shades of burgundy and forest green, were arranged in cozy clusters around low coffee tables. The tables, made of rich, dark wood, bore the marks of countless cups and glasses, but they gave each table character, a lived-in feel that made this place feel more like a home away from home rather than a sterile shop.

Along one wall, a sturdy wooden bar stood sentinel, its surface worn smooth by years of use. Behind it stood an impressive array of liquor bottles, their amber and crystal hues promising a myriad of flavors and possibilities. Shelves to the left of the bar were lined with an eclectic mix of books and board games, inviting patrons to linger and explore. Potted plants, lush and verdant, were scattered throughout the space, adding a touch of nature that our wolf sides yearned for.

The morning crowd hummed around us, a mix of humans and Shifters, each absorbed in their own world, unaware of the tension knotting between me and Ryan.

I leaned back, my gaze coming back to the door. "I'm pretty sure Ronnie operates on his own time."

Ryan's jaw clenched. He hated waiting, hated not being in control. And he especially hated dealing with Ronnie Bishop.

As I scanned the room, my eyes landed on Sofia behind the bar. She was hard to miss; her curly red hair was a fiery beacon. She moved with an effortless grace, serving customers with a smile that didn't quite reach her eyes today. I knew that smile; it was the one she wore when her mind was miles away, probably worrying about her brother, Jase.

Sofia caught my eye and gave a subtle nod, her way of letting me know she was there if we needed her. She had been through hell and back with us, and I was fucking lucky to have her as my friend. Sofia turned to hand a tray of drinks to Julie, one of the waitresses who worked here.

Ryan leaned back in his chair, his gaze flickering between the door, the room, and me. That was Ryan—always assessing for threats. Anyone who walked into the bar and didn't already know who he was, would have had no trouble in clocking him as the most dangerous person in here. It wasn't just his physical presence—though that certainly was impressive with his six-foot two frame, taut muscles honed from hours upon hours of training and fighting, dark hair, and smouldering blue eyes that could pin you in place with one look—no, it was the way he emanated strength and menace. When Ryan walked into a place, everyone knew it. A deep inner instinct put you on alert, urged you to run because you were in the presence of an apex predator at his peak. It didn't help that he'd been on edge since Ronnie Bishop's call this morning. Ryan did not like Ronnie, a human leader of a bike gang. Ronnie dealt in information and the last time we met, Ryan had been appalled at how much Ronnie knew about our Shifter world and what was going on in the local Packs. He also didn't like the way Ronnie looked at me, although Ronnie seemed to be much more focused on Shya, the daughter of the Bridgetown Pack Alphas. I understood his need to shield me from everything, especially with his wolf urging him to protect me at all costs. Our mate bond was still so new, and it didn't help that I'd recently been kidnapped by my ex, Seth, and had a sociopathic werewolf, Carl, try to kill me. But I didn't want Ryan—or the Pack—to see me as weak. That I couldn't handle myself and had to rely on my mate all the time. I was stepping into some pretty big fucking shoes. This Pack had been Jem's. Everyone was looking at me to see if I could live up to the Parker name.

The bell above the door jingled, snapping me out of my thoughts. Ronnie Bishop sauntered in, his presence shifting the atmosphere of the room. Sofia's gaze flicked towards him, a flash of recognition—and something else, maybe caution—crossing her features before she turned her attention back to the customers.

I watched as Ronnie made his way through the bar, his eyes locked on ours. There was an air of confidence about him that bordered on arrogance, the kind that came from knowing too much and fearing too little. Ryan's posture stiffened, his protectiveness over me flaring up like a warning signal.

"It's go time," I whispered.

Ronnie's eyes found mine as he approached, a smirk playing on his lips.

Ryan leaned forward and put his arms on the table. His muscles bulged, and the green sheen that flared in his eyes whenever he was angry, flashed in warning. He was pissed and was letting Ronnie know about it.

Ronnie slid into the chair opposite us. "Mai, Ryan," he greeted, his voice smooth as silk. "Thanks for meeting me on such short notice."

I forced a smile. "You said it was important."

"It is. I'm here to call in my favor. I'm being framed."

Ryan frowned. "Really? You mean there are some things you don't do?"

Ronnie's eyes darkened. "Actually yes. I don't deal in ripple. But someone is making it look like I do."

The word sent a shiver down my spine. Ripple: the drug that had been wreaking havoc in the Shifter community. First down south and in the conclave cities—those joint human and Shifter cities—and now up north. There were no big cities up here but we had human-only and Shifter-only towns and those, like ours and Bridgetown, where the two mixed together. Ripple was the first drug that affected Shifters and it was spreading like wildfire.

Ryan scoffed. "And you expect us to believe that?"

"Yeah, I do." Ronnie said, glaring at Ryan. "I got no reason to lie. I won't touch the stuff and don't let anyone under me touch it either. My guys know the rules. We deal in pretty much everything else, but we don't go near ripple."

"I didn't see you as a person with a line. Let me guess, it's not so much the drug as you being worried the Packs will come after you?"

Ronnie's face stayed relaxed. "You can think what you want, Ryan. I didn't come here looking for your approval. You're right, though. I know the Alphas up here are getting real antsy about this stuff. They're looking hard at where it's coming from and who's involved. And it's not just them. My contacts say the Wolf Council is interested and is snooping around. I ain't a fool. I know how the Council deals with anyone they deem a threat."

He wasn't wrong. The Wolf Council was our governing body, overseeing all werewolf Packs in North America. Although they gave the Packs a lot of freedom, they were ultimately responsible for maintaining order among the Packs, enforcing laws, and keeping the peace between Shifters and humans. They feared a war between our species above all else and were known to be ruthless in shutting down any threat to the Packs, the Council, or the current status quo between us and humans.

I studied him, trying to gauge his sincerity. "Why come to us?"

"Because you owe me a favor," Ronnie reminded us. "And I need someone with your... connections to help me clear my name. If a Pack clears me, it might hold off the Council from declaring war on me and my businesses."

Ryan and I exchanged a glance. Ronnie was right, we did owe him. He'd given us vital information a few days ago about Tristan's planned attack on the Bridgetown Alphas, Michael and Camille. We'd used this information to stop the attack and prevent Tristan from taking over the Bridgetown Pack. It meant we now had a friendly Pack on our borders, and not one that was working with Brock to destroy us. Plus, we were running our own investigation into ripple. I'd seen first-hand the effects ripple had on Shifters. Last week, we'd gone with Michael to meet one of his Pack, Arabella, who'd started taking the drug. In less than two weeks, she'd gone from a vibrant, happy, ambitious young woman to a shell of a creature; sunken eyes, shallow skin, thinking only of her next hit, and completely unable to Shift to her wolf form. It was devastating for her and her sister, Noreen. If this was replicated throughout our communities, Shifters would be decimated within two years.

Helping Ronnie was a no-brainer. Following this thread could give us another lead and direct us to the real suppliers behind the ripple crisis. It was an opportunity we couldn't ignore.

"What do you need from us?" I asked.

Ronnie leaned back, his gaze calculating. "Find out who's framing me. I have my suspicions, but I need proof. I'll deal with it from there."

I nodded. "Okay. In the meantime, I have another favor to ask."

Ryan tensed. He was not happy about this, but he knew me well enough to know I was going to ask Ronnie for this. We had to use every resource we had, even if that meant owing Ronnie even more.

"Yeah?" Ronnie raised an eyebrow.

"My brother Jem. Brock called three days ago. Said Jem was alive, and that Brock is the only person who knows where he is. He wants... something important in return for the information." I wasn't about to tell Ronnie all of our secrets. Knowing him, he'd find out himself soon, anyway. "We have four days to give it to him."

"And you want me to find Jem first?"

"I want to know if Brock is telling the truth. Is Jem still alive? Or is it all bullshit?"

Ryan tapped a finger against the table. "Brock will call back. Probably in the next couple of days. When he does, he'll expect us to ask for proof of life. We need to know if whatever proof he gives us is the real deal or not. And we need to know where Brock is keeping Jem so we can get to him before we have to hand over the thing he wants."

My heart skipped a beat. Brock's claim that my brother was alive had been haunting me since we heard it. Ryan's brothers were all trying to find Jem, as well as track down the source of the drugs coming into our territory. Having Ronnie use his contacts and resources as well gave us the best chance of finding Jem. If he was alive. I had to keep reminding myself that Brock's claim was probably bullshit, but the tiny spark of hope that it had ignited was proving hard to ignore.

Ronnie rubbed a hand over his jaw. "Brock hates you." He looked at Ryan. "He's consumed by his hatred. Right now, all he wants is revenge. You killed his dad, and he needs to make you pay. Even if you give him what he wants, he'll probably kill Jem anyway."

"All the more reason for us to find Jem, if he is alive, before the timer runs out."

Ronnie nodded. "Understood. I'll see what I can do." He stood, his chair scraping against the floor. "I'll be in touch."

As he left, the tension in the air eased slightly, but it was far from gone. Ryan ran a hand through his hair, his expression dark.

"I don't trust him," he said flatly.

"I know," I replied, my mind racing. "But he's a resource we can't afford to ignore."

Ryan's blue eyes met mine, filled with a mix of frustration and resolve. "I'd do anything for you. For this Pack. If Jem is alive, we'll find him," he said. "I promise."

Chapter Two

Mai

Sofia waved at Ryan and me from behind the counter as we made our way to the exit.

"Call me later!" she called out.

I smiled and gave a wave back, pushing open the heavy wooden door, and hearing the bell jingle. The morning air was crisp and fresh, filled with the scents of pine and maple. I took a deep breath, savoring the smells. I still couldn't believe we were here, back in Three Rivers.

Ryan and I headed to his sleek, black pickup, parked just down the street. I could feel the eyes of everyone on us as we walked, their curiosity overwhelming. Ever since Ryan and I had been publicly announced as the new Alpha pair, we'd been getting plenty of speculative looks and hushed whispers from Pack members.

It made sense. For years, Jem and Hayley had led the Three Rivers Pack. Then, everything changed in a blink. Jem was gone, Hayley revealed as a traitor. Brock, Alpha for such a short time, was now on the run. And Ryan and I now held the Alpha positions.

It was understandable that people were unsure about us, this newly bonded pair who were suddenly taking the reins. It didn't help that I'd only been back a few days after being gone for four years. There had been so many changes in such a short amount of time. Now they were wondering what kind of Alphas we would be, if we were even ready for the responsibility. Hell, even I wasn't sure.

"I feel like we're in a fishbowl," I muttered, slipping my hand into Ryan's as we walked along the street.

He squeezed my hand. "Comes with the territory," he said, a slight edge to his voice.

Ryan opened the passenger door for me, his eyes meeting mine as I slid into the seat, sending a little shiver down my spine.

As Ryan started the truck, his hand found mine, his thumb gently stroking my skin. "We'll get used to this," he said quietly.

I nodded.

We drove in silence to the Alpha compound. Two of our new enforcers, Rafael and Ava, stood guard on either side of the gate. They were part of the Renegades, what the Pack was calling those that supported and fought with me and Ryan at the Pack Meet two days ago to challenge Brock and Hayley and win the Alpha position of the Pack. They had risked their lives for us, had proven their loyalty beyond doubt, and I would never forget that. I smiled at them, and Rafael and Ava bowed their heads respectfully as we passed through. The gesture made my stomach flip. I wasn't used to people deferring to me this way. To them, we were the new, rightful leaders of the Pack. To me, I was still Jem's little sister. The one who'd run away when Ryan had rejected me in front of everyone four years ago.

Winding through the compound, we passed the other homes reserved for the Pack's hierarchy, including the house where the Shaw brothers lived, and where me and Ryan had been staying since we got back. Ryan drove straight past it, though, toward the end of the road where the largest house of all stood—the official residence of the Alpha pair.

Ryan brought the truck to a stop in the circular driveway. I stared up at the imposing three-story structure, a knot in my chest. This place held so many complicated memories.

It had been a house of horrors under Oliver's reign, a place to be feared. After Jem and Hayley became the Alphas, they had transformed it into a home. But I'd only spent a few days there before Jem was supposedly murdered there.

Stepping through those doors felt viscerally wrong. It was acknowledging that we really were the Alphas now, but to me this had been Jem's home. And a small, loyal part of me balked at the idea of anyone else taking his place. Especially me. The younger sister who'd disappeared on him.

Beside me, Ryan closed his door and came around to open mine, jolting me from my thoughts. His blue eyes were filled with understanding as they met mine. I'd been putting off going into the house since we got back from the Meet. It was too much; too much responsibility, too many memories, too many nightmares where I pictured Jem dying in that house. But I had to face it. Being in the house sent a message to the Pack that we were here, we were serious about being the Alphas, and we were ready to rule.

Ryan reached out, his hand gently cupping my chin and lifting it, so I met his eyes. "Hey," he said softly, "I know being here is hard."

I leaned into his touch, closing my eyes for a moment. When I opened them, I could see my own pain reflected in his gaze. "It feels wrong," I whispered, voicing the thoughts that had been haunting me. "Being here, taking Jem's place. After everything…"

Ryan's thumb brushed over my cheekbone, catching a tear I hadn't realized had fallen. "We're not taking Jem's place. We're honoring his legacy, continuing what he started. He would be proud of you."

I wanted to believe him. But the guilt and grief were too fresh, too raw. "I left, Ryan. I left you, I left him, I left the Pack. How can I lead them now?"

Ryan pulled me into his arms, holding me tight against his chest. I could feel the steady beat of his heart, the warmth of his body seeping into mine. "You came back," he murmured into my hair. "You're here now, when the Pack needs you most. That's what matters. We'll take it slow."

I nodded, swallowing down the lump in my throat. Ryan was right. We'd take this one step at a time. Ryan enclosed my hand in his, and we walked through the door together.

When I first came here, it had had a cozy and welcoming feel to it. Now, the pastel rugs had been removed and the bookshelves lining the walls had been gutted of their books. I guess Brock wasn't a big reader.

"We'll refill them," Ryan promised, following my gaze to the empty shelves. He knew I loved to read. There hadn't been much time lately for books, though.

We walked past the living room, where I'd seen Jem again after my four years away. I blinked back the tears as I thought about how tightly he'd hugged me and how safe I'd felt in his arms. Here the room was the same, with its high ceilings and large windows that let in plenty of natural light.

A door opened, and Sylvie came rushing toward me from the kitchen.

"Oh, Mai! Ryan!" She caught me in a brief hug, stepping back to look at my face. "You're here! I'm so sorry about your brother."

In her early forties, Sylvie's short brown hair looked ruffled today, like she had taken less time with it than usual, but she still had her three earrings in each ear. Her face was pale and drawn, and there were tears in her eyes. It reminded me that I wasn't the only one grieving. Sylvie had been the chef and housekeeper for Jem and Hayley.

"Thank you, Sylvie. How have you been? Did Brock and Hayley treat you okay?"

"Oh, don't you worry about me. What's important is that you're here. You and Ryan are the Alphas now, just the way Jem wanted it."

I glanced at Ryan, who was smiling warming at Sylvie. I didn't know her well, but Jem had trusted her, and Ryan and his brothers liked her.

"Thank you, Sylvie," Ryan said. "If you need anything—"

"I'll ask. Now on you go," Sylvie tilted her head toward the hall on the left. "The others are already waiting."

I followed Ryan down the corridor to a set of carved wooden double doors and couldn't help but admire his sculpted ass as he walked ahead of me. I still had to pinch myself that Ryan was really mine. He pushed the doors open, revealing a spacious study with floor-to-ceiling bookshelves lining the walls. In the center sat a large, rectangular table surrounded by his brothers—Mason, Derek, and Sam.

Mason, with his close-cropped black hair and piercing blue eyes, sat to the right. His leanly muscular frame was tense, and he fidgeted with a small rubber ball, rolling it between his fingers.

Derek, the new Beta of the Three Rivers Pack, sat across from Mason. His military background was always on show in his posture and his short brown haircut. Gray eyes, sharp and observant, scanned the room as we entered.

Next to Derek was Sam, his twin brother. Though they shared the same muscular build, Sam's shoulder-length brown hair and easy-going grin always set him apart. As the peacekeeper among the brothers, Sam's ability to see the bigger picture often clashed with Mason's focus on immediate consequences.

Jase was also there, perched excitedly on the edge of his seat. He wasn't old enough to be an enforcer yet—at nineteen he still had a year to go before he could apply, but he had earned my trust.

"Morning," Ryan greeted them.

Jase jumped up to grab me a chair, beaming. "Hey Mai! How's it going?" His enthusiasm was infectious. I couldn't help but smile back as I sat down.

"Not too bad so far. We'll see if that changes after this meeting."

My attempt to lighten the undercurrent of tension thrumming through the room didn't work. No one, apart from Jase, even cracked a smile.

Ryan cut right to business. "Derek, what's the latest on surveillance around the compound?"

"I've tripled patrols for now and set up a rotating sentry system. No scents have been picked up on the perimeter."

Derek had become an expert at intelligence gathering and counter-surveillance tactics during his years in the army. Those skills were proving invaluable now.

Ryan nodded. "Good. And the rest of Three Rivers' security?"

"We've increased foot and vehicle patrols of the streets and have eyes keeping watch on key areas—the school, town hall, commercial strip."

"It's vital we tighten security, at least until the dust settles."

Mason chimed in next. "Sam and I have reached out to our PI contacts across the region and put them on alert. If anyone connected to the Three Rivers passes through their territory, we'll know about it. Might help us map their movements."

I felt a swell of gratitude for the brothers' quick, decisive actions. With their help shoring up defenses, Ryan and I could focus on figuring out our next moves. Suddenly, I didn't feel so alone. Because, to be honest, what the fuck did I know about being an Alpha? Ryan had been Jem's Beta, he knew how this all worked. Me? A week ago, I'd been working as a website designer.

My eyes drifted around the study. It still didn't feel quite real, being in the inner sanctum discussing Pack security protocols. I had gone from a wolf on the run, to part of this tight-knit circle now steering the future of the Three Rivers Pack. I felt overwhelmed and totally out of my league.

My gaze stopped on a tumbler on Jem's, well, I guess now mine and Ryan's, desk. It was black with a metal rim and the words Three Rivers Bottley Bar, etched onto the side in silver. But Jem wasn't here anymore, he wasn't going to walk in the door and say, 'don't worry, I'll take care of everything.' Ryan and I were the Alphas now, and I had to accept that.

Chapter Three

MAI

Maybe I just had to start small. Make a decision to signal that this wasn't Jem's, Hayley's, or Oliver's Pack anymore. That there was a new way of doing things, even if I didn't know exactly what that was yet. Though there was one thing that I'd been thinking about for a while.

"The walls around the compound," I interrupted. "I want them gone."

Ryan stiffened, surprise flickering across his features. "What do you mean, gone?"

I straightened in my seat. "I mean demolished, taken down completely. No more gates and barriers separating us from the rest of the Pack."

Understanding dawned on Sam's face. "You want to show unity. Bringing the Pack together, instead of the leaders being behind closed walls."

"Yes, exactly. I don't want to be locked away in the big house separate from everyone else. If we're going to be the Alphas of this Pack, we need to be among our people."

We all looked at Ryan.

"It's an interesting idea..." he began slowly. "But those walls have kept previous Alphas safe for generations. It's a place where the whole Pack can run to if we come under attack. Perhaps we should take more time to think this through."

I sat up straighter to meet Ryan's gaze head-on. "It's never been used as a safe haven for the Pack, and it didn't keep Jem safe. All it has done has created a barrier between the Alphas and the enforcers and the rest of the Pack. The walls need to come down. We need to show everyone that we are not like the other Alphas. This is a new start. For the whole Pack."

Sam cocked his head to one side. "There are definitely pros and cons to weigh. But it could be a powerful symbol to start off your reign."

Ryan frowned. I knew he was picturing worst-case scenarios—assassins breaching our home, other Packs slipping past to attack at night. But his over-protectiveness couldn't rule every decision we made as Alphas.

"Ryan," I said firmly. "This is important."

He let out a breath, his shoulders losing some of their rigidity. "Alright. We'll take down the walls."

I blinked. Ryan agreeing to one of my ideas this quickly was practically unheard of.

"But we double the guards," he stipulated. "And I want Derek to do a full security assessment before any demolition starts."

"Deal," I agreed, before he could change his mind.

"I'll start the planning and logistics," Derek said briskly, making a note on his phone. "What's next?"

Next was figuring out how the hell to shut down the spread of ripple, investigating the potential origins of the drug shipments and who could be behind them.

And then there was the question of my brother Jem, and whether Brock's claim that he was alive had any truth to it. We'd jumped into the deep end, essentially fighting a war on two fronts.

"Ronnie thinks he's being framed as the supplier of ripple in the region. He's asked us to look into it," said Ryan.

"And you agreed?" Mason growled, as he twirled a pen through his fingers.

Mason was not a big fan of Ronnie's. Ronnie had been Shya's contact, and he'd dropped some hints that he'd like to be much more. It pissed Mason off to no end. I suspected that Shya was Mason's fated mate, but he was taking it extra slow due to Tristan gaslighting Shya for months. Tristan, like Brock, was still out there and everyone thought Tristan still had plans to make Shya his.

"He cashed in his favor. Plus, it's a new lead on ripple. We'd be idiots to ignore it," Ryan replied calmly, staring his brother down. Mason lowered his eyes and nodded.

Derek leaned forward. "I'll put some feelers out. If someone is trying to frame Ronnie as a ripple supplier, we'll catch whispers of it."

"What about Jem?" I asked, a little hesitantly. "Has anyone found anything?"

Mason and Sam exchanged an uneasy glance. "We're chasing down every rumor," Sam assured me. "But so far, nothing concrete. If Brock has him, no-one knows about it."

"Someone must. Have you talked to Brock's enforcers? The ones who were here that night when Hayley..." I paused, unable to continue that thought. "What do they say happened to Jem's body?"

"They're talking, but it's not making much sense. Two of them took Jem's body to the cage room and locked him in a cage on Brock's orders. Brock apparently went to see the body later that night—Paulo, one of the enforcers, saw Brock go into the room at midnight. He came out again at two. When Paulo was passing the cage room the next morning on his way out, the door was open, but there was nothing there. No-one saw what happened to Jem's body. No-one knows anything."

"Apart from Brock."

"Apart from Brock," Derek confirmed, as he turned to face me. "Mai, you gotta know, if any of us had thought for a second that Jem wasn't dead, we'd have gotten him out of there, or we'd have died next to him."

I did know that. They loved Jem as much as I did.

"You think he's dead? That Brock's fucking with us?"

He hesitated before replying. "I just don't want you to get your hopes up."

Ryan's phone rang. "I have to take this." He kissed the end of my nose, then picked up his phone and left the room.

Sam looked at me. "Brock will call again. He knows there is no way we'd nominate him without proof of what he's saying. He'll call and we'll work out if he really has Jem or not."

I tried not to let the crushing disappointment show on my face. But Sam seemed to sense it, anyway.

"We'll keep digging, too. We have allies across the territory on the lookout. Someone's bound to turn up a real lead sooner or later."

We didn't have later though. We had to nominate someone for the Wolf Council in four days, and if I had to choose Brock so I could get Jem back, I'd do it in a heartbeat. I'd just have to convince Ryan it was the right thing to do.

Sam glanced toward the door and then back at me. "How are you holding up? How are things with Ryan? You guys settling in okay?"

I leaned back in my chair. "It'll take some getting used to, this whole Alpha gig."

Sam nodded. "And things with Ryan, all going okay?" his tone was casual, but Sam kept glancing at the door where Ryan had gone to take his call.

"What's going on, Sam? What are you worried about?"

He was silent for a moment. Mason shifted uncomfortably; Derek crossed his arms, a glower on his face, but he didn't say anything either.

"Well?"

"You have to understand that Ryan and his wolf were forged to be Alphas. After our mom died, I know you know that Dad drank and checked out on all dad duties. He disappeared for days on end. There was no money, no food; we were all slowly starving, and at risk of losing our house. Ryan tried to bring him back to us, to cure him of the bottle, to save him, but Dad didn't want to be saved and he died not long after. Ryan has never forgiven himself for that, for failing to save Dad. And then it all fell on Ryan. He didn't have to, he could have dumped us in the forest, made it on his own, but he chose to stay and look after us. He used to get up at three a.m., Shift, and head out to find us food. Oliver had decreed the year before that hunting in the fifteen miles around Three Rivers was reserved for him and his enforcers. They killed any they caught or suspected of hunting there. Ryan had to range further and further to find us food. He usually managed a rabbit or two. It didn't fill our bellies, but it made a dent, and Jem helped out when he could.

"Then Digit found Ryan when he was rooting through the trash cans behind the school. Digit was an enforcer, and what Digit wanted, Digit got. He made Ryan work for him; said if he didn't, then Digit would start paying visits to our house at night. That he'd had an eye on Ryan's brothers for a while, that he liked little boys and their innocent faces, and if Ryan wanted to keep Digit's eye off us, then Ryan had better do what he was told."

I recoiled. I remembered Digit, remembered how everyone avoided him, how he took what he wanted from all the stores in town, never paying for anything. Everyone was scared of him and what he would do if you drew his attention.

"Did he...?" I didn't know how to ask Sam if Digit came to visit their house.

Sam shook his head. "We were some of the lucky ones. We had Ryan, and he made sure Digit stayed away."

I sighed in relief.

"The work from Digit was irregular at first, but Ryan was good at it and Digit was soon throwing jobs at Ryan. Digit's main problem was that he was lazy as fuck. He'd made it as an enforcer and thought that meant everyone and their aunt Louise should lick his fucking shoes. Anyone disrespected him? He sent Ryan to show them the error of their ways. Someone owed him money, and anyone could owe Digit money, you just had to look at him the wrong way and he'd fine you a hundred dollars, and he sent Ryan to collect. And if Oliver ordered Digit to actually get off his ass and do something, if he could get away with it, he'd send Ryan instead. Ryan hated it, hated the things he did to the people Digit sent him after, but for all his faults, and there were a fuckload, Digit paid money. It meant we finally had food on the table, finally had clothes that fit and shoes on our feet. It meant the house was safe, and we weren't about to get kicked out onto the streets. It changed Ryan, though."

My heart ached for Ryan and the things he must have seen, and the things he must have done to keep his brothers safe. "I never knew."

"He didn't want you to. He didn't want any of us to know. Ryan quit the day Jem defeated Brock's father and became Beta. Ryan became an enforcer to watch Jem's back, but it also meant he now had a steady paycheck coming in. Not that Digit took it well, but Ryan was an enforcer too and equal to him in the hierarchy." Sam sighed, glancing at his brothers. "It took Ryan two months to realize that I'd started working for Digit instead."

"You?"

Sam nodded. "I was young, saw Ryan had cash in his pocket and I wanted some of that. I had dreams of being the bad-ass enforcer my brother was, and I thought running jobs for Digit would be the first step."

"What happened?"

"Digit started to pay me more attention. A touch here, a squeeze there. I didn't like it, or how it made me feel. I wanted out but didn't know how to do it. Then Digit started to siphon off guns from Oliver's deals. He was selling on the side, and I became his favorite for running those guns to his buyers outside the Pack. One night, a deal went bad. I managed to escape, but Digit was not the forgiving type. By the time I made it home, my arm was broken in four places, and I had a face that was bluer than the Nauru flag. Ryan scented my blood, found me in the bathroom, and made me tell him everything."

I blinked slowly. "What did Ryan do?" I already knew. I'd remembered what had happened to Digit, but I wanted to hear it from Sam.

"Ryan took me with him. He said he didn't want me to have nightmares about Digit. We went to his house, and Digit laughed when Ryan confronted him. Said if he couldn't have Ryan as his grunt, he'd take his brothers, in each and every way, one by one. Digit said he was going to get Oliver to sign off on us working for him. I have no doubt, Mai, none at all, that Oliver would have agreed."

"What did Ryan do?" I repeated.

Sam glanced at the door again before continuing. "Digit was the first person Ryan killed. It was a brutal fight, but Ryan was efficient, methodical. Digit was a threat to us, so Digit had to die. After, there wasn't much left of Digit." He looked away and paused for a moment. "Ryan covered it up. Made sure it couldn't be traced back to any of us."

Oh, my beautiful Ryan. I wanted to go to him, to hug him for the loss of his innocence, for all the things he'd been through. I wanted to take it all away.

"Ryan always had a strong protective streak, but after that it went into overdrive. If he viewed you as his—his brothers, his family, his mate—he would do anything, and I mean anything, Mai, to ensure that you were safe, that he didn't lose any of us the way he lost Dad. Then…"

"Then I ran away," I finished for him. "He lost me. For four years."

Sam nodded. "He was a shell of himself after that. Ryan threw himself into making sure we were looked after, that Jem was secure in his position and then he went searching for you. He'd be gone months at a time, looking for you, but he always came back empty-handed."

"I got good at running and hiding," I murmured.

"Mai," Sam glanced at his brothers, "we want you to understand that Ryan's protective instinct is more pronounced than usual for a werewolf. Even more than for an Alpha. He is driven to do anything to protect those he loves, and for years you have been the sole object of his obsession. Now that he has you, it might calm down."

"But it might not?"

Sam wiggled his hand in a maybe, maybe not gesture. "With all the threats you've faced since you've been back, things might be amplified instead."

Why was he telling me this? My eyes widened. "He won't hurt me." My voice was firm, angry that Sam might even think it.

"He would never hurt you, Mai," Sam agreed. "We all know that. But we don't know how he's going to react. We just want to you to be prepared."

CHAPTER FOUR

RYAN

The afternoon air was heating up as Mai, Jase, Derek, and I walked up to the bungalow on Elm Street. According to Thomas, our Pack doctor, the werewolf who lived here—one Norman Adler—had been brought in showing signs of advanced ripple addiction. Norman wasn't in a state to answer our questions—Thomas had him locked down in his medical room and said Norman was ranting about dust storms and living in an iron recycling plant on the planet Mars.

Evelyn and Ava had come to see me this morning after my phone call with Thomas. I'd put them in charge of the Renegades, those werewolves that fought for us at the Meet. They were our core enforcers now. Usually, enforcers would be running down an errand like this, but Mai and I had agreed that right now we needed those we trusted to be out in the Three Rivers, showing the Pack that things were settling down, there was order and safety here. Too many would be wary of me and Mai right now, not sure what sort of Alphas we were going to be, but they might feel more comfortable with the Renegades around—people they'd known their whole lives. People they knew and trusted. Mason and Sam had headed back to their PI agency to see what they could dig up on who was framing Ronnie, and Jem's whereabouts. With the rest of the Renegades guarding those of Brock's enforcers that we captured, until Mai and I decided what to do with them, that left Mai, Jase, Derek and me this task.

I scanned the quiet street as Derek picked the lock on the front door. We were hoping Norman's home might still hold some clues about where he got the ripple.

The door clicked open, and we stepped inside, hit immediately by the stale air and an unwashed stench. Mai wrinkled her nose in distaste. "You'd think with our enhanced senses, people would be more inclined to open a window now and then."

The living room was cramped and cluttered, overflowing ashtrays and discarded takeout containers littering every surface. The sagging couch had clearly seen better days.

"Derek, Jase, search the bedrooms. Mai and I will take the living room and kitchen."

We split up, Derek and Jase heading towards the back of the house. In the living room, unopened mail piled up on a small, cluttered table, and children's toys were left lying around. Derek has done a background check on Norman. He worked at a local car loan business. He'd not found his mate yet, but up until a month ago he had been living with a human woman and her two kids. The woman apparently left a month ago, reconciling with the children's father and heading out west to be with him.

I began rifling through the stack of bills and letters, looking for anything that might point to a dealer or a place where Norman could have gotten the ripple. Mai was opening and closing kitchen cabinets, her movements efficient and focused.

"Find anything?" she asked.

"Just bills and junk mail so far."

Mai came back to the living room and started sifting through a pile of magazines and newspapers stacked haphazardly on a side table. A used needle fell out of the papers and onto the floor.

Mai squatted down and reached out to it.

My wolf nearly jumped out of my skin. "Don't touch it!" I growled, pushing him back down.

I've got this.

The needle could still have drops of ripple in it, and I didn't want Mai anywhere near that thing.

"I'm not an idiot, Ryan." Mai's hand reached past the needle to a fallen piece of paper. She scooped the needle onto the paper and brought it close to her nose.

"It's ripple," she confirmed. "The smell is the same as in Arabella's room."

At least we knew now for sure that Norman had been taking ripple. But my wolf was deeply unhappy. This wasn't a safe place for our mate.

I glanced around the living room. "There's nothing else useful here."

Mai didn't look up from the table. "We haven't checked everything yet. There could be something hidden."

"Derek and I can handle it. Why don't you head back with Jase?"

Her head snapped up, eyes blazing. "Head back? You think I can't handle this?"

"That's not what I'm saying. I just—" I started, but she cut me off.

"You just what? Want to protect me from everything, to the extent that I can't even do my job?"

"No, it's not about that." It was so about that. "I just don't think there's anything here. You could be of more use—"

"Sitting at home, reading magazines, perhaps?" Her voice was sugar sweet.

"Yes. No. Not magazines. Reports. Doing background checks. That sort of thing."

Mai stared at me, her eyes blazing. She knew exactly what I meant. "We're the Alphas, Ryan Shaw. You and me both. I know this is hard for you, but I don't hide away at home. Ripple is going to destroy our Pack. My brother might be out there in the hands of that sick fuck, Brock. And you, you are not going to put me in a marshmallow room, where I couldn't get hurt even if I tripped over, and shut me out of these investigations. If you can't see that, how are we supposed to rule this Pack together?"

My wolf growled inside of me. It wasn't that we thought Mai couldn't handle herself, but the thought of losing her scared us shitless. We'd lost her once, when she ran from me after I rejected her. Four years without her and now that we had her back, my wolf went crazy whenever she left the room. Her being kidnapped by Seth, then giving herself up to Brock to try to save Sofia's life, hadn't helped calm either of us. My wolf thought maybe a marshmallow room was a great fucking idea. Besides, that was what this was all for, wasn't it? Win the Pack so we could mold it into a killing, fighting machine that would put itself between any danger and our mate. We'd learned long ago the importance of Pack. With both parents gone, I had three younger brothers to feed and clothe, and I did what I had to, to make sure they were okay. Then my best friend, Jem, saw what was happening, and he helped out. We wouldn't have survived if it wasn't for him. That was Pack. Now I had hundreds of werewolves under my command, and I was going to make damn sure that we changed this Pack into one where every single member would protect the others. That way, they'd protect Mai, and if we ever had pups, they would protect them. I just needed to do it without Mai realizing why I was doing it. There wasn't a doubt in my mind that she'd leave me if she thought I believed she couldn't handle herself.

Derek and Jase reappeared from the back of the house, their expressions tense.

"Everything okay in here?" Derek asked, glancing between Mai and me.

"Fine," Mai replied, though her body language said otherwise.

Derek studied us both for a moment longer, before saying, "Good, coz we found something." He held up a pair of jeans and a crumpled receipt. "I found these in his hamper. The jeans reek of ripple. And this receipt was in the back pocket."

I scanned the list of items, my gaze snagging on a name scrawled near the bottom. "Bradford Hayes?"

Derek nodded. "He's human. A low-level dealer downtown."

Finally, a real lead. I felt a spark of hope—this could be the break we needed.

"So what now? We bring this Bradford guy in for questioning?" Jase asked eagerly.

"Ryan and Derek will track down Bradford," Mai said curtly. "Jase, you and me are going to go and talk to Norman's work colleagues."

Without looking at me, Mai strode out of the door. She was pissed, of that I had no doubts. Jase glanced at me quickly, then looked at Derek. Derek jerked his head towards the door, and Jase ran after Mai.

Derek and I sat in silence, parked downtown on a dingy corner, waiting for Bradford to show up.

My thoughts kept drifting back to Mai. I knew she was right—it was vital we found a way to make this work. I'd seen the damage an unstable Alpha pair could do to a Pack. If Jem and Hayley hadn't been at each other's throats all the time, there was no way Brock could have convinced Hayley to do what she did. And without a stable Pack, I'd have no hope of forging us all into an elite force. I had to stop trying to side-line her, but the thought of anything happening to her made me want to burn the fucking world down.

"So, how are things going with you and Mai?" Derek asked casually. "From the way she tore out of there earlier, I'm guessing not awesome."

I glared out the window. "We're working through some things."

Derek held up his hands in mock surrender, though his eyes sparked with humor. "We all knew you were going to suck at being her partner. We just didn't think you could mess it up this quick."

My hands clenched into fists. He could fucking talk.

"Really helpful," I bit out. "Let me know when you finally admit that Sofia is your mate, then maybe you can start doling out relationship advice."

Derek flushed. "This isn't about me and Sofia. I'm just trying to look out for you, bro. You can't do what Jem and Hayley did and try to hide your arguments. It affected the whole Pack. We need the two of you to be on the same page. We want you to be happy, you and Mai. So stop fucking it up."

I knew Derek meant well, but I was in no mood for his meddling. Not when I knew he was right, and I was fucking this up.

I took a deep breath, running a hand over my face. Derek was my brother. He had my back, always.

"I have to protect her, I have to keep her safe, but every decision is a fucking battle. I'm trying to find the line between what I want to do, and what I know will push her away."

"She's independent, she always has been, bro. That's what we all love about Mai. Your protective streak has always been strong, and add to that the mating bond, and everything is amplified. It forces you to be freakishly over-protective."

"This is different," I admitted.

Derek laughed. "They all say that."

"No, this is different, Derek," I insisted. "I can't lose her, not again. I wouldn't survive it. But if I don't protect her, I could lose her, and if I do protect her, she might leave me."

Derek placed a hand on my shoulder, squeezing gently. "Yeah, that's fucked up, but you need to find a way. I have faith in you, bro. You and Mai. You're our Alphas now and the whole fucking Pack is relying on you to work this out."

I turned round to face him. "Is that your idea of a pep talk? 'Don't fuck it up'?"

He grinned at me. "Yup. It's short, it's sweet, it rolls off the tongue and covers all bases. I might it get embossed on a T-shirt."

"Great, Derek. Great fucking help you are."

After twenty minutes, Derek suddenly sat upright, gaze fixed down the street. "There. That's him."

I followed Derek's line of sight to see a short, slightly overweight guy in an oversized hoodie standing on the corner. His head swiveled side to side as he talked to a glassy-eyed human teenager. Even from here, I could make out the small pills exchanging hands.

We waited until the kid had pocketed his purchase and scurried off. Then, as one, we stepped out of the car. Bradford's head jerked up, eyes blowing wide. Before we could react, he turned and sprinted down the nearest alley.

"Dammit," Derek growled, as we set off after him. Garbage cans and debris flashed by as we followed Bradford through the dingy concrete canyon. Up ahead, I saw him duck through a hole in a chain-link fence. I put on a burst of speed, closing the gap. With a grunt, I swung through the ragged opening just as Bradford disappeared around the corner of a crumbling brick building.

I could sense Derek right on my heels. We rounded the building side by side, nearly slamming into Bradford cowering against the wall. A towering fence loomed behind him—a dead end. He was trapped.

I stalked toward him. "We just want to talk, Bradford."

Bradford shrank back against the bricks, hands on his knees, wheezing from the effort of running. "Look man, I got nothing to say."

In a flash, I had his shirt twisted in my fist, just enough to convey I meant business. "I think you do, Bradford. You're dealing in ripple. You're dealing to Shifters."

"Nah, man! I wouldn't do that. I ain't stupid."

"Yeah, how about Norman Adler? You know him?"

"Norman? Nah, I don't know no Norman."

Derek held out his phone. On it there was a photo of Norman that Thomas had sent to us.

I leaned closer to Bradford and growled, "Try again."

Bradford blinked. "Oh, yeah. Norman, right. I know Norman. Good guy. Bought some stuff from me, sure."

"Ripple?"

Bradford's eyes shifted to the side.

"Bradford, I'm about done playing nice."

"Okay, okay. Yeah, he bought some ripple."

"The ripple shipments. Where are they coming from?"

"I swear I don't know!" Bradford wheezed.

"Derek, hold him. I'm going to get our hand drill." I showed Bradford my teeth. "It works really well on bones."

"Okay, okay!" Bradford threw his hands up. "Don't hurt me, okay? There's this guy, calls himself Ghost. He's the one moving the major product. Rumor is he works for this biker gang guy. Named Reggie Billet or something."

I released Bradford.

"Ronnie Bishop?"

"Yeah, man. That's it. Ronnie Bishop."

"What else do you know about Ghost?" Derek pressed. "Where's he operating from?"

Bradford just shook his head frantically, still gasping from trying to run from us. "That's all I got, I promise! No one knows who Ghost is."

"How do you get your supplies?"

"It just turns up. I start running low, the next day, the product will be on my doorstep. I don't know how they know. They just do. It's like they're ghosts, man. Watching all the time, never seen. That's why the main man is called Ghost, you know."

"And the money you make? How do you get it to them?"

Bradford shrugged. "The day after the product arrives, I leave the money in an envelope taped under a bench in Cotton Park."

Maybe we could set up a sting. If Bradford was running low, we could watch his house and stakeout the bench. We could catch them in the act.

"When did you last get a restock?"

"Two days ago."

"And how often do you run low?"

Bradford held up his hands in an *I don't know* gesture. "Depends on my clients, man. Could be a week. Could be a month."

Fuck! Frustrated, I stepped back, running a hand through my hair. Another dead end.

"Show me your phone," Derek ordered.

I knew he wanted to check if Bradford was telling the truth. We'd have to run all the numbers but maybe we'd get lucky and hit one that could be traced to the guys supplying ripple.

Bradford pulled out his phone. Derek swiped it out of his hands. "Hey!"

I grabbed Bradford's shirt and hauled him against the wall. "You know who I am?"

"S...sure," he stuttered. "You're the new Alpha."

"That's right. I'm the Alpha. And the new rule for the Three Rivers is that this is a drug-free territory. No more, not even for the humans. You're going to drop off any drugs you have at the Alpha Compound, then you're going to have to find a new job, Bradford. Or I'll put you down. There won't be another warning."

He stared at me wide eyed and then nodded. I released him and he almost tripped over himself in his hurry to get away.

I watched him scamper down the alley, then turned to Derek. "Put enforcers on his house. I want it watched twenty-four-seven."

Derek nodded. "At least we have a name now."

"You heard of him?"

"Nope. But we'll find him, Ryan. And when we do..."

He was right, when we found Ghost, he was going to be in a world of hurt.

CHAPTER FIVE

MAI

The Wheel Deal Car Loans sign flickered erratically as Jase and I pulled into the parking lot, the garish light seeming to mimic my own unsettled state of mind. I took a deep breath, trying to push down the argument with Ryan that was still roiling inside me. I knew he loved me, but his overprotectiveness was unbearable sometimes. We were supposed to be partners, equals in leading this Pack. Yet at every turn, he sought to shield me, to take the dangerous roles while keeping me safely in the shadows. It was maddening. I wanted to kiss him and kick him in his perfect fucking jaw at the same time.

Jase glanced at me tentatively as we got out of the car. "You okay?"

I sighed, raking a hand through my hair. "Of course."

He didn't look convinced.

"Really, Jase, there is nothing for you to worry about."

Jase nodded, and I knew I wasn't fooling him. He would be discrete, though. The last thing I needed was the Pack whispering about discord between their new Alpha pair. Ryan and I would work through this somehow. We had to, for everyone's sake, his included—if we didn't, he'd have to hire a good surgeon to wire his jaw back in place.

Steeling myself, I pushed through the front door of the rundown building, a little bell tinkling overhead to announce our arrival. The interior was a study in contrasts—posters of luxury cars and dream vacations stuck onto dingy walls amid worn furniture. The atmosphere felt strangely suspended between ambition and weary resignation.

All chatter stopped as we walked in, and the whispered "It's the Alpha," fanned out. A dozen wary gazes swiveled our way. I could smell the apprehension from the workers clustered in the cramped office space. Their expressions ran the gamut from dutifully blank to thinly veiled dread. It struck me then how terrifying I must seem to them, an unknown and unproven Alpha sweeping in unannounced.

From the uneasy glances Jase and I received, I gathered my glower wasn't inspiring much confidence. This wasn't how I wanted our Pack to look at us—with distrust and trepidation. I had to fix that, starting now. I tamped down on the anger still simmering within me, not wanting to give these people any more cause for fear.

"My name is Mai. We're not here to make any trouble. We're just looking for some information about Norman."

Finally, a tentative voice broke the heavy silence. "Is Norman okay?"

I turned to see a lanky young man, his height accentuated by his slender build, watching us from a cautious distance. His posture was slightly hunched, as if carrying an invisible weight on his shoulders. His eyes, large and expressive beneath a mop of untidy brown hair, flickered with a mix of curiosity and unease. Worry was etched deeply into his boyish features, the kind of worry that spoke of genuine personal concern rather than mere professional obligation. Kyle, his nametag declared in plain, unassuming font.

I softened my voice, hoping to set him at ease. "Kyle, right? I'd like to ask you a few questions about him, if that's okay. Somewhere private."

Surprise flickered across Kyle's face, but he nodded. "Yeah, okay. We can talk in the break room."

"Jase, see what you can find out from the others."

He nodded at me, and I turned and followed Kyle down a short hallway to a dingy, windowless room containing a few rickety chairs and a coffee machine that looked older than me. He perched tentatively on the edge of a chair, while I took the one opposite.

"So…" Kyle began hesitantly. "Is Norman okay? We were all real worried when he didn't show up for work."

"He's safe. He's with Thomas and getting the help he needs," I assured him. Kyle visibly relaxed.

"That's good to hear. Norman's a real decent guy, you know? Always ready to help out when someone's having car trouble or anything. He doesn't deserve whatever's happening to him."

I studied the young man thoughtfully. "It sounds like you two were close."

Kyle gave a sad little smile. "Yeah, I guess we were. He was nice to me. Helped me out when I started here. Showed me the ropes, you know? He didn't really have anyone else since Marsey left."

"What happened with Marsey?" I asked gently. "It seems her leaving really affected Norman."

Kyle glanced down at his clasped hands. "I probably shouldn't speak ill of her. But Norman was real good to Marsey and those kids. Treated them like his own family. He was even saving up to buy a ring, wanted to make it official."

Kyle shook his head bitterly. "But I guess Marsey got bored or something, slumming it with a Shifter. She up and left without warning, went running back to her ex out west. Took the kids. It tore Norman up. He started drinking, missing work. He was depressed as hell."

In the sterile facts Derek had told us about Norman's life, it was easy to overlook the human heartbreak at the root of his downward spiral.

"When did you notice him start to change?"

"A couple of weeks after Marsey left. At first it was just the drinking, coming in late looking like shit, not having shaved or washed. But then..." Kyle hesitated, like he was debating whether to continue.

"It's okay, you can tell me. Anything you say here, I'll keep confidential."

Kyle glanced uneasily at the door before answering. "Well, Norman started talking kinda crazy. Paranoid stuff about people watching him and whispering lies about him. His moods were all over the place—pissed off one minute, laughing the next. It wasn't like him at all. I think he'd started using whatever new drug is going around. Messed him up bad."

"Do you know where Norman got the drugs?"

Kyle shook his head slowly. "I have no idea. I asked him once, when it was getting really bad. But he just muttered something about ghosts and demons. Wasn't making any sense."

"You've helped more than you know, Kyle. Truly. If you do happen to hear anything that could help us find the suppliers, please let me know. Anything at all."

Kyle kept his gaze on the ground, but he nodded. "I will. I want to do right by Norman. He deserves that."

I thanked Kyle and gave him my number, hoping he might remember some clue that could unravel this mystery. I went back to reception where Jase was talking to some of the others. He heard me coming and walked towards me.

"They don't know anything, but those two are acting particularly dodgy."

Jase jerked his head toward the doorway where two other young employees lingered.

I paused, watching the pair. The shorter one, Garth according to his name tag, was a wiry young man with sharp, angular features. His hair was cropped close to his head, and his eyes, a piercing shade of green, flickered with a mix of fear and defiance.

Next to him stood Liam, a head taller and with a broader build that suggested physical strength. His face was round, with a softness to it that suggested he hadn't stopped growing. His hair was a tousled mass of dirty blond, falling haphazardly over his forehead, and his green eyes shifted nervously, avoiding direct contact with everyone.

Garth and Liam exchanged an uneasy glance between themselves, but it was the smell of fear coming off them both that convinced me that Jase was right.

I went over to them and kept my tone gentle but firm. "There will be no judgment or punishment. But if you have any information about where Norman got the drugs, it could help save lives."

Garth's words spilled out in an anxious rush. "We only tried it once, the other night, after things ended with my girl. Bradford sold it to us. Over on Cotton Street. Please don't make them fire us!"

I exchanged a pointed look with Jase. This changed things. These two needed a medical evaluation, and we had to shut down Bradford, fast.

"Thank you for your honesty," I told them. "You won't get fired, I promise, but you both need to come with us, get checked out by a doctor. Just to be safe."

Garth and Liam didn't argue as we ushered them out to the car. I was hoping that we'd gotten to them in time, before the hooks of ripple addiction sank too deep.

CHAPTER SIX

MAI

Thomas must have heard the car pull up, because he emerged onto the porch just as we were getting out, Garth and Liam trailing uncertainly behind us. Despite the bulging muscles clearly evident even beneath his loose-fitting shirt, Thomas was a gentle giant. People were often intimidated by his size—at six foot five he loomed over most of us—but after five minutes with Thomas, you were completely at ease. He had a way about him, perfect for his profession, that made you feel safe in his presence.

"Mai, Jase, good to see you both," Thomas nodded to me, his eyes lowered, and shook Jase's hand. I was struck again by how strange it felt to have people treat me like the Alpha. Before, I'm sure Thomas would have hugged me. Now, he couldn't look me in the eyes. I grieved the loss of that contact, of being able to physically express my friendship with others, and wondered if this was why we had Alpha pairs, so that one person didn't have to live the loneliness that being the head of a Pack created. Then Thomas turned to the two young men standing awkwardly behind us and said, "And who do we have here?"

I glanced back at Garth and Liam, who were hovering by the car as if debating making a run for it. "This is Garth and Liam. They work with Norman. They both took ripple."

"Man, it was one time!" Garth whined, but Liam shushed him.

"I was hoping you could examine them, make sure the drug hasn't caused any permanent damage."

Understanding lit Thomas's eyes. "Of course, bring them on in." He turned and headed into the house, calling over his shoulder, "Wally's just putting the finishing touches on his famous lasagne if you all want to stay for dinner."

Jase's eyes lit up at the prospect. We'd missed lunch and I had heard his stomach rumbling all the way here.

Garth and Liam hesitated at the door, shooting quick looks back at the driveway.

I stepped toward them. "You'll be safe here, I promise. Thomas is a great doctor, he'll take good care of you both." Garth gave a short nod and headed inside, Liam following.

You would never have known that just a few days ago Brock's enforcers had attacked the house and me and Jase had fought them off. Thomas and Wally had cleared all the debris and scrubbed the blood from the floors. It looked as immaculate as it had the first time I'd come here.

Thomas led Garth and Liam to the back room he had converted into a clinic for his patients, while Jase sprawled onto the overstuffed floral couch in the living room with a contented sigh. "Sofia's coming over too, you know. Her and Wally have been planning this dinner for the last couple of days."

I smiled, sinking into the cushion beside him. It would be good to see Sofia. I'd been meaning to make some proper time for her and me, but since we'd been back and officially declared the Alphas, I'd been too busy with Pack business, the ripple situation, and Brock's ultimatum, to see my best friend.

As if summoned by my thoughts, Sofia breezed through the front door without knocking, arms laden with dishes piled precariously high.

"Mai, Jase!" she greeted brightly. "What are you guys doing here? Please tell me you're staying for dinner. Wally and I have made enough food to feed the entire Pack!"

Jase jumped up and took the dishes from her. "Smells amazing!"

He carried the dishes through to the kitchen as Sofia collapsed onto the couch next to me, kicking her feet up with the casual air of someone who has come to feel entirely at home. She and Jase had spent a lot of time hiding here after Brock took over.

"Rough day?" she asked sympathetically, no doubt scenting my weariness.

I shrugged, aiming for nonchalance. "Not the easiest. But we may have caught a break. At least enough to keep following the thread, see where it leads."

Sofia nodded, her gaze sharpening with interest. But whatever questions she had would have to wait, as Wally swept into the room, wearing a frilly pink apron and a grin.

"Dinner's in the oven, and the cocktails are ready!" he declared with theatrical exuberance. "Mai, Jase, so glad you're joining us. We could use some sane company around here for once." He winked at Sofia, who stuck out her tongue in response.

"Thank you for having us over," I began, but Wally immediately waved away my thanks.

"Nonsense, the more the merrier."

Thomas emerged from his clinic, looking pleased. "Garth and Liam are doing well, considering the circumstances," he reported. "There are some signs of dependancy. I'm going to keep them here under observation and run more tests. I'm hopeful that we have got to them in time, but the next few days will be vital."

I let out a breath I'd been holding. Not the best outcome, but not the worst either.

At that moment, my phone buzzed loudly on the coffee table, startling us all. An incoming call from Ryan flashed across the screen. I felt a swoop of nerves in my stomach. I was still angry with him, and I was suddenly hyper-aware of Sofia and Wally's gazes fixed on me.

"Ryan," I answered.

"Where are you? I swung by the house, but it's empty."

I knew he worried every time I wasn't with him. In the last month, I'd been kidnapped, held hostage, and taken by a cold-blooded killer. His words to me were tightly controlled, but I could feel the tinge of panic through our bond. It was going to take time for him to trust that I would be okay whenever he wasn't there.

"I'm at Thomas and Wally's with Jase and Sofia," I explained calmly. "Everything's fine."

He knew I was safe here with Thomas and Wally and the Miller siblings. Thomas might be a gentle giant, but he worked out daily. It was almost bordering on an obsession, but he had reason. He and Wally escaped another Pack, one that was none too happy that they were mated to each other. I knew Thomas was determined that no one hurt Wally again, even if he had to go against his firmly held belief that only fools resorted to violence. A throb of relief pulsed down my bond with Ryan. He was silent for a moment, and I imagined him running a hand through his perpetually tousled hair the way he did when gathering his thoughts.

"Look, I just wanted to say...I'm sorry about earlier. You were right, I need to stop trying to shove you into some box labeled 'fragile, handle with care.' I know you can take care of yourself."

Okay, first he'd given in to my request to remove the walls around the Alpha compound. Now he was apologizing and admitting I was right. He was trying really hard to make this work. I appreciated it, I really did, but I wasn't sure it would be that easy. I didn't know if we'd be able to find a balance. Maybe it started with me meeting him halfway.

"We're still figuring this out."

I heard Ryan release a breath. "Yeah, we are. But we'll get there." The warmth in his voice sent a pleasant tingle through me.

"Invite him over for dinner!" Wally called. Werewolf hearing sucked sometimes.

"Did you hear that?" I asked Ryan.

"Does the invite extend to me?" I heard Derek say in the background.

"Of course!" Wally replied.

"You know, I don't think this is our conversation anymore," I whispered to Ryan, knowing full well everyone could hear me.

"No," Ryan agreed. "I'm pretty sure I can get them to clear out if I tell you exactly what I'm thinking of doing to you later on."

Mmm. I suddenly really wanted to know what he was thinking.

"Oh, fuck no!" Derek's voice came over the line, as I heard him get out of a car and slam the door.

I laughed. "Well, that seemed to work."

"We'll be over soon. I love you."

"I love you, too."

I hung up as Wally said, "Awww, you guys are so cute. I soooo would not have cleared out, though."

CHAPTER SEVEN

MAI

Ryan and Derek arrived just as we were sitting down to eat. A ripple of excitement passed through me at the sight of Ryan, his tousled hair and deep, blue eyes stirring something primal inside me. Our bond hummed contentedly. He strode toward me, his gaze locked with mine, the intensity in his eyes melting away any remnants of the day's frustrations.

"Hey, baby," he leaned down, his lips brushing against my mouth in a gesture that gave me the warm fuzzies inside.

"Dinner's ready!" Wally called out. "Time for kisses later, children!"

"You can count on it," Ryan murmured against my ear.

We walked to the table as Wally, still decked out in his frilly pink apron, paraded in with a massive tray of lasagne. "A feast for your eyes and bellies, folks! This here's one of my many culinary masterpieces!"

Thomas followed, a grin on his face, carrying two baskets of garlic bread. "Don't let it get to his head, but he's not wrong."

We sat around the table, the tantalizing aroma of tomato sauce and melted cheese filling the air.

Derek waited until Sofia sat down, then grabbed the chair next to her. "How did the Bar hold up without their star manager? Did they beg you to come back after your disappearing act?"

Sofia and Jase had to lie low at Wally and Thomas's house when Brock took over. Brock knew Sofia was my best friend, and we'd been trying to keep Sofia and Jase safe. Not that it worked out that way.

Sofia, pausing as she served lasagne onto her plate, eyed him warily. "They were just fine. I know you think it's different on planet Derek, but down here not everything falls apart when you disappear on them. People cope. They move on. No big deal."

Mmm, I wasn't sure she was still talking about the Bar. I knew for a fact the owners did not cope well. They lived out of town and had given Sofia free rein. They loved her and would do anything to make sure she stayed on.

"Planet Derek?"

"Yeah," Sofia started to wave the serving spoon, still full of lasagne, around as she spoke, "Planet Derek, where everything is all about Derek and what he wants, when he wants it. He wants to go on a date, he goes on a date. He wants to ghost someone, he ghosts them. He wants to crook his finger and then expects that person to fall over themselves running back to him. Planet Derek."

Wally's eyes widened as he tracked the spoon's movements.

Derek leaned back in the chair and smiled smugly at Sofia. "I thought it was no big deal."

Sofia flushed. "It wasn't a big deal. I learned my lesson and have no intention of ever repeating it."

"You'll change your mind."

I honestly thought Sofia's head was going to explode. She whirled to face Derek, holding the spoon threateningly in his face. "I will never, Derek Shaw, never ever change my mind. I would rather be trapped in a cage with a hundred face-eating rats than go on another date with you."

Sofia had had a phobia of rats since I'd known her. As teenagers, I'd pointed out she was a fuck-off werewolf, who could kill a rat with one bite, but she was having none of it, insisting they were evil rodents with whiskers that would tickle your face just as they ate it.

Derek grinned at her. "You seem to have given another date with me a lot of thought."

Everyone in the room could see what was coming next. I'd never seen Wally move so fast. He jumped up and grabbed the spoon from Sofia.

"I love you, Sof, but I've just scrubbed these walls and floors of blood. I do not intend to be on my hands and knees again for such an unfun reason anytime soon!"

Jase leaned forward and rubbed his jaw. "Derek, I hope you realize that Wally just saved you. Sofia has a mean right hand with cooking utensils."

Sofia looked appalled. "That was one time! And it was an accident. I wouldn't have hit you with the potato masher if you hadn't been trying to sneak up on me."

"Sneak up on you? You're a werewolf. You smelled me and the fact that I'd just eaten the last piece of your favorite chocolate before I'd even set foot in the room!"

"The fact that you pinched my chocolate is completely unrelated."

Wally leaned down and whispered loudly in Sofia's ear, "Oh, honey, no-one, and I mean absolutely no-one, believes that!"

Ryan raised his glass in a toast. "To chocolate and misbehaving brothers." He glanced meaningfully at Derek, but he only had eyes for Sofia. Not that she noticed. She was pointedly ignoring him.

"To chocolate and misbehaving brothers," echoed the group, glasses clinking together in a semblance of harmony.

Ryan pushed a stray strand of my hair behind my ear. "Next time, we leave the kids at home, and go for a date night, just you and me."

I grinned at him. "Deal."

It wasn't until Wally had cleared up dessert that Ryan asked for updates. "Derek, any news on the Ronnie situation?"

Derek wiped his mouth on his napkin before answering. "Ronnie runs a highly lucrative operation out of Haxton. His gang runs a tight ship, and I gotta say, he has links to all the major players in the region. He deals mainly in information and he's good at it, but he has his fingers in lots of pies. Not drugs, though. Not until six months ago. After that, there's a paper trail linking him to drug shipments coming into the northeast. Two weeks ago, a large shipment of ripple was found in a storage locker in the territory of the Westwoods Pack. The locker was registered to one of Ronnie's companies."

"You think Ronnie really is being framed? Or that he's in this up to his neck and is looking at us to give him an escape?"

"Ronnie is clever, but above all, he's careful. Shrewd. It doesn't fit his MO to register the locker in a company that could so easily be traced back to him."

"Then the question is back to who is framing Ronnie and why?" I asked.

Derek shrugged. "Could be revenge for something Ronnie has done, or information he has passed on. Could be another player wanting Ronnie out of the way so they can muscle in on his operations. Or someone in his gang looking to move up. He's the type of man who has made a lot of enemies."

"Keep digging. Don't rule out anything yet. I want to know if Ronnie is playing us," said Ryan.

Derek nodded. "I've got Waylen on this. If there is anything to be found, he'll get it."

"Waylen Jones?" I asked. I went to school with a human called Waylen. It wasn't a common name around here.

"Yeah, you know him?"

"Sure. He was in my year at school. Sat behind me in math. Skinny guy, always fidgeting. Good with computers."

Ryan snorted. "That's an understatement. We tracked him down two years ago after he hacked into the Pack's mainframe and downloaded the blueprints for the entire Three Rivers. Said he wanted to know if it was true that there was an underground tunnel from the Pack compound to Bridgetown. Turned out he had a secret girlfriend in Bridgetown and wanted to sneak over there without his brother finding out. He was paranoid that his brother, who's six foot three and played quarterback in high school, would follow him on his trips over there, realize the girlfriend was hot and steal her off Waylen."

I glanced from Derek to Ryan. "Is there a tunnel?"

"No," Ryan smiled at me. "As we told Waylen when we picked him up. He didn't believe us. Still doesn't. Even though he's been working for Sam and Mason at their PI firm for the last two years and has been all over the compound top to bottom trying to find it."

"He hacked into the Pack's mainframe, and you gave him a job?" Wally asked.

"Hell, yes. Rather he was working for us than against us."

Just then, Ryan's phone rang.

"Apologies," he said to Thomas and Wally as he pulled his phone out and hit the accept button. I could hear Sam's voice through the phone. "We've got something. A potential lead."

Mason chimed in, his tone urgent. "We've got into Brock's financial records. Six months ago, he bought a property just outside our territory. It's isolated, off the grid. Perfect for hiding someone."

My breath caught as the room fell silent, every pair of eyes fixed on the phone. This could be where Jem was being held.

"We need to check it out," I said, my voice steady despite the racing of my heart.

Ryan nodded. "Keep digging. See if you can get plans or images of the property. We need to know what we'll be walking in to."

"Will do," replied Mason.

"Once we have those, I'll go and scout round the property," Sam said.

"Scouting only, Sam. Do not engage. We'll put a team together and go in first thing tomorrow."

"Copy that."

Ryan hung up as a spark of hope ignited in my chest. If Jem was alive and he was there, he could be home by lunchtime tomorrow.

Ryan must have seen it on my face. "We haven't had proof of life yet, Mai. This might be a storage barn for Brock's action figure collection for all we know."

"I know. It's hard not to hope, though."

"If he's alive, we'll find him, Mai," Ryan whispered, his hand finding mine, squeezing gently.

If he was alive. Or was Brock just fucking with us? That was the question.

Chapter Eight

RYAN

Mai hadn't wanted to stay at the Alpha House, and I hadn't wanted to push it, not yet. I led Mai into my bedroom, a space that had always been more than just a room to me. The king-sized bed at the center acted like a silent promise of comfort and intimacy now that Mai was with me. Full-length windows framed one side, offering a view of the moonlit gardens outside.

My thoughts drifted to Derek, out there in the night, gathering information on Ghost. Mason and Sam were at their office, digging into information about Brock's property, then Sam was going scouting. It was a relief, knowing we weren't in this alone, that my brothers had our backs. Yet, I couldn't help but feel a twinge of satisfaction that tonight, it was just Mai and me in this house.

"I like it here," Mai said softly, flopping on the bed with careless grace. This house was where we first crossed that line, I finally got to sink my cock into her, to possess every part of her, and seal our mate bond.

I moved around, turning on lamps, letting the warm light chase away the shadows and create a cozy glow. I wanted to see her for what

I had planned. Mai shot me an appreciative smile as she stretched leisurely across the bed, the soft lamplight accentuating her curves in all the right ways.

"We should take advantage of the privacy while it lasts."

Her thoughts were mirroring mine and her suggestive tone sent a spear of desire through me, but we had some things to discuss before I could fuck her senseless.

"We need to talk about moving to the Alpha house," I said, watching her closely.

She looked away. "I know it's important," she started. "But there's something about this place, your room...it feels safe, Ryan."

I understood her reluctance. The Alpha house wasn't just a home; it was a symbol, a responsibility. And for someone like Mai, who was used to being alone, used to being on the run, it was a big step. But it was a step we needed to take, for the Pack, for our position as Alphas.

"It's not just a house, Mai," I replied gently, choosing my words with care. "It's a statement. It tells the Pack, and the world, that we're here to stay, that we're in charge."

Mai climbed off the bed and walked toward me. "I know, Ryan. It's just...this room, it's where we started. It's hard to let go. And it feels so final, moving there. Like it's the closing of a chapter in my life, and the start of a scary, new one."

I reached out as she got near me, pulling her into my arms. "We'll make the Alpha House ours, Mai. We'll fill it with new memories, good memories. But this room, this house, it will always be a part of us. No matter where we are."

She nodded, but it wasn't convincing.

"I want to be there tomorrow. I want to be part of the team that search's Brock's property."

Oh, hell no. There was no fucking way she was going. The very idea of it set my teeth on edge, but I had to tread carefully here. "Mai, it's risky. If both Alphas are off territory at the same time—"

"It's Jem. I have to be there," she interjected, her voice firm, as she stepped out of my embrace and started to pace around the room.

I loved her determination, but right now it was a pain in my ass. How could I tell her that my wolf wouldn't stand for it? That he wanted to claim her, chain her up, and guard her from everything? If I let him have his way, she'd find it suffocating, intolerable. That was why I had to sculpt this Pack into a cohesive, fighting unit. We had to bring the Pack together. There had been too much instability, too much violence under Oliver. And Jem and Haley's rocky relationship had done so much fucking underlying damage to the Pack bonds.

My wolf chuffed in agreement. We needed to make this Pack stable; that was the only way to make sure Mai was safe. And if I had the whole Pack protecting her, she wouldn't always feel it was me trying to wrap her in cotton wool. She wouldn't find me suffocating. She wouldn't leave me.

"I know, but we're not even sure if Jem is alive," I countered. "We need to think about the Pack. Brock is still out there. Not everyone has accepted us as Alphas. There are still some who supported Brock. It's not a good idea for both of us to leave the Three Rivers territory right now. We can't afford to leave the Pack vulnerable."

Mai's brow furrowed as she sighed. "I hate that you're right," she admitted, her voice softer. "I want to be there, in case Jem..."

"I get it, Mai," I said, taking her hands in mine.

She looked up at me, her big brown eyes earnest and intense. "You go. I'll stay and hold down the fort. It's the smart move."

Thank fuck for that. "If he's there, I'll bring him back to you. I promise."

———

I gave her one last look, wanting to memorize every detail of her body before claiming her. No more distractions. She was mine now. I stalked toward her and my cock, already hard, twitched when her eyes widened, her breathing hitched, and her pulse sped up.

That's right. I'm hunting you. There's no escape.

She stood still as I approached, eyes watching my every move. I grabbed her and captured her mouth in a kiss. I couldn't get enough of her, so I plunged my tongue deeper. Our tongues tangled together, and she met me stroke for stroke, her hands gripping my hair tightly as she arched into me.

I slipped my hand beneath her shirt, feeling the warmth of her skin against mine, and traced my fingers along her collarbone, slowly working my way down to the valley between her breasts. Her sweet, fucking breasts. I needed to see them.

I pulled her top off her, unclipped her bra and watched as her tits bounced free. They were so pert, so fucking inviting.

"Mine," I growled, as my fingers tweaked her hardened nipples. A shiver ran through her body, and she moaned.

Hell, yeah.

My hand moved to the button of her pants, and I worked it open slowly, savoring the anticipation of what lay beneath. As I slipped my hand inside, I could hear her heart racing. She gasped as my fingers found their way into her panties. Her scent, of honeysuckle, mint, and aspen leaves was intoxicating; it was a heady mix of arousal and need that had me on the edge already.

"Fuck, you're already wet for me," I murmured against her skin, my voice thick with lust.

She nodded, her breath coming in short pants now, and I could feel her tremble beneath my touch. I slid a finger inside her slowly, watching her face as I delved deeper, feeling the tight heat of her body gripping me. She was perfect—tight and wet and ready for me. As I thrust my finger in and out, she let out a moan that vibrated through my body, making me even harder.

I circled her nipples with my tongue before taking one in my mouth and sucking and grazing my teeth on it ever so delicately. She gasped as I switched and paid the same attention to her other nipple.

I needed to hear her moan for me again. I moved lower, quickly stripping off her pants, and pushed her on to the bed. She giggled as she landed on the mattress, then went still as I hovered my mouth over her panties, at just the right spot. Breathing out, I let my hot breath touch her there and she writhed with impatience. Chuckling, I started to lick her through the silky material of her panties. My wolf's instincts demanded that I claim her now, that if I didn't take her right then and there, we would both go crazy. But some part of me held back. I wanted to make sure she felt every last ounce of pleasure. I grabbed her thighs and tossed them over my shoulders.

As my tongue stroked her throbbing clit through the damp fabric, she moaned loudly, and I smiled. There it was. My cock throbbed in response.

"You want more?" I asked, smiling wickedly at her whimper as I pulled her panties to one side and slid a finger inside her again.

She nodded vigorously, looking down at me with lust-filled eyes and biting her delicious bottom lip. Her cheeks looked flushed, and the scent of her honeyed arousal made my cock twitch relentlessly in my jeans. I quickly shoved them down and took out my cock in one swift move.

I stroked my shaft slowly, watching her eyes widen as she watched me. My fingers slid along the length of it, coating my own hand in pre-cum.

"Ryan," she moaned.

"You like that, do you? Watching me touch myself and thinking about me plunging into you again and again."

Her breath hitched.

I didn't waste another second; I pulled off the rest of her clothes, gave myself a moment to admire the fucking beauty that she was, then went to the small fridge in the corner, opened the freezer compartment and put five ice cubes in a glass.

Mai eyed me suspiciously. "What are they for?"

"Guess."

Her eyes widened. "You don't honestly think you're going to—"

"I don't think. I know. And you're going to love it, Mai."

I picked up a cube. "Lie back."

She only hesitated for a moment, then did as I commanded. Fuck, I loved that about her. Willing to try anything.

I held the ice cube tight in my palm over her naked body. I felt the ice melt and watched it drip from my palm onto her hot skin. She gasped as the icy water splashed on her stomach. I moved my hand, trailing the water up and around her breasts. She was panting now, her eyes half-lidded with desire. Kneeling next to her, I placed the cube against her skin.

"Oh!"

I grinned as her eyes flew open in delight.

"Like it?"

She nodded. The cube melted against her skin and I traced her contours with it, sliding it up, around and over first one nipple, then the other.

"Oh, fuck!" she whimpered.

I bent over and took her free nipple in my mouth, switching them over so she had ice, then my hot mouth on her. Her nipples were so erect, so wet from the icy water, it was fucking amazing. I was going to come right there.

"Ready for more?" I whispered.

"Goddess, yes!"

I popped the ice cube in my mouth, then closed my lips around her clit.

"Ryan!" she cried, and I knew she wasn't going to last long. I used my tongue to stroke the cube against her clit.

Her taste was on my tongue, scorching hot and sweet at the same time. She was perfect—in every sense of the word.

I grabbed another ice cube and gently pushed it inside of her. Her whole body shook, shivering with wave after wave of pleasure.

"That's so...fuck, Ryan, that feels so amazing!"

I rose up and slid into her. She cried as her walls stretched around me like a glove.

My wolf nearly purred with satisfaction at the silky delight of being deep inside our mate again. The heat from her pussy enveloped me, then the ice cube started to melt, sending spikes of icy water around my cock.

Mai started to move her hips against me urgently.

She was so fucking responsive, so eager to take my cock, and every sound she made only drove me further into the depths of desire.

I needed to be deeper inside of her. I slid out, laughing as she moaned in disappointment, before I flipped her over. I pulled her hips up, so her ass was in the air, and positioned her so her knees were on the very edge of the bed, and she had to balance there.

"Stay there," I ordered, then got off the bed, stood behind her and, holding her in place with my hands on her hips, thrust into her again. Her whole body spasmed under me. Then she started to move, her hips rising to meet mine with each thrust. Our rhythm was fast but smooth now, every grind sending waves of heat coursing through my body. I slowed down my thrusts, drawing out her pleasure for as long as I could stand it. She was so fucking wet her juices were dripping off my balls. When she started to groan again, I felt her walls clench against my cock and knew she was about to come apart. I grabbed another ice cube, bent over her, and rubbed it against her swollen clit. Then I pounded into her as she cried out, moaning and writhing. I fucking loved that I could do this to her. Spurred on by the added friction, we moved together faster and faster. Every thrust seemed to drive us both closer to insanity.

"Oh my Goddess, Ryan," she whispered huskily. "I can't take any more. I'm going to—"

She came on a loud shout of my name. Her inner walls contracted around me, sending streams of her cum coating my throbbing shaft, making me lose all control. I bucked into her as her release triggered my own, and I held her tight against me as we both tumbled over the edge together into ecstasy.

Chapter Nine

RYAN

Brock's property was nestled in a secluded section of forest, hidden from prying eyes. I had taken Derek, Mason, Sam, Rafael and Ava with me. Ava was decisive, cool under pressure and didn't stand any crap from others. Rafael was the joker of the Renegades, always quick to laugh and tease, but when needed, he proved to be serious and deadly. Both her and Rafael were werewolves we could trust.

Despite Sam's scouting report, asserting the area appeared deserted, I knew better than to lower our guard. In dealing with Brock, complacency was not an option.

As we neared the clearing that housed Brock's property, I signaled for a halt. The tree line provided a natural cover, allowing us a moment to check it out. Mist clung to the ground, creating a ghostly veil that partially obscured the house and barn. Their shapes loomed, spectral and foreboding, as if emerging from a dream.

"Perimeter's clear," Sam whispered, his gaze sweeping the dense tree line, ears straining for any sound out of place.

Mason, standing a step behind, only had eyes for the target. "Two main buildings—the house and the barn. We'll need to be thorough, check every possible hiding spot." His voice was a low murmur, barely audible above the rustling leaves.

"Derek," I turned to face them, "you're with me. We'll take the house."

Derek's response was a simple jerk of his chin.

"Mason, Sam, cover the barn." I glanced at them, noting the subtle shift in their stance, ready for action.

"Ava, Rafael, guard our backs. Make sure no-one sneaks up on us while we're inside." I looked at each of them in turn. "And remember, stay sharp. Brock's never been one to leave things to chance."

Splitting up was risky, but it doubled our speed while minimizing our exposure. We'd sweep each building simultaneously, converge on any discoveries, and get the hell out. A clean, surgical strike.

Rafael and Ava vanished into the ghostly mist, their silhouettes quickly swallowed by the morning fog. Mason and Sam were next, their footsteps muffled, as they moved towards the barn, a fusion of stealth and strength.

Derek and I approached the house, our boots crunching softly on the gravel pathway, the sound jarring in the predawn stillness. The house loomed before us, an unassuming structure cloaked in the morning fog. It had a wooden exterior, once painted in what must have been a bright blue but now faded by the elements. Vines crept up one side, nature's fingers trying to reclaim what man had placed here.

My hand reached for the door, cool against my skin. I slipped into that dark place in my mind I went to on missions, my senses sharpened, and my movements controlled, deliberate. Derek gave a curt nod; he was ready.

Inside, the house was a canvas of minimalism and neglect. The living room, small and confined, melded seamlessly into a cramped kitchen. The air was stale, the scent of disuse heavy. A faint, underlying odor of mold lingered. I inhaled deeply, sifting through the layers of smells for anything out of place, any hint of Jem.

Sparse furnishings dotted the space—a threadbare sofa, a coffee table marred with rings from forgotten cups, a small box television.

Derek and I moved in sync, our footsteps silent on the wooden floor. My eyes scanned every inch, every corner.

We moved to the kitchen. Its counters were clear, save for a few utensils and a lone, dusty kettle. My eyes lingered on a small kitchen knife, its blade catching the dim light.

Derek, a few steps behind, paused to examine the countertop, running his finger along the surface.

"Too clean," he muttered, almost to himself. His observation was spot on; the kettle was dusty, but the countertop was immaculate, hinting at a deliberate attempt to erase some traces. But of what?

Room by room, we continued our search. The bedrooms were unremarkable, their beds empty and disused. Closets stood bare, a few hangers swaying slightly as we passed by. The air here was cooler, the scent sterile and controlled, as if someone had gone to great lengths to leave no trace behind.

"Nothing," Derek said, his voice echoing my own frustration. We moved back through the house in silence, each step heavier than the last.

Outside, the early morning light had begun to chase away the shadows, revealing the reality of our situation. The property, once a beacon of hope in our search for Jem, now felt like a barren wasteland of disappointment.

Sam and Mason appeared from the direction of the barn. Their expressions were grim, and it was clear they had no better news than we did.

"The barn's clear," Sam reported. "No sign of Brock or Jem. No traces, no scents. I don't know if either of them have ever even been here."

Mason, usually the stoic one, allowed a rare flicker of annoyance to cross his features. "We checked every stall, every loft, every nook and cranny. Nothing. If Jem was here, there's no evidence left. No scent either."

Fuck! I was going to have to break the news to Mai. I knew I told her not to get her hopes up, but our bond told me she was desperate that we would find Jem.

"We'll search the house again," I ordered. "Look for anything—papers, receipts, phones, anything that could give us a clue to Brock's whereabouts."

My phone vibrated in my pocket. I dragged it out. Unknown number. Okay, I'll play. I hit the answer button.

"Who is this?"

"Ryan Shaw, this is Kara Adelaide, Alpha of the Cocrane Pack."

I paused. I'd met Kara when I'd gone to the Cocrane Pack searching for Mai after Seth had kidnapped her. Kara and Ajak, the Alphas, had refused to help me find them, but after I left the meeting Kara had sent a girl after me who had given me an idea of where to look. The tip had been right, and I'd reached Mai just in time. I'd gotten the impression that Kara had been fond of Mai when Mai lived with the Cocrane Pack.

"Kara, this is a surprise."

"I wanted to congratulate you on becoming Alphas of the Three Rivers Pack. I trust Mai is well?"

"Mai is doing great, thank you."

"Please tell Mai that I am sorry about what happened with Seth."

"If you text me a number, I can give it to Mai and you can tell her yourself."

Mai had told me that she liked Kara. If she was ready to talk to her, it would be good for Mai to have more friends. Someone she could talk to about this whole Alpha thing.

"I would appreciate that. However, that is not the reason I'm calling."

"Oh?"

"The Cocrane Pack would like to enter into a no-hostilities pact with the Three Rivers Pack. We harbor no ill feelings about the death of our Packmate, Seth. It was a righteous kill."

Well, that was a surprise. A no-hostilities pact meant that both Packs would guarantee not to attack the other. Sometimes it was the first step toward a full alliance, where each Pack would support and aid each other, and pledge to defend the other Pack if it was attacked.

"That's an interesting offer, Kara. I will need to discuss it with my mate."

"Of course. That brings me to another piece of news. As I'm sure you are aware, Michael and Camille of the Bridgetown Pack sent Korrin home to us after he interfered in your challenge to be Alphas of the Three Rivers. As punishment, I am letting you know that Korrin, along with eight of our wolves that were with him, have been officially banished from our Pack. Their Pack bonds have been destroyed. His interference with your Alpha challenge went against all our Shifter laws."

Fuck! This call wasn't about offering a pact. This was about covering their own asses. Kara was telling me that Korrin was in the wind. I knew Kara and Ajak would punish Korrin, but I had thought that punishment would be within their Pack and they would keep a tight leash on him from now on. By banishing Korrin, he could do anything, be anywhere. And Kara wanted to make sure that there was no blowback on her Pack.

"Can we expect an attack?" I asked, my voice hard.

Kara paused. "Korrin is still...upset at the death of his son. He is passionate, should I say, about revenge."

Great. This was just what we needed right now.

"I appreciate you letting me know."

"Be careful, Ryan. And protect Mai."

She hung up before I could reply.

I pocketed the phone and walked into the house. I should have killed Korrin when we had the chance. He'd tried to ambush us on our way back from our first meeting with Ronnie Bishop. He'd managed to ram our car off the road and in the ensuring fight, Sam and Mason had been badly hurt. Thomas had had to put Sam into a coma for a few days while he healed. I'd fought Korrin and broken his leg. I should have killed him, but Mai didn't want to kill a man when he was defeated and couldn't fight back. Or maybe it was because she and I had killed Korrin's son. Did she feel guilty? She had nothing to feel guilty about. Seth was psychotic. He would have killed her.

"Ryan, check this out."

Derek's voice snapped me back to the present. He stood in the office, a neatly arranged room with a desk dominating the space. The desk was clear apart from a computer resting on top, its screen glowing softly in the dim room. Derek turned the screen so we could all see.

Brock's smug face was on it, his eyes gleaming with malice. Derek hit play and Brock's voice came out of the speakers. "Looking for something?"

His voice, dripping with condescension, sent a ripple of anger through me. He was taunting us, playing games with Mai's feelings and Jem's life as if they were nothing but pawns in his twisted agenda.

"You really thought it would be this easy?" Brock continued, his smirk widening. "You've got a lot to learn. If you want Jem, you know what you have to do. Time's ticking."

Mason's hand squeezed my shoulder. "We'll find him," he said firmly, though I could hear the doubt lurking beneath. "There's still time."

I wanted to believe him, to find solace in his assurance. But the reality was that Brock had outsmarted us. Again. And now Jem's life hung in the balance, if he was even alive. This could all be a ruse by Brock to fuck with us and keep us off-kilter. To fuck with Mai's emotions and draw out her grief. Brock had given Mai hope, and now I had to go home and crush it.

Chapter Ten

MAI

The soothing familiarity of Jem's old study wrapped around me like a warm embrace as I stood in the doorway, taking in the quiet stillness. Sylvie wasn't here, but she'd left a food platter in the fridge, and I'd noticed fresh flowers in the hallway. Stepping inside the study, I let the oak door close behind me with a soft thud that echoed in the large, book-lined room. This had been Jem's sanctuary, a place where the duties and stresses of the Pack could be momentarily set aside. Brock hadn't had time to gut it, and the scent of Sylvie here told me that whatever changes he'd made, she had undone. And now, it was mine.

I moved further into the room, my fingers trailing over the leather spines of books, loving the feel and scent of them. Jem's presence, while gone, still lingered here, whispers of him woven into the very walls. Photos in simple frames dotted the room: Jem and Hayley at the annual Moon Dance, some of the enforcers after a successful hunt, a candid shot of Ryan and Jem drinking at Bottley Bar, a photo of me and Jem playing football taken just before our parents died. Each captured moment was a glimpse into his life, into who he was and what was important to him.

I sank down into the plush leather chair behind the desk, the faint scent of sandalwood—the scent of my brother—still clinging to it.

I leaned back, tilting my face up to the light streaming in through the windows behind me. The warm rays splashed across my face. Was Jem really dead? Or was he out there somewhere, in Brock's hands? Every passing hour twisted my anxiety tighter.

A polite rap at the door stopped my thoughts from spiraling.

"Come in," I called, straightening in my seat.

The door opened, and Jase poked his head in, an uncertain smile flickering across his boyish face. "Hey, sorry to bother you. Just wanted to check if you need anything?"

Jase's presence brought a small smile to my lips. I beckoned him inside. "You're not bothering me. Come on in."

Jase stepped into the study, softly shutting the door behind him. He stood awkwardly for a moment, hands behind his back, as his eyes roamed the room before settling on me.

"Nice digs," he said, a hint of awe in his tone as he took in the dark wood, the floor-to-ceiling bookshelves brimming with volumes, the plush rugs underfoot. "Swanky."

I let out a short laugh. "It's not really my taste. A bit too formal and serious, but I can see why Jem liked it."

Jase moved closer to the desk where I sat. "Yeah, it fits him. Kinda old-fashioned but in a distinguished gentleman kinda way."

"You never came in here before?"

Jase shook his head. "I had no reason to come here. My parents came a few times when Oliver was Alpha. After that, with Jem and

Hayley, I had no problems, nothing I needed to discuss with the Alphas."

I looked around the room, thinking that I wanted to change that. I wanted this to be an open place for people to come and chat and just talk about everyday things, not just when they had an issue only an Alpha could resolve.

"Anyways," Jase said, breaking the moment, "how're you holding up?"

I gave a small shrug. "Hanging in there. Trying not to think about..." I trailed off, but Jase understood.

"If Jem's there, Ryan will find him."

"I know. I just wish I was there, too. But Ryan was right. We can't risk leaving the Pack unprotected." Even as I said the words, they tasted bitter. My brother was out there, and my place was here dealing with paperwork and Pack business.

Jase perched on the edge of the desk. "For what it's worth, I think you and Ryan are a fucking great team. You've got this Alpha stuff down."

I grimaced. The boy wonder was trying to pep me up.

Jase's expression hardened. "I'm serious. You're one of the strongest people I know, Mai. Whatever happens with Jem, Brock, all of this crazy stuff...you've got this."

I couldn't stand having Jase try to cheer me up. I was his Alpha, I was supposed to look after him. "What're you doing here, anyway? Shouldn't you be at work at this time of day?"

Jase shrugged, unconcerned. "I quit."

I blinked. "You what now?"

"I quit. I wasn't going to be a delivery boy forever, and this is more important."

"This being?"

"Watching your back."

A warm fuzzy feeling spread through my chest. But still. Watching my back would put him in danger. He'd already been through a lot supporting me and Ryan. If it wasn't for us, he never would have had both his ankles broken. I wasn't sure I felt comfortable with little Jase Miller being a target for me. I started to reply when hurried footsteps and a quick rap at the door had us both twisting around.

"We'll talk about this later," I said quietly before raising my voice again. "Come in."

The door burst open and Evelyn strode in, slightly breathless. In her mid-thirties, with a slender build with defined muscles, and long dark brown hair that she usually wore in a braid, Evelyn had been a staunch supporter of me and Ryan, even letting us crash at her cousin's place when we were hiding from Brock and Hayley.

"Evelyn?" I questioned, rising from my seat. "Everything okay?"

She closed the door swiftly behind her before facing us, her expression grim.

"I just got a tipoff that there's a ripple pickup at the farmer's market. This morning."

Her words dropped like stones in the quiet room. I stiffened, exchanging a startled look with Jase.

"The farmer's market?" I repeated. "That's in the middle of town. Are you sure?"

Evelyn nodded. "My contact is one of the stall owners. Said they'd seen suspicious activity in the last few weeks. He thinks they're using one of the stalls as a front for the exchange."

Before I left, the farmer's market had been a cornerstone of the Three Rivers community. A lot of trade happened in the market. Three Rivers was a convergence point between the smaller towns further north, and the big cities in the south. Most goods passed through here and the market was a key place for trades to happen. If the stall owner was right, this could be our chance to finally get a solid lead on Ghost.

My mind kicked into gear as the pieces fell into place. "We need to intercept that pickup."

Evelyn's eyes gleamed. She knew the opportunity this presented. "I can pull in maybe five Renegades that are nearby."

I nodded. "Do it. We'll meet them there."

"I want to come," Jase said. Something in his tone stopped my immediate reaction that he should stay here. Jase wanted to be an enforcer for the Pack, had proven himself on a number of occasions. If he could get his ankles broken and still want to do this, then he would find a way. Maybe watching my back wasn't such a bad idea; at least that way I'd be able to keep an eye on him. I still wanted to talk to him about quitting his job, though.

"Alright, get the car ready. We need to move fast."

As Jase sprinted from the room, I turned to Evelyn. "Make sure your team is ready, but keep it quiet. We don't want word getting back to Ghost's people and spooking them. If they get there before us, tell our enforcers not to engage, just observe for now."

Evelyn nodded, already typing rapidly into her phone. I strode from the study, my earlier uncertainty burned away by pure, propulsive purpose. This could be it—our chance to finally gain ground against Ghost and his ripple.

Chapter Eleven

Mai

I jumped into the pickup, Jase driving as we sped from the compound. Evelyn sat silently in the backseat, tapping messages on her phone to the other Renegades. My heart thudded loudly in my chest as I tried to calm the anger that was bubbling up inside. How fucking dare they be trading this stuff in Three Rivers.

"What's the plan?" Jase asked, navigating a sharp turn.

"Stopping that ripple shipment has to be priority one. We can't risk more of it getting out. But this is also a golden chance to get one of Ghost's contacts. If we can grab just one dealer, we may finally get some real intel on Ghost."

"It won't be easy. If we're right, these will be serious people," Evelyn commented from behind us.

"We'll hopefully have the element of surprise on our side. Evelyn, your team is in place?"

"Yes, I have five Renegades on standby near the market," she confirmed.

"Good. We wait until the deal is done, then grab one of the dealers. We need to do this as quickly and quietly as possible. The market will be full of people; we don't want any bystanders injured."

Jase pulled the pickup into a side alley a block from the market entrance. We headed for the main street, the din of the bustling market washing over us: vendors hawking fresh breads and produce, the murmur of lively conversations, laughter and yips as children, in both human and wolf forms, chased each other round the legs of adults.

I scanned the crowded stalls and shoppers. Evelyn nudged me, then tilted her head at a vegetable stall near the fountain. A plump, silver-haired woman was working the stall, bagging potatoes for a customer with a broad smile. The image of wholesome community spirit.

"I'll be stationed over there," Evelyn pointed to an entrance to an alleyway, next to a hat stand.

There were four main exits from the market: the entrance we had come through, a wide arch leading to a busy street on the opposite side, a narrower passage snaking between the sun-bleached stalls to the south, and an open black gate at the northern end. Smaller alleyways, like the one Evelyn had chosen, branched off at irregular intervals, offering refuge from the bustling crowd.

I gestured to Jase that he should blend into the browsing shoppers. Near the fountain, a group of musicians had gathered, the jaunty melody of a fiddle intertwining with the deep thrum of a bass. The music added to the Market's lively atmosphere, but it also meant an extra challenge in monitoring the area for threats.

We all kept a casual distance from the produce stall and waited. Shoppers came and went. Most of them chatted with the vendor, bought something and moved on. Nothing suspicious.

It wasn't long, though, before the whispers started.

"Is that...?"

"Have you seen who's here?"

"Is she going to buy something, do you think?"

Damn it. This fish bowl thing was not helping.

My eyes found Evelyn. I jerked my chin toward the west exit. Evelyn set off immediately. I walked slowly, taking my time to nod to the stall owners. I'd been had and now I had to play the Alpha role. Jase followed behind, doing what he promised and watching my back.

It took about ten minutes for me to reach the west gate.

Evelyn was waiting for me and Jase.

"Any news?" I asked.

Evelyn checked her phone. "Nothing suspicious at the stall."

"Good. I'm sorry about this, turns out I'm a hinderance. Too many people recognize me and are curious about the new Alpha and what I'm doing here. Any dealers won't come near this place while I'm around."

"It'll settle down. People are nervous right now. After Jem, after Brock and Hayley. They're not sure yet of you and Ryan," Jase said.

"Jase is right. Things will settle down," Evelyn agreed.

"Can your team handle this?" I asked her.

"Of course." She nodded to our left. "The Coffee Emporium is just over there. They have seating upstairs where you can look out over most of the market. You can keep an eye on the situation from there, if you like."

I followed Evelyn's gaze to see the three-story coffee shop on the edge of the market.

Jase grinned. "Just don't tell Sofia we went in there. It's her stiffest competition."

⁂

Jase and I bought a couple of coffees—extra cream for me, and black for the enforcer-wannabe—and took seats on the third floor next to a large window with a view over the market. I had a good view of the vegetable stall.

I spotted them after twenty minutes. Two men wound their way through the bustling crowd, their movements sharp and deliberate, cutting a clear path toward the vegetable stall. The first, a bulky figure, had the build of a seasoned brawler. His beard, unkempt and peppered with gray, jutted from his jawline, giving him a grizzled, almost bear-like appearance. His eyes, sharp and scanning, darted over the throng, hinting at a person used to danger. He wore a thick, leather jacket despite the mild weather, its surface scuffed and scarred, as though it had seen its share of scuffles.

The other was leaner, almost wiry, with a head completely shaven. His gait was peculiar—a slight limp in his left leg, as if nursing an old injury or a poorly healed fracture. He wore a faded black t-shirt that clung to his sinewy frame, and his arms were sleeved with tattoos, intricate designs that snaked from his wrists up to his hidden shoulders. One particularly noticeable tattoo, a snarling wolf, seemed to leap out from his forearm as he moved. Around his waist was a distinctive belt, studded with metal and adorned with a large, ornate buckle depicting a serpent coiled around a skull. His eyes, like his companion's, were alert, constantly flicking over the faces in the crowd.

I watched as they approached the silver-haired vendor. She gave them a subtle nod, her expression betraying nothing as they exchanged quiet words. Then, with casual nonchalance, the bearded man slipped her an envelope. In turn, she passed him a small, dark blue haversack. The ripple payload.

It was a slick, discreet exchange, over in moments. Then the two men turned and left the stall in separate directions, vanishing into the milling crowds.

From this viewpoint, I could see five Renegades emerge from their spots and spring into action. I was guessing the sixth had been ordered to watch the stallowner.

My eyes tracked Grizzly Adams; he was the one with the ripple. He headed to a bottleneck, where people were pushed together between two popular stalls that each had customers three deep waiting their turn. Evelyn wasn't far behind him. Grizzly passed through the crowds, then walked past a teenage girl in a green hoodie. If I'd blinked, I would have missed it. The teenager had an identical dark blue haversack, and they did a switch as they passed each other. Evelyn was too far behind; she had at least five people between her and Grizzly.

"Did you see that?" Jase asked, rising out of his chair for a better look.

"Yeah." I kept my eye trained on Evelyn, waiting to see if she followed the teenager or Grizzly. The teenager veered left, keeping two people next to her as she walked past Evelyn. Grizzly kept going. I held my breath as Evelyn followed Grizzly.

Fuck!

I took off, taking the stairs two at a time, Jase right behind me. We burst out in the street.

"There!" Jase pointed to a stall selling 'authentic Three Rivers Forest' candles. The girl in the green hoodie was sniffing one of the candles. She pulled a face, put the candle back and set off toward the north end of the market.

"Text Evelyn. Tell her the mark made a switch. She needs to keep following and see where he goes. Me and you will try to get the ripple. Stay close, Jase. We don't know how many more of them are here."

I didn't want to be walking us into a trap, but if I did, the closer Jase was, the more likely I could protect him.

As if reading my thoughts, Jase looked at me out of the corner of his eye. "I'm supposed to be watching your back, Mai, not the other way round."

Mmm, I was going to have to learn to be more subtle about this.

We trailed the girl in the green hoodie for the next twenty minutes. She didn't seem to be in a rush to leave the market; tasting the free food samples, trying on scarfs and hats, and smelling candles, perfumes and soaps. She didn't buy anything though and kept moving north.

As she got near the northern gate, Jase asked, "What do we do when she leaves the market?"

Otter's Road ran perpendicular to the market's northern gate. It was a quiet road; perfect for a pickup if she had someone in a car waiting for her. We couldn't let the girl get in a car. We had to take her before that happened.

"Get ahead of her. Wait just outside the gate. Take her when she comes out. I'll keep following in case she heads in a different direction."

Jase nodded, his eyes hardening with determination. He quickened his pace, weaving through the crowd with the agility of a wolf on the hunt. I watched as he slipped through the northern gate and took up a position just outside, partially concealed by a stack of empty crates.

I kept my eyes locked on the girl in the green hoodie, matching her leisurely pace as she made her way towards the exit. She paused at a stall selling handcrafted jewelry, admiring a pair of silver earrings, but after a moment, she moved on, heading straight for the gate where Jase waited.

As she stepped through the threshold, Jase lunged forward, grabbing her arm in an iron grip. The girl yelped in surprise, instantly trying to wrench herself free. I surged forward, closing the distance in a heartbeat.

The girl was quick, twisting like an eel in Jase's grasp. She lashed out with her free hand, aiming a wild punch at his face. Jase ducked, but the movement loosened his hold, and she managed to slip free.

I was on her in an instant, tackling her to the ground. We hit the cobblestones hard; the impact knocking the air from my lungs. The girl thrashed beneath me, her elbow catching me in the ribs. I grunted, tightening my hold.

Jase was there a second later, pinning her legs as I fought to restrain her arms. She was strong, fueled by desperation and adrenaline.

As we struggled, her hoodie fell back, revealing a shock of bright blue hair. I don't know if it was her hair, or her scent that finally penetrated Jase's brain, but he recognized her.

"Amara?" Jase's voice was strangled with disbelief.

The girl, Amara, went still beneath us, her eyes wide with fear and shock.

"Jase?"

"What the hell are you doing?" Jase demanded, his voice shaking.

"You know her?" I asked, not loosening my hold on Amara's arms.

Jase swallowed hard, his jaw clenching. "She's my ex-girlfriend."

Chapter Twelve

MAI

So, this was awkward. I wasn't letting her up though and scanned the crowds that were starting to gather around us.

"I haven't seen her in months, but..." Jase continued as he shook his head, as if trying to clear it. "Amara, what the fuck have you gotten yourself into?"

"What have I gotten into? What the hell are you doing? Last I heard you were a delivery boy. Now you're attacking random women at the market!"

"We need to get her out of here," I said, not liking the murmurs around us. I was going to have to pull the Alpha card soon to stop anyone from interfering. Then the fact that we took a girl from the market would be all over the Three Rivers, and Ghost would know we were closing in.

A car screeched to a halt in front of us, and Evelyn leaned out. "Need a ride?"

"Goddess, yes!" I pulled the girl up, twisting her arm behind her back. "Try anything and I'll break it."

The girl turned her head to sneer at me before saying to Jase, "This your new girlfriend? Bit of a bitch, ain't she?"

"Actually—"

I shut him up with a look. I had probably been recognised but on the off chance that I hadn't, I didn't want everyone with werewolf hearing to overhear who I was.

I hauled the girl into the back of the car, making sure to snag the haversack from the ground, and followed her in. Jase jumped in the other side, boxing Amara between us, and Evelyn hit the gas.

"What happened?" I asked Evelyn as we turned off Otter Road and headed to the Alpha compound.

"We lost the dealers. They both headed straight for an exit and were picked up by different cars. We managed to get the plate for one, and I've sent it to Shaw Investigations to see if they can track it down. We did manage to get the stall holder. Woman named Greta. My team is taking her to the cage room now. I figured if the other two were picked up at the exits, maybe your mark would be too. So I jumped in the car and headed round."

Amara was looking from Evelyn to me to Jase. "Cage room?" she squeaked. "Are you guys working for the new Alphas?" Her eyes widened. "Fuck! Let me out now! I don't want anything to do with the new fucking Alphas. I heard they're worse than that old one, Oliver. Jase, you gotta help me! I don't want to end up wolf meat for their next meal!"

I turned my gaze on her and let my wolf out a bit. I don't know what she saw in my eyes, but she cringed away from me.

"Fuck! You're her, aren't you? Fuck!"

Jase snorted. "You always did know how to make a memorable first impression, Amara."

Her scent changed; before she was angry but now waves of extreme fear were rolling off her.

"This isn't funny, Jase. You don't know... you don't know."

"Relax, Amara. I don't know what you've heard or who you've heard it from, but we don't really eat wolves. Ask Jase. You know what kind of person he is. Would he be here, working for me, if we were that bad?"

"You don't understand. You have to let me go," she said quietly. "Please. I can't be seen with you."

"Why?"

She shook her head, eyes downcast. A single tear trickled down her cheek.

What was going on?

"Evelyn, change of plan, take us to Thomas's."

I didn't want to come in hard with Amara, and Thomas and Jase might be our best bet to get her to open up.

Evelyn pulled the car up to the curb outside Thomas's house. As we climbed out, the front door opened, and Thomas stepped out. I don't know how it did it, but he always knew when I arrived. I kept a firm grip on Amara's arm, but she didn't resist.

"Mai, Jase, Evelyn," he greeted with a nod. His gaze settled on Amara, who was still wedged between us, her shoulders hunched and her eyes down, though they were darting nervously. "Amara, isn't it?"

She nodded.

"Have you met Amara before?" I asked.

Thomas frowned. "No, but I knew her parents."

"Knew?"

"Yes, they died last year."

"I see. Well, Amara's...involved in a situation we're investigating. We were hoping you could help us out."

Thomas's expression softened, and he stepped aside, gesturing for us to enter. "Of course. Please, come in."

As we crossed the threshold, Wally emerged from the kitchen. He raised an eyebrow at the sight of Amara, but gave me a wicked grin. "Mai, always a pleasure. Are you back for more of my delicious lasagne, or time with my sparking personality?"

I returned the smile, feeling a little of the tension ease from my shoulders. "As much as I love them both, Wally, we need to borrow Thomas's expertise."

Wally dramatically put a hand on his heart, "Ah, you wound me, Mai. I always knew you liked Thomas more than me!"

Amara was staring wide-eyed at Wally, as if she had no idea what she'd walked in to. Wally caught her looking and winked at her.

"Come, please," said Thomas, "before Wally starts listing all the ways that he's better and prettier than me—all of which will be true, by the way."

Thomas led us down the hall to his medical room. "Amara, why don't you and Jase wait in here for a moment? I just need to speak with Mai."

Amara hesitated, her gaze flicking to Jase uncertainly. I gave Jase a pointed look. "Keep an eye on her, make sure she doesn't try to run off. We won't be long."

Jase nodded and guided Amara into the room, closing the door firmly behind them.

Evelyn and I followed Thomas out into his garden, making sure we were out of earshot.

"What can I do to help?" Thomas asked, turning to face me.

"We caught Amara with this." I held up the blue haversack, opening it to reveal several bags of small, round red pills, each one marked with a distinctive three-wave emblem. "We think this is ripple. I was hoping you could run some tests, see what you can find out about it."

Thomas took the haversack, examining the pills with a furrowed brow, before opening one of the bags and cautiously sniffing inside.

The strong scent of salt and a dark, musky smell wafted out.

"I'll do what I can, Mai. I have some equipment here that should help me get started."

"Thank you, Thomas." I hesitated, glancing towards the closed door. "There's something else. Amara...she's scared, really scared. More than just being caught. I was hoping you and Jase might be able to get her to talk, find out what has her so terrified. How she ended up involved in all this."

"I'll do my best." Thomas's expression softened. "Unfortunately, I have bad news. Norman Adler killed himself this morning."

"The addict whose home we searched?"

Thomas nodded.

Fuck! Fuck fuckity fuck fuck!

"What about Garth and Liam?"

"It's touch and go. Liam is recovering, but Garth is not out of the woods yet. He can't Shift which is a worrying sign after only one dose. But we'll get to the bottom of this, Mai, one way or another. Now, I suggest you head out through the side gate, unless you want Wally to insist on feeding you and regaling you with his many finer points."

"That doesn't sound so bad. But I do need to take a rain check. Next time?"

"Next time," Thomas agreed.

With a final nod, Evelyn and I headed for the side gate, my mind already racing with the next steps. We had lost our first Pack member to ripple, but we now had the drugs and a potential witness. But I couldn't shake the feeling that we were still only scratching the surface of something much larger and more sinister.

Chapter Thirteen

Mai

I sank into one of the plush leather armchairs in Jem's study. Greta, the human stall vendor, was secured in the cage room downstairs. Ryan and his brothers had come back about an hour ago with the news that Jem was not at Brock's property and the bastard had left a message just for us.

Frustration and despair clawed at my insides. Every lead, every hope, seemed to slip through our fingers like sand. Time was running out, and with each passing hour, the chance of finding Jem grew dimmer. A feeling of hopelessness sat on my chest, like a lead weight, threatening to drown me.

Shift. Run.

My wolf wanted out. It had been a while since we'd been able to be in wolf form, and she was getting impatient.

Not yet. Soon.

She rubbed against my insides, making her displeasure known, but I didn't have time right now.

Soon, I repeated, and she went quiet.

Ryan stood at the bay window, staring out into the forest, deep in thought. He was working through his anger that he hadn't found Jem, that I'd gone to the market without telling him, had followed drug dealers, and ended up in a fight with a teenager. If we were going to be the Alphas we needed to be, then we were going to have to find a way to make this work. I needed to be able to make on-the-spot decisions, and he needed to trust that I'd be okay.

Ryan shifted to the side, and my eyes fell on his perfect ass. It was honed, pert, and oh-so-touchable; I wanted to nibble on it, then clasp it tight as he drove his cock into me. Goddess, his whole fucking body was so beautiful, strong muscles sculpted from hours of training and fighting. And it was all mine.

"We're running out of time," Mason said, interrupting my thoughts as he paced before the cold fireplace.

No shit.

"Taking Amara to Thomas was not the best idea. She could have had vital information we need to stop Ghost and shut down ripple here. We need her here so we can interrogate her."

"She isn't a hard-core dealer, Mason. She's a scared teenage girl."

"But we don't know what information she has. In operations like this, intel is often time-sensitive. Whatever she eventually gives us might be too late. Getting it now might give us the piece that cripples Ghost's operation and saves countless lives down the road."

My jaw tightened. I stared at Mason, and he immediately lowered his gaze.

"Is that the kind of Alpha you want me to be?" I asked. "Willing to torture a child? I won't inflict that on someone just because it's convenient. Every member of this Pack matters."

Mason grimaced, raking a hand through his dark hair.

Ryan finally turned to face us. "Mai's right. We have to show the Pack what sort of Alphas we intend to be. And torturing Amara is not it."

I looked at Ryan, really looked at him for the first time since he got back and told me the news that Jem hadn't been there. He was paler than usual. I checked our bond and pulses of tiredness shot through it. He looked worn out. Since we took over, he'd been balancing searching for Jem with trying to stabilize our Pack and protect me at the same time.

I stood up, walked out the door and across the hall into the kitchen.

Sylvie was sitting at the breakfast bar, flicking through recipe books and writing in a notebook in front of her.

"Ah, Mai, I'm glad you're here. Do you think hamburger soup sounds like something you would want to try?"

I pulled a face.

"No? No, I didn't think so either. I'll keep looking. Can I get you anything?"

"Ryan needs something to eat. Is there anything I can grab from the fridge?"

"Och no. Don't you bother yourself with that. I'll bring something in right away, something you can all eat. It's my job to feed you all up after what you've been through."

I stepped toward the fridge. "Oh, don't worry. You keep searching for alternatives to hamburger soup. I can just grab something."

Sylvie held up her pen threateningly. "Step away from the fridge, before I have to use force. And I will, you know! Go and sit down. I'll bring you all food in a moment!"

I froze, then smiled. This was the first time since we got back that someone had talked to me like the old Mai and not the Alpha. It shocked me just how much I appreciated it.

I nodded my head to her, a smile still on my face, and walked back to the study. I went straight to Evelyn, who was seated on the sofa beneath the bay windows. "Did you recognize those dealers back at the market?"

"No," replied Evelyn, her green eyes darkened with concern. "I've never seen them before."

Derek spoke up from where he was leaning against the desk, brows furrowed in concentration as his eyes flickered over his tablet screen.

"I'm pulling the security footage from the market," he said. "I should have something in a minute."

There was a knock on the door and then Sylvie walked in carrying a tray piled high with meat sandwiches, chips and salad.

Ryan's stomach grumbled in response.

"Sylvie, you're a star!" I said. "Thank you."

"It's no problem at all. That's what I'm here for. There's plenty more as well, so eat up, all of you."

The others thanked her as she left the room. I was relieved to see Ryan walk over, take a plate, and fill it with food. Then he put the plate in front of me.

"You need to eat." I pushed the plate toward him.

"And I will, after you."

"Ryan!"

"Mai."

"Can one of you take a bite so the rest of us can eat, please?" Sam chipped in, a grin on his face.

I sighed and took a bite of a ham sandwich. The ham melted in my mouth and I almost moaned with pleasure.

"Does she get that look on her face when you put things in her mouth, bro?" Sam teased Ryan.

Ryan glowered at his brother. "How about I slam my fist into your mouth and see what kind of face you pull?"

Derek and Mason laughed. This was what we needed to break the tension in here. Food and laughter. And to forget for a moment that we were Alphas. It felt good to know that we would still have these times, when our closest family and friends didn't defer but still felt they could tease us.

"Your turn," I said to Ryan, my mouth still full of food.

He filled another plate and sat down at the desk to eat.

Silence invaded the room as we ate. Werewolves took our food seriously.

After ten minutes, I'd eaten enough to voice a question. "Any news on the car that picked up one of the dealers?"

Sam wiped his mouth. "Nothing doing. We didn't have enough of the plate number to get a match. I have some of my guys going through all the partial matches. It's gonna take some time, though."

"I think I have something," said Derek. "The image quality is grainy, but take a look."

He passed over his tablet. A blurry black-and-white video materialized, showing the crowded farmer's market. Derek fast-forwarded until the time stamp matched the confrontation with the dealers. We watched the grainy shapes move across the screen, tension mounting as it all played out.

"That's it. There are no cameras on the exits that the men used."

"I don't recognize either of them," Ryan said in frustration. "Let's see what we can get out of the stall owner. Mai, Derek, you're with me."

I nodded, rising from my chair with renewed determination. Hopefully, Greta could give us a lead.

The temperature plunged as we descended into the basement, the sterile lights casting shadows across the concrete walls. This area was reserved for containing unstable or dangerous members of the Pack; it was supposed to be cool and calming, far removed from the activity of the main house. The isolation prickled my skin, though, evoking memories of Brock holding me down here not long ago.

Greta sat calmly on the floor of the farthest cell, her legs folded into a supple lotus position despite her age. Iron-gray hair was scraped back in a tight bun, sharp eyes peering out at us. They fixed unnervingly on me as we approached.

"Well, if it isn't the Alpha pair themselves, to what do I owe the honor?" she said dryly, her accent betraying Eastern European roots.

"Let's not play games, Greta," I said, folding my arms across my chest. "You're going to tell us everything you know about Ghost and his new drug shipments."

The woman's wrinkled face remained impassive. "I run a vegetable stand, nothing more."

Ryan stepped forward and leaned his shoulder against the bars. "I'm not buying the innocent old lady act," he said in a low voice. "You're a conduit for Ghost's ripple distribution in this area. You're going to give us everything you know."

Greta met his menacing stare, entirely unmoved. "Or you'll do what, exactly? Kill a helpless human woman? I think your mate might take issue with those methods. I hear she couldn't even order Korrin dead after he ambushed you on a road."

Her pale eyes slid to me knowingly.

She was right. If I couldn't sanction Korrin's death, or Amara's torture, I wasn't willing to sanction the killing of Greta, either. Of course, she didn't know that. Not for sure. I felt my frustration rising, but kept my tone level.

"You don't know me. Or what I'm capable of. I've seen what ripple does to Shifters. I know what it will do to our communities. I'm pretty sure you do too. So, don't make assumptions about me. I will do whatever it takes to get ripple shut down. If that means the torture and death of one old lady…" I shrugged, hoping she wouldn't see through my bluff. "I'm not going to lose any sleep over it."

Greta considered me for a long moment, then flicked her gaze to first Ryan and then Derek, before sighing. "Very well. I will tell you what I know. But I warn you, it's not much."

She shifted on the floor, wincing slightly as she unfolded her legs. "Two years ago, a man approached me with a business proposal. My stall would become a transfer point for certain deliveries he arranged. I was to receive a crate with his delivery every Saturday morning. It would arrive on my back porch before dawn. Sometime later, another man would come to the market to retrieve it. The pick-up men were always men, very rarely were they the same."

"And you didn't think these deliveries were suspicious?" Derek asked.

"I learned long ago not to ask dangerous questions," Greta replied calmly. "The compensation was generous. I provided a simple service."

"But you knew it was drugs?"

Greta shrugged. "I suspected, but I didn't get to be my age by looking in boxes I'm being paid handsomely not to open."

"Two years? They're using already established drug lines to ship ripple in," Ryan said.

Greta smiled wryly. "I suspect that also. Your mate is right, I have heard about ripple and what it does. I don't know for certain if, or when, they switched out the usual drugs for ripple, though."

My fingers curled impatiently around the bars. "You must have some useful information. Who was your initial contact? How were you paid?"

The woman considered for a moment. "My initial contact was someone called Elias. A wolf, though not from your Pack. He handled all the details. About a year into our arrangement, I was informed by one of the pick-up men that Elias had met an...unfortunate end, but the deliveries would continue as normal."

"And you never saw or heard from anyone after that?" Ryan pressed.

Greta shook her head. "Only the weekly pick-up men. Whoever has taken over Elias' operation keeps their identity well hidden."

Derek and I exchanged a look. We needed to dig up details about this Elias.

I opened my mouth to ask another question when my cell phone suddenly vibrated in my pocket. I hesitated, then drew it out, frowning when I didn't recognize the number.

"I'll be back," I said quietly to Ryan and Derek before slipping from the room.

"Hello?" I answered cautiously, pressing the phone to my ear as I moved down the shadowy corridor for privacy.

Static hissed across the line, followed by muffled noises that put my senses on high alert. Then a voice I never imagined hearing again spoke my name.

"Mai?"

My heart stuttered. "J-Jem?"

"Listen closely," the voice continued. "I don't have long before..." His words dissolved into a violent coughing fit.

"Jem, are you okay? Where are you?"

His breathing was labored on the line when he regained composure.

"I'm alive...for now."

"How do I know it's really you?"

There was another coughing fit, then the voice said, "Remember our apartment, Mai? When mom and dad were alive? When you were five, I promised you I'd sneak into the kitchen at midnight for a week to make you an ice cream sundae. You insisted on coming with me. We got away with it for two nights, but on the third night, Mom caught us. You remember how we got out of it?"

"We pretended to be sleepwalking," I whispered.

"That's right. No way Mom bought it, but she went along with it and guided us back to bed."

I could feel tears running down my cheeks. This really was Jem. He really was alive.

"I'll get you out of this," I promised.

Jem coughed again, his voice getting weaker. "Don't. Protect the Pack. That's your job now."

Before I could respond, another voice replaced Jem's on the line. My blood ran cold at the silky tones.

"Now, now. Don't listen to him, Mai. Not if you ever want to see him again."

"You fuck-face! Put Jem back on the line!"

"Really, Mai, is that how you talk to your Wolf Council representative? We'll have to do something about your manners soon. So, how is Alphahood treating you? Finding it as easy as you thought?"

"Let Jem go!" I demanded harshly.

"Of course. Just as soon as I have a seat on the Wolf Council. You have precisely forty-eight hours left to uphold your end of the deal. Don't let Jem down."

My jaw tightened, fury raging through my veins.

"And if we don't?" I challenged.

"Then your beloved brother will finally meet a rather grisly demise. I'll send him to you after. What's left of him, anyway."

Chapter Fourteen

Mai

The basement hallway was eerily quiet, the kind of stillness that seeped into your bones and made every whisper seem like a shout. I stood there, numb, the phone call with Brock still replaying in my mind.

Jem was alive. I'd spoken to him, his voice a mixture of pain and defiance. The relief was overwhelming, yet it mingled with fear and uncertainty.

Ryan and Derek came out of the cage room. Ryan's eyes met mine. He could read the turmoil on my face and through our bond as easily as if I'd shouted it.

"What happened?" Ryan demanded.

I drew in a shaky breath. "It was Brock. He called…" The words felt like shards of glass in my mouth. "Jem's alive. I talked to him. He's alive, Ryan."

The news hit Ryan like a physical blow. Before he could respond, the pounding of footsteps echoed down the hallway.

Mason appeared, his face etched with urgency. "Korrin's attacking," he said, his voice strained, "He's gone after Bottley Bar. Sofia's there."

Without a word, Derek sprinted up the stairs.

My stomach dropped. Korrin. Seth's father. He wanted revenge on me and Ryan for killing his son. And now, Sofia, my best friend and someone I considered a sister, was in danger because of us, because of me.

"Korrin's trying to draw you out," Mason said, his jaw clenched. "He wants you away from the compound."

I gritted my teeth. Korrin was using our own people as bait to lure us into his trap.

"We need to go," I said, determination steeling my voice. Ryan, standing nearby, nodded in agreement, his eyes dark with resolve.

Mason hesitated. "No. That's what he wants. You should stay here. Let me, Derek, and Sam handle this."

I shook my head. "We're Alphas, Mason. This is the job. We can't hide in here while the Pack is being attacked. Our place is out there, defending them."

"We lead from the front." Ryan growled, and I could feel his anger through our bond.

Mason gave a curt nod. "Let's move, then."

Urgency surged through us as Ryan, Mason, and I bolted upstairs, our footsteps resounding in the otherwise silent compound. At the front door, we ran into Evelyn, Jase, and Sam. Their faces were taut with the same mix of determination and dread that churned in my gut.

"Where's Amara?" I barked at Jase.

"She's with Thomas and Wally. Sam says Sofia's in danger?"

"Come," Ryan ordered, and Jase ran after us.

We climbed into two SUVs parked in the driveway, the engines roaring to life as soon as we jumped in. Evelyn and Jase jumped in one car. Sam drove me, Ryan and Mason. Tension crackled in the confined space; every muscle in my body tensed for the impending confrontation.

As we sped through the streets, Mason's phone buzzed incessantly with updates, his fingers flying over the screen as he relayed the information.

"They're inside the bar," Mason's voice cut through the thick silence, his eyes fixed on the glowing screen. "Korrin and his crew. He has eight people with him. Sofia and some of the customers are fighting back. It's chaos in there."

My heart hammered against my ribcage. Guilt gnawed at me; my past had spilled over, endangering those I cared about.

Ryan's hand found mine, squeezing tightly.

"Kara called me earlier. Her and Ajak banished Korrin and his crew from the Cocrane Pack."

I swung my head toward Ryan. "Why didn't you tell me?"

"I didn't keep it from you intentionally. Kara called when we were at Brock's property. I was going to tell you after we'd talked to Greta. I didn't think Korrin would attack so soon."

If Kara banished Korrin, then she had to know that Korrin would head straight here. She had cut his leash, and now there was nothing holding Korrin back.

"She wanted to ally the Cocrane Pack with the Three Rivers under a no-hostilities pact."

I snorted. "Yeah, right. She was covering her ass more like it. Telling us she'd set Korrin loose, and then offering the pact to make sure there were no repercussions for her."

"I thought the same thing."

"We'll take it, though. We'd be fools not to. It could come in handy in the future."

Ryan looked at me. "You're getting the hang of this Alpha gig."

"We're almost there," Sam said, his voice steady.

Ryan squeezed my hand. "When we get in there, stay behind me, Mai."

I opened my mouth to argue, but a green sheen flared in his eyes as he cut me off. "I mean it. You said if this was going to work between us, then I had to let you be in danger. I'm trying, Mai, but it isn't going to happen overnight. Stay behind me, or I'll pick you up and run you out of there myself."

I sat back, my frustration mounting. Korrin was here because of me, and Ryan was telling me to let others handle it.

Mason's phone buzzed. "Derek's arrived."

"Tell me he hasn't stormed in there. Tell me he's waiting for us to arrive so we can make a plan and hit it together?"

Mason's phone buzzed again. "I'd love to tell you that, bro. But Derek is going to be Derek."

"Fuck!"

The streets were empty as we neared Bottley Bar; the Three Rivers folk knew to run if there was an attack. Our two SUVs skidded to a halt in a cloud of dust beside the building. The sounds of the ongoing battle were immediate and intense—the snarling of wolves, the clash of bodies, the shouts and cries of pain and rage.

We jumped out of the car. I could feel my wolf, close to the surface, responding to the scent of blood and the sounds of our Pack in danger.

"Mai—" Ryan started.

"Don't. I'll keep behind you, but I'm not staying out here. Sofia's my best friend. I'm the Alpha, Ryan, just like you. My place is in there."

Ryan nodded once, but I didn't need our bond to tell me how unhappy he or his wolf were about this.

"We've sent the call out," Mason said. "Our enforcers will be here in five minutes."

"Too long," Ryan replied, his eyes scanning the Bar. "Evelyn, Jase, stay out here. Mop up any of Korrin's crew that tries to escape. Help any of ours that come out and send in the other enforcers when they get here. The rest of us, we go in now. Sam, head for the back exit. Mason, try to get as many of our people out as possible. We hit them hard. Aim for Korrin. He's the one driving this."

Jase scowled at the ground. I knew he was angry he was being made to stay out here with his sister inside, but he didn't complain.

We burst through the doors of Bottley Bar, the scene before us a maelstrom of snarls, blood, and chaos.

Shattered glass crunched under my feet, the acrid scent of smoke filling my nostrils. Ryan surged forward, flinging bodies left and right, clearing the way for the rest of us. A wolf lunged towards me, teeth bared, but I sidestepped and delivered a swift kick to its ribs. It yelped in pain and stumbled away, only to be met with Mason's fist as he came charging in behind me.

We fought our way through the throngs of Korrin's men. In front of me and to the left, Sam, full of rage, rammed his fist into the nose of one of Korrin's crew. The nose broke and blood splattered over my face and dripped from my forehead.

Lovely.

I strode forward, trying to see Korrin. The further in we went, the more the bar was in chaos, furniture broken and upturned, games, books, broken bottles spilled across the room. The scent of alcohol and blood was everywhere. Bodies lay crumpled on the ground, some twitching in agony, others still. Julie, the waitress who worked with Sofia, lay on the ground, her side torn open. A teenage boy huddled under a table that was still standing, whimpering and cradling an arm that was hanging at an odd angle.

Two of ours, a male middle-aged werewolf with two-day stubble and tattoos up his arms, and a pretty twenty-something woman that I thought I recognized from high school, were taking on one of Korrin's crew in wolf form. The wolf was snapping at them, driving them back toward the wall. The woman picked up a broken bottle from the floor and swung it at the wolf. It shied away, and the man took advantage and drove his knee into the wolf's head, knocking it out.

A roar to my left spun me round. Korrin was standing in the center of the room, his face twisted into a snarl as he fought with Sofia and Derek.

For a moment I paused, just watching the beauty of them fighting together. Derek was trying to fend off Korrin and protect Sofia at the same time. He moved with a beautiful grace, his army training on full display. Sofia was trying to help Derek, kicking out at Korrin, then dancing back.

I ran forward. Sofia looked up, relief and terror warring in her gaze when she saw me. Derek, perhaps alerted by the change in her scent, turned to see if I was a new threat. Korrin darted past him and jabbed his fist into Sofia's throat. She staggered back, choking, gasping for breath and clutching her neck.

Derek slammed into Korrin, flying across the ground.

"Protect Sofia," I barked at him.

Derek didn't hesitate; he ran toward Sofia.

Korrin rolled to his feet and saw me. I bared my teeth, every fiber of my being thrumming with rage. I could sense Ryan behind me; his presence felt more than seen.

Korrin turned towards us, a wicked grin spreading across his face as he took us in. "Finally, the Alphas themselves have graced us with their presence," he sneered.

My wolf growled within me, demanding that I tear him limb from limb.

Okay then.

I launching myself at Korrin. Ryan was quicker, though. He collided with Korrin with a sickening thud, the force of his blow sending them both spinning. Ryan landed furthest from me. Seeing this, Korrin stepped back, and before I could block him, he punched me in my gut. I managed to twist into it and the blow landed on my hip. It felt like a jackhammer. I staggered back, falling into an upturned table.

Then Ryan was there. His muscles rippling through his T-shirt as he delivered a sharp kick to Korrin's ribs. Korrin responded with a vicious uppercut. Ryan kept his movements fluid and precise, with a flurry of jabs and kicks. Blood glistened on both their faces as they exchanged blows, the sound of flesh hitting flesh filling the air. Korrin was a skilled fighter, but Ryan was faster, stronger, and an Alpha.

To my right, Sofia was on the floor, still gasping. Derek was crouched over her, protecting her from the battle around them. Out of the corner of my eye, I saw a wolf launch itself at them. I dashed forward as Derek's hand darted out and caught the wolf by its neck. He swung the wolf with one hand and slammed it into the wall. The wolf snarled, tore itself free, and went for Derek. I reached Sofia just as a woman came out of the shadows, her foot aiming for my head. I leaned back just in time; her foot passing an inch from my nose. I pulled on the Pack bonds, five-inch claws extending from my fingers, and slashed into her back as she twisted away.

A body went flying past me, landing on his back on a nearby table. Korrin. Ryan had thrown him across half the bar. The table splintered beneath Korrin's weight. He rolled though, so quick, grabbed a broken whiskey bottle, and before I could blink, he slid over to Sofia, hauled her up and held the jagged edge to Sofia's throat.

"One more move and I'll slit her throat," he threatened.

My heart pounded as I stared at Sofia's terrified face. Ryan was at my side, his rage setting our bond afire as Derek stood over the unconscious body of the wolf he'd been fighting, his every muscle taut with the strain of holding himself back. It was the first time that I'd seen Derek look scared. We were stuck, unable to take action without endangering her life.

"This is the least I can do to pay you back for the pain you caused by murdering my son. I'm going to take everyone you care about before coming for you."

Derek's vicious snarl sounded behind me, and I knew I had seconds before he launched himself at Korrin.

Korrin's grin widened as he saw our hesitation. "That's right," he said, pressing the broken bottle closer to Sofia's neck, breaking the skin. The scent of her blood filled the air as Sofia whimpered, and I knew we had to act. I couldn't just stand and watch. But any move we made would be too slow. Korrin would kill Sofia before we could get to them.

Talia fucking Johnson, the Wolf Council member, appeared out of nowhere behind Korrin. How the hell had she managed to get here so fast?

"You always were a coward, Korrin. Attacking a bar worker? Really? Not man enough to come for the Alphas?" I said, hoping to keep his attention on me until Ryan and Derek could get a bit closer.

"You fucking bitch! You've no idea what I'm capable of. I'm gonna make you watch as I remove her head, knowing that this is what I'm going to do to you, Mai."

Ryan and Derek were edging closer, then Talia moved, coming up fast behind Korrin. Suddenly aware of a new threat behind him, he loosened his grip as he turned.

I sprinted toward them as Sofia slipped her hands between her neck and the broken bottle and pushed. Korrin, realizing she was trying to break free, jabbed the bottle towards her, but it was too late. Ryan and Derek reached them at the same time. Ryan's claws extended, and he punched them into Korrin's throat. It was brutal and efficient and I knew without a doubt that Korrin wouldn't survive it.

Derek hauled Sofia away as Korrin grabbed at his neck, gargling blood, and sank to the floor. He lifted his arm, pointed at me, and tried to say something.

"Bitsssss."

Ryan bent down and snapped his neck in one twist.

I turned to see Derek gather Sofia up in his arms and kiss her.

Oh wow.

I think my jaw hit the floor.

Sofia was kissing him back. It was like they had completely forgotten everyone else here. I saw the moment that Sofia realized what she was doing. Her eyes flung open; she pushed Derek back and then punched him square on the jaw with her uninjured hand.

"Oof," Derek's head snapped back, and then he grinned at her. Sofia scowled at him, like really scowled, like she was trying to make his head explode just with her thoughts. Then she turned away, cradling her bloody hand.

Ryan was next to me in an instant.

"You okay?" he said, patting me all over, looking for injuries.

I nodded, touching a deep cut on the side of his face.

He took my hand and kissed it, the relief humming through the bond overwhelming me.

"You killed him." I expected to feel guilt and sadness about that, but all I felt was a grim satisfaction. He'd attacked our Pack and for that he had to pay.

"I'll kill everyone who's a threat to you."

Chapter Fifteen

RYAN

I used to like being in Jem's study, talking through strategies with Jem and my brothers. Today, though, there was too much going on inside my head for me to feel its calming influence.

With Korrin down, his crew, or what were left of it, made a run for it, but the Renegades mopped them up. We'd have to decide what to do with them. They'd been exiled from the Cocrane Pack so we couldn't send them back there. Talia had offered to arrange transportation to Adarcan Prison, a jail run by the Wolf Council. Shifters referred to it by its nickname, The Kennel, but most Wolf Council members were not impressed by that name. It was going to take a few days to arrange, though.

Thomas had arrived on site shortly after the end of the fight. He'd enlisted Wally in helping him treat the wounded, a role Wally dove in to, just like he did with anything that would make his mate's life easier.

Sofia's hands would heal, but it would take a few days. Derek and Jase had taken her home to the apartment she had above the Bar. She'd been upset at the state Bottley's was in, but Mai had assured her we'd fix it up in no time.

"We need to focus on Jem," Mai said, her voice soft. "Brock's proof of life...I spoke to him, Ryan. I heard his voice. Jem's out there, and we have to find him."

The mention of Jem steeled my resolve. He was more than just my former Alpha; he was my best friend, my brother in all but blood. "We will," I assured her.

Mai nodded. "I want to believe that, I really do, but we need a Plan B. We need to consider what we do if we can't find him in time. We'll need to nominate Brock for the Wolf Council."

The idea caught me off guard. "Nominate Brock? After everything he's done? You can't be serious."

"Of course, I'm serious. It might be the only way to find Jem."

"Brock on the Wolf Council, Mai? You know what he's aiming for," I said, my voice edged with concern. "He's made it clear he wants to rule over all the Packs in North America. That kind of power in his hands..."

Mai's expression was resolute. "I know, Ryan. I know what he wants. But that's a fight for another day. We have time. We know what he plans, and we can work to stop him. But right now, our priority has to be Jem. We have to do whatever we need to to get him back."

I started pacing. "If Brock gains a foothold in the Council, the power he could wield...and if he succeeds in his plans to take over the Council, then it's not just about Jem anymore. It's about the future of all Packs."

She leaned her head back and closed her eyes. She looked tired, really tired. "We can't tackle everything at once. Yes, Brock's ambitions are dangerous, but right now, the only thing that matters is finding Jem."

She needed to be in bed. Not arguing about this with me.

"Ronnie's right, Mai. Even if we nominate Brock, chances are he'll kill Jem, anyway."

"It's a chance we have to take. We have to get my brother back."

I let out a slow breath. If it made her sleep better, or sleep at all, I'd agree to anything right now. "Alright. We keep trying to find Jem, but if we need to nominate Brock to get him back, we will."

Mai nodded, opening her eyes. "We bring Jem home, then we'll deal with Brock. One battle at a time." She paused. "Well, two I suppose. We have to tackle the ripple situation at the same time. But after that, then we'll deal with Brock." She tilted her head to one side. "And take down the compound walls, recruit more enforcers, stabilize the Pack, root out the rest of Brock's supporters, get more help for Thomas, and make sure Mason doesn't start a war with Bridgetown over Shya."

Plus, mold this Pack into a motherfucking army. "You didn't think this Alpha gig was going to be easy, did you?"

"I thought we'd get the Pack back from Brock and Hayley and then I'd get to go away for a spa weekend with Sofia."

I laughed, then picked her up and sat down so she was snuggled on my lap. My cock went hard at having her so close. "There's no spa weekend with Sofia. You owe me ten weekends, just you and me, before you can even think about going away without me."

"Mmmm," she purred. "What kind of weekends were you thinking about?"

"Naked ones. Definitely naked ones."

She blinked up at me, an innocent look on her face. I wasn't buying it for a second.

"Won't that be a bit cold?"

"If you get cold, I'll let you go on top, make you do all the work. That'll warm you up."

She opened her mouth, and I was dying to know what she was about to say, when her phone went off.

She pulled it out of her pocket and I saw the screen flash *Jase* before she answered it.

"Mai?"

"I'm here. You okay?"

"It's Amara. If I text you directions, can you come down here?"

She glanced at me, and I nodded. "We'll be there, Jase. Are you in danger?"

"No. It's not that, but it would be good if you could come."

Fifteen minutes later, we pulled up at the end of a cul-de-sac. The houses here were old and rundown, with broken gates and peeling paint. There was a gap of about fifteen feet between two of the houses, and a narrow trail snaked between them. It led into the forest. Mai and I exchanged a glance, both of us on high alert as we got out of the car and followed Jase's scent into the forest.

I hadn't been this way in years, not since I was an enforcer for Oliver and did patrols round here. The path wound through the trees and gnarled roots, and I caught the musty odor of ancient stone on the air. Mai's cute button nose wrinkled as she caught the scent, too. The ruins of an old temple slowly came into view, with its crumbling walls and partially collapsed roof.

"Sofia and me used to come here to play," Mai whispered. "Her mom told us it was an old temple for the Dark Goddess. Did you know that we used to worship both the Dark Goddess and the Moon Goddess, but that long ago our Alphas made a deal with the Moon Goddess to only worship her in exchange for greater powers and protections? The Dark Goddess, on hearing this, cursed the protections so that they would wear away with time. She warned the Pack that unless we went back to worshipping her, we would slowly die out."

I raised my eyebrows at her.

"I didn't say I believed it. But it certainly made playing here more exciting."

We followed Jase's scent to a small, hidden entrance on the side of the ruins. Mai walked over to the wall and ran her fingertips over a marking. "See?"

I looked closer and saw Mai's initials.

MP&SM BFF

"Best friends forever?" I guessed.

She nodded, a small smile on her face. My eyes fell on a heart just below it with the initials RS&MP inscribed inside of it. I cast a smug look at Mai and she blushed. She was so fucking adorable.

With a nod to Mai, I stepped inside, into what had to be the main chamber of the temple. The interior was just as deteriorated as the outside, with debris and rubble littering the floor. Strange, faded runes and symbols were painted on the walls.

In the center of the chamber stood a large, circular altar, now broken and covered in leaves.

Jase was crouched down to the left of the altar. He looked up as we entered, relief washing over his face.

Against the far wall, Amara sat on the floor, her arms wrapped protectively around a young boy. He looked to be around six or seven years old, but it was hard to tell; he was scrawny and thin so could be older or younger. The child was fast asleep, his head nestled against Amara's chest. Even in slumber, the resemblance between the two was striking. The boy had the same rich skin as Amara, and his small face held the same delicate features—a button nose, full lips, and long, curling lashes that rested against his cheeks. I looked at Amara again, sitting there in her oversized green hoodie. I was betting she was just as skinny as the child and was trying to hide it.

Mai took a step forward, her voice low and gentle. "Amara, it's okay. We're here to help."

Amara tightened her hold on the boy, her gaze darting between Mai, Jase, and me, but she didn't say anything.

Jase stood up slowly, his hands held out in a placating gesture, and made his way over to us.

His voice was soft as he spoke. "She ran away from Thomas and Wally's house," he explained. "I followed her. She went to a house on Callisto Avenue. She was inside for maybe ten minutes, then came out with the boy and brought him here."

"You know who he is?" I asked, though it was obvious they were related.

"It's Ben, Amara's brother."

I glanced at the sleeping child, the pieces of the puzzle starting to fall into place.

"After their parents died, Amara was left to support Ben. She couldn't find any jobs that paid enough. They got kicked out of their home, and she's been struggling to find enough food for them both."

I glanced over at the girl with the bright blue hair and her sleeping brother. I recognized that look in her eyes, that desperation and fear that you won't be able to feed your siblings that day. I knew what it was like to live off scraps or not eat at all so that your brothers could eat. I'd only gotten through it because Jem had helped out when he could.

"She's been working as a drug runner for the last two months because it pays, and she can finally feed her brother. The dealers know her situation. They know about Ben."

Jase's voice dropped even lower. "Amara was scared that someone saw her being taken by me and Mai yesterday and that word would get around. She thought the dealers might do something to Ben to make sure that she doesn't talk. So she left tonight to fetch Ben and move him somewhere safer."

I looked around at the ruins, taking in the crumbling walls and the debris-strewn floor. This was hardly a safe place for either of them.

"She's refusing to tell me anything about the dealers, in case we shut them down. If they get shut down, Amara has no money coming in and no way to get food for her brother."

Amara glowered at us, a stubborn look on her face. With her werewolf hearing, she could hear every word Jase was saying.

Mai stepped forward and crouched down in front of Amara. Her voice was gentle but firm as she spoke. "Amara, if you come with us, we will make sure Ben has more food than he knows what to do with. Neither of you will ever go hungry again. I promise."

Amara's gaze flickered between Mai and me, uncertainty and distrust plain on her face. It was a look I knew all too well, the look of someone who had been let down too many times, who had learned the hard way that trust was a luxury they couldn't afford.

"Amara, listen to me," Jase said. "Mai and Ryan are the real deal. You can trust them. They really will do everything in their power to help you and Ben. And if you can't trust them, trust me. I know things didn't end well between us, but you know me. You know I won't lie to you about this, not when it might put you and Ben in danger."

Amara's eyes searched Jase's face, then she sighed.

"Alright."

In a gesture that spoke volumes about the depth of her trust in Jase, she gently shifted Ben in her arms and held him out for Jase to take.

As Jase reached for the boy, Ben stirred, his eyes fluttering open. He looked around, taking in the unfamiliar faces. He was immediately on edge, burying deeper into his sister's arms. "Mara, who're they?"

Amara's hand gently smoothed Ben's curls. "They're friends, Ben. They aren't here to hurt us."

Ben blinked. "You think that, but you can never be sure. Everyone can hurt us."

I felt Mai's reaction through the bond; her sadness that such a young boy had learned this lesson and her desire to make sure no-one hurt this boy ever again.

"Hey, Benny," Jase called. "Remember me?"

Ben nodded. "Yeah, you're the dickhead that Mara dumped."

I burst out laughing at the look of shock on Jase's face.

"We're going to have to work on your language," Jase replied, shooting an annoyed look at Amara. "How about we go outside for a bit? I saw a soccer ball out there. I'll let you have a three goal advantage?"

Ben laughed, delighted, all thoughts of people hurting him gone. "You are so going down! Three goals? Should have gone for ten, dickhead!"

Jase narrowed his eyes at Amara, but she only shrugged at him. Jase followed Ben outside, Ben's excited chatter fading into the distance.

Left alone with Mai and me, Amara took a deep breath. She seemed to be steeling herself for what she was about to say. "I don't know much about ripple or the dealers," she began, her voice low and hesitant. "I was approached two months ago by this guy I went to school with, Markus Remny. He always was an ass. But he knew I was struggling. He said I could make some real money."

She paused, her face twisting into a grimace. "He's been my sole contact. He calls, tells me when and where. I do it."

Fuck, another dead end.

"You said he went to school with you?" Mai asked. "You ever hang out, catch up on old times?"

Amara nodded slowly. "Twice. I wanted more info about his bosses. I wanted to find out what I was getting into."

"Anything he let slip?"

"The second time, he was talking on the phone, telling someone that they had to go to the new place. Said it was at 589 Denison. I went and checked it out the next day, but it was just a big warehouse. Locked tight. No-one about. No way in that I could find."

I nodded. I'd text Derek and get him on it as soon as we left here.

Amara's face turned wary. "That's all I know. Is it enough? Is it enough to protect and feed Ben?"

I looked down at her, still sitting on the dirty floor. "Amara, even if you had nothing to give us, it would have been enough."

Amara's eyes widened, and for a moment, she looked impossibly young and vulnerable. Then, to my surprise, tears began to stream down her face. She angrily swiped at them.

"Don't tell, Jase. I'm too fucking badass to cry," she muttered, but her voice was thick with emotion.

CHAPTER SIXTEEN

RYAN

We took Amara and Ben back to Thomas and Wally's. I wanted to get Ben checked over. As soon as we explained the situation, Wally went all mother-hen on them. He declared that they were both moving in and set up a room upstairs for them to share until Thomas could clear out the storage room in the back and give them a room each. Amara seemed happy with the idea. Ben was over the moon, especially when Wally showed him their fully stocked fridge and Thomas took him on a tour of his medical office, showing him all the equipment, and embellished stories about which tools were used to amputate limbs.

After that, Wally took them both upstairs, while Thomas asked us into his office.

"You sure you don't mind them staying here?" Mai asked.

Thomas waved his hand. "Are you kidding? Have you seen how happy Wally is? I'd be banned to the sofa for a month if I said no."

"Well, you know where we are if there are any issues."

"That I do. I'm sure it won't be necessary, though. The reason I asked you in here is that I analyzed the ripple you gave me."

"You found something?"

"Maybe. I'm not done with it yet. But my preliminary findings show that ripple's active ingredient is stable in both liquid and solid forms. This means it can be administered in various forms—injected, via pills, or even inhaled. Injected or inhaled, the effects will be felt rapidly. With a pill, it might take longer to kick in but the effect will be longer-lasting. From a scientific point of view, it is quite the remarkable to create something like this that effects Shifters so reliably. We've been trying to achieve this for decades with no success. The person who designed this really is a genius."

Shifters had an unpredictable relationship with most drugs. Unlike alcohol, which affected us just like humans, how we reacted to other substances was very individualized.

"As you know, Shifters typically have a complex and variable response to drugs," Thomas continued. "What might cause a euphoric high in one Shifter, could have absolutely no effect on another. Even within families, reactions can differ wildly. A painkiller that works wonders for one child might do nothing for their sibling."

Mai nodded. "I remembered hallucinating for hours after taking a painkiller in school for period pains because that's what worked for the humans, while Jem took the same ones when he broke his wrist skating boarding and it had no effect at all. He had to Shift three times until his wrist healed, and he was in agony each time."

"Exactly. This unpredictability has been both a blessing and a curse. On one hand, it's made treating Shifter patients with conventional medicines challenging. On the other, it's largely protected our community from widespread drug abuse issues that plague human society."

Thomas's eyes gleamed with a mix of scientific fascination and concern. "But ripple...ripple changes everything. It's the first drug we've encountered that appears to have a consistent, powerful effect on all Shifters, regardless of individual physiology. That's what makes it so dangerous—and so intriguing from a scientific standpoint. I honestly have no idea how they have managed it."

He leaned forward, his voice lowering slightly. "The implications of this are staggering, Mai. If we could understand how ripple achieves this universal effect, we might be able to develop medicines that could reliably treat Shifter illnesses and injuries. But in the wrong hands, as we're seeing now, it's a recipe for disaster."

Someone had cracked a code we'd been struggling with for generations. If we could get our hands on that person, could convince them to turn their mind to treating and preventing illness, to healing rather than destroying, the breakthroughs they might accomplish could be phenomenal. First though, we had to eliminate their latest creation.

"Anything else?" I asked.

"There is one more thing—I've managed to identify a high concentration of a synthetic pheromone compound. I believe it is this that's making ripple highly addictive to Shifters. This compound is derived from a rare botanical source, likely a genetically modified or hybrid plant, which requires specialized greenhouse conditions to grow. Such facilities would most likely be found in urban areas with access to advanced horticultural technology and discreet locations."

My mind whirled, thinking through the implications.

"Is that helpful?" Thomas asked.

I nodded. "It narrows it down, gives us a place to start looking. Thank you."

"As I said, I'm not done yet. I'll let you know anything else I find out."

<hr>

By the time we got home, Talia Johnson was there, waiting in her black SUV.

Mai glanced at me. "We can ignore her. Pretend we don't see her."

I was tempted. Mai was exhausted, and she needed sleep. "I seem to remember you trying that with me once." She'd closed her eyes and counted to three, saying I wasn't really there and would disappear when she opened them again. It had been cute as hell. "How did that work out for you?"

"Not good," Mai admitted grudgingly, crossing her arms over her chest.

I was sure Talia wouldn't let us ignore her, either. "We might as well get it over and done with. No way is Talia here by accident, and I want to know what the fuck she's really doing in our territory."

Talia was a striking figure, her skin a rich shade of ebony that seemed to glow under the lights. Her eyes, a piercing amber color, took everything in at once, assessing and calculating. This evening, she wore a perfectly tailored light-pink suit; the fabric clinging to her lean, muscular frame. A silver wolf-head pin gleamed on her lapel, a symbol of her position within the Council.

She swept into our study with an air of authority, her eyes scanning the space like she owned it. I was already regretting my decision not to ignore her; Talia was a wild card, and it was never good when the Wolf Council showed an interest in your Pack.

"Thank you for seeing me, Mai Parker, Ryan Shaw," she said, her voice smooth and confident.

Talia had an annoying habit of always saying everyone's surnames. I briefly wondered if she said her partner's full name when she was getting fucked.

"Talia Johnson," Mai replied, and I knew she was copying Talia to get a rise out of her.

"Regarding the attack on your coffee shop in town. I have done a preliminary investigation and I can confirm that Korrin attacked you and your Pack. There will be no consequences for his death."

I sat at the desk, considering Talia's comments. I didn't give a fuck if there were consequences for Korrin's death. He was a threat to Mai, and he needed to die.

"Why are you here, Talia?" I asked.

She paced to the left, glancing out of the window at the forest beyond before answering. "I'm here to offer my assistance to your Pack in dealing with the ripple crisis in the area. I'm sure you could use the Council's help."

Mai eyed her warily. "Thank you for the offer, but we are handling it."

Talia's gaze didn't falter. "I have the resources and the connections to make a difference. And whether you like it or not, you need me."

It was Talia's way of saying that we were stuck with her. The Wolf Council was involved, and no one said no to the Wolf Council. Not if they wanted to live. I was going to have to do something about the

Council. My wolf would not tolerate any threats to Mai's safety. But first we had to have a stable Pack behind us.

Talia's confident stance didn't waver as she looked directly at Mai, her gaze piercing and unrelenting. "Let's start with the witches. I need to know everything you have on the witches, particularly their involvement with your Pack."

Mai met Talia's gaze, a flash of defiance in her eyes before she spoke. "There is no involvement with our Pack. We know the law. Witches are not allowed to live or practice in the North East, not since Simon Webster tried to create a spell to put all werewolves under his control."

"But you have had contact with a witch?" Talia pushed.

Mai tilted her head, a haunted look in her eyes. "Seth, my ex-boyfriend, was working with a witch. They tried to break my bond with the Three Rivers Pack. I never got a good look at the witch. I couldn't even tell you if it was a man or a woman. Seth claimed that the witch showed him that my bond was impure, that it was tainted in some way. I got the impression that the witch had manipulated his perception, but I have no proof of that."

I felt a surge of anger at the thought, my fists clenching involuntarily.

"Arabella, a member of the Bridgetown Pack, claimed that she only felt pure when she was high on ripple," Mai continued. "Is there a link? Is that why you're here? You think the witches are part of ripple's creation? That they're doing something to it to make the werewolves think they are only pure when they're on it."

Talia's eyes narrowed. "It's a possibility," she admitted. "At the moment, we don't know. We don't have enough evidence, but the correlation is alarming."

She paused, her gaze shifting between Mai and me. "What's more concerning are the reports we've been receiving. There's unrest among many Packs. Werewolves are claiming their bonds feel impure, and they're seeking ways to sever these connections. It's possible the witches are casting spells on ripple, making Shifters feel this way. It's a pattern that's emerging, and it's spreading fast."

Mai's expression hardened. "If that's true, we have to stop it. If werewolves start to break their Pack bonds, it will be chaos."

Mai was right. The Pack bonds were there for a reason. We were pack animals; we needed the security and safety of our Packs, they kept us grounded, stopped us from going rogue. Alphas kept us in line and made sure we did nothing to upset the peace with the human communities.

Talia nodded. "Exactly. This isn't only a ripple crisis or a witch problem. It's an attack on the fundamental nature of our bonds, the very essence of what makes a Pack. And it's a crisis we need to address head-on."

"Where do we start?" I asked.

Talia smiled, showing her teeth. "I have information that all production of ripple in the northeast has been consolidated into a new lab. I don't know where it is yet, but I'll need backup in order to shut it down. When I discover the location, do you want in?"

My eyes flashed. Unlike Talia, I knew exactly where this new lab was. And if Amara's info was good, it was right under our noses, in our territory. Of course I fucking wanted in.

Chapter Seventeen

MAI

It was two a.m. when we pulled up near 589 Denison. The building was based in an industrial area and at this time of night, it was deserted. Derek had spent the last few hours digging into this place. It looked like it had been bought six months ago, but the new owners only started operating out of it in the last few weeks. Right before Brock and Hayley took over the Pack. Whether that meant Brock knew about it, or even sanctioned it, we didn't know. He was certainly involved in ripple somehow. Hayley had implied that Brock had been supplying her with the drug, but we didn't know where he had been getting it from.

I stared ahead at the building. Towering warehouses and factories loomed on either side, their windows dark and lifeless. The only sound was the occasional whisper of the wind, carrying with it the faint, lingering scents of diesel and metal. I couldn't help but imagine how different this place must be during the day, filled with the rumble of trucks and the chatter of workers going about their business.

But now, in the stillness of the early hours, it was as if the entire district had exhaled and fallen into a deep, restful slumber.

We got out and stalked toward the suspected ripple lab. I couldn't help but feel a sense of unease; the building looked just like its neighbors, its exterior pristine and unassuming, designed to blend seamlessly with its surroundings.

"It looks so ordinary," I whispered to Ryan, my voice barely audible in the stillness of the night. "Hard to believe they've set up a ripple lab inside."

Ryan nodded, his eyes narrowed as he surveyed the building. "That's what makes it the perfect cover," he muttered. "No one would suspect a thing."

I shivered, and not just from the cool night air. The thought of what they were doing in there filled me with dread. If what Talia said was true, it had the potential to destroy not just our Pack but all Shifter communities. We had to put an end to this. Not just here, but wherever they made this stuff.

Ryan's hand found mine in the darkness. I squeezed back, letting the familiar strength of his grip ground me. We were running short on people for an op like this. We needed to recruit more enforcers as a matter of urgency. Our enforcers were guarding what was left of Korrin's crew, monitoring the routes in and out of the Three Rivers against another attack—people were understandably jittery about an attack in the heart of our territory and we needed to show we were protecting the Pack—and helping Thomas with the injured from the attack.

With the enforcers occupied, that left the Shaw brothers, Jase and Talia to back up me and Ryan. Ryan had split us into teams before we left the compound—him and me, Derek with Mason and Sam, and Talia with Jase. The goal was to shut this lab down so they were never able to make ripple again. We had to send a message. We had to make sure the dealers knew we were coming for them, and that ripple wasn't welcome here.

Beside us, Talia moved with predatory grace, her amber eyes scanning the shadows.

"We take this place down. I want no trace of ripple here by the morning." Ryan's voice was a low growl.

Talia nodded, her expression all business. "I don't need to remind you how dangerous ripple is to Shifter communities. We need to make sure this facility is no longer an option for whoever is running ripple. We have information that all the labs in this area have been consolidated into this one. We take it out and we'll be able to set back their operations for months."

"Derek, Sam, and Mason, you're Team Two," Ryan said, his eyes scanning the building. "Go round the back. Talia and Jase, Team Three. Come in from the east. Mai and me are Team One. We'll hit the front."

Ryan had already told us this back at the house. The plan was simple. Mason, Sam, and Derek would set fire to the building, drawing out the guards. The rest of us would get in, make sure there wasn't anyone else inside, then destroy the building and the equipment.

The wind shifted and the smell of chemicals drifted over us, mixed with a strange metallic tang that set my wolf on edge.

"No problem," replied Mason, twirling a knife in his hand.

Sam grinned at us. I got the impression he was going to enjoy this.

Derek nodded at me and Ryan. Then the brothers melted into the night.

"Come on, Jase," Talia ordered. "Let's see what you can do."

Talia and Jase headed toward the left of the building, while Ryan and I made for the main entrance. I could feel the adrenaline pumping through my veins, a wild, exhilarating rush.

Ryan shattered the glass door with ease and we stepped through into a dimly lit corridor. The air was thick, heavy with a mix of chemicals and stale, recycled oxygen. Each breath felt like inhaling a synthetic cloud. My wolf whined, wanting to be back in the clean, fresh air of our forest. There was no going back, though. Not yet.

We moved in sync down the main corridor. A sudden movement at the end of the corridor caught my eye. I looked up just as a massive, snarling wolf emerged from round a corner.

Okay, so they had guards in wolf and human form. The wolf's fur bristled at the sight of us. He, and from the size of him, he was definitely a he, bared his teeth and snarled.

Oh shit!

The wolf charged towards us, his claws scraping against the concrete floor. Ryan shoved me back as he darted in front of me, his body tense and ready to fight. But the wolf was quick. With a powerful leap, he sailed over our heads, twisting mid-air to land behind us, blocking our exit.

It also meant that despite Ryan's attempts to protect me, I was now face-to-face with the snarling beast, his hot breath hitting my skin. Fear and adrenaline surged as the wolf came at me. I threw myself back as the wolf hit me, using his momentum to kick up and flip us so I landed on top of the wolf. Ryan was there in a second, clamping his arm around the wolf's neck while I twisted us so the wolf was on its side. I lay my body across him, stopping him from attacking us with his claws. He jerked and writhed, trying to throw me off, then started to thrash wildly as Ryan squeezed down on his windpipe. I held on, knowing if it got free, his claws would eviscerate me.

It felt like forever, but then with a final, desperate whine, the wolf went limp, his body sagging.

"You okay?" Ryan asked as we both stood up.

"You stepped in front of me!"

"Did I?" Ryan's face was one of complete innocence.

I wasn't buying it. "Yes, you did! You need to stop trying to protect me all the time."

"I must have tripped."

"Into a fighting stance, right in front of me?"

He grinned at me. "I'm always ready to fight."

He looked so cocky and I just wanted to wipe that grin off his face, but now was not the time.

"We need to keep moving," I said, my voice low and urgent. "We'll talk about this later."

Ryan winked. "Can't wait, baby. Will you be wearing that frown when we do? Only, fair warning, I have to heroically resist kissing you whenever you frown at me like that."

"Let's move," I grumbled, knowing now was not the time to kick him in his throat.

Ryan motioned me to a door on the left. I put my ear against it, then shook my head to tell him there was no one inside. Ryan swung the door open. It was empty, just a sterile room with benches on their sides and vials and beakers scattered across the desks.

We pressed on. The next room was larger, and I immediately knew that this was the heart of the operation. Rows of high-tech equipment buzzed and whirred, lights flickering on their displays.

Tubes and wires snaked across the floor like mechanical vines, feeding the machines that churned out small, red pills, with the three wave emblem stamped on them.

I could hear Ryan's low growl, a primal sound barely contained. The sight of the lab ignited a fury in us both. This was where they made the ripple, the drug that had hooked Arabella and Norman, that was causing so much pain and destruction all across the Shifter communities.

Gunfire echoed down the corridor, abruptly cut off, and the smell of smoke was starting to waft along the corridors. If we wanted to destroy this place, we had to be quick.

We moved methodically, Ryan ripping cords from sockets, me shattering glassware and smashing equipment.

"What do we do with the ripple?" I asked, nodding toward the bags of red pills.

"Leave it. It'll burn with the rest of this place. We can't afford anyone else getting their hands on it."

I nodded, just as the lights flickered and plunged us into darkness. The lab, moments ago a hub of destruction, was now a cave of shadows, our only light the faint glow of emergency exit signs. The sudden plunge into darkness sharpened my senses, heightening every sound and movement.

The sounds of fighting were closer now.

Adrenaline surged, my wolf close to the surface.

The dim emergency lighting flickered as two figures burst into the room. Guards, both human, one tall and lanky with a shock of red hair, the other shorter but solidly built, with close-cropped dark hair, charged toward us.

Not even a hello first. Well, that was just rude.

The tall guard swung a heavy baton, aiming for Ryan's head. With swift precision, Ryan ducked and slammed his fist into the guard's gut. The guard doubled over, gasping for air, as Ryan brought his knee up into the man's face. I heard the crack of his nose breaking as the second guard came straight at me. I leaped over a table. My wolf was snarling inside. As I landed, I bounced up and back, using the table to pivot in the air, and delivered a quick, powerful kick to the guard's head as he chased after me. His body went limp, and he collapsed to the ground.

A yell pierced the air.

Jase.

The sound was filled with pain and urgency. Ryan and I exchanged glances.

"Go. I'll finish up here. I'll be right behind you," Ryan ordered.

Chapter Eighteen

MAI

I charged down the corridor, the sound of my footsteps echoing in the empty space. There, to the right, sounds of snarling. I charged down another corridor, then burst into a room on the left.

The space had probably once been an office, but whoever was running this ripple lab had stripped it of everything apart from an overturned desk in front of the window. In the far corner, an old, stained mattress lay on the ground, surrounded by a few tattered rags. It was the scene in the center of the room that held my attention, though. Jase had his back to the mattress and was fending off a huge brown wolf. The wolf had its jaws around Jase' arm, tearing into his flesh. Blood was scattered across the dusty floor, where Jase had tried to shake the wolf off. Jase kicked out, hitting the wolf in its chest. The wolf's grip broke, but in that split second I saw it readying itself to launch at Jase's neck.

I sprinted forward, desperate to help, but already knew the distance was too far. I was never going to reach Jase in time. With a vicious snarl, the wolf opened its jaws and lunged.

Suddenly, a blinding flash of light filled the room. The wolf yelped in pain, its body thrown against the wall.

What the hell?

I turned, my eyes wide with shock, to see a frail teenage girl huddled in the corner. Her hands were outstretched, trembling with the effort of the magic she had just unleashed.

The girl couldn't have been more than sixteen. Her face was gaunt, and she had drab, dirty blonde hair that looked like it hadn't been brushed in months. Her thin body was covered in bruises, and to be honest, I was surprised she was standing; she seemed so weak. Yet in that moment, she had found the strength to save Jase's life. As the light in the room faded, the girl's eyes fluttered closed, and she collapsed to the ground, her energy spent.

I rushed to Jase's side, my hands shaking as I assessed his injuries. His arm was torn up, and he was losing a lot of blood. He was barely conscious, his breathing shallow and labored.

"Jase?"

"The girl," he whispered, his voice hoarse with pain. "Don't...don't hurt her."

"The witch, you mean?" He knew witches weren't supposed to be here, knew it was a death sentence to practice magic in the north. If Talia found her, she'd kill her on the spot.

"Please, Mai."

I nodded. "I won't, Jase. I promise. Just hold on, okay? Hold on."

I pulled on the Pack bonds, not sure what to do, just knowing that I needed to take his pain away. My hands suddenly felt hot. Like I'd stuck them in the oven hot. I stared at them for a moment, wondering what to do.

Put hands on the pup, my wolf nudged me.

Right.

I lay my hands over Jase's wound. He gasped, then his face smoothed out, his eyes closed, and his body went limp in my arms.

Damn it. Was that supposed to happen?

Mason ran into the room, his eyes taking it all in at a glance.

"You hurt?"

"No. It's Jase."

Mason strode forward to help me stem the blood still pouring out of Jase's forearm. These awesome Alpha powers didn't seem to extend to actually healing people. I'd have liked to have a word with whoever made that deal with one of the Goddesses.

"Who's the girl?" Mason asked as he put pressure on Jase's wound.

"A witch. One that saved Jase."

Mason raised an eyebrow. "Really?"

"Do you think you can get Jase and the girl to Thomas's? Without Talia seeing you?"

He scoffed, a smile playing on his lips. "You insult me, Mai. Of course I can. Where is the head honcho, anyway?"

That was a good question. Talia was supposed to be watching Jase's back. I hoped she wasn't dead somewhere. We'd have a hell of a time explaining that to the Wolf Council.

"Get them to Thomas's. I'll search for Talia," I said, standing up, and with one last glance at Jase and the girl, ran out the room.

The faint scent of Talia—jasmine petals and coconut—guided me back along the corridor, turning left at a junction, up a set of stairs and into a side room. This room hadn't been cleared out. Three computers sat on a long, sturdy desk at the front of the room. Papers were strewn all over the floor, and Talia was decidedly not dead. She was stooped over one of the computers, her fingers flying over the keyboard, a flash drive plugged into it.

"What the actual fuck are you doing?"

She didn't flinch, her eyes glued to the screen. "Getting what I came for," she responded coolly.

Fury punched into me. This was never about shutting down the lab. Whatever Talia was here for was on that computer.

"The whole mission was a setup?" My voice was cold. "You used us as a distraction?"

Talia finally looked up, meeting my gaze unflinchingly. "Yes. This information is vital. It's bigger than just shutting down one lab."

I clenched my fists, trying to contain the rage boiling inside me. "And Jase? You were his team. It was your job to watch his back!"

"He was a means to an end," she stated flatly. "Sometimes sacrifices are necessary."

"Sacrifices?" My voice cracked with emotion. "He's a kid, Talia. He's a member of my Pack."

She unplugged the flash drive and pocketed it. "Mai Parker, you need to learn to see the bigger picture if you want to be a good Alpha. Ripple is a threat to all Shifters. What I've found here could lead us to the source. It could identify the witches that are involved in this."

I stepped closer, my wolf snarling inside me. "I don't give a fuck about your bigger picture. You put one of my Pack in danger. I want you out of Three Rivers. Now."

Talia sighed, her expression unyielding. "You're being short-sighted. This isn't about one werewolf or one Pack. Ripple is destroying our entire community. The ends justify the means, no matter how harsh it may seem at the time."

I shook my head, disgust and anger mixing in a turbulent storm. "Whoever taught you that really fucked with your head, Talia. I don't operate that way. And I won't start now. Leave."

For a moment, we stood there, Talia frowning at me, a look of disappointment etched into her face. Me, I was trying not to rip her head off. Then, with a curt nod, Talia brushed past me and disappeared into the darkness of the corridor.

Chapter Nineteen

Mai

The tires of Ryan's car protested as we took the last turn onto the driveway leading to Thomas and Wally's house. I could feel the tension and exhaustion in my body, my knuckles white from gripping the door handle too hard. Next to me, Ryan was grim-faced.

It had been a long night and I couldn't remember the last time I'd slept. We'd moved all the guards out of the building. Sam and Derek were taking them to Sam and Mason's PI agency—they had a couple of holding rooms there that would contain them while they were interrogated. I doubted if the guards knew anything that would lead us to Ghost but you never knew.

We'd then stoked the fires in the building and watched it burn. Ryan had stopped the firefighters when they'd arrived, and only let them in when it looked like the fire would spread to the adjoining buildings. We both stank of smoke and chemicals now but at least they wouldn't be making ripple in that lab again.

I pulled my phone from my pocket with a shaky hand. Sofia answered on the second ring.

"Mai! What time is it?" she asked, her voice sleepy.

"Jase is hurt. He's at Thomas's place now. Can you come?"

Sofia didn't even hesitate. "On my way."

Ryan pulled up next to Thomas's faded blue pickup truck and killed the engine. Before Ryan could even open his door, Wally was striding out of the house.

I jumped out, just as Wally said, "He's stable. It's nasty though, and he lost a lot of blood."

"And the girl?" Ryan asked. I'd filled him in while we were watching the flames take over the building.

Wally hesitated. "You know what she is?"

"We know she's a witch. We also know she saved Jase's life," I replied.

"The Wolf Council will go crazy if they find out about her! You sure about this?"

I sighed. "I don't know what we'll do with her yet. I want to talk to her before we make any decisions."

"Well, she's in a worse way than Jase. Thomas says she's highly malnourished and has been badly beaten over a period of time."

I closed my eyes briefly, a flashback of Seth's fists hammering into my ribs hitting me.

Adrenaline spiked in me, and my heart beat wildly for a moment. Ryan was by my side in an instant. His warm arms wrapping me against his hard body. "You're safe, Mai. Seth is dead. He can't harm you."

I swallowed. I had no idea where that came from.

"Sorry, I just—"

"Don't you be sorry, Mai!" Wally interrupted. "You, girl, have nothing to be sorry for. It was all that piece of shit dickhead. He's the one that needs to be sorry. If, you know, he wasn't already dead, I'd make sure of it. Do you think the Moon Goddess frowns on us going and rekilling dead Shifters? Even if it's for a good fucking reason?"

He was rambling. That meant he was nervous. I put my hand on his arm and he stopped talking immediately.

"Thank you, Wally."

Ryan took my hand, and we followed Wally into the house. He led us down the hall and into the back, where Thomas kept his office and medical rooms.

Thomas was sitting behind his desk, writing notes on a laptop, but stood as soon as we walked in.

"Mai, Ryan," he nodded to both of us, keeping his eyes down. "You'll want to see Jase first, I suppose?"

Thomas knew me too well. "Yes. Please."

He opened a sliding door into a larger medical bay with two beds on each side of the room.

"You've expanded this," I observed.

"Well, turns out I've had need of more beds lately. I'm keeping my suppliers very happy, though, with all my new orders."

Hmmm. He was right; since I'd been back, the Pack injury count had risen considerably. We needed to make sure we paid for it out of Pack funds.

The witch was on the bed to the left. She was still unconscious, but her face was clean and she had some bandages across her body. Mason stood next to her, probably guarding her and guarding the rest of us from her. Who knew how she was going to react when she woke up. Mason nodded to me and Ryan.

Jase was in the right-hand bed and gave me a pained smile when he saw me. His injured arm was heavily bandaged and his other arm was hooked up to a drip.

Amara was slumped in a chair next to Jase. She looked tired, her blue hair a shock of color in this room.

"Did you find Talia? Is she okay?" Jase asked, leaning forward, his voice still weak. The boy wonder was worried about her. Knowing Jase, he was feeling guilty that he wasn't able to protect her. I should have punched Talia when I saw her.

"Talia's fine. Don't worry about her."

Jase relaxed back against the bed.

"You caught the fucking asshole who did this, right?" Amara demanded.

Thomas immediately stepped forward. "Amara has been a great help to me and Wally. Despite her appalling bedside manner, she has a natural instinct for doctoring. If she learned to think before she spoke, especially to her Alphas, she might live long enough to make a good doctor one day."

Amara snorted.

"Give us the room, Amara," Ryan ordered.

She glanced at Jace, and seeing no help there, she huffed, stood up, and strode out.

Thomas shut the door behind her. "She isn't talking about what her and Ben have been through. Wally and I are trying to help them feel safe first, before we start prying."

I nodded, as Ryan asked, "Jase, can you tell us what happened?"

As I got closer to the bed, the smell of antiseptic mingling with the metallic tang of blood made my stomach churn. Suddenly I felt too hot and took off my jacket and put it on the chair.

Ryan sent a sharp look my way. "You okay?"

"I'm fine," I replied, swallowing down the nausea. "I just need some fresh air."

He nodded, turning back to Jase. I walked back through the house and out the front door. Amara and Wally were nowhere to be seen. The early morning air was cool against my face as I looked up at the sky. It was still dark, with only a hint of pink and orange on the horizon. I took deep breaths, trying to calm my racing heart.

Would this get easier? Seeing people I loved getting hurt, knowing that they were putting their lives on the line for us, for our Pack? Would I ever be able to shrug this off and continue to make decisions that put them in harm's way? Did I want to be the type of Alpha who could just shrug it off?

Sofia's blue Ford Raptor tore into the driveway. It screeched to a halt, and Sofia jumped out.

"He's okay." I jerked my chin toward the door. "He's with Thomas and Ryan."

Sofia nodded and ran inside. I walked in behind her, needing a moment before I saw Jase again. Instead, I headed for the second-floor bathroom. It was a nice room, small, with a vase of daisies next to the sink. At my parents' funeral, Ryan had picked a daisy and given it to me. I'd kept it, along with his jacket that he'd draped over me, and an eagle's feather he'd given to me later. All little mementoes that had kept me linked to Ryan, even when I was far away.

I splashed water on my face and looked at myself in the mirror.

Silly human feelings.

My wolf was not impressed. I'd used the resources I had, to do what needed to be done to protect the Pack; that was all that mattered.

I felt so fucking tired. I sat down, leaning my back against the wall. Maybe I'd just close my eyes for a minute.

"Mai? You okay?" Sofia's voice, laced with concern, called from the hallway.

"I'm fine," I croaked. "Just...needed a minute."

Sofia let herself in, her expression immediately flooding with sympathy as she sat next to me.

"Jase is going to be just fine." She knew me too well. "He's telling Ryan what happened."

"I'm sorry, Sofia. We got information from Talia—you know, the werewolf from the Wolf Council that showed up after our Alpha challenge?"

Sofia's eyes went guarded as she nodded. She didn't like Talia or the Wolf Council any more than I did.

"She said she had information on the main ripple lab in the northeast. We worked out it was here, in Three Rivers. We went to shut it down. Talia was supposed to be watching Jase's back. It was a ruse, though. She was using us as a distraction. She wanted the information in the computers at the lab. She ditched Jase in order to get it, and he got attacked."

I gently touched Sofia's hand. "I'm so sorry, Sofia. It was our call. We shouldn't have trusted Talia, and your brother got hurt because of it."

Sofia studied my face. "Jase has wanted to be an enforcer since he was six years old. This is his dream, Mai. And to be an enforcer for you and Ryan, that's everything he's ever wanted. He loves you both, you know that. He'll do anything for you. You made the best decision you could, given the information you had. You are not responsible for Talia fucking Johnson's actions. Jase is alive. He's going to have a wicked scar that the girls are gonna love. And you now know not to trust the Wolf Council. It could have been a fuckload worse."

I leaned my head on her shoulder. "You're the best, you know that?"

"Oh, I know. Please make sure you tell me at least once a day, though. I'm sure that's part of the best friends' agreement."

"Soooo," I said after a moment. "We gonna talk about you and Derek kissing?"

Sofia's face went carefully blank. "There was no me and him smooching. He kissed me. I punched him. End of story."

She was wrong. For a minute there, she had totally been kissing him back.

"There's nothing between him and Shya, you know."

Sofia was silent for a moment. "Nothing now, or nothing then?"

"Nothing period. Not then, not now. He's not interested in Shya, and she certainly isn't interested in him that way."

"Then why, Mai? Why did he ghost me? We had one date, and it was…it was incredible," she whispered. "But after that, it was like he was a different person. He didn't respond to my texts or my calls. It was like I didn't exist. I can't…I can't trust my heart to someone who did that to me."

"I know he had his reasons, Sofia." The Derek I knew would never treat anyone, and especially not Sofia, that way. "I don't know if they're good reasons or not. But don't you owe it to yourself to find out? He's definitely not ghosting you anymore. Why don't you ask him?"

She sighed. "Because I'm not ready to hear what he has to say. I just want to smack him each time he opens his mouth. I'm so angry with him. I like this anger, though. It got me through the nights when all I can think about is his body next to mine, or when I breathe in his scent and feel like nothing will ever harm me, you know? I don't know who I'll be if I let it go."

"This won't be forever. You'll be ready at some point." I stroked her hair. "And I'll be here, no matter what, angry Sofia or heartbroken Sofia, scared of face-eating rats Sofia or madly in love Sofia."

"Okay, so maybe you're the best!"

I grinned. I was glad I was back here and had Sofia by my side again.

"So," Sofia said, sitting up and looking at me. "Are you and Ryan going to get pregnant or what?"

I blinked, frozen at the very thought.

"Pregnant? Don't be absurd!"

"Really? Isn't that the next step? Find your fated mate, seal the bond, have lots of big, fat puppies? I bet Ryan wants them. Or at least wants to indulge as much as possible in the process of making them."

Female werewolves could only get pregnant during the three days around a full moon. Our immune systems meant we didn't catch the sexually transmitted diseases that ran through the human communities, so we often had no need for contraception. With Seth, my ex-boyfriend, I'd been extra careful. As a werewolf, I was hyper-sensitive to when the full moon was. I could feel it in my bones, so getting pregnant by mistake was highly unlikely.

The door opened, and we both looked up to see Wally standing there.

"Preggers?" he squeaked.

"Shhhhh!" I gestured him into the room. "Keep your voice down!" The last thing I needed was for Ryan to overhear and get the wrong idea.

"Oh my goddess, oh my goddess, oh my goddess!"

"I'm not pregnant!"

Wally looked at me, his hands on his hips. "Denial. That's okay. Completely normal. I'll do the excitement for both of us! Oh, Goddess, I'm already thinking of baby socks knitting patterns!"

The mere suggestion sent my anxiety sky-rocketing. "No. No babies. Or puppies. Or wolf cubs. No small wolves. Nope."

"Ah, rambling. Also completely normal." Wally winked at me.

Sofia grinned at me. "Just you wait. You'll change your tune. And in the meantime, just enjoy the nightly thirty-six orgasms that Ryan gives you."

We found Ryan in the kitchen, speaking in hushed tones with Thomas, Derek, and Mason. I hadn't heard Derek arrive. The men looked up when Sofia, Wally, and I entered.

"How're our patients doing?" I asked.

"They're resting now," Thomas reported. "I've got them both on some pain meds. They just need rest."

I nodded. Jase was in good hands with Thomas.

I could feel Ryan's eyes on me, looking me up and down. A pulse of concern shot along our bond. I glanced over at him and smiled. "I'm fine."

He didn't look convinced, but he nodded and turned to Derek. "Any news?"

Derek was staring at Sofia, but she was looking everywhere but at him.

"Waylen's been hitting the caffeine hard and digging into that werewolf, Elias, who Greta named as her initial contact," Derek said. "Turns out he was a member of the Bridgetown Pack."

Ryan frowned. "We'll need to pay them a visit, see what they know about Elias and his drug operation before he died. Maybe someone over there will have a lead on Ghost."

He turned to Mason and Derek. "I want you two to head over there, see what you can find out. I'll call Michael and Camille and get you permission. Make it clear you're following a lead. I don't want to start any trouble."

Derek nodded, but I saw the glint in Mason's eye before he turned his head away. Going to Bridgetown would give him the chance to see Shya again. His wolf was probably going crazy, with her being so far away. Not that Shya wanted anything to do with Mason. She felt there was no future for them, not with her the Bridgetown Alphas' daughter, and Mason committed to the Three Rivers Pack.

"I should get home," Sofia said, interrupting my thoughts.

Thomas glanced at his watch. "It's nearly eight. I want to keep an eye on Jase, at least for another few hours. You're very welcome to stay if you want to. Or if you have things to do today, you can come back later? He's out of danger, Sofia."

Sofia glanced at Derek, then back at Thomas. "I'll stay, if that's okay. I've got a couple more hours before I need to head back to take over for the lunch run."

Ryan strode toward me, his warm, strong arms pulling me into him.

"Let's get you home."

I nodded absently. I felt stretched taut, like my very soul was wearing away. I rubbed my face, realizing how utterly exhausted I felt.

"I'll get your coat," Wally announced, hurrying out of the kitchen.

I gave Sofia a quick hug. "Text me with updates. I want to know how Jase is doing."

"Sure," she agreed, as Ryan steered me toward the corridor.

Wally met us by the front door, handing me my jacket. "Get some rest, the both of you. Mai, we'll talk later, girl."

I mustered a tired smile before slipping into the car. As Ryan rounded the car, I placed my jacket on my knees, and my hand brushed against the box shape in my jacket pocket. I pulled it out, then quickly stuffed it back in. It was a pregnancy test. Wally must have slipped it in there.

I was going to kill him.

Chapter Twenty

Mai

"It's time, Mai." Ryan said gently. "We need to sleep at the Alpha House tonight."

Er, no. I was so not ready for that yet.

He must have seen my answer on my face.

"It's okay. I have a plan."

"A plan? To get me to move in there?" I shook my head. "I love you, Ryan Shaw, but there is no plan in the whole fucking world that is going to make me want to go there instead of your bedroom."

He looked smug. "We'll see. Step one; get you relaxed."

He pulled off the main road and stopped at the edge of the forest. I sat there, not moving. From here, I could see the boundary of the Alpha Compound, and the top of the Alpha House. From here, it seemed to loom over us, taunting me with its memories.

Ryan opened my door and held out his hand. "Come on."

"What are we doing here?"

"Running."

I blinked. "Running?"

"When was the last time you Shifted, Mai?"

Oh. "I...I don't know."

"Exactly. You've been so caught up in becoming Alpha, so focussed on Jem and Brock, on ripple and what's it doing to all of us, that you're not taking care of yourself. You're a werewolf—"

"I know perfectly well what I am, Ryan."

"Do you?" he asked softly. "You're part wolf. You need to let her out, you need to keep yourself open to her. You're not just a human or a wolf, Mai. You're something special. A blend of the two, but that means you can't afford to ignore either side of yourself. If you do, you'll slowly become weaker, you'll feel incomplete. You want to be a good Alpha? You need to be whole, to embrace every part of who you are."

See? Good mate. Clever mate.

My wolf agreed, and I realized with a startling clarity that they were right. I'd been so caught up in the chaos and drama of the mess that was our lives recently that I had neglected my wolf, pushed her aside, even when she'd been telling me what I needed.

"Fuck. I really hate it when you're right."

Ryan smirked at me. "No, you don't."

I glared at him, knowing he was right. Again.

"You ready?" he asked.

Yes, my wolf replied.

Ryan stepped back, stripped and began to Shift, his body blurring as it reformed into the shape of a massive, gray wolf. His fur was thick and lush, gleaming in the dappled sunlight that filtered through the trees.

I closed my eyes, reaching deep within myself to find my own wolf. She was there, waiting, eager to be set free. I let her take control and felt my bones crack and muscles stretch and shrink, reshaping themselves. My skin felt like one big itch for a moment as fur sprouted along my body. Then it was over; I was standing on four paws, my senses sharpened, and my mind focussed solely on the rhythms of the forest.

My wolf chuffed in happiness, and took off running, paws pounding against the soft earth, Ryan following close behind. The stress and worry that seemed part of me, now fell with each stride, replaced by a pure, unadulterated joy of not thinking, not plotting or planning, but just being here, in the moment. The wind ruffled through my fur, carrying with it the scents of the forest—rich soil, leaves that were starting their autumnal changes, small animals scurrying through the underbrush.

I ran and ran, following the trails left by my Pack. I could smell them here, the threads of other werewolves, following the same path over and over again. It was comforting, knowing my Pack had come this way for hundreds of years. I ran until my lungs burned and my muscles ached, until I felt like a part of my soul had been filled up, the missing piece clicking back into place. I was whole again, human and wolf, Alpha and Pack member, all parts of myself working together.

Lost in the simple pleasure of the run, I almost didn't notice Ryan coming up fast behind me until he pounced, his larger form crashing into my back and sending us both tumbling to the ground in a tangle of fur and limbs. I leaped to my feet, shaking off the impact, and saw Ryan standing a few feet away, his tail wagging and his tongue lolling in a wolfish grin.

Oh, so that's how he wanted to play it? I bared my teeth in a playful snarl and took off, darting between the trees and leaping over fallen logs. I could hear Ryan behind me, his paws thudding against the ground as he gave chase.

We wove through the forest, a game of chase that made my heart sing with wild abandon. It felt so right; this was where I belonged, with the feel of the earth beneath my paws, the rush of the wind past my ears, the thrill of being pursued by my mate.

Of course, I couldn't just let him win.

I zipped past a dense thicket, veered left then right; doubling back, lying in wait. As Ryan came barreling past, I leaped out, catching him by surprise and sending us both rolling across a patch of soft moss. The look of shock on his lupine face was priceless, and I let out a yip of triumph.

Got you.

He huffed, and I bounded away, my tail held high in a clear challenge. I heard him get to his feet and dart after me.

My wolf grinned. She was already thinking of how to lay the next trap for him.

Chapter Twenty-One

MAI

The moment Ryan and I stepped through the front door of the Alpha House, a new wave of exhaustion washed over me. We'd been out for a few hours, chasing and playing. We'd Shifted back and headed back to the compound. I felt better, whole again; but even my wolf couldn't erase the weariness that came with too much stress and too little sleep. Ryan's hand felt warm against my skin, and he cupped my face and kissed me softly. My wolf stirred.

Mate. Ours.

Yes, I agreed.

Ryan and me needed this. We needed alone time, without anyone else around, without any pressures or roles or duties. Without being the Alphas of the Three Rivers. We needed the chance to just be Ryan and Mai again. And right now, I just wanted to curl up with him and sleep for a year.

"Hey," Ryan said softly, his fingers gently brushing mine as we stood in the foyer. His touch sent shivers up my spine. "You alright?"

"Yeah," I breathed out, my voice barely above a whisper. "I just...let's go back to the Shaw house. I miss the comfort of your room. I feel safe there."

Ryan's eyes darkened, and a mischievous grin tugged at the corner of his lips. "Mmmm. I have a better idea," he said, his voice low and seductive. "Step two: we make new, good memories in the Alpha House. Memories that will make you feel just as safe here."

I raised an eyebrow, intrigued. "What exactly do you have in mind?" I asked, trying to suppress the flutter in my stomach as all thoughts of sleep fled. Our bond flared to life, and I swallowed hard, feeling for a moment everything that he was.

"Fun things, Mai," he replied, his tone playful yet possessive. "Fun, naked, things in every room."

With a devilish smirk, Ryan took my hand and led me further into the empty house, our footsteps echoing throughout the space. The anticipation built within me, creating a delicious tension as I tried to imagine what he had planned for us.

The moment we entered the kitchen, he murmured, "Trust me," as his hands moved down to my waist before swiftly lifting me up onto the cool granite surface of the kitchen island. The sensation sent a shiver through my body. He whipped my top off, then my bra, so I was naked from the waist up. He hesitated, his eyes roaming possessively over me.

"So beautiful. And all mine," he growled.

My breath caught as I realized he was solely focused on me and me alone. For him, there was nothing else in this world. I was his prey and part of me knew that an apex predator had me in its sights. I wanted to run, to hide, but I couldn't move. He had me pinned just with his gaze.

"Lie down."

Right now, Ryan was all Alpha male, possessive and radiating authority, and I knew I would do anything he said. I lay back against the cool granite top. "Good. Now keep your hands above your head."

I intertwined my fingers and rested them on the smooth surface above my head.

"Promise you won't move them," he added, his gaze locked onto mine, searching for any sign of hesitation.

"I promise," I whispered, my heart pounding in my chest. The vulnerability of being in this position, of being completely at his mercy, set my core on fire.

As Ryan leaned down to capture my lips, I allowed myself to get lost in the moment, reveling in the heat of our connection. The scent of him, pine needles and musk, enveloped me like a warm embrace, making me feel safe and cherished.

"Ryan," I murmured, my voice thick with desire as he trailed his fingers along my neck and down my sides, leaving a trail of goosebumps in their wake. I felt a shiver of anticipation run through me.

"Shhh," he murmured, his lips curving into a wicked grin that sent a fresh wave of arousal coursing through me. "Save your energy, Mai. You're going to need it."

I squirmed beneath his touch as he slowly peeled off my jeans, and then dragged my panties down my legs and over my ankles. His movements were deliberate and unhurried. I wriggled, wanting to touch him, to feel his heat under my hands, but I'd promised not to move my arms.

"Patience, beautiful," Ryan chastised gently, his breath warm against my ear as he leaned in to press a series of feather-light kisses along the curve of my throat. "We have hours, and I plan on making you beg. A lot."

He kneeled down by my ankles and started to tease me with his lips and tongue, trailing kisses and licks up my legs.

My body arching towards him of its own accord, desperate for him to get to the good spots. He chuckled, and continued his slow ascent of my legs, kissing and licking around my core, getting closer and then sliding away. It was torture. I just wanted to grab his head and move it where I wanted. I balled my hands into tight fists, trying my best to control my body's yearning for his touch.

"Say it, Mai," he demanded, his blue eyes sparkling with amusement. "I can see how wet you are, how much you want me. But you're going to have to beg for it."

I lasted another moment, before I couldn't take it anymore.

"Please, Ryan, suck my clit, I want to feel your tongue on me, inside of me," I heard the desperation in my voice, but I didn't care. All I wanted right now was to feel his hot mouth on me.

"There, that wasn't so hard, was it?" he murmured, before finally giving me what I wanted. His tongue flicked over my clit before encircling it, then sliding rapidly over it up and down with the expertise of the only person who knew my body completely. I looked down at him and watched him as he kissed and sucked my clit, flicking his tongue over it, before sinking it deep inside me. It was pure pleasure. I was so wound up, every touch of his tongue made me moan and quiver. My breathing grew shallower as he used his tongue to press inside me ever-so-slightly, finding the most sensitive place before sliding away yet again. Sensing that I was close, he pressed on just a little harder without increasing the tempo of his strokes. I felt like I was going to come apart. My entire body was on fire, every inch of me screaming to release the tension that was building within me. He reached up and pinched one of my nipples, and the combination sent me over the edge, high into orgasmic bliss.

I arched my neck and let out a gasping cry as my spine stiffened and my release crashed over me in a wave of ecstasy.

I came down from the high slowly. The counter top was cool against my heated skin. I looked down at Ryan standing over me, his face full of male satisfaction.

"Don't think for a second that I'm done with you, yet."

Um, yay!

"Come with me," he murmured, his voice low and seductive, as he held out his hand. I gripped it and slid off the countertop.

"I'm naked," I pointed out.

Ryan grinned at me. "I know."

He pulled me toward the door.

"Where are we going?"

"You'll see," he replied with a mysterious grin.

We tiptoed through the house. The lights were off, and I could only hear the sounds of our heartbeats and our soft breathing. The cool air brushing against my bare nipples made me shiver. Ryan guided me into the study. "We're making new memories, remember," he said, the hunger in his gaze making my heart race.

I nodded as he pulled me close, pressing his lips to mine in a kiss that left me craving more. My hands clung to his broad shoulders as he backed me up against the bookcase.

"Touch me, Mai," he ordered, his hot breath sending shivers down my spine.

Oh, fuck, yes!

I obliged, taking off his shirt and exploring the hard planes of his chest, circling his nipples before trailing lower to unbutton his jeans. He groaned as my fingers brushed against the massive bulge beneath the denim. Opening his pants, I slid my fingers beneath the elastic of his boxers and found his shaft. He groaned, warm breath tickling the sensitive spot behind my ear.

"I love it when you touch me," he murmured against my skin as I began stroking him in a lazy rhythm, taking him in my hand, squeezing gently. I teasingly ran my thumb over the sensitive tip of his penis, loving the way he moaned in response. I gave his length one last stroke before kneeling down and taking him into my warm mouth. My tongue explored his steel-hard length, tracing every vein and ridge on the underside of his cock as though committing them to memory. I moaned as I took him deeper, feeling his precum hitting the back of my throat, and savoring the taste of my mate. He moaned and tangled his fingers in my hair, guiding me as I worked him with my mouth and hands.

I felt a wave of desire building within me as I enjoyed the sounds coming from his lips. I loved the feel of him sliding in and out of my mouth, the sounds of me sucking deeply and him moaning. His cock twitched. Then he reached down, grasped me under my arms, and lifted me up. I whined in disappointment, but Ryan just chuckled, then sat me on the desk. The smooth wood surface was cool against my butt and I hitched in a breath as Ryan spread my legs wide.

"Remember, you need to beg, Mai," he ordered, as he picked up one of my legs and threw it over his shoulder. I gripped the desk, bracing myself for what was to come. Ryan traced a finger along my slit, his thumb stroking my clit as he circled his fingers around my entrance. He dipped them inside, just the tips of his finger, then withdrew.

I moaned.

He did it again, driving me crazy with his teasing. I needed to feel him all the way inside of me.

"Ryan," I gasped.

"Yes?"

He teased me with his fingers, never going more than an inch inside.

"Say it, Mai."

"Please, please, Ryan."

"There's my good girl."

He plunged three fingers in and I cried and arched toward him when he hit my g-spot. My fingers gripped the desk as I thought of his cock sliding into my wet core. I'd never wanted anyone as much as I wanted him right now.

"Please, Ryan. Please fuck me," I breathed.

He growled deeply, and before I could draw another breath, he removed his fingers and drove deep within me in one powerful thrust. His cock hit the end of my vagina, filling me to the hilt; it felt so right, like it belonged inside me. I closed my eyes as he pulled out almost all the way, leaving just his head still inside. He rocked back and forth, teasing me with just the tip of his cock this time.

I opened my eyes. Ryan lifted an eyebrow at me.

I gave in. "Please, Ryan."

He grinned, then plunged back inside of me, filling me entirely yet again.

I trembled around him, loving every minute of his forceful, single-minded passion. He slid out, then thrust inside me again. The desk creaked against the force of his thrusts as he pounded into me.

"Harder," I begged, feeling another orgasm building within me. He leaned back, changing the angle, and reached up with one hand to knead my breast. Then he gave in to my request, driving into me even harder. I gasped each time he thrust inside, his cock sending a deep vibration through me that threatened to consume us both. I reveled in it. In all of him, in knowing that he was mine. Only mine.

"I'm going to come," I moaned.

He immediately slowed. "You need to beg for that."

"Ryan!" I complained.

"Beg, Mai. I want to hear you beg to come."

"Fuck!" I couldn't stand it any longer. My body was quivering with need. "Please, Ryan. Please make me come!" I panted.

He laughed. He fucking laughed. I didn't have time to get pissed about it, though, as he drove into me with such force and energy that my mind went blank with pleasure. We reached the edge together. I grabbed the desk edge on either side of me and held on as the first wave of pleasure swept through me. My inside walls tightened, my hands opening and closing against the desk, unable to find purchase. My orgasm hit me like a tidal wave, rocking my body hard, pulling a scream from my lips. Ryan's fingers dug into my hips, holding me still as he continued to thrust within me through the waves of my climax. Our bond flared to life, and for a moment, I could feel his utter awe. He loved me, worshipped my body, and had plans to do this every day, several times a day, for the rest of our lives.

Chapter Twenty-Two

RYAN

The late morning light filtered through the floor-to-ceiling windows of the Alpha House kitchen, casting a warm glow over the granite-topped island where Mai and I sat eating lunch. We'd gotten about two hours of sleep before my phone started ringing. Sylvie had stopped by, stocked up the fridge and left us a pre-made lunch of salmon and cheese sandwiches. I was enjoying the serene quietness of the kitchen, of being here with Mai. Not talking, just being near each other. I sipped my coffee, and thought about going down on Mai this morning, right here, on the countertop, and how fucking gorgeous she looked when she came with my tongue inside of her.

Mai, seemingly lost in her own thoughts, played with her food, picking it up, then putting it down again without taking a bite. I reached over, covering her hand with mine, feeling the connection that always seemed to calm the storm inside me. She looked up, offering me a faint smile that didn't quite reach her eyes. Something was on her mind, something more than the usual Pack troubles.

Before I could ask, Mai's head turned at the sound of the front door swinging open.

Derek and Mason strode into the kitchen, their expressions a mix of fatigue and tension. Mason's jaw was set in a hard line, and his eyes had a distant, angry look. Whatever had happened in Bridgetown, it was clear he wasn't happy. The question was, was his unhappiness to do with what he found out, or with Shya?

"How did it go in Bridgetown?" I asked.

Derek leaned against the counter. "We talked to a few of Elias' friends, if you can call them that. Elias was not the sort to have friends. More like people he often fucked over. None of them were exactly heartbroken about him being dead." Derek eyed the sandwiches on the table, and I nodded. He picked one up before continuing. "We managed to find out that Elias was deep into supplying drugs in the northeast. He was a major dealer. Had the supply lines set up and secure, had runners and low-level dealers working for him. He was an established player. Then about two years ago, this Ghost character came into the picture."

I put down my mug of coffee. "Ghost?"

"Yeah, he started muscling in on Elias' operations. Elias was none too happy. Apparently Ghost wanted to monopolize the drug routes into the northeast. He eventually came to Elias and told him that he had the resources and the backing to take over and Elias should give it up."

"I'm guessing Elias didn't respond too well to that?"

Derek shook his head. "Fuck no. Elias hit back and hit back hard. It started six months of war between the two."

"And Michael and Camille knew nothing about it?" I found that hard to believe. They prided themselves on having a territory that not only welcomed human tourists, but encouraged them to visit. They stomped down on any threats that would scare the tourists away and having a drug turf war happening in their territory would be high on their list of no-nos.

"Nope, but get this," Mason chimed in from where he stood by the window. "Tristan was the Beta then. It was his responsibility and according to Elias' contacts, Tristan apparently knew all about it and covered it up."

No wonder Mason was in a bad mood. Just saying Tristan's name set off the rage inside him these days. Tristan had convinced Michael and Camille that he was Shya's fated mate. Hell, he'd even convinced Shya of it for a while. He'd gaslit them all, and when Shya realized, she'd told her parents. They'd taken Tristan's side and told her that she just needed time to accept him. Back then, Tristan had been their golden boy. The trusted Beta who would be a perfect match for their only daughter. Eventually, the truth had come out, but Shya was scarred by the whole thing and had no interest in trusting another wolf ever again. Unfortunately, Mason entered the picture soon after, and was having a hell of a time trying to convince Shya that he was really her fated mate and that she should give him a shot. Tristan had escaped the last time we'd fought him. He was still out there, and still claiming that Shya was going to be his.

I tapped my fingers on the countertop. "Tristan was covering for one of them."

Mason nodded.

"Which one, Elias or Ghost?" Mai asked.

Derek shrugged. "Without asking Tristan, we don't know. The war ended when Elias was found dead in his home about eighteen months ago. Since then, Ghost has taken over all his routes and contacts."

"Any clues at all as to Ghost's identity?"

"No. No one knows who he is, but two people saw Elias arguing with Tristan the day before he died."

Tristan. Was it a coincidence? Was he working with Ghost, or was he Ghost?

For fuck's sake. Each time we made progress, it just threw up more questions.

We'd need to get in touch with Michael and Camille, see if they had any more intel on what Tristan was up to these days.

My phone buzzed. It was a text from Sam.

Waylen's got something.

CHAPTER TWENTY-THREE

MAI

The underground parking lot of Shaw Investigations was a cavernous space, the concrete walls echoing the soft purr of our SUV as Ryan skillfully maneuvered into a parking spot.

The space was lined with a variety of cars, some sleek and modern, others rugged and utilitarian, each one telling its own story of the people who worked above.

Surveillance cameras dotted the ceiling, their unblinking eyes a silent testament to the security measures in place. I noticed a keypad next to the elevator, requiring a code for access—a further layer of protection.

We walked to the elevator, its doors a gleaming metal that reflected our images back at us. I glanced at Ryan, noticing the way his eyes were constantly scanning the area. That was Ryan, always ready, always alert. Derek and Mason shared a look, an unspoken understanding passing between them. This was their world, one of secrets and shadows, and we were stepping into it.

The elevator itself was modern, the interior sleek and polished. A small security camera was nestled in the corner, and a panel of buttons glowed softly in the dim light. As the doors closed, sealing us in, I felt a thrill of anticipation. I'd finally get to see inside the inner workings of their top secret PI firm.

We went up in silence, the soft hum of the elevator the only sound. Ryan stood close to me, his hand brushing against me, sending a jolt through my entire body. Our bond was still so new, and it flared to life almost randomly at the moment. The image of Ryan lifting my skirt and fucking me right here sprang into my head. Ryan turned his head and looked at me, his eyes half-lidded, an expression of utmost smugness on his face. He knew exactly what I was thinking.

The elevator came to a stop with a gentle ding; the doors sliding open to reveal the firm's reception. Behind a long desk sat a young man with a sharp suit and sharper eyes. He assessed us with a quick, professional glance, his smile polite yet guarded.

"Good morning, Mr. Shaw," he said, his voice respectful and attentive. "Welcome back. You have a few messages waiting for you." He handed Mason a small stack of papers, his movements precise and efficient.

Mason nodded, taking the messages. "Thank you, Dean. Anything urgent?"

"No, sir. Everything is under control," Dean replied, his eyes briefly flickering to Ryan and me, before immediately looking at the floor.

Mason turned to us. "Dean, you already met my brother, but this is Mai Parker. They're our new Pack Alphas."

Dean inclined his head, his expression a mix of respect and curiosity. "It's an honor to meet you. Welcome to Shaw Investigations."

"Thank you, Dean. It's nice to be here."

As Dean pressed a button under his desk, I heard the soft click of a lock disengaging on the door behind him.

We walked through the door and down a corridor into an open office space. There were about ten people in here, all busy working away on their respective tasks. No one looked at us directly, but I caught more than one giving us the side-eye. I was never going to get used to this. Ryan took my hand; that's all he had to do to settle my thoughts. I wondered if he knew the power he had over me now. I braced for the panic that should come with that thought, but nothing happened.

Huh.

I actually loved the thought that he could do this to me. When the hell had that happened?

As we walked through the office, I studied the people here, curious to see who would work in a PI agency. There was a mix of men and women, their ages ranging from fresh-faced interns to seasoned veterans. One woman, with sleek black hair pulled back in a tight bun, was examining a series of photographs pinned to the wall. As we walked past, she straightened and inclined her head, before quietly murmuring, "Alpha Mai, Alpha Ryan, welcome."

Next to her, a young man was poring over multiple computer screens, his fingers flying over the keyboard. He stood up as we approached and turned to face us fully, his eyes down. "It's an honor to have you here, Alphas," he said, his voice steady despite the scent of his nervousness reaching me.

Further along, a man and a woman were having a low-voiced discussion over a cluttered desk. The man, tall with a weathered face and salt-and-pepper hair, gestured at a map spread out before them.

The woman, younger and with an air of fierce determination, shook her head and pointed to the left-hand corner of the map.

Just past them, a lean, middle-aged man detached himself from a group huddled around a whiteboard.

"Alpha Mai, Alpha Ryan," he addressed us first, bowing his head slightly. Then, turning to Mason, he continued, "Mason, got a minute?"

Mason turned to him, a questioning look in his eyes. "Something urgent, Jeff?"

The man, Jeff, shook his head. "No, nothing pressing. Just wanted to run some findings by you, but it can wait."

"Alright, catch me after the meeting with Sam and Waylen," Mason replied, his voice steady and reassuring.

Jeff nodded, giving us a brief, polite smile before returning to his group, leaving us to continue our tour.

Ryan, walking beside me, let his gaze wander over the room. I could sense that he approved. "I haven't been in a while," he murmured to me, his deep voice barely above a whisper. "They've put in place a few changes since I was last here."

Mason, leading our small procession, glanced back with a hint of pride in his eyes. He was in his element here, the calm, composed commander amidst a sea of information and strategy. "We like to stay on top of things. Efficiency is key in our line of work," he said, rolling a tennis ball between his hands.

Finally, we reached Mason's office. The space was a perfect representation of him—organized, no-nonsense, yet with personal touches that spoke of a life beyond the job. He placed the tennis ball on the desk amongst neatly stacked papers, two computer screens, and small things he could fidget with dotted around the space. I saw three tennis balls, a fidget spinner, and a book hook with different colored skulls.

My eyes were drawn to a photo pinned to his corkboard, a candid shot of the Shaw brothers, arms slung over each other's shoulders, grinning widely. The image transported me back to a day six years ago, a memory so vivid it felt like yesterday.

It had been a warm summer afternoon, and the Shaws had come over. Things were getting bad under Oliver, and Ryan and Jem were just starting to plot their takeover. Ryan had brought his brothers over, and he and Jem had rustled up some cheap burgers and hot dogs to feed us all. We'd gone out to the small park behind our apartment. The sun had been high in the sky, casting a golden glow over everything.

I remembered how teenage Ryan had manned the grill, proudly wearing a "Kiss the Cook" apron. I had so wanted to kiss him, had thought I could use his apron as an excuse if he was horrified, but I couldn't get the courage to do it. Instead, I just watched his face light up with a broad smile as he flipped burgers and hot dogs. Mason, Sam, and Derek had been messing about in a heated game of Frisbee, their competitive spirits on full display as they dove and leaped to outdo each other. Back then, Ryan had been quick to laugh, and I knew he loved to see his brothers having fun.

Jem had taken that photo after we'd all eaten. Ryan, Mason, Sam, and Derek, the Shaw brothers, arms around each other, their faces so young and carefree.

So much had changed in six years. They still looked alike, in the shape of their noses, and the set of their jaws, but now they were serious, dangerous predators. When one of the Shaw brothers looked at you, it pushed all the oxygen out of your lungs. Each of them could make you feel like you were the only thing in the whole world that interested them. They were focused, single-minded, and relentless.

Ryan leaned closer to me. "I'm proud of all of them. They've each built something important. Something that makes a difference."

Mason shrugged. "We do what we have to do, for the Pack, for our family."

"And we all try not to make a mess while doing it," Derek winked at me.

"Have you guys finished the tour yet? I'm getting lonely in here!" A voice called from the office across the hallway. I turned to see Sam poking his head around the door.

I laughed and walked into his office. It was the same size as Mason's, with a large desk littered with papers and three laptops, walls adorned with Star Wars posters, and a cozy area for private conversations.

Sitting in a brown leather chair in front of the desk with a laptop on his knees was Waylen Jones. He was just how I remembered him from school. Waylen looked up at me, his face breaking into a grin that was part playful, part mischievous. "Mai Parker, as I live and breathe."

He hadn't changed much since our school days—still skinny, his frame almost swallowed by the oversized black T-shirt he wore. His hazelnut hair was a tousled mess, as if he'd just run his hands through it, and lime-green owlish glasses perched precariously on the bridge of his nose, magnifying his keen eyes.

He stood up and stretched, a series of pops emanating from his back. His movements were restless, his fingers tapping rhythmically on the side of his leg as if to an unheard beat.

"I see you've come to see the wizard behind the curtain," he said with a wry smile, pushing his glasses up.

I couldn't help but smile back. "Waylen, still trying to hack the world, one system at a time?"

"Always," he replied, his tone light but confident.

"You guys know each other?" Sam asked, a hint of surprise in his voice.

"Yeah, Waylen sat behind me in math," I said, returning my focus to Sam. "He was a pain; he used to drive our teacher crazy with his constant questions."

"I prefer the term 'intellectually curious'. And, I might add, those questions led me to where I am today."

"And that's him being modest," Mason interjected. "Waylen's the best hacker we've got. Probably the best in the state."

Waylen shrugged, a small smirk playing on his lips. "I just do what I do best—uncover secrets and unravel mysteries. It's all in a day's work."

Ryan gestured at Waylen's laptop. "Sam says you have something for us?"

Waylen's expression shifted, a mix of frustration and determination coloring his features. "I've been digging, but Ghost is a ghost in more than just name. It's like the freaking guy doesn't exist," he admitted, his hands moving constantly as he spoke. "Every time I get close to that fucker, it's like 'poof' he disappears on me. I'm going to get him, though. No one outruns Waylen the Wizard."

"But you have found something?" asked Derek.

"Yeah, I've been going back through all the intel you guys collected. You remember Bradford Hayes?"

"The human drug dealer that me and Ryan ran down?"

"That's the one. According to your briefing, Bradford first put you onto the name of Ghost, and claimed that Ghost was working for Ronnie Bishop."

"Yeah, we know all this."

"Ah, but in your notes, you said that Bradford didn't know Ronnie's name. Called him Reggie Billet, and only once you mentioned Ronnie Bishop, did he confirm it."

Ryan nodded. "That's right."

"Which makes you think that he didn't really know Ronnie at all, and only heard the name tossed around once in a while, right?"

"You got a point in there somewhere, wizard boy?" Mason asked.

"I'm getting there," Waylen replied, bounding up and down on his feet.

"Bradford Hayes is human. He has a cousin, one Otto Hayes. Bradford and Otto are tight. They went to school together, they used to live together, they even co-own a pickup truck."

"Yeah, so?"

"So, Otto Hayes works for..." Waylen paused, with a big grin on his face. "Drum roll, please."

"Waylen, get on with it," ordered Sam.

"Ronnie Bishop. Otto has been working for Ronnie for the last five years. There is no way Bradford Hayes didn't know exactly who Ronnie was."

Ryan and Derek looked at each other.

"Hayes lied to us," said Derek.

"I knew that shithead got caught too easily. We need to pay Bradford another visit."

Chapter Twenty-Four

RYAN

Bradford's house was a modest two-story brick house with a neatly trimmed lawn and faded siding. The driveway was empty, and curtains drawn. This afternoon, it was just another sleepy house on a sleepy block, giving no hints as to the occupant within.

"No movement, no lookouts that I can see," Derek muttered.

I nodded. "Stay alert."

My muscles tensed as we crossed the street. The intel we'd squeezed out of Bradford Hayes at our last encounter had been vague. If his aim had been to misdirect us, to drop Ronnie's name and make us think we'd squeezed it out of him, why had he given us Ghost's name too? It has been our first clue, the first time we'd had a name to go on. It didn't make sense.

We climbed the front steps cautiously. The faint glow of a television screen flickered behind the drawn living room curtains. I exchanged a glance with Derek, then pounded a fist on the door.

For a long moment, silence. Then came the scrambling of footsteps, followed by the metallic grind of locks being hastily turned. The door jerked open an inch, a pair of beady eyes peering out.

"Fuck, man!" Bradford registered who we were, and tried to slam the door shut.

I didn't hesitate. Gripping the knob, I threw my shoulder against the wood. It burst inward with a crack, the chain lock snapping from the frame. We spilled into the house on Bradford's heels. He sprinted for the back of the house and let out a yelp as Derek tackled him to the faded carpet. In seconds, we had him up and dumped on the leather sofa.

"Check the house," I told Derek. "I'll keep an eye on him."

Derek swept through the first floor while I stood over a cringing Bradford. This floor of the house was small, I could see most of it from where I stood—living room, kitchen, utility closet. It only took Derek a moment to verify we were alone. He disappeared upstairs, then returned to the living room a few moments later.

"It's clear," Derek said.

We both stood over Bradford. His leg jittered nervously, eyes darting between us.

I dragged over a chair and settled down so we were eye to eye. Bradford shrunk back against the couch, looking like he wanted to disappear into the upholstery. Up close, I could see the sheen of nervous sweat beading his sallow skin. He reeked of fear and cheap cologne.

"Please," he stammered. "I already told you everything I know. I stopped dealing, I swear. Just like you told me. The drugs, man, they aren't coming from me!"

"Oh, we know." I kept my tone casual. Deceptive. "You're small time, Bradford. A bottom feeder. This is way over your head."

He nodded rapidly. "Yeah, yeah exactly! I'm nobody, just a small-time dealer trying to get by."

I leaned forward, holding his gaze. "But you know things. About Ronnie Bishop. About Ghost." I paused, letting the names settle between us. "I'm thinking you know more than you've let on."

Bradford's throat bobbed as he swallowed. "I don't, I swear! I told you about Ronnie, just like you asked. He's the guy you're looking for. He's the one running ripple into the territory."

"Really? How's your cousin, Bradford? Otto, right?"

Bradford froze, then swallowed loudly.

"Otto?" he squeaked.

Out of the corner of my eye, I saw Derek move to stand directly in Bradford's eyeline. He shifted, subtly emphasizing the hard lines of muscle beneath his shirt. A classic interrogation tactic. Push, then threaten.

"Yeah, Otto. He works over in Haxton, doesn't he?"

Bradford's gaze darted from me to Derek and back again. "Yeah, yeah. Otto works out there."

"Uh-huh. And how does he like working for Ronnie? A good job, is it?"

Bradford bolted up and ran for the door.

Derek was on him in an instant, tripping him up and sending Bradford sprawling on the floor. Bradford scrambled up. Derek slammed his boot down on top of Bradford's back, pinning him to the ground.

"Going somewhere, Hayes?" I was out of patience with this scumbag.

"I don't know nothing!" Bradford pleaded, his face squashed on the carpet.

"You pretended not to know who Ronnie Bishop was. What name did he give us, Derek?"

"Reggie Billet."

"Oh yeah. You dropped Ghost's name, then told us he was really working for *Reggie* and that *Reggie* was running the show. You had the name just a little off, just enough for us to believe that you didn't know it was Ronnie you were talking about. Why the theatrics, Bradford?"

Bradford's body went limp as he laughed. A low chuckle that got louder.

"You finally worked it out, did you? Took you long enough."

Derek hauled him up off the floor and slammed Bradford into the wall. Derek's forearm cut across Bradford's neck, letting in just the bare, minimal amount of air.

I stood up and stalked toward them.

"You're going to tell us what the fuck you know, Bradford."

Bradford grinned back at me.

"I'm a low-level dealer. You think I know fuck? No, man. I just do what I do."

I motioned to Derek to let him go.

Bradford collapsed forward, holding his neck.

"You told us about Ghost. Why?"

He gasped in a breath before he replied. "Coz I needed some cred with you. You had to believe I knew what I was talking about. I dropped Ghost's name to make sure you believed me, then I could steer you to Ronnie."

Bradford thought we already knew about Ghost. He had no idea it had been the first time we'd heard his name.

"Start at the beginning. Why did you want to blame Ronnie for the ripple?"

Bradford looked back up at me. "It wasn't my idea to blame Ronnie."

No shit.

"I was just following orders."

I went very still. "Orders from who?"

Derek cracked his knuckles, the sound loud in the room. Bradford flinched.

"Who ordered you to blame Ronnie Bishop?" I repeated. My voice was cold steel.

"Who do you think? The true werewolf, the true Alpha, told me to do it. Said anyone comes sniffing around, make sure I have you clueless fuckers chasing your asses looking at Ronnie."

Derek frowned back at me. The true Alpha?

"The Alpha?"

Bradford grunted. "Yeah, man, him. The true Alpha."

I went very still, ice trickling down my spine. The true Alpha. There was only one wolf Bradford might refer to by that title here in Three Rivers.

Brock.

Rage ignited inside me, white-hot and visceral. It took every ounce of self-control not to seize Bradford by his scrawny neck and shake him until his teeth rattled. Brock was involved in this, had his bloody paws all over it. Not just supplying Hayley with it, but he was involved in flooding our streets with that poison, destroying lives, families, our whole damn community. And he was setting up Ronnie to take the fall.

"And where will I find this true Alpha of yours?"

Bradford grinned at me. "I've no idea, man. He's everywhere, he's nowhere."

Fuck!

We needed a break. We still had no clue where Brock was, or who the fuck was Ghost. My hands curled into fists. Brock had framed Ronnie—was Ronnie in on this? Was this just a distraction to delay us? We'd split our resources chasing after Ghost, trying to find out who he was, instead of focussing everything on Brock. We were out of time and out of leads. Brock was going to kill Jem if we didn't nominate him tomorrow. The urge to tear Brock apart with my bare hands, make him suffer for every life he'd ruined, pulsed inside me, primitive and feral.

But I couldn't give into it. Not yet. I needed to be smart, keep a clear head. Use this rage as fuel rather than let it control me.

I exhaled slowly, regaining my composure before turning back to Bradford.

"You're coming with us."

"What?" Bradford snapped his head between me and Derek. "No way, man."

I stepped up close to him. "Yes way, man. I'm not letting you scurry back to your *Alpha* and tell him we've worked it out. You're going to spend some time in our cage rooms and once this mess is settled, I'll think about what the fuck to do with you."

Chapter Twenty-Five

MAI

I sat beside Jase's bed, watching the steady rise and fall of his chest as he slept. Thomas had assured me that his arm was healing, but the sight of the bandages covering his body still made my stomach churn. I couldn't help but feel responsible, even though I knew, logically, that Jase had been doing his duty as a member of the Pack. If he wanted to be an enforcer, this is what he would face on a daily basis.

Jase stirred, his eyes fluttering open. He managed a smile when he saw me. "Hey. You been here long?"

"Long enough to hear you whisper Amara's name in your sleep. On your thoughts, is she?"

"What? No! Definitely not!"

I grinned at him. Looked like I'd hit a nerve. I didn't point out that I was just teasing and all he'd done was snore. Instead, I asked, "How are you feeling?"

Jase sat up and swung his legs off the bed. He moved his bandaged arm around, testing it out, then grinned at me. "Better. Don't worry, I'll be up and watching your back again in no time."

I tried to return his smile, but it felt forced. "I know you will, Jase. But I hate seeing you get hurt. The life of an enforcer is dangerous and violent, Jase. Next time you might not be so lucky. What was the worst thing that happened on your delivery job? Did a little old lady chase you down the street with her cane because you forgot her prune juice?"

Jase shook his head. "You're not going to persuade me to give it up, Mai. I know the job is dangerous. But it's also about standing up for the weaker members of our Pack, protecting those who can't protect themselves. I was younger than you and Sofia, but I still saw the damage Oliver caused when he was Alpha."

Oliver had been a vicious, unhinged asshole that used the Pack to sell guns, often faulty ones, and let his enforcers do what they liked. They made sure that anyone they didn't like suffered.

"I want to do some good, Mai. I believe in what you and Ryan are trying to build here. It's what this Pack deserves and I'm going to do everything I can to support you. So, no, I'm not going to change my mind about being an enforcer. I'm going to work hard, I'm going to train more and I'll be the best damn enforcer this Pack has seen."

I sighed, knowing I wasn't going to be able to talk him out of it.

A soft whimper from the corner of the room drew my attention. The teenage witch we'd rescued from the lab was stirring. Her eyes flew open suddenly, wide with fear as she took in her unfamiliar surroundings. She tried to sit up, but her frail body seemed to struggle with the effort.

Jase jumped off his bed, and approached her, hands up and voice gentle. "Hey, it's okay. You're safe now. No one's going to hurt you here."

The girl's gaze darted between Jase and me, uncertainty etched on her gaunt features. Her eyes lingered on Jase for a moment, and a flicker of recognition passed over her face. "You...you're the one from the lab," she whispered, her voice hoarse. Her accent was odd, not one I recognized, and I'd traveled all over in my four years away. "Your moon star was bright. I couldn't let it go out."

Moon star? *Okaaay.*

Jase nodded, a grateful smile on his lips. "That's right. You were incredibly brave back there. Thank you."

I stood up slowly, not wanting to startle her. "I'm Mai, and this is Jase. Can you tell us your name?"

The girl hesitated for a moment. "Esme," she said finally, her voice barely above a whisper. "My name is Esme."

Good, a name was a start. "How old are you, Esme?"

She glanced at Jase, then back at me. "There have been seventeen summer solstices since I arrived here."

Seventeen? That surprised me. I'd put her at fifteen tops.

There was a soft knock at the door and Thomas walked in. Normally he was an imposing figure, tall with bulging muscles, but he had hunched his shoulders and made himself appear smaller, a technique he used when dealing with vulnerable patients.

Thomas approached Esme cautiously, his steps measured and slow. He crouched down beside her bed, bringing himself to her eye level. "Hello there," he said, his deep voice warm and soothing. "I'm Thomas. How are you feeling?"

Esme's eyes widened slightly, but she didn't seem to mind Thomas being here too. "I am not injured," she managed, her voice still weak.

Thomas nodded, a kind smile on his face. "That's good to hear. You've been through quite an ordeal." He paused for a moment, studying her face. "Would you like something to eat? I'm sure you must be hungry."

At the mention of food, Esme's eyes lit up, but she nodded guardedly, as if not wanting us to know just how hungry she was.

We made our way to the kitchen, Thomas leading the way, with me and Jase following and Esme a few steps behind us. I knew that Esme might not feel comfortable having anyone behind her. Her steps were wobbly though, and I could hear her falter more than once. I wanted to turn and help her, but the first time Thomas looked over his shoulder at me and shook his head.

The enticing aroma of freshly baked bread and chili beckoned us forward. Wally was in the kitchen stirring a large pot, wearing his favorite frilly pink apron. He turned as we walked in. "Just in time! I've got food ready for you."

Esme hesitated in the doorway as the rest of us sat at the kitchen table.

"Wally, this is Esme," I said, introducing them.

"Pleased to meet you, young Esme," Wally smiled at her, then turned back to the pot. "I hope you like chilli, I'm made way too much food again."

We all made ourselves busy, looking anywhere but at Esme. After a moment, she made her way over and sat in a chair at the other end of the table.

Wally served up generous portions of the steaming chili, accompanied by thick slices of crusty bread. He placed a bowl in front of Esme, who stared at the food with a mixture of hunger and disbelief.

As soon as Wally stepped back, Esme grabbed the spoon and began to devour the chili. She tore off pieces of the bread, dunking them into the chili and stuffing them into her mouth, barely pausing to breathe between bites.

"You should slow down, Esme," Thomas warned gently. "Too much too quickly and you'll make yourself sick."

Esme looked up at Thomas, then took a deep breath and deliberately slowed down her movements.

After Esme had emptied her bowl, and said no when Wally asked if she wanted more, I leaned forward. "Esme, do you know where you are right now?"

Esme glanced around, taking in her surroundings. "Yes. I'm in a kitchen."

"I mean, do you know where in the country you are?"

She thought about it. "Somewhere in the north. They moved me around a lot, but it's colder up here than the last place they kept me. It's easier for my magic to trickle like a broken tap, drip, drip, drip, they don't notice I keep my sleeping room cold. I like the cold. It keeps the bad smells away, and the bad men. They don't like it chilly."

My heart clenched at the thought of her being "kept" anywhere or who the bad men were. "Can you tell us what you were doing at the lab where we found you?"

Esme's gaze dropped to her empty bowl, and she seemed to shrink into herself. "My coven...they were no good. They were supposed to protect me. That's what covens do, yes?"

I nodded. "Yes, covens are like Packs. They are supposed to protect their members. Did your coven not protect you, Esme?"

"They did not! My uncle sold me to werewolves two summer solstices ago." Her voice was barely above a whisper. "I was taken to different places. Here and there, there and here again. Never good places. Not family, not home. Just bad men and bad smells. They make me cast a spell on these wave pills, over and over and over and over. Wherever they take me, that's what I have to do. Or no food for Esme. No sleep for Esme. No happy Esme."

My wolf snorted in disgust. *Mistreated pup. Kill those who did this.*

I paused. It was interesting that my wolf saw Esme, a witch, as a pup. She felt connected to her. Why? And why would a coven sell one of their own, and to werewolves of all people?

I reached out and gently touched Esme's hand, trying to offer some comfort. "Esme, do you know what the spell you cast on the pills does?"

Esme nodded, a haunted look in her eyes. "It makes wolves go all gray. But not in a good way. Their bonds become torn, black and shriveled. That's what they see, even if it's not really there. Poor little wolves, they break the bonds, try and make new ones, but the old ones, they are good, they just don't see it anymore. The spell it makes messes with their minds, makes them doubt the people they care about most. It is an evil thing. That I know. Yes, that I know."

She shuddered, and something I couldn't make out flickered across her face. "But if Esme doesn't do the spell, bad things happen. Bad men, bad smells. Pain. Hunger. These things became Esme, Esme becomes them."

I heard Jase's sharp intake of breath beside me.

I squeezed Esme's hand, trying to pour all the reassurance I could into the gesture. "Esme, I want you to know that what they did to you was wrong. No one deserves to be treated like that, and no one has the right to force you to use your magic against your will."

Esme's eyes glistened with unshed tears, and she gave me a small, tentative nod.

I looked at Esme, trying to keep my voice gentle as I asked, "How did you know to do this spell? Did you create it yourself?"

Esme shook her head vehemently, her eyes wide with a mixture of fear and disgust. "No, I told you it is an evil thing. My coven...my uncle, he taught it to me before they accepted money for me." Her voice trembled as she continued, "The werewolves who paid, they came. They wanted a witch who knew this spell. My uncle, he showed them me. Special Esme, special me."

A cold chill ran down my spine at the implications of her words. At the way her family, her coven, had used her. This wasn't just a case of a witch being sold and exploited; it was a premeditated plan to use Esme's magic to sow discord and mistrust among werewolves, to break our Pack bonds. Was this a witch plan, or a werewolf one? Why would werewolves agree to this?

Jase's face hardened, his jaw clenching with barely contained anger. "They knew exactly what they were doing," he growled, his hands curling into fists. "This whole operation, it's not just about the pills. It's about tearing apart our communities."

I turned back to Esme, my mind racing with questions. "Esme, is there a way to reverse the spell, to reverse the effects?"

She tilted her head to one side and seemed to consider my question. "My uncle said that all spells have a counter. Spells can go one way, then the other. Topsy turvy. Turvy topsy. So, yes, it is possible."

I leaned forward, holding my breath. "And do you know the counter spell?"

"Oh no! No one taught that to Esme. Maybe it is waiting, silent little mouse spell, waiting to be found."

Well, that sucked. A reverse spell would have come in handy right about now.

"What about the werewolves who bought you? Do you know their names? Or the ones who kept you in the lab?"

Esme's face fell, and she seemed to shrink into herself once more. "No. No names. They were careful, tippy-toe careful, not to say names around Esme."

She wrapped her arms around herself, as if trying to hold herself together. "Code words, they used. Bad men were scared that I might try to use magic against them if I knew their true names." She laughed then, a bitter sound. "I would have, too!"

They were trying to cover their tracks, making sure that even if Esme escaped, she wouldn't be able to identify them.

"I might be able to help with that," Wally said, pulling out his phone. "I've been collecting photos of some of the werewolves we've encountered, trying to build a database of those we can't trust. Maybe you could take a look and see if you recognize anyone?"

Esme nodded hesitantly. Wally handed her his phone, and she began scrolling through the images, her brow furrowed in concentration.

I caught Wally's eye and gave him an appreciative nod.

Wally grinned, a mischievous twinkle in his eye. "I'm not just a pretty face, you know," he quipped, trying to lighten the mood. "I've got brains to match these fabulous eyes." He fluttered his eyelashes at me, making me laugh.

Esme scrolled through the photos. Then she suddenly stopped, her finger hovering over the screen. "This one," she said, pointing to a stern-faced man with cold eyes. "And this one too," she added, indicating another photo.

Then Esme's finger landed on a third photo. "Ah-ha! Yes, indeed, ah-ha! It's an ah-ha moment!" she whispered, her voice trembling slightly. "I only saw him once, but he was the big boss man. The others, scared little lambs, they were, when he came calling. He said that they had consolidated—it's a big word, consolidated, but he used it, so I can use it too."

"What did they consolidate, Esme?" I asked gently.

"All the labs into one. He said, I overheard him talking, that they could up production with the consolidated—I like that word now, even if he did say it first—lab and it would make it easier, not having to move Esme around all the time, from lab to lab to lab to lab. Always on the move."

That matched what Talia had said.

Wally leaned in, studying the photo closely. "Are you sure, Esme? You only saw him the one time?"

Esme nodded, her gaze still fixed on the screen. "I remember this face. Big boss man. Like the whole sparkly world owes him and he will take it and burn it and eat it all up. But my brother will stop him. I don't have a brother yet, not yet, but I will." She touched the screen with her pinky finger. "They called him a name. Esme doesn't remember, but it was like a phantom, white and scary, there and then gone."

Wally turned the phone around so I could see the photo, and my heart nearly stopped. There, staring back at me from the screen, was Brock.

I dug out my phone and called Ryan.

"I know who Ghost really is."

CHAPTER TWENTY-SIX

MAI

I felt myself relaxing into the passenger seat of Ryan's car. The soft hum of the engine and the gentle motion of the car were soothing, and for a moment I didn't have to think, didn't have to plot or plan. I could just be me.

I glanced over at Ryan, taking in the strong line of his jaw and the way his hands gripped the steering wheel with quiet confidence.

Ryan caught my gaze and smiled, his eyes warm and tender. "You okay?" he asked, his voice low and comforting.

I sighed, leaning my head back against the seat. "It's just this. Being Alpha...it's a lot, you know? The responsibility, the constant pressure...it's never-ending."

Ryan reached over and took my hand, interlacing our fingers. His touch was grounding, a reminder that I wasn't alone in this. "It won't always be this way. It'll get easier."

I squeezed his hand, feeling a surge of gratitude and love. "I don't know what I'd do without you."

Ryan lifted our joined hands and pressed a soft kiss to my knuckles. "You'll never have to find out. I'm here, always."

We passed through the gates of the Alpha compound, the familiar sight bringing a sense of homecoming, which surprised me. Was I getting used to being here? Was I starting to feel that this was home?

Ryan parked outside the Alpha House, climbed out, then came round and opened my door. His frame blocked out the lights from the house, and for a second my breath caught. His muscles strained against his shirt, and I stilled as he stared right at me, his gaze laser-focused like I was the most interesting thing in the entire world. Some deep part of me wanted me to run. It knew what he could do, that if I made one false move, he could kill me in an instant. But he was mine, and there would be no more running. Ryan held out his hand and pulled me effortlessly out of the car.

As we stepped through the door, I stopped dead in my tracks. The once-empty bookshelves that lined the walls were now filled to the brim with books—not just any books, but titles from my favorite authors, the ones I read under my covers, or secretly on my phone.

I turned to Ryan. "You did this? For me?"

Ryan grinned, looking very pleased with himself. "You like it?"

"Like it?" I stared up at the shelves, my mouth hanging open. "You need to fetch help, Ryan. Book TBR drowning is occurring."

He laughed and slid his arm round my waist, pulling me to him.

"I can definitely help with that." He kissed me, his tongue teasing my lips apart. It wasn't a long kiss, just a promise of what was to come, before he stepped back and let me explore my gift.

"How did you know which books to get? Oh, my Goddess, that's Rina Meyors' new book! I've been waiting for weeks for this to come out!"

"Well, I may have hacked into your phone again, to see your wish list and the books you've been reading."

I spun round, ready to yell at him, but then found I didn't care. Not if I got all these beautiful books.

Ryan led me over to the shelves, pointing out two that were still empty. "These are for you to fill with whatever books you like. I've set up an account at the local bookstore, so you can go and pick out anything that catches your eye. Consider it an ongoing gift. I've already worked out where I can build more bookcases."

"Ryan, this is too much."

"Nothing is too much, Mai. Nothing. Get used to being spoiled. This is just the start."

I ran my fingers along the spines of the books, marveling at the titles. Some were old favorites, books I had read and reread. But others were new releases, books I had been eagerly anticipating but hadn't had the chance to buy yet.

"This is incredible. You're incredible." I breathed, feeling overwhelmed by the thoughtfulness of the gesture.

Ryan pressed a kiss to my forehead. "That's a problem I can live with. Seeing you happy...that's all I want."

I grabbed three books from the shelves, eager to dive into the new worlds and stories they held. Ryan and I settled onto the sofa in the study, our bodies naturally curling towards each other. As I flicked through the pages, inhaling the comforting scent of new books, Ryan's voice broke through my reverie.

"Before you get completely lost in those," he said, his tone serious. "I'm pretty sure Brock is the one framing Ronnie."

I looked up sharply, my heart skipping a beat. "Brock? But why would he do that?"

Ryan sighed, running a hand through his hair. "I don't know. I feel like we're still missing some pieces of this."

"Shya once said that there was no love lost between Brock and Ronnie. She was banking on Ronnie helping us before because he'd do anything to get back at Brock. Maybe it goes both ways."

"Maybe."

"Okay, so let's go back to the start. What do we know?" I lifted my hand and counted the points off on each finger. "One, Brock wants to be nominated to the Wolf Council. That's his goal for now. His end goal seems to be taking over the Council and basically ruling all of the north as some ridiculous Wolf King. Two, we know he's Ghost and is involved in the production and spread of ripple. Three, he's been working with the witches to cast a spell on ripple, making it highly addictive to Shifters, and making Shifters want to break their Pack bonds because they come to see them as impure."

"If the Shifter communities are overrun by this drug, society as we know it will break down. We'll have rogue wolves that are addicted to ripple, can't Shift and don't have the Pack bonds to keep them grounded. It'll only be a matter of time before they start attacking humans. So how does that fit in to Brock becoming a Wolf King?"

"What if we did nominate him? He gets on the Wolf Council. We know he's linked to the witches. What if there's a spell to reverse the effects of ripple and break the addiction? Esme said that it was possible. Then he's poised to become the savior in all this, swooping in with a counter-spell, stopping all the rogue wolves, mending the Pack bonds. He's suddenly a hero."

I felt a chill run down my spine. "That would give him a lot of power on the Council. He might even be in a position to take it over. But why would the witches agree to this?"

"If I was him, I'd offer them free rein in the north-east again to do what they liked. Plus, they'd be allied with the new Wolf King. That would give them a lot of power."

Ryan pulled out his phone and sent a quick text.

"What are you doing?"

"Putting extra security round Thomas's house. If Brock realizes we have Esme, he might try and get her back."

I closed my eyes, feeling the weight of the situation pressing down on me.

"You still think this will get easier?" I asked, feeling so tired all of a sudden.

Ryan pulled me into his arms, holding me close. "It will. I don't know when, but it will, I promise. We can do this."

I soaked in his heat and let myself relax into him. The deadline to nominate Brock for the Wolf Council was tomorrow. With what we now suspected, could I really give in to Brock's demands? But if we refused and hadn't found Jem before then, we'd be sacrificing my brother. I'd just got him back; there was no way I could lose him again. The Pack, fuck, it felt like it was the whole Shifter community or my brother. I knew what Jem would say; he had told me when he called, but I honestly had no idea if I could make that choice.

"You need distracting. I can feel your brain ticking."

"You feel my brain ticking?" I looked up at him and smiled. "Really?"

"Really," he said. "That or I have ants crawling up my back." He did a mock shudder.

"I don't think I can stop my brain ticking," I laughed.

His eyes went dark and green sparks flitted across them. "I know how."

Yes, please!

Ryan took my hand and led me up to our bedroom. I thought he was going to lead me to the bed, but he kept going, through the room and into the bathroom.

I eyed the shower. Shower sex with Ryan was mind-blowing.

"Nope. Not shower sex tonight," Ryan said, reading my mind. "I want you to watch me fucking you."

"I do watch you."

I wasn't lying; I loved looking into his eyes as he took me.

"No, I want you to watch yourself while I fuck you."

What?

He turned me round to face the huge mirror hanging over the double sink, and stood behind me, looking at our reflection.

"I don't know—"

"You don't have to know, Mai," Ryan interrupted. "I know. Strip."

I hesitated, and Ryan took a step toward me. "Now, Mai."

Okay then. I could do this. The idea of sex with Ryan wasn't something I was going to turn down. Plus, I could always close my eyes.

I stripped, throwing my clothes in the corner. Ryan did the same, and I took a moment to admire his freaking amazing body. His hard muscles, his perfect jawline, his massive cock. I still couldn't believe it was all mine. I just wanted to touch and lick him all over.

"Hands on the edge of the sink, Mai."

I did as he said.

"Spread your legs for me."

I opened my legs and tilted my butt back. Ryan trailed a finger lightly across my butt, sending a shiver through me.

"So fucking beautiful. Before I'm done with you, you're going to see it too."

"See what?" I gasped as he kicked my legs wider still.

"How beautiful you are. How beautiful you look when you have me inside of you. How your face lights up when I'm fucking you, whether I fuck you slow, or hard, or fast, whether I tease you or let you have what you want."

I felt a spasm in my core at his words, and heat ignited inside of me.

"I—"

"Quiet, now. Watch."

Ryan grabbed my hips, lined himself up, and then looked at me in the mirror.

"You're going to stay very still, Mai. No moving, no bucking. You're going to watch yourself get fucked by me, and there is nothing you are going to do except enjoy it. Understood?"

I nodded, catching his gaze; I couldn't tear my eyes away from him.

He inched his way inside of me. I could feel my pussy expanding as he forced his way in. His cock felt amazing, the size of it filling me completely, bit by bit.

"You like that," he stated.

Damn fucking right, I liked it. I nodded, unable to speak.

"No, Mai. Look at your face. Look at the delight on it when I'm inside of you."

I looked at myself and froze. He wasn't wrong. My expression looking back at me was not one I'd seen in a mirror before. It was one of pure joy, pure certainty that what I was doing, what I was feeling, was the most amazing thing, the rightest thing in the world.

Ryan slid out, hesitated for a moment, then slid back in, tantalisingly slowly. I watched as my eyes went half-lidded from the feelings of pleasure coursing through me.

He traced his fingertips down my back, along my butt, then gripped my hips tightly.

"You ready?"

"Always," I moaned.

Ryan started slowly, then steadily increased his pace. Sliding out completely, then slamming back inside of me. He stopped there each time, when he filled me to the hilt, eyes never leaving mine, before sliding back out again. It was intimate and so deeply personal, like he was seeing into the depth of my soul.

I was desperate to buck against him, to increase the friction, to move in any way. But each time I tried to, Ryan's fingertips would dig into my hips, reminding me to stay in place. It was torture. Sweet, delicious torture.

I glanced down, seeing my breasts jiggle with each thrust of Ryan's. My nipples were hard and erect.

He was having none of it. He grabbed my hair, wrapped it round one hand, and yanked my head up.

"Look, Mai!" he ordered.

So I did. I watched myself as he fucked me. "Mmmm, you just got a hell of a lot wetter, Mai. You like what you see, don't you?"

I did like it. I was fascinated by it. I watched my face relax; it looked blissful, so fucking happy, and I didn't recognize myself.

"This is what I see every time I fuck you, Mai. You, my fated mate, so perfectly happy every time you take my cock. You get off on it. You need it, Mai, as much as I need to be inside of you, feeling you so fucking wet as I drive my cock into you over and over. In a minute, you're going to come all over my cock and your face is going to be the most beautiful thing you've ever seen. You love this, Mai. Admit it."

"Yes," I agreed, unable to form any other words. The pressure was building; I could feel my orgasm coming. I was going to come, and I was going to watch myself while I did it.

All thoughts left me; it was just Ryan and me. The wet, slapping sounds of him fucking me, and my face, so delightfully happy, so eager to be fucked by him. I would do anything for this feeling, anything Ryan asked of me, just to feel his cock filling me, to feel him slide in and out of my pussy. I wanted more. I was desperate to move now, to slam down on his cock just as he was driving into me, to urge him on. My hips bucked, but Ryan held me in place, keeping me still. He went faster, increasing his speed, pounding into me again and again, until I couldn't take it any longer. The feeling of absolute bliss erupted inside of me.

"Yes," I cried, as I watched myself do exactly what he said and came all over his cock.

I woke up around two am. I was curled into Ryan, my back against his chest. His arms were wrapped round me, his legs over mine, pinning me in place. I would have thought this position, this statement that I was his, would make me feel uncomfortable. But I felt safe, like I was exactly where I was supposed to be. My wolf rubbed up against my insides, letting me know she was happy. She quieted, content where she was. I don't know if some sense in him alerted Ryan to me being awake, but before I knew it, he'd wrapped his hand around my breast. The warmth of his palm soaked into my skin, and he leisurely swiped his thumb across my nipple.

Mmmm. This was nice.

I arched my back into him, and without a word, he slipped inside.

Oh my. The shock of him suddenly being there sent little spasms through my pussy. It was delicious and so fucking amazing I thought I might come on the spot.

Then he moved his hips, pulling out, then slowly inching his way back in. He took his time; his hands caressed every curve of my body, sending shivers down my spine with every stroke. I could feel his warm breath on my skin. Though I was surrounded by darkness, the bedroom seemed to glow with the intensity of our connection. His cock slid in and out of me, hitting all the right spots. His fingers found my nipples, tweaking and rolling, causing spikes of pleasure to cascade through my body. He took his time, like we had all the time in the world, and each time he slid inside of me, it sent jolts of pleasure from my core to my very soul. He kissed my neck, his teeth grazing my skin just a little, sending a thrill of excitement shivering through me. I moved against him, urging him to go faster, but he just chuckled in my ear. He was letting me know that this time he was in charge. He knew exactly what to do to send me over the edge, but he'd decide when I could orgasm. His rhythm increased slowly. His hand gripped my neck, pulling me back, forcing me to look into his eyes. I was lost in the heat of his gaze, yearning for that one moment of release. My body arched up against his, my pussy pulsating around his cock, my hips bucking, begging for more. I could feel my climax building from the deep, steady strokes of his hips, and the constant magic of his fingers on my nipples.

"Now, Mai," he ordered.

My eyes rolled as I let go and moaned loudly, my orgasm crashing over me like a tidal wave. I clenched around him, my inner walls gripping his cock, milking him of every last drop of pleasure. He maintained his pace, riding out my orgasm with me, his eyes never leaving mine, as he came hard.

I rode the high with him. Then rested my head against his shoulder and promptly fell asleep with him still inside of me.

Chapter Twenty-Seven

RYAN

I gripped the steering wheel, maneuvering my black SUV along the winding road that led to Bridgetown. Mai was in the passenger seat next to me. Mason sat silently in the back, his gaze fixed out the window. The faint hint of Mai's jasmine perfume mingled with the earthy pine scent wafting in through the cracked open windows and part of me wanted to swing the car over, order Mason to fuck off, then kiss every inch of her, and sink my cock into her fucking amazing pussy. But we had a job to do. Today was the day we nominated someone for the Wolf Council. We had until twenty-two hundred to find Jem.

We were headed to the Bridgetown Pack to meet with Michael and Camille. As our Beta, Derek was in charge back at Three Rivers. I hated leaving him behind, but I needed someone I trusted to look after things while Mai and I were away. Derek was beyond capable; he'd stepped up as acting Beta numerous times when Jem was alive, and I'd been away searching for Mai. Still, unease gnawed at me. We were entering foreign territory, and I felt the absence of my Pack bonds keenly, like something vital was missing. My wolf was unsettled and didn't like it. He wanted us to turn around, take Mai back to the safety of our home, our territory.

As we got closer, I could see the vibrancy and life pulsing through the town. Flowers bloomed from every window box, shops displayed wares proudly behind gleaming windows, and people milled about the tidy streets. Under Michael and Camille's leadership, the place was a prospering community that drew both humans and werewolves.

We followed the winding streets until the facade of their Alpha House emerged. I pulled up in front of the building and put the car in park.

I inhaled deeply as we got out, sorting through the mingling scents of unfamiliar wolves and humans. The air was thick with scents, far more than I'd encountered at the Alpha House before. There were several vehicles parked along the street, and groups of people milled about the front lawn. Laughter and chatter filled the air, punctuated by the occasional excited squeal or shout.

A group of three women and two men hurried past us, their arms full of bolts of fabric in various shades of red, cream, and gold. They were discussing color schemes and floral arrangements, their voices rising with enthusiasm. Two men followed close behind, carrying large wooden crates that clinked and rattled with the unmistakable sound of glassware.

The front door swung open, and Michael stepped out onto the porch, his sharp First Nation features set in a polite smile. Beside him stood Camille, her chestnut hair swept back in a neat chignon that highlighted her graceful neck and the delicate curve of her jaw. They made a striking pair—Michael's tall, lean frame softened by Camille's taut elegance. Both of them exuded an air of calm authority.

"Ryan, Mai, welcome," Michael greeted, his gravelly voice warm. Camille nodded, in her usual reserved but not unfriendly way.

"Mason, you've returned," Michael continued, and his voice was a lot colder now. "Camille and I have said all we intend to say about the matter."

Mason folded his arms across his chest and stared directly at Michael. It was a challenge. "I'm aware," he replied gruffly.

What the hell happened when Mason and Derek came here? And why the hell hadn't Mason given us a heads up?

A scuffling sound emerged from behind Michael and Camille, followed by a teenage voice. "Tucker, it's mine!"

"Not again," Michael sighed, stepping aside to reveal two boys in the foyer. The taller of the two clutched a book to his chest, glaring down at the smaller one.

"I just want to look at it!" the younger boy insisted, jumping up to try to snatch the book. He was all spindly limbs and tousled hair.

The older boy held it out of reach. "Tucker, you got ice cream over one book and then jelly all over the last one I was reading. Just let me read in peace!"

"Enough, both of you," Camille interjected, her voice sharp. "We have guests, in case you didn't notice."

The boys looked over at us, recognition flashing across their faces.

"Ryan! Mai!" Tucker exclaimed, his grin growing even wider. He darted over to give me a quick hug before bouncing over to Mai. He ignored Mason. Henry hung back, offering us a polite smile and nod, just like his mother.

"Sorry," Henry said sheepishly. "We didn't mean to interrupt."

"No need to apologize, Henry," I assured him. "It's always good to see you two."

I meant it. I liked Michael's boys.

Tucker was already chattering excitedly to Mai. "Did you bring presents? You have to see the go karting track dad made for me out back, it's so cool! And Henry got another new book, but he won't share it." He looked up innocently at Mai. "Maybe you can make him?"

Yeah, he wasn't fooling anyone here.

Mai laughed as Henry rolled his eyes in exasperation. Camille placed a gentle hand on Tucker's shoulder. "Alright, let Mai and Ryan come inside. You can pester them later."

Tucker sighed dramatically but allowed Camille to usher him down the hall. Henry shot us an apologetic look before following. I bit back a laugh. Tucker always had a way of lifting everyone's mood.

Michael waved us into the spacious central hallway. "My apologies for the disruption. Tucker is full of energy today."

"Just today?" Mai teased as we followed Michael.

Michael dipped his head at Mai and smiled. "Good point. This is Tucker every day, as you all well know, having spent some time here. It just feels more taxing today because of all the arrangements."

"Arrangements?"

"Yes, Shya is to be mated to Edmond. I'm not sure you've met him yet. His work takes him traveling every now and again."

Mason didn't seem in the least bit surprised. Just extremely pissed off.

"When the fuck did that happen?" I blinked, trying not to laugh as the words tumbled out of Mai's mouth. She definitely hadn't quite got the hang of this Alpha diplomacy thing yet.

Michael and Camille looked taken aback at Mai's outburst. I placed my hand on the small of Mai's back.

"My apologies," Mai said quickly. "It was surprising news, that is all. And when is the, er, happy event?"

Camille seemed slightly mollified when she replied, "We're going to have the ceremony in two weeks. So, as you can imagine, the place is abuzz with preparations and Tucker is a little more overexcited than usual."

We followed the Bridgetown Alphas through the hall. The inside of the house was just the same as the last time we were here, as sleek and modern as the exterior, yet punctuated by warm accents and furnishings that lent a certain hominess. Michael led us straight to a set of carved wooden doors which opened into an expansive study. Floor-to-ceiling bookshelves lined two walls, packed to the brim with leather-bound volumes. In the center sat an imposing antique desk, meticulously organized. Two plush leather couches faced each other near the windows, angled to take in the view of the gardens outside.

"Can we offer you any refreshments?" Camille asked, motioning us to sit down.

Mai sat down on the nearest couch. "No, thank you." I sat next to her as Mason stood behind us both, watching our backs. He wasn't the only one who hadn't forgotten that Mai and I had been attacked in this study by one of the Bridgetown Pack.

I leaned forward, elbows braced on my knees. Time to get down to business. "We have an update on Brock."

Michael and Camille's attention sharpened, their postures tensing. I quickly summarized our findings, along with Talia's warning about ripple making Shifters feel impure to the extent that they were breaking their Pack bonds.

Mai finished for me. "And we're pretty certain Brock is framing Ronnie for the ripple shipments."

"Are you sure about this? You have the proof?"

Mai shook her head. "Not yet, but it all adds up. And we still don't know where he disappeared to after Jem took over Three Rivers. All of this could have been years in the planning."

"I'll be damned," Michael muttered. "Nothing suggested Brock was capable of this. If it's true, he's cleverer than we gave him credit for."

Camille smoothed her skirt. "I'm having difficulty believing Brock, or indeed any werewolf, is capable of spearheading something so destructive to our kind. What's his motive?"

"We think it's about a power grab. Ripple gives him immense power over the Shifter communities. We know he's working with the witches. It's speculation at the moment, but if they have a spell to reverse the effects of ripple, to mend the bonds, then he can unveil it at the right moment and be the hero of the Shifter community."

"His ultimate goal is to rule the northern Packs," Mai continued. "With ripple, he can weaken them, create chaos. Leaving the door open for him to step in and take over."

Michael and Camille glanced uneasily at each other.

"Do you have any clues as to Tristan's whereabouts?" I asked. "He's a known associate of Brock's. If ripple is involved, he likely is too."

Michael grimaced. "Unfortunately, we have yet to locate Tristan since his disappearance last month. However—"

"We've received intelligence he is still fixated on our daughter," Camille interjected, her tone tinged with steel. "He taunts her periodically with messages, insisting she's meant to be his mate."

Out of the corner of my eye, I saw Mason stiffen.

"It's one of the reasons why it's important that she is mated to Edmond as soon as possible. It will protect the succession of our family and bring much needed stability to this Pack."

I'd forgotten that Alphas in the Bridgetown Pack tended to pass the role on to their children. Other Packs fought it out, but Michael's family had been Alphas here for the last hundred years. Shya, as the oldest, was next in line. It was a good political move, mating her to someone within the Pack. Of course, if it was my mate, I'd burn the world down before I'd let her mate with someone else. And if I knew my brother, he definitely had plans to do the same. This changed things. Whatever Mason did, we couldn't afford to have a hostile Pack on our borders, not right now.

Chapter Twenty-Eight

RYAN

"We'll look into Tristan's potential ripple connections," Michael continued. "Your theory makes sense. He's shown himself capable of great duplicity."

"Thank you." Mai's eyes followed a group of children on the other side of the study windows, playing tag on the back lawn. "I was wondering if you'd seen any more of AJ?"

"AJ?"

"The bear Shifter that attacked Tucker."

AJ had been working for Tristan. His family had been cursed by witches, so that their bear forms were insane. There was no rational thought when they Shifted, they just wanted to destroy and kill. From what Mai had told me, AJ was haunted by it, but Tristan was holding his mate hostage, forcing AJ to do whatever Tristan wanted.

"No," Camille said. "We have regular patrols in the forest now, and none have picked up his scent."

"Good. That's good." Despite her words, Mai looked troubled.

"So," Michael leaned back in his chair, "how are you finding Alphahood? Settling in okay?"

"Yes, thank you." Mai glanced at me. I knew what she wanted to ask, so gave a slight nod. "Would you mind if we picked your brains about the partial Shifts?"

Camille glanced between us. "Of course. Here, the knowledge is passed down from one generation to the next, but your Pack has had many disruptions in recent years. It must be confusing for you both, learning about all the powers you now have access to on the fly, as it were."

I smiled wryly. "It's one of the disadvantages to having your succession determined by combat. When there is a change in Alpha, the one with that knowledge is either dead or not feeling particularly inclined to pass it on."

"Well, anytime you have questions, we're more than happy to answer them for you."

A soft knock sounded at the door. It cracked open to reveal Shya, her curly auburn hair framing sharp green eyes. She slipped inside without waiting for a response, Tucker in her arms.

"Sorry to interrupt, Father," she began. "Hello Ryan, hello, Mai." She smiled broadly at Mai. Like her brother, she completely ignored Mason.

"Tucker fell while trying to climb the bookshelf in Henry's room. He wanted to get to the top, where Henry had hidden his book." She quickly added, "He's fine, just a little shaken up, but he wanted you, Mom."

Camille opened her arms, and Shya placed Tucker on Camille's lap.

"How are you doing?" she asked softly.

"I just wanted the book! I don't understand what's so good about it. Why does he prefer a book to me? A book, Mom! I'm fun. More than words on stupid dead wood!"

"You are fun, buddy. Too much fun. Henry gets Tucker-overload. Just like you get sugar overload, right? You still love sugar, you still want sugar, you just need a time-out from sugar every now and again."

"Tucker-overload?"

"Yes, honey, Tucker-overload."

Tucker seemed to think about this. "Okay, I can help him manage his Tucker-overload. But only if you tell me a story."

Camille smiled. "Ah, blackmail is it?"

"No, negotiation. Dad says it's important to be a good negotiator."

Camille shot a look at her mate. "Did he now? Very well. A short story, then you go and apologize to your brother."

Tucker grinned widely and settled in on his mom's lap.

"Have you heard the myth about the True Shift?"

Tucker shook his head. I frowned; I hadn't heard this one. I glanced over at Mai, and she shook her head; she hadn't heard it either. Oliver had a lot to answer for. So many of our tales and history had been lost when he took over the Pack. It was something we had to try to get back. I'd need to talk to some of the elder Pack members, see what we could put together.

"In ancient times, the True Shift was given as both a gift and a test from the Dark Goddess. It was the perfect blend of wolf and human, a colossal being of immense power. It was said that the gift would come to you when you most needed it—whether out of survival, or love, or revenge, the Dark Goddess would respond to all calls. Over time, an elite Pack was created from all those who had been given the gift.

They were called the Lunar Guardians. They protected all werewolves. Fought wars against other Shifters. Patrolled our boundaries and kept us all safe. But one Guardian, Madrick, used this gift against his own people. He wanted to be the Alpha of all Alphas, the King of the Wolves, and he used his gift to take over Pack after Pack. The other Guardians were complacent. They had grown lazy, only coming to help when there was a big battle for which they knew they'd be honored as heroes. They thought many issues were now beneath them, and they let smaller problems fester and poison the Packs. They did not see the danger, and failed to protect those that needed it the most. Too late, the rest of the Guardians realized what Madrick was doing. They rallied for a final battle and managed to kill Madrick. But the Dark Goddess, furious at what the Guardians had become, removed her gift. She aged them until their backs were bent and their teeth had fallen out as punishment for failing her. And the Lunar Guardians were no more."

My wolf paced restlessly inside of me. There was something about this story that he didn't like, but I couldn't work out what.

"So, the Guardians were evil?" Tucker asked.

Camille shook her head. "No. No more than you or me. Unlike the Moon Goddess, the Dark Goddess likes to test us. She bestowed the gift on any who needed it badly enough, but it was what they did with it that counted. An evil werewolf might use the gift for good, and a good one might use it for evil. She is one who judges your deeds, not what is in your heart."

"But the Moon Goddess, she judges what is in your heart, not your deeds?"

"So it is said."

Tucker frowned. "But then you get judged twice! One judges you for what you want to do, and the other for what you actually do! That's not fair!"

Michael laughed. "Yes, they'll get you coming and going, Tucker. Let that be a lesson for you to stop trying to steal your brother's books!"

Mai leaned forward. "You know, we don't follow the Dark One, just the Moon Goddess. I don't think I've heard about the True Shift before. Do you believe it's possible? To shift into a true werewolf, and not just our human and wolf forms?"

"My grandmother told me that when she was little, her parents found the bones of a True Shifter," Michael said. "It was supposed to be ten feet tall, with a huge skull and jaws that could crush a bear in one bite!"

"Yes, but your grandmother had the gift for exaggeration," teased Camille. "Right up to her deathbed when she insisted that the brownies she cooked were so good that the Dark Goddess herself had come to visit and traded the recipe for the secret to eternal youth. And your grandmother claimed to have misplaced the piece of paper where she wrote down the secret."

Mai laughed as Michael sighed. "Those were some damn fine brownies."

I didn't laugh. I couldn't. I'd just worked out what about the story had my wolf so agitated. Bradford had called Brock the True Werewolf. At the time, I'd assumed he'd meant the rightful Alpha, but what if he'd meant it in this sense? What if Brock had made a deal with the Dark Goddess and could shift into the True Werewolf form? It would explain why so many followed him. And if I was right, we were fucked.

Chapter Twenty-Nine

Mai

Ryan was sitting stiffly next to me, and I got a pulse of something through our bond. I couldn't quite work out what it was; concern, worry? I wasn't sure, and it was gone before I could work it out.

With the story told, Camille had sent a reluctant Tucker to say sorry to Henry, and Michael turned his attention back to us, his gaze flickering between Ryan and me. "So, what are your plans now? How do you intend to proceed with this information about Brock?"

Ryan shrugged. "First, we're going to Ronnie's. We made a deal with him, and he ought to know what's happening. Plus, he's proven resourceful in the past; he might have insights that could help us piece together more of what Brock's up to."

Shya's eyes widened, a determined glint entering her green irises. "I'll go with you."

The response was immediate and unanimous. "Absolutely not," Michael and Mason said in unison, their voices ringing with authority.

Shya whirled on Mason, her auburn curls bouncing with the sudden movement. "You have no say in this, Mason. It's my decision."

Before Mason could respond, Michael interjected, his tone firm. "Ronnie is too dangerous, Shya. I can't allow it."

Mason folded his arms with a smug look on his face. I almost shook my head at him. He still had a lot to learn about women. If Ryan had done that to me, I'd find inventive ways to wipe that look off his face, probably with a swift kick to his jaw. But Shya wasn't backing down. She faced her father, chin lifted defiantly. "Dad, if you're really grooming me to take over the Bridgetown Pack someday, you have to let me do things like this. I have unfinished business with Ronnie. I need to see this through."

I could see the struggle in Michael's eyes—the desire to protect his daughter warring with the knowledge that she needed to learn and grow as a future Alpha.

Finally, Michael sighed, his shoulders sagging slightly. "Fine."

Mason opened his mouth to argue, but Ryan shook his head and he closed it with a loud click. He was not happy.

Michael fixed Mason with a stern look. "Protect her at all costs."

Mason's face was stony as he replied, "Of course."

Interesting. As the Alphas, it was me and Ryan that Michael should ask to keep Shya safe, not Mason. Michael might not approve of Mason's feelings for his daughter, but he seemed quite happy to take advantage of them to ensure she was protected.

The rumble of the engine filled the tense silence as we drove, leaving the territory of the Bridgetown Pack behind. Ryan's eyes were firmly on the winding road ahead. Mason sat in the passenger seat, his gaze alternating between the side-view mirror and the road, his fingers busy rolling a tennis ball between his hands. Shya and I were in the back, an awkward silence hanging in the air.

I stared out of the window, trying not to think about Jem, about Brock, or about ripple and the danger it posed to Shifters. For some reason, I kept coming back to the idea of kids. Did I want them? I'd never given it any thought. After Ryan rejected me four years ago, I never even considered it. What about Ryan? I had no idea if he wanted them, either. With everything that had happened since I got back, it wasn't a conversation that had come up. My phone buzzed. I glanced down to see a text from Sofia.

Hey chickie, u okay? Did u reach 36 yet today?

I shook my head, smiling as I swiped the notification away. Another buzz. This time from Wally.

Girl, let me know if u need anything! Here for u no matter what xoxo

Sofia waited exactly two minutes before she sent the next one.

So what did u decide? To pup or not to pup?

I silenced my phone, but knew I wouldn't get away with it for long. Both Sofia and Wally were going to bug me until I talked to them. I don't know why they'd picked now, with everything going on right now, to start asking about babies of all things. But maybe that was it, with everything that was going on right now, they needed something like this as a distraction.

I stole a glance at Shya. I bet she didn't get asked about babies. Not yet, anyway. No, she was on a mission today, that much was clear. She had gotten in the car with a small package wrapped in brown paper and ignored all Mason's questions as to what was in it.

"So, Edmond, huh?" I asked, ever so casually.

Shay slid her eyes to me. "I don't want to talk about it."

I held up my hands. "Sure, no problem."

I took my cue from Sofia and waited exactly two minutes. "So, is he nice? Smart? Big muscles?" I lowered my voice, "A hot-rod in bed?"

A loud bang came from the front. I leaned forward to see Mason drop pieces of an exploded tennis ball on the floor of the car. Fuck me, he'd popped the tennis ball with his bare hands!

"I know you all suspect that Mason is my fated mate," Shya sighed, "but at one stage, Tristan had me convinced that he was. I may have feelings for Mason, but I can't trust them. I won't trust my judgement in this. So, I will do as my parents think best. Edmond is a good match for the future of our Pack."

"Shya—" Mason growled as he turned in his seat.

"This is not the time to talk about it. You had your say, Mason. And no matter how growly your voice gets, how perfect your ass is, or how many contractions in my pussy it causes, I am not changing my mind!"

Okay, then.

I leaned over to her and whispered, "So exactly how many contractions in your pussy does Mason's ass cause?"

"Oh, fucking hell!" she said stiffly as she closed her eyes. Shya's face had gone bright red. "I can't believe I just said that! If you could never mention it again, that would be much appreciated."

I grinned at her. "Sure. It'll cost you a girls' night out when this thing with Brock is finished, though."

"Done."

"I'm going to mention it again. Many, many times," Mason drawled from the front seat.

"I hate you, Mason Shaw."

"Yes, but your pussy doesn't hate me. If I have to win you over one body part at a time, I will."

Shya growled next to me, crossed her arms and with a glower on her face, turned to look outside.

The buildings of Haxton emerged up ahead, the sprawling town unfurling before us. Ryan navigated the streets with practiced ease until we pulled up near a biker repair shop sandwiched between two larger buildings. I spotted Ronnie's tattooed and leather-clad gang members milling about the place.

One of the men ambled over as we got out of the car. He was tall and broad-shouldered, with a shaved head and arms covered in sleeves of colorful tattoos. His leather vest hung open, revealing a white tank top stretched tight over bulging muscles.

"You the folks from Three Rivers?" he asked in a gravelly voice, his piercing gaze sizing us up.

"That's right," Ryan replied evenly. "We're here to see Ronnie."

The man nodded, scratching at his beard stubble. "Figured. Boss said you'd be stopping by."

He jerked his head in a follow me gesture and started towards the garage entrance. I caught a glint of metal tucked into the back of his jeans. The sight sent a prickle of apprehension down my spine. These men were dangerous, even to Shifters.

I moved closer to Ryan as we entered the dim garage behind the man, the smells of oil and gasoline thick in the air.

He led us to a door marked 'Office' in faded letters.

Without knocking, he pushed inside, announcing gruffly, "The wolves from Three Rivers are here."

Ronnie was seated behind a tidy oak desk. He looked up from some paperwork with an expectant smile, and his gaze went straight to Shya.

"Shya! Glad you could make it. I appreciate you coming all this way to deliver that package."

Shya nodded, avoiding looking at the rest of us. "Of course. I owed you a favor and I keep my word."

Ronnie winked at Shya. "That you do. And I intend to collect the rest of the favor soon."

Out of the corner of my eye, I noticed Mason clenching and unclenching his fists. Mason had burst the ball he'd brought to keep his hands busy. The fidget toys and tennis balls that he used to help him think also kept him calm.

Ronnie finally glanced at Ryan and me. "So, have you found out who's framing me yet?"

"Yeah. Brock Madden."

Ronnie's expression hardened instantly, his voice dropping. "Brock? You're sure about this?" He leaned forward intently, the flirtatious demeanor vanishing.

"We found this out from a low-level drug dealer in our area, Bradford Hayes. We believe he has a cousin working for you, Otto?" Ryan said.

"Yeah, I know Otto." Ronnie picked up his phone and spoke quickly. "Round up Otto Hayes for me. I want him here for questioning in thirty."

A clipped, "Yes, boss," came through the line before Ronnie hung up and looked at me. "Bradford steered you toward Brock?"

I nodded. "All the clues point to a person named Ghost being the major player in the ripple drug trade here. We think that Brock is Ghost. Framing you takes the target off his own back, and given you and Brock have history, I imagine he's more than happy to put that target on yours."

Ronnie was silent for a moment, his jaw clenched tight. When he responded, his words were clipped and sharp. "That fucking asshole. I should've known he'd try something like this." He slammed a fist on his desk, making us all jump.

"Hey," Shya said gently. "We're going to figure this out. Brock won't get away with it."

Ronnie's fists slowly uncurled at her words. He drew in a long breath before meeting our eyes again, his anger tempered but still simmering beneath the surface. "You're damn right he won't. I'm with you all the way on taking that fuckhead down."

Surprise trickled through me. From what I knew about Ronnie, he preferred to stay neutral, especially in Shifter disputes. His primary business was information. He went places and talked to people that others couldn't get access to, precisely because he was neutral and wasn't seen to be taking sides. Brock must have really pissed him off.

If his plan had worked, and the Wolf Council believed that Ronnie was involved in moving ripple into the northeast, they wouldn't have hesitated in killing Ronnie and dismantling his businesses. Maybe Brock had finally fucked-up. He'd been one step ahead of us all this time, but pissing Ronnie off and having Ronnie and his less-than-legal resources come out on our side would be invaluable in uncovering Brock's operation and his location.

"I appreciated you all coming over here. I know your time is running short," Ronnie continued. "I may have a piece of intel for you." He leaned forward. "Word on the street is there's been some unusual activity out near the old forestry station about thirty miles north of the human town of Runford. Folks have seen armed guards patrolling the area. I did some digging. Shifters, known associates of Brock, come and go at all hours. Turns out the station got purchased a few months back by a company called Blackthorn Holdings. It looks like a shell corporation. My guys are still working on who the real owner is."

I gripped Ryan's hand, hope and fear swirling inside me.

"I figured you'd want to check it out. Could be where Brock's keeping Jem." He slid a scrap of paper across the desk towards me, an address and a crude map sketched on it.

"Thank you, Ronnie," I said. "If this pans out—"

"You'll owe me another favor."

I glanced at Ryan, then nodded. I'd agree to owe Ronnie a hundred favors if we found Jem at this address.

"Agreed. I appreciate you looking into this for us."

He gave a curt nod, his eyes flickering to Shya briefly. "I look after my allies."

Mason shifted next to me, the glower on his face getting deeper, if that was even possible.

"Are you going to attack the old forestry station?" Ronnie asked.

Ryan nodded. "I'll get my tech guy to see what he can dig up, but yeah, barring any surprises, we're going in."

"Me and my men will be ready."

"You'll go in with us?" I asked.

Ronnie replied curtly. "We'll be there."

Chapter Thirty

MAI

With five hours left to find Jem, I wanted to strategize with Ryan. Work out what the fuck we were going to do. But as we pulled up to the main house and climbed out of the SUV, I knew it was going to have to wait.

Standing on the front steps was a figure I'd hoped not to see anytime soon. Talia. Just the stern set of her shoulders made my muscles tense.

"Talia," Ryan greeted with a nod as we approached.

"You've got some nerve," I said. I could feel my wolf pulling on me, wanting to be let out to teach her a lesson in protecting Pack members.

"Ryan Shaw. Mai Parker," Talia ignored the hostile reception, but her gaze lingered on me a beat too long. "I have some developments to discuss. Shall we?"

She headed inside without waiting for a response. With a shared look of resignation, Ryan and I followed her towards Jem's old study.

"Let's skip the pretenses. I know you paid Ronnie Bishop a visit earlier today."

I bristled, crossing my arms defensively. "Are you keeping tabs on Ronnie or on us?"

Talia swung her gaze to me. "The Wolf Council keeps tabs on everybody, and I make it my business to know where certain people go."

"We're certain people?"

She inclined her head. "You keep interesting contacts."

I was done playing this game. "What exactly do you want from us this time?" I asked bluntly.

"Believe it or not, I'm just here to talk."

I snorted in disbelief. So far, Talia's definition of 'talk' meant manipulating us.

"Are you going to ask how Jase is doing?" I asked.

Something flashed across her eyes; I wasn't sure if it was anger or guilt, though.

"He's recovering well, no thanks to you."

"For what it's worth, I am sorry about what happened to him. If there had been another way—"

"You should have found another way. Manipulating us and letting Jase get hurt does not enamor the Wolf Council to us."

Talia's face shut down and her eyes went cold. "We don't need to enamor ourselves to anyone. You need to understand that the Wolf Council is more powerful than any one Pack. We work for werewolves as a whole, and if we need to destroy a Pack to protect the rest, we'll do it with a spring in our step and sleep well afterwards."

I stared at her, believing every word. The Wolf Council looked to the big picture, no matter the cost to individuals.

Ryan cleared his throat. "Now that you're here, you've saved us a phone call. We have reason to believe Brock Madden is the leader of the ripple operation. The one they call Ghost."

Talia's expression remained impassive. "Not Ronnie Bishop?"

"No."

"And your proof?"

Ryan's jaw tightened. We both knew we had nothing concrete. Just hunches and circumstantial evidence.

Talia gave a curt nod at our telling silence. "Thought so. We need more before we can move against Brock Madden. I want to confirm everything before we move. This is too important; we can't risk getting it wrong and tipping them off."

"We're working on it," Ryan said tersely.

"Work faster. But that's not actually why I'm here." Talia straightened, her tone business-like. "Your nomination for the Wolf Council seat is due in a few hours."

No shit. It was all I could think about. There was no way we were telling Talia about Brock's blackmail. If she got involved, her priority would be stopping Brock; she wouldn't care if Jem died in the process.

"Whoever you nominate will have substantial influence shaping Council policy," Talia pressed on. "The Council is currently split into factions. Different groups want different things. Your nominee will be able to sway the votes on a number of crucial issues coming before the Council in the next four years. Their vote could be crucial in which side comes out on top."

"You want us to nominate someone who will support your side?"

"I want you to be aware of how important this role is. Not just for your Pack, but for Shifters all across the Americas."

I shrugged. "You see the big picture, Talia. We're small pups in the den. The Three Rivers is our top priority."

"That might be so, but the nominee will be dealing with wide-ranging issues. Including issues critically important to the Three Rivers Pack."

"Such as the ripple crisis," Ryan finished for her.

"Precisely." Talia began to pace, her movements sharp and precise. "The Council seat would give the nominee a direct line into ongoing investigations, access to intel and resources. They will be heavily involved in stopping ripple, shutting down its supply, and investigating the witches."

I glanced at Ryan, knowing what he was thinking. If we nominated Brock to the Wolf Council, he would have access to all investigations into himself. He would know where the Wolf Council was going to look and have plenty of time to move his operations before they got there. He could manipulate the investigations, tamper with evidence. He'd be in a position to protect the ripple business and ensure its survival until he had consolidated his position and could appear to be the hero in putting a stop to it all.

"Did you have someone in mind?" I asked.

Talia gave me an appraising look. "Yes. I believe it would make strategic sense for you and Ryan Shaw to nominate yourselves. Joint nominations are allowed for fated mates. You could split the term, trade off attending sessions."

I sucked in a breath, blindsided by the suggestion. Up and leave the Pack? The notion filled me with instant dread. We'd only just taken control back from Brock and Hayley. The Pack's foundation was still fragile, vulnerable. How could we abandon them all now?

"It would also establish you both as rising powers, put you in the inner circle influencing regional policy."

"We'll need to discuss this and weigh our options," Ryan said calmly. Too calmly for my liking. He couldn't possibly be considering it, could he?

Talia inclined her head. "Naturally. Your decision is due at twenty-two hundred. I'll be back in a couple of hours to set up."

Wait, what fresh hell was this? "Set up?" I asked.

"Yes, the decision will be broadcast to the Wolf Council. That way, there is no confusion, and we eliminate the possibility of you trying to change your minds after. We have learned the hard way that Alphas sometimes try to backtrack on their decisions. Broadcasting the decision nicely precludes such a situation. So, consider it carefully. Tonight is the start of a new era for your Pack and the Wolf Council."

With that, she swept out of the study. Summoning a heroic level of patience, I waited until she was out of earshot before rounding on Ryan.

"Please tell me you aren't seriously thinking about this," I hissed in disbelief.

Ryan held up a placating hand. "Let's talk it through, Mai."

I began to pace, emotions churning violently inside me. "What's there to talk about? We finally have a chance to bring stability back to the Pack. They need us here, not off playing politics at the Council. I thought we agreed we'd nominate Brock if we couldn't find Jem in time."

Ryan's eyes flashed. "This is about more than just the Three Rivers Pack. Ripple is spreading everywhere, destroying Shifter lives. We have a shot at shaping how the Council tackles this crisis."

"I left the Three Rivers before, Ryan. I'm not leaving it again." I meant it too. There was no more running for me. This was my home, and I'd die here.

Ryan stood abruptly, his impressive frame towering over me. "I'm thinking about our people. This could help protect them in the long run."

I narrowed my eyes and briefly considered kicking him in the head. I don't know what he felt pulse along our bond, but he took a deep breath, stepped back and softened his tone.

"I'll go wherever you go. You're stuck with me whether you like it or not. But Mai, the Council seat would give us leverage, resources. We could make a difference at the Council."

"We can make a difference here. To people like Sofia and Jase. To all the Normans, Garths and Liams. To the humans in the Three Rivers. You remember the Three Rivers motel, Ryan? It was supposed to be this shiny new business when it opened, but now it's just a run-down shack. The Three Rivers have so much trade coming in and out of here. But the humans here don't thrive. None of the previous Alphas, not even Jem, thought much about them. I want to change that. They might not be werewolves, but they are still part of the Three Rivers. We could change things for so many people here." My shoulders slumped, anger draining away, only to be replaced by a hollow sense of uncertainty. Despite what I'd just said, Ryan wasn't wrong. We needed help, badly. Especially if ripple was about to flood our communities. But the thought of walking away, leaving the Pack when we fought so hard to get it back...it went against every instinct I had running through me.

Ryan took my hand gently in his. "We don't need to decide anything right now. We have time to find Jem, to come up with another way."

As Ryan enfolded me in his arms, I nodded and let out a shaky breath, soaking in the comfort of his arms around me.

"I should call Jase, check on how he's recovering."

"Mai—"

"I won't be long." I needed to hear that Jase was okay. Needed to know that our Pack, our family, was safe.

Ryan looked like he wanted to object, but in the end simply pulled me close once more, placing a kiss on my forehead.

The hallway was dim and silent as I slipped out. Heading down the corridor, I took out my phone and dialed Jase.

He picked up on the second ring. His voice sounded tired, but not in pain. "Mai! We were just talking about you."

"Should I be worried?"

"Most definitely. I was filling Sofia in on what a hard boss you are."

Sofia's laughter echoed from behind him. "Liar. He was singing your praises as usual."

"How are you holding up?" I asked gently.

"Never better," he proclaimed. "Can't wait to get out of Thomas's. Wally keeps forcing me to eat his delicious cooking and I'm scared I'm going to put on fifty pounds and be too big to fit out the door."

His bravado should have made me smile, but I couldn't bring myself to match his lighthearted tone. The memory of seeing him on the floor, bleeding, was still too raw.

Jase seemed to sense the shift in my mood. "I'm alright, Mai. Really."

I kept my tone light. "I should let you rest. Just had to hear for myself that you were out of trouble. Again. This is getting to be a bad habit of yours, you know, you getting injured. Bet that job at Takymora's is looking pretty good right about now."

"No chance. I'll be out of here first thing tomorrow. Nothing's gonna stop me watching your back."

That was just what I was afraid of.

CHAPTER THIRTY-ONE

RYAN

The stale coffee did little to sharpen my focus as I stared down at the detailed schematics laid out across the dining room table. Around me, the low murmur of voices droned on, my enforcers immersed in debate over entry points and extraction routes. I should have been right there with them, laser focused on finalizing our plans to raid the old forestry station north of town. Instead, my mind kept drifting. To what Camille had said about the True Shift. Was it possible? Or a kid's story? What could I do if I had that power? What would it mean for our Pack, for Mai? I'd be able to protect her better, could make sure that no one ever threatened her again. How had Brock done it? If he had managed to make a deal with the Dark Goddess, it could change everything. Right now, all I had was myths, legends, and guesses.

I shook my head, attempting to steer my thoughts back to the task at hand, and cleared my throat. The chatter in the room died down as all eyes turned my way.

"Waylen, what have you been able to find about the site?"

Waylen perked up from his slouched posture, pushing his green glasses up his nose. "I haven't gotten much from satellite images, nothing recent anyway. But I did manage to enhance and stitch together some older aerial shots to get a rough blueprint of the station's layout."

He pointed to a section of the crude map laid out on the table. "From what I can tell, there are a few structures that could be used for holding prisoners. This larger outbuilding here, or some of the storage sheds over in this area."

I saw Mai lean forward as she studied the spots Waylen had pointed to. I knew finding any trace of Jem was her top priority in all this, however slim the odds. The fierce hope in her eyes made my chest ache. I wished I could promise her that we'd bring her brother home safe. But I knew better than to make guarantees I couldn't keep.

"Waylen also managed to dig up ownership records for that shell company, Blackthorn Holdings," Derek added gruffly. "Took some creative hacking, but he was able to follow the trail back to a distant cousin of Brock's."

I nodded, unsurprised, but we needed concrete evidence tying him to the ripple operation.

"Hopefully this raid can not only get us Jem, but maybe there's some paperwork we can use to link Brock to his other operations." I said. "Anything you can retrieve linking Brock directly to distribution could be the proof we need to take to the Wolf Council."

"I'll sweep their system when we're in," Waylen assured me. Tech geniuses like him were invaluable for missions like this.

"You're going?" Mai asked, sounding surprised.

Waylen flicked his gaze between me, Sam, and Mason before frowning slightly at Mai. "Just because I'm the tech guy doesn't mean I sit in a dark room all day. You werewolves don't get to have all the fun!"

"He'll be well protected, Mai," Sam smiled at her. "And we've found him to be crucial in the field. He can access computers on site, bypass security systems and hack almost anything we put in front of him. It saves time, and in previous cases, saved lives."

Mai nodded, but she still looked uncomfortable with the idea.

"Sam, you're next." He'd headed out there as soon as I texted him the details and had got back about ten minutes ago.

"The area is crawling with goons, that's for sure. I saw fifteen to twenty guards around the perimeter."

The numbers were higher than I'd hoped, but not surprising. Brock would guard his secrets fiercely.

"How many enforcers can we spare?" asked Mai.

Mason squeezed a tennis ball in one hand. He was going to burst another one in a minute. He'd been working on the damn thing ever since we dropped Shya back home. "Not many. There are fifteen Renegades. We know we can rely on them, which is why they are either guarding the growing amount of prisoners we have or watching our borders. Korrin's attack has unsettled a lot of people. They thought with Brock and Hayley gone, the chaos of the last few weeks had passed. They're scared. An attack right in the heart of the Three Rivers has made some question if you're both up to the Alpha job."

Fabulous. Just what we needed right now.

"Keep them on the borders. We need to secure the Pack and make sure there are no more attacks. But Brock is the priority. Then we'll address any doubts in the Pack."

Mason nodded. "We can probably spare five Renegades. After this latest crisis is over, we'll increase recruitment. We've had a lot of interest but haven't had time to assess their loyalty or their skills. We'll take another five from our agency. The rest are on mission down south, following the ripple supply lines."

Five Renegades, five of Sam and Mason's guys, plus me and my brothers, that made fourteen. Fifteen if you included Waylen, but he wasn't a fighter. Plus however many men Ronnie took with him. The element of surprise would work in our favor—Brock had no reason to expect us to come crashing through his doors unannounced.

I glanced at Mai, knowing she was about to lose her shit.

"You can't come, Mai. You need to be here."

I started counting in my head, one, tw—

"You are out of your fucking mind, Ryan Shaw, if you think I'm staying behind while you walk in there. Not this time."

"Okay."

Mai paused, her mouth open to argue with me more. "Okay?" she said, her voice full of suspicion.

"I can't stop you from going. We just need to work out who will stay. As Mason pointed out, the Pack is nervous right now. We need someone who can settle nerves, someone with authority. Talia and the Wolf Council will also need an answer in three hours. So whoever stays behind will need to be trusted to give our nomination."

She looked at me sharply, and I knew she'd realized that it could only be her. She folded her arms across her chest and glared at me.

"Don't think I can't see how neatly you're maneuvering me into staying."

"So, you will stay?"

"Fine," she bit out the word.

I nodded, trying not to show how fucking relieved both me and my wolf were that she wouldn't be part of this fight.

"Alright, we move out in thirty. Get anything you need and meet me by the cars." I swept my gaze over each of my brothers and enforcers, watching their spines straighten and chins lift at my words. They were ready. So was I.

Chapter Thirty-Two

RYAN

I peered through the dense foliage, my eyes picking up the subtle signs of activity ahead—fresh tire tracks cutting through the underbrush, the smell of cigarette smoke wafting on the breeze. We were close.

Around me, my team was poised and ready, their bodies tense with anticipation. Derek, Sam, Mason, Evelyn, Ava, and Rafael had all shifted into their wolf forms, their bodies blending seamlessly into the dense foliage. Waylen, the only human in our group, kneeled beside me, his face set with determination.

I glanced at my phone. We had forty-five minutes until Mai was set to nominate Brock for the Wolf Council seat. Forty-five minutes to find Jem and get him to safety. If he was even in there.

I turned, my voice low but firm. "This is it. Our last chance. We go in hard and fast, no hesitation. We find Jem, and we get him out. Understood?"

A chorus of soft growls and nods answered me. Waylen met my gaze, his eyes glinting with a fierce loyalty. "Let's do this."

I was about to give the signal to move when a familiar scent caught my attention. Ronnie emerged from the shadows to the east, his broad shoulders filling out his leather jacket.

"Wasn't sure you were going to show," I said, keeping my voice low as I appraised him.

Ronnie's lips curled into a smirk. "You should know by now, Ryan. I always show up when there's something in it for me. I've got ten men with me. All good fighters. They'll follow your lead."

The old forestry station loomed before us, a weathered two-story structure that had seen better days. Its wooden walls were discolored and worn, showing years of neglect and exposure to the elements. Several windows were boarded up, giving the building an air of abandonment and disrepair.

Surrounding the main building were a handful of smaller outbuildings, likely used for storage or equipment back when the station was operational. Now, they stood silent and empty, their doors slightly ajar and their interiors cloaked in shadows.

Despite the station's dilapidated appearance, there were signs of recent activity. Footprints in the soft earth led to and from the buildings. Barriers had been put up around the perimeter, and armed guards and Shifters patrolled the grounds. They moved with a sense of purpose, their eyes alert.

The presence of such heavy security was a good indication that something was here that needed guarding. But was it Jem, was it connected to ripple, or was it something else?

We would have to be swift and decisive, using the wooded surroundings to our advantage.

I looked at the wolves behind me. "We move in two minutes. Ronnie?"

"I'll tell my men," he replied, before slipping through the trees.

I turned to Waylen. "Stay close to Mason. We don't know what we're walking into, but he'll make sure you get in and out safely."

Waylen grinned at me. "Don't worry, boss. This is gonna be fun," he said, his hand resting on the hilt of his knife.

I shook my head. Despite being a human, he was as reckless as my brothers.

I checked my phone one last time. Thirty-eight minutes until the nomination.

I raised my hand, two fingers extended. The signal to move.

The moment we breached the perimeter, all hell broke loose.

Brock's men seemed to materialize out of nowhere; there was a fuckload of them, more than we thought. Maybe forty of the fuckers. Where did Brock get this many? Were they paid mercenaries or some of the men Tristan had taken from Bridgetown? I didn't have time to think. They swarmed us from all sides, humans and wolves in a sea of snarling faces and flashing claws.

I pulled on my Pack bonds, Shifting my hands so they were tipped with claws that could tear through flesh and bone, then lunged at the nearest attacker, a burly man who stank of pumped up adrenaline. I sidestepped round him, grabbing his arm and twisting it behind his back until I heard the pop of his shoulder dislocating. He howled in pain, and I dropped him. Two wolves were on me in an instant, their claws raking across my back, tearing through my jacket and leaving burning trails of pain in their wake. I whirled around, slashing at their faces. Blood sprayed across my vision, hot and sticky, but I didn't stop.

I couldn't stop. Every second counted, every heartbeat bringing us closer to the moment when Mai would have to make her choice.

The air was filled with the sounds of growls and the clash of bodies, the scent of blood and sweat heavy in the air. I could hear the sharp crack of gunfire, the yelps of pain as bullets found their marks.

I caught a glimpse of Derek, his massive black form tearing through the enemy ranks like a juggernaut. Ava and Rafael fought back-to-back, their movements perfectly synchronized as they took down one opponent after another. Even Waylen was holding his own, his knife flashing in the fading light as Mason protected him and he danced around the attackers, lunging in when he saw an opening with a graceful, deadly precision.

A wolf slammed into the back of my legs, yanking me off balance. I hit the ground hard; the breath knocked from my lungs. The wolf above me snarled.

It should have gone for the kill rather than showboating.

I caught its head between my hands, and twisted, breaking its neck.

I rolled to my feet, my chest heaving as I scanned the chaos around me. We were making progress, but it wasn't enough.

For every enemy we took down, it seemed like two more took their place. They pressed in from all sides, a relentless tide of fury and aggression.

A sharp howl of pain caught my attention, and I whipped my head around to see Sam stumble, his hind leg buckling beneath him as a wolf latched onto his thigh. Derek was there in an instant, his powerful jaws clamping down on the attacker's neck and dragging him away, but the damage was done. Sam's blood pooled on the ground and he staggered and fell. Derek ripped out the attacker's throat, then dashed back to stand guard over Sam.

Nearby, Evelyn was grappling with a human as he tried to slash at her underbelly with a fucking sword. She was holding her own, but I could see the fatigue setting in, her movements becoming slower, more labored.

Ronnie's men were taking hits, their numbers dwindling as Brock's forces continued their assault. I saw at least five of them on the ground, two of them not moving. The odds were shifting against us, the balance of power tipping in the wrong direction.

CHAPTER THIRTY-THREE

MAI

I paced the length of the Alpha House's living room, my nerves stretched taut. Jase stood by the window, his eyes constantly scanning the surrounding area for any signs of trouble. I liked that he was here; it felt like I wasn't entirely alone in this.

Talia had arrived half an hour ago and was now bustling around the room, setting up the equipment that would link us to the Wolf Council. I had considered not letting her in, but there was no escaping this. Talia had reiterated to me, several times now, that once I announced my decision, there would be no way to reverse it. The thought made my stomach churn, the finality of it all sinking in like a lead weight.

My mind drifted to Ryan and his brothers, out there risking their lives to find Jem. I had to believe that they would be safe, that they would find him in time. The thought of losing any of them, of the price we might have to pay for this gambit, made me want to throw up.

"They'll be okay, Mai," Jase said softly, as if reading my thoughts. He moved to stand beside me. "Your mate is one fuck off badass, and the Shaws are the best fighters in the north. They've got this."

Talia straightened up from the equipment, her face grim. "It's all set up. The Council will be able to see and hear everything once the link is established."

I swallowed hard, my mouth suddenly dry. "How much time do we have?"

"Ten minutes. Have you made your decision? Once you make your choice, there's no going back."

"I am aware, Talia, thank you. I think that's the eighth time you've reminded me."

The truth was, I still had no fucking clue who I was going to nominate. I turned my back on her and closed my eyes for a moment, Ryan's parting words echoing in my mind. "I trust you, Mai," he had said, his eyes boring into mine, making me feel like I was the only person in the whole world. "No matter what happens, no matter who you choose, it'll be the right choice."

He had kissed my forehead then, a gentle touch that said more than words ever could. No matter what I decided, he'd back me. I loved the trust he had in me, but I wasn't sure it was deserved. Right now, I didn't have a fucking clue what I was going to do. Nominate Brock and further his scheme to be a Wolf King, or don't and sentence my brother to death? Even if I could live with that decision, who the hell would I nominate instead of Brock? Talia wanted it to be me and Ryan. Ryan seemed open to the idea. We could do a lot of good, make a lot of changes if we were on the Wolf Council, but it would mean leaving Three Rivers. I'd shed blood getting this Pack back; it felt wrong to just walk away from it even if it would be to make sure it, and all Shifter communities, were protected.

The minutes ticked by, each one feeling like an eternity. I could feel Jase and Talia watching me pace. They were waiting for me to make a decision, to choose the path that would shape the future of this Pack and the whole Shifter community. How the hell had this happened? A month ago, I'd been a website designer living in Cocrane. Now it felt like whatever I chose in this moment would change history.

So, no fucking pressure then.

My wolf was no help. She was asleep, confident, like Ryan, that I'd make the right choice.

I was so lost in my thoughts that I barely registered Talia's voice cutting through the silence. "It's time. Everything is set up. Please, take a seat so we can begin the proceedings with the Wolf Council."

I blinked, my eyes focusing on the chair she gestured to. It looked innocuous enough, just a simple armchair positioned in front of the cameras. But to me, it felt like a throne, a seat of power that I wasn't ready to occupy.

With a deep breath, I moved towards the chair, each step feeling heavy and leaden. I checked my phone one last time, hoping against hope that there would be a message from Ryan, some sign that he had found Jem and that everything would be alright.

The screen remained blank, taunting me with its emptiness.

Shitting hell!

Just as I was about to set the phone aside, it buzzed in my hand.

Finally! Thank fuck!

But as I opened the message, my blood ran cold.

Not Ryan. Brock.

Hope ur ready for the big announcement. Remember, it better be my name you say or Jem really dies this time. I'll be watching.

How the hell would Brock be watching? This was supposed to be closed proceedings for the Wolf Council. Brock had to have contacts and help from people on the Council.

I felt sick; the bile rising in my throat. My hands shook as I set the phone down, my mind reeling.

I looked up at Talia and Jase. Talia was staring at me dispassionately, a slight frown on her face. Jase's was etched with concern. He knew something was wrong.

I couldn't take it anymore. The walls of the room felt like they were closing in on me, Brock's threat and the impending decision crushing the air from my lungs.

"Excuse me," I managed to choke out, getting to my feet carefully, so neither Jase nor Talia got suspicious. "I just need a moment."

"Mai Parker, it's time; you don't have a moment."

"Watch me, Talia Johnson, watch me take a moment," I said as I left the room.

My feet carried me to the bathroom on instinct alone. I barely made it to the toilet before the nausea overtook me. I retched, my stomach heaving as I emptied its contents into the bowl. The bile burned my throat, tears stinging my eyes as I gasped for breath.

I took a shaky breath, wiping my mouth with the back of my hand, then pushed myself to my feet, my legs trembling beneath me. I flushed the toilet and moved to the sink, splashing cold water on my face and rinsing the taste of bile from my mouth.

Uck.

I smelled Jase just before there was a soft knock on the door.

"Mai?" Jase's voice was muffled through the wood, but I could hear the concern in his tone. "Are you alright?"

I cleared my throat, keeping my voice steady. "I'm fine, Jase. I'll be out in a second."

"Are you sure?" He sounded unconvinced.

"I'm sure," I said, injecting as much confidence into my words as I could muster.

There was a pause, and for a moment I thought he might push the issue. But then I heard his footsteps retreating.

I turned back to the mirror. Could I nominate Brock knowing now what it would mean for this Pack, for all werewolves? Would I sacrifice them all in order to get Jem back? Would Jem ever forgive me if I did? I shook my head.

Nope, it didn't make the answers suddenly fall into my brain.

Fuckity fuck fuck!

My reflection caught my eye. Ryan thought I could do this. He wanted me to see what he saw when he looked at me. An Alpha. A strong, bad-ass Alpha. I couldn't fall apart, not now. I had to be strong; I had a job to do. I'd fought and killed for this position, and I would do it to the best of my abilities.

With a final nod to myself, I turned and strode out of the bathroom, my head held high.

The living room was silent as I entered, all eyes on me. All twenty-seven members of the Wolf Council were already present on the screen, their faces solemn and expectant.

I had never met any of them before, but the reputation of the Council was not something to take lightly. I found myself studying some of their faces, trying to glean some insight into their characters.

In the center of the screen were two elders, a man and a woman. The woman's silver hair was pulled back in a severe bun, her gray eyes seeming to see straight through me. The man, with his neatly trimmed beard and sharp suit, looked every inch the politician, his expression unreadable.

To their right was a rugged-looking man, his face tanned and lined. I had the impression that this was a man who spent a lot of time outdoors.

Next to him was a striking blonde woman, with sleek hair and a designer dress. She peered at me with a look that reminded me of an eagle sizing up a mouse.

On the far left was a younger man, maybe mid-twenties. He looked bored, like he had much more important things to do, and he was annoyed at having to be here.

Opposite him was a man whose hulking frame seemed to dominate his screen. He was a bear of a man, with broad shoulders and a barrel chest that strained against the fabric of his shirt. He sat perfectly still, his massive hands folded in front of him, but there was a coiled energy about him that suggested he could spring into action at any moment. Every inch of him radiated power and authority, and I had no doubt that when he spoke, the other members of the Council would listen.

As I studied their faces, I knew I was being evaluated in turn.

I refused to let my nerves show. I wasn't a web designer anymore. I was the Alpha of the Three Rivers Pack, and I had earned my place at this table.

I lifted my chin higher and looked directly into the camera. I was here as an equal, as someone worthy of their respect.

"Mai Parker, take a seat." The silver-haired woman's voice rang with authority.

I took my seat in front of the cameras, my spine straight and my expression neutral. I would not let them see my fear, my doubts.

I was ready.

Talia moved to my side so that she could be seen on the screen. She opened her mouth, but the woman cut her off. "Not the whole ceremony today, Talia. We're all busy. We are here to hear the nomination for the Wolf Council. And then I, for one, have another meeting to get to."

Talia's face showed none of her displeasure, but I caught the scent of her annoyance.

"As you wish." Talia bowed her head slightly. "Mai Parker, on behalf of the Three Rivers Pack, who is your nomination for the Wolf Council?"

I took one last glance at my phone. Still nothing.

Shit!

This was it; I had to say a name.

Chapter Thirty-Four

RYAN

Desperation fueled me as I fought my way towards the main building, my mind racing. We needed to change tactics.

The outbuildings. If we could lure some of Brock's men inside, funnel them into a bottleneck, we could take them out more easily. It would buy us time, give us a chance to regroup and push forward.

I caught Derek's eye across the battlefield, signaling my intentions with a sharp nod towards the nearest outbuilding. He bared his teeth in acknowledgment. I charged over to him, smashing through a wolf standing in my way. Bending, I scooped up Sam and slung him over my shoulder. Derek surged forward, clearing a path.

"With me!" I roared, my voice cutting through the din of the fight and alerting our fighters to the change in plan.

We broke away from the main battle, sprinting towards an outbuilding on the left. It was long and narrow, with a rusted tin roof that had partially collapsed in on itself. The walls were made of weathered planks, some of which had rotted away, leaving gaping holes. Not ideal, but it would have to do.

I adjusted Sam's weight on my shoulder. The sound of footsteps followed behind us, the snarls of pursuit as some of Brock's men took the bait.

I reached the door first, my shoulder slamming into the wood with enough force to splinter the frame. I ducked inside, setting Sam down gently against the wall.

Derek and the others ran in behind me, then turned to face the fighters coming after us. Waylen went straight for Sam and stood over him, his knife ready for anyone that went their way. Ronnie and his final two men came to stand beside me.

I jumped straight up, grabbed a beam with one hand, and swung myself up into the rafters. I ran along the wood back toward the door as wolves piled in beneath me.

Ava and Rafael were a blur of motion, their lithe forms weaving through the attackers. I dived off the beam and crashed into the wolves streaming in through the broken door. Rage boiled inside me, a searing, white-hot fury that threatened to consume me. It fueled my every move, my every strike, as I tore through the wolves. The confined space worked to our advantage, limiting the enemies' ability to surround us. Derek and Mason used their brute strength to drive those inside back toward me, where I slashed and clawed them into a bloody pile of bodies.

But even as we thinned their numbers, I knew it wasn't enough. We were running out of time, the precious seconds slipping away.

If Jem was here, I had to find him. I had to end this before it was too late.

I let out a roar that shook the very foundations of the building, a primal, savage sound that seemed to come from somewhere deep inside me. It was a rallying cry, a call to arms, and my Pack answered it with howls of their own.

I charged out of the outbuilding and smashed into the wolves that stood between me and my mate's brother.

We fought like demons, like creatures possessed, a Pack driven by a desperate need to save one of our own. I could feel the blood dripping down my face, could taste it on my tongue, but only one thing mattered. For Mai, I had to save Jem.

And then, suddenly, it was over. The last of Brock's men fell to the ground, his throat torn out by Derek's powerful jaws. The silence that followed was deafening, broken only by our ragged breathing and the soft whimpers of the wounded.

I stood there for a moment, my chest heaving, my body drenched in sweat and blood. I looked around at the carnage we had wrought, at the bodies that littered the floor, and felt a grim sense of satisfaction that we were still standing and Brock's men were not. I Shifted my hands back to human and pulled out my phone. We were late. Mai was due to give the nomination two minutes ago.

Fuck!

I could only hope she'd found a way to delay.

I wiped the blood from my eyes and turned to my Pack, my voice hoarse but steady.

"Search the buildings," I ordered. "Every room, every corner."

I could feel their determination through the Pack bonds as they sprung into action. I headed left, toward a cluster of smaller outbuildings, and had just got to the first one when I heard it—a howl, loud and urgent, coming from the direction of the main building.

Derek.

He had found something.

I took off at a dead run, my heart pounding in my chest as I raced towards the sound. I burst through the doors of the main building, following the scent of Derek's adrenaline and the faint, yet unmistakable scent of Jem.

I found Derek standing at the top of a narrow staircase, his dark wolf form tense and alert. His ears were pricked forward.

He looked at me, his gray eyes gleaming in the dim light, and let out a soft whine. Then he turned and bounded down the stairs.

I didn't hesitate. I plunged down the stairs, taking them three at a time, my senses straining for any sign of Jem. The scent was stronger now, a blend of earth and coconut.

I reached the bottom and found myself in a small, damp cellar. The air was thick with the smell of mold and decay, and the only light came from a single, flickering bulb hanging from the ceiling. A dead guard lay to the side, his blood still pooling out beneath him.

And there, in the corner, was Jem. He was lying still, his body thin and battered. Derek was beside him, his large wolf body standing protectively over Jem's fragile form.

I approached slowly. Derek looked up at me, let out a soft whine, then nudged Jem gently with his nose.

Jem stirred at the touch, his eyes fluttering open. They were glazed and unfocused, but when they settled on me, I saw a flicker of recognition.

"Ryan?" he whispered, his voice weak and hoarse.

"I'm here," I said. "We've got you. You're safe now."

Derek let out a soft whine and pressed his nose against Jem's cheek, his tail wagging slowly. Jem reached up with a trembling hand and tangled his fingers in Derek's fur.

We'd done it. We'd found him. He was alive, and I was bringing him home to Mai. I pulled out my phone and hit Mai's name.

It rang once, twice, three times. Each second felt like an eternity. We had to be on time.

CHAPTER THIRTY-FIVE

MAI

"Well?" Talia prompted me.

"Our nomination for the Wolf Council seat is...Sam Shaw."

I said the only name that popped into my head. The only choice, really. The only one who had the skills and the big-picture worldview that this role required and someone we knew would protect the Three Rivers at all costs. Me and Ryan, our place was here. My bond with this land, the Three Rivers territory, thrummed in response to that thought and I knew I'd made the right decision.

"Can you repeat that?" said the hulking bear of a man, leaning forward so his face filled his box on the screen.

Had I just signed my brother's death warrant? I closed my eyes and sent a quick prayer to the Goddess that Ryan had found Jem. "We nominate Sam Shaw," I confirmed.

"We thank the Three Rivers Pack for their nomination," the silver-haired elder said. "We look forward to working with Mr. Shaw.

Talia will do the initial on-boarding training and we expect to see him in person in front of the Wolf Council in three days."

Fuck! I had just changed Sam's life without even talking to him. He had family here; he ran a business here, and I'd signed him up for a four-year term.

My phone rang. Ryan.

"Excuse me, I have to take this." I said to the Council before standing up and walking out of the living room.

I ducked into the study and shut the door.

"Please tell me you have him."

"I have him."

My heart missed a beat.

"Say that again." I needed to be sure I hadn't misheard.

"I have him, Mai."

Oh, thank the Goddess! I slumped against the wall, not even trying to stop the tears streaming down my face.

"He's not in great shape, but he's alive. We'll take him straight to Thomas's."

"What about you?"

"Some injuries. Sam's pretty banged up, but we've stopped the bleeding. Waylen will stay here with a team to sift through any papers and laptops they can find."

"And Brock?"

"No," I heard the anger vibrating in Ryan's voice, "that fucker wasn't on site."

It was too much to hope that we'd get lucky enough to get Jem and Brock.

"Did I call in time?" he asked. "Did you nominate Brock?"

I shook my head, relief coursing through me. Relief at Jem being found, at stopping Brock's plans, at least for now, at Ryan being safe.

"You missed the nomination by a couple of minutes. But I didn't go for Brock."

"Thank f—"

"Ryan, it's Sam! We've got to move, now!" a voice in the background yelled.

"I gotta go, Mai. Meet us at Thomas's." The line went dead.

I took a deep breath to compose myself before heading back to the living room. I walked in and found that the Wolf Council link had already been disconnected, the screen now dark and silent. Another laptop stood open on the table. Talia was busy dismantling the rest of the equipment, her movements efficient and practiced.

Her eyes narrowed slightly as I walked in. "I hope you know what you're doing, Mai Parker."

I met her gaze, refusing to be intimidated. "I do."

Talia raised an eyebrow. "And this Sam Shaw? Why him?"

"Because Sam is the best person for this role. He has the skills, the experience, and the integrity that the Wolf Council needs. You're damn lucky to have him."

"That remains to be seen."

I stepped closer to her and lowered my voice. "Let me be clear, Talia. If you ever pull a stunt on Sam like the one you pulled at the lab? Then, fuck politics. You won't just have the whole Three Rivers Pack to answer to, you'll have me. There are no second chances, Talia. You get Sam hurt, and I'll make sure you hurt in return."

Talia's eyes flashed with anger, but her voice was calm when she answered. "I'll be sure to keep that in mind."

I bared my teeth at her. "You do that, Talia Johnson."

I turned to face Jase. "Ryan found Jem," I said. "He's alive."

Jase let out a sigh of relief. "Thank the Goddess," he murmured.

I turned back to Talia, my expression serious. "Brock's been trying to blackmail us into nominating him to the Wolf Council," I said. "It turns out that Hayley didn't finish the job and Brock has been keeping Jem alive to force our hand. He has big plans for the Wolf Council and getting a seat on it was just the first step. He won't give up. This isn't going to be the end of it, Talia. The Wolf Council needs to be prepared."

"The Wolf Council can look after itself. I'd be more worried about yourselves, if I were you. I've had dealings with Brock Madden in the past, and if you've managed to thwart his plans, I doubt he'll let that go easily."

"We can handle Brock."

Talia tilted her head to one side. "The Brock Madden I met was ruthless. If you've crossed him, he won't stop until he's made you pay."

A sense of unease spread across my stomach at her words. But I pushed it down, focusing on the task at hand.

"Are you done here?"

Talia moved over to the open laptop. "Not yet. You have documents to sign."

"Documents?"

"Yes. They must be signed within a hour of the nomination. You have the Official Nomination Form, the Candidate Verification Form, the Alpha Endorsement Form, the Confidentiality Agreement, the Terms of Service Agreement, and the Oath of Allegiance. It shouldn't take too long."

Talia was wrong. It took fucking forever. Page after page had to be annotated with my initials and each document needed at least five signatures. By the time we were done, I wanted to throw the laptop against the wall.

As Talia clicked the computer closed, I stood up. "Your business is done here, Talia. It's time for you to leave the Three Rivers. I want you out of our territory."

Talia's lips quirked in a small, humorless smile. "You would do good to remember that the Wolf Council considers all Packs, all territories, as under our control."

I stared at her, not rising to the bait.

Talia nodded. "You're learning, Mai Parker. You might survive this yet. As you wish, I'll leave your territory, but I'll be close by." She reached into her pocket and pulled out a business card, holding it out to me. "Give this to Sam Shaw," she said. "Have him call me. He has his own documents to sign and we have a lot to go over."

I took the card, glancing down at the embossed letters on the front and the wolf insignia that matched her pin. When I looked back up, Talia was already heading for the door, her bag slung over her shoulder.

"Don't forget what I said about Brock Madden, Mai Parker," she called back, not bothering to turn around. "Watch your backs."

With that, she was gone; the door closing behind her with a soft click.

I turned to Jase, my expression grim. "Let's go," I said. "We need to get to Thomas's."

Chapter Thirty-Six

MAI

I rushed into Thomas's house with Jase right behind me. I couldn't believe they really found him, that Jem was really alive. I wanted to laugh and cry at the same time. I wanted to see Jem with my own eyes, to hug him and tell him how much I'd missed him.

Ryan was sitting on the couch when I ran into the living room, a bloody towel in his hand. He was shirtless, his muscular chest and abs glistening with sweat and smeared with blood. His blue eyes, usually so bright and intense, looked tired and filled with worry.

As soon as he saw me, Ryan dropped the towel and strode over, his powerful legs covering the distance in just a few steps. He wrapped his strong arms around me, pulling me into a tight hug. I breathed in his scent; it always settled me.

"Thomas is with Jem in one of the upstairs guest rooms," Ryan said, his deep voice rumbling in his chest. "There wasn't enough space in the medical office."

I pulled back, searching his face. "How is he?"

Ryan's jaw clenched. "It's not good, Mai. But he's alive."

I let out a shaky breath, relief and fear warring inside me. "And Sam?"

"Things got a bit dicey with Sam for a moment," Ryan admitted. "But he's going to be fine. He's out back with Wally and Amara. They're helping him to Shift to speed up the healing process."

"Amara? She's helping?" Jase interrupted.

Ryan nodded, a small smile tugging at his lips. "Yeah, Thomas wasn't kidding. She's got some skills."

"What about the rest of the team?" I asked.

Ryan's expression was somber. "We lost two, and have a few injuries. Thomas is going to see them next."

Before I could respond, Thomas's voice called out from upstairs. "Mai? Ryan? Can you come up here, please?"

I didn't hesitate. I rushed up the stairs, my heart pounding in my chest. Thomas met us at the door to the guest room. "Mai, I need you to take a moment before you go in there. Jem is stable for now, but he needs rest," Thomas's voice was low and gentle. "You need to be prepared for what you see in there. Jem's been starved and beaten, and he's lost his mate. Mentally and physically, he has a lot of healing to do. Right now, he's too weak to Shift. He needs food and sleep before he'll be strong enough for that."

I felt tears prick at the corners of my eyes, my chest tightening with emotion.

I swallowed past the lump in my throat. "I understand."

Ryan came to stand beside me. "Ready?"

I nodded, and together we followed Thomas into the room.

Jem was lying on the bed, his eyes closed and his chest rising and falling with each shallow breath. An IV drip was connected to his arm.

His torso was bare, and I could see his ribs protruding beneath his skin. Bruises of various colors mottled his chest and stomach.

Even though Thomas had warned me, it was still a shock to see him like this. Gone was the vibrant, confident Alpha, so full of life and power, that I'd last seen. Instead, his body was wrecked, his face pale and gaunt. He looked to have aged ten years. I sat down on the chair beside the bed, and careful not to disturb the IV line, I reached out and took his hand in mine.

The moment my skin touched his, Jem's eyes snapped open. For a split second, I saw confusion and fear in their depths before they hardened with fury. A vicious snarl tore from his throat as he lunged at me, his teeth bared.

I flinched back, just as Ryan hauled me out of the chair.

Jem's attack was uncoordinated and clumsy, though. He tumbled off the bed, his body hitting the floor with a sickening thud.

Thomas rushed forward, dropping to his knees beside Jem. "Get her out of here!"

"No!" I didn't want to go. I finally had my brother back; I wasn't going to leave him now. I struggled against Ryan's arm, but he held me firm and moved us towards the door.

I looked over Ryan's shoulder to see Jem's face contorting. He was trying to Shift, his features twisting and morphing into something halfway between man and wolf. But the change wouldn't hold, and his body snapped back to human. He snarled again, trying to get to me, but Thomas held him back as Ryan closed the door.

"Put me down, Ryan!"

He ignored me, carrying me downstairs despite my protests. I wanted to go back, to help Jem.

"Mai, you can't be in there right now," Ryan said firmly, setting me down in the kitchen. "He's not in his right mind; he could hurt you."

I stopped fighting him. "I don't understand," I whispered. "Why would he react like that?"

"He's been through a lot. It's going to take time for him to heal."

I looked up at him, a sudden thought occurring to me. "Do you think he's on ripple? That could explain his behavior."

Ryan shook his head. "I didn't smell it on him. Whatever that was, I don't think ripple is the issue."

I frowned, remembering the way Jem's face had contorted as he tried to Shift. "When I left the room, it looked like he was trying to partially Shift, but it wasn't working. His features kept changing back and forth."

"Only Alphas can use the energy from the Pack bonds to do that. Jem's not the Alpha of the Three Rivers anymore; he no longer has access to that power. It's going to take him time to get used to that."

For fuck's sake. Could it get any shittier for my brother?

I climbed onto Ryan's lap, needing him to hold me. Without a word, he knew what I needed. His strong arms wrapped around me, and he held me that like, my head resting on his shoulder, until Thomas walked in ten minutes later.

"Jem's settled and is sleeping for now," he said, rubbing a hand over his face. "Mai, I need you to be out of the house before he wakes up."

I stared at him, feeling a mix of confusion and hurt. "What? Why?"

Thomas sighed, pulling out a chair and sitting down heavily. "I've seen this once before. It's a very rare set of circumstances. But essentially it comes down to the fact that Jem is too weak right now to keep his wolf under control."

I shook my head, not understanding. "But what's wrong with his wolf? Jem's wolf is not only one of the strongest I know but also one of the gentlest."

I twisted round to face Ryan. "You remember that time when we were kids, when Jem's wolf found that box of abandoned kittens in the woods? Most wolves would have either ignored them or eaten them. Instead, he carried them, one by one, in his jaws, over two miles to our apartment. It took him over three hours to get them all."

"I remember," Ryan grunted. "Those damn things followed him around whenever he Shifted to his wolf. What happened to them?"

"We couldn't feed them, hell we could barely feed ourselves at that point. Jem found homes for them, but it took a long time for his wolf to forgive Jem for giving them up."

"Mai, you have to understand," Thomas said, putting his arms on the table. "Jem, the man, knows that you're his sister. He loves you. He wants to protect you. He wants you to be happy. But right now, his wolf only sees the person who killed his mate."

I felt like I had been punched in the gut. Why hadn't I thought of that? I'd been so focused on getting Jem back, I hadn't thought about how he would feel seeing me again.

"When Jem is stronger, he'll be able to control his wolf," Thomas continued gently. "But right now, he's too weak. He's locked in a battle with his wolf; trying to stop him from attacking you."

It was like my world was crumbling around me. After all the pain we had gone through to get Jem back, and now his wolf wanted me dead.

Ryan slipped his hand round the back of my neck and pulled me closer to him. "We'll figure this out, Mai. It won't always be like this."

I wanted to believe him, but I wasn't so sure. I knew myself and my own wolf, and no matter the circumstances, I would never be able to forgive someone who took Ryan from me.

A noise at the door had us all turning round. Esme was hovering at the entrance to the kitchen. She was clean at last, and her dirty blonde hair that looked so drab and lifeless before, now bounced a little as she looked at me with gentle, shy eyes.

"I can help," she said quietly, her voice barely above a whisper. "I overheard. I can do good this time, cast a spell that will make the wolf sleep for two days. The man can heal and get strong before he has to face his wolf again."

I stared at her, thinking. The idea of using magic on Jem made me uncomfortable, but if it could help him...

Thomas nodded thoughtfully. "I've seen it done before. Down south where witches can still practice. It's a safe and effective way to give Jem the time he needs to recover."

I glanced at Ryan, seeking his opinion. He met my gaze and shrugged; it was up to me. Jem was my brother.

"Thomas, do you think Jem is able to make this decision if you asked him?"

"No, he's not in any state to understand this."

I looked at Esme. Did I trust her? She could do anything to my brother without us knowing. I'd be putting my brother's life in her hands.

Trust the pup, my wolf urged me.

You sure?

My wolf didn't reply. She'd already said what she thought.

"Okay, do it."

A smile lit up Esme's face. "Yes, I will do good this time."

Thomas stood up. "I'll be there the whole time, Mai. I'll keep a close eye on her."

I watched them go, my heart heavy with worry and hope.

Chapter Thirty-Seven

RYAN

Mai looked so small, so scared, sitting there. I wanted to take this pain away from her. I'd do fucking anything, so she didn't look like this ever again.

I turned as Sam hobbled in the back door, followed by Amara and Wally. Through the open door, I could see Ben doing a piss-poor job at hiding in the bushes. He'd been spying on them, though they didn't need to be werewolves to know he was there. Two paws were visible under the leaves and his tail kept wagging, causing the entire bush to shake. Without parents to teach him, he'd obviously missed out on some vital lessons. I'd have to take him into the woods and show him how to be the predator he was born to be.

Derek, his phone pressed to his ear, was in front of Ben. Sam was vulnerable while he was Shifting from one form to another, and while we trusted Wally, Amara was still an unknown. Derek must have been watching over Sam while he Shifted.

Sam's face was pale as he limped past me and eased himself into a chair. Wally grabbed a glass of water.

"See? You're looking better, already," he said, placing the water in front of Sam. "A few more Shifts and you'll be running round after all the delinquent pups again."

Sam managed a weak grin at Wally's words.

"How are you really doing?" asked Mai.

Sam shrugged, wincing slightly at the movement, but then grinned at Mai. "A little near-death experience isn't going to slow me down," he said, then paused as if thinking. "Although the limp might."

That pulled a small smile from Mai, and I felt a of surge of gratitude for my brother.

Wally patted Sam's shoulder gently. "I'm sure it's perfectly normal after the injury you had—"

"Yeah," Amara snorted. "It was fucking hideous! Your leg was half hanging off!"

Sam's face paled even further, but Wally waved off Amara's comment. "I'll get Thomas to take a look at it after you've Shifted a couple more times. For now, the only thing you need is some of my cooking."

Sam's stomach grumbled as if on cue.

"Male werewolves and their stomachs," Amara shook her head wistfully. "They're never happy unless they've got a full belly!"

"No, that we are not," agreed Wally. "So, I'd better get on it *tout de suite*, and you, Amara, can give me a hand by running to the shops." Wally handed her a shopping list and a credit card.

I raised my eyebrows at Wally; that was awful trusting of him.

Amara seemed to think so too; she stared at the card for a moment before reaching out carefully and taking it, like she thought it was a trick and Wally would snatch it back any second.

"Sure," she said, heading for the door. "I'll be back soon."

Just as Amara went out the front door, Derek strode into the kitchen, his face grim. "Ryan, I've got Ronnie on the phone. To say he's pissed would be a colossal motherfucking understatement."

I sighed, running a hand through my hair. I couldn't blame Ronnie for being angry. Only two of his men had walked out of the forestry station of their own accord. The rest had to be carried out. If I were in his shoes, I'd be furious too. I nodded to Derek and took the phone.

"Ronnie."

"I lost two men, Ryan. Two good men. And three more have serious injuries. We're talking life-changing stuff here."

I closed my eyes, feeling the weight of those losses. They might not have been Pack, but they fought with us. "I'm sorry, Ronnie. I truly am."

"I know that, Ryan. And I'm glad you found your boy. But I'm pissed as hell that Brock wasn't there. I went in expecting to take him down, and instead, we walked into a fucking bloodbath."

"Brock's a slippery bastard, but we'll find him, I promise you that."

"I want in from now on, Ryan. I want revenge for what he did to my men."

I nodded, even though Ronnie couldn't see me. "I understand. We'll keep you in the loop."

"You better. I heard Mai didn't nominate Brock for the council. Thank fuck for that."

I frowned, wondering where Ronnie kept getting his information from. He always knew more than he should.

"She made a good choice. Smart even."

I glanced at Mai. She looked sheepishly away, and I narrowed my eyes. With everything that had happened, I hadn't had time to talk to her about who she nominated in the end. Of course, it wouldn't be a good idea to let Ronnie know that I was fucking clueless about it.

"Well, I'm glad we surprised you."

Ronnie laughed, the sound low and gruff. "I mean it, Ryan. It was a smart move."

With that, the line went dead.

Ronnie was obviously not one for goodbyes.

"Well, I for one," said Sam, "feel sorry for whatever poor fucking sucker Mai nominated. Who'd want to be thrown into that pit of vipers?"

Mai looked at Sam, her expression guilty. "Yeah. About that..."

Everyone in the room paused and turned to look at Mai, then swiveled their heads to look at Sam. Sam's jaw dropped open as he realized who she'd nominated.

Mai was a fucking genius, and the Wolf Council didn't have a clue what was going to hit them. I couldn't help it; I burst out laughing.

Chapter Thirty-Eight

MAI

I stood in the kitchen with Wally, watching the scene unfolding in the garden. Sam paced back and forth; his limp more pronounced with every step. He seemed oblivious to the pain, too caught up in his ranting to notice.

Ryan was trying to calm Sam down, his hands held up in a placating gesture, but so far, it looked like Sam wasn't having it.

Guilt gnawed at my stomach; I was the cause of this. I had chosen Sam without even discussing it with him first. I stood by my choice; Sam was one of the best of us and he'd kick ass on the Council. But I'd upended his life without a second thought, and I couldn't blame him for being angry.

Wally's voice pulled me from my thoughts. "Don't worry about Sam," he said, his tone reassuring. "He'll get over it. He's just a little surprised right now."

A little? That was an understatement.

I sighed, turning away from the window to face Wally. "I'm not so sure,."

"You did what you thought was best for the Pack, Mai. You did your job as Alpha. Sam knows that. He just needs some time to adjust to the idea."

I wanted to believe Wally, but the guilt was still slugging around in my stomach. Was this the type of Alpha I wanted to be? Moving members of my Pack around like pieces on a chessboard with no thought to their desires and feelings? Was this what it took to be an Alpha? Was I making the role my own, or was it molding me into someone I didn't recognize?

Wally interrupted my spiraling thoughts by placing a plate of food in front of me. "Eat," he ordered, his tone brooking no argument. "I'll make a proper meal when Amara gets back, but this'll do for now."

I raised my eyebrows at him, a small smirk playing on my lips. "Is that how you speak to your Alpha now, Wally?"

Wally gave me a look that clearly said he wasn't impressed. "Just like Thomas is in charge in there," Wally pointed down the corridor to the medical room, "in this kitchen, I'm in charge and I won't hear a word to say I'm not!"

He stood up tall, and even though he was only about five foot nine, with me sitting down he seemed for a moment to loom over me in the way I remembered Jem doing to me when we were little, and mom and dad had just died. He'd do the same thing, put food in front of me and order me to eat, standing over me to make sure I did it. I'd gone through a stage of not wanting to eat, not wanting to do anything after our parents died. Jem brought me back though, insisted on me eating, made me tag along with him whenever he went out. It didn't take long for me to realize that if I went with him, I'd get to see Ryan. Soon, I was waiting impatiently by the door before Jem was ready to leave.

I picked up the sandwich, ham by the smell of it, and without taking my eyes off Wally, I carefully put it in my mouth and chewed.

Wally's face lit up. "Good. You need to remember, Mai, our fearsome and beautiful leader, that in here, I get to take care of everyone. Especially you. You haven't stopped since you and Ryan took over as Alphas. I know Sylvie is doing a fine job, she always does, but when you are here, in my domain, I am not going to let her down. And especially, especially now..." He trailed off, giving me a pointed look. Oh my bloody Goddess, he was fattening me up in case I got pregnant anytime soon.

I wanted to shut this baby thing down now, but Wally wasn't wrong. I needed to take the time to stop and eat more regularly. I had been running myself ragged, trying to prove that I could be the Alpha my Pack needed.

I rolled my eyes but put another bite in my mouth.

The door slammed open and Sam came stomping into the kitchen, his face a mask of anger and frustration. He didn't even glance in my direction as he limped through the room, heading straight for the front door.

Ryan and Derek followed Sam in. We all watched as Sam disappeared through the door, letting it fall shut behind him.

"He'll come around," Ryan said. "Just give him time."

I nodded. I wanted to believe him, but I couldn't shake the feeling that Sam was never going to forgive me. There was no saying no to the Council. I hadn't left him any choice. He had three days to recover, put his affairs in order, work out what he and Mason were going to do with their PI agency and leave the Three Rivers.

A sound made me look up. Jem stood in the doorway. He looked even more frail than he did lying on the bed. He stared straight at me, his gaze boring into mine, and his voice was hoarse when he asked. "What the fuck did you do, Mai?"

Chapter Thirty-Nine

MAI

I jerked up from the kitchen chair, my heart pounding in my chest as I faced Jem. Thomas appeared in the doorway, gently guiding Jem into the kitchen. Despite Thomas pulling out a chair for him, Jem refused to sit down, instead grabbing onto the back of a chair to steady himself.

"Esme's spell went well," Thomas said, his voice soft but strained. "But it took a lot out of her. She's resting upstairs now."

Jem's gaze never left my face. But at least he wasn't attacking me, which was definitely a step forward.

"What did you do, Mai?" Jem repeated, his voice harsh.

I frowned, not sure what he was asking. "Um, Esme cast a spell to put your wolf to sleep for a couple of days," I said, trying to keep my voice steady. "It was the only way to—"

"I know that," he snapped. Ryan's face went blank, and I knew he was about to come to my defense.

I shook my head once at Ryan, telling him I'd handle this.

"I'm not talking about the spell. I want to know about Hayley."

My heart skipped a beat at the mention of Hayley's name. I had been dreading this moment, knowing that, eventually, we would have to have this conversation, but I hadn't thought it would be so soon.

Ryan moved to stand between Jem and me, but I gently pushed him back. "It's okay, Ryan."

I could feel Ryan's muscles coiled tightly under my hands. Neither Ryan nor his wolf liked the way this was going, but Ryan loved Jem like a brother. I couldn't let them get into a fight over this.

"You want to know about Hayley?" I asked Jem.

"Yes."

"About how I...about how..." I trailed off, appalled at the thought of having to tell Jem how I killed his mate.

Jem studied my face for a long moment, his expression unreadable. Then, without taking his eyes off of me, he ordered, "Everyone out. Now. I want to talk to Mai and Ryan alone."

No one moved.

Well, this was awkward.

Thomas, Wally, and Derek all glanced at me. Jem wasn't their Alpha anymore, and they needed the go-ahead from either me or Ryan before they obeyed. I'd been so hell-bent on getting Jem back that I hadn't thought past that, or about how Jem would fit into the Pack hierarchy now.

I gave a curt nod, giving them permission to leave. They didn't hesitate, filing out of the kitchen, leaving Jem alone with me and Ryan.

As soon as they were gone, Jem slumped into the chair. He ran a hand over his face, and the scent of his exhaustion and sadness filled the room. My wolf whined inside of me, wanting to go and comfort him.

Too dangerous.

She snorted. Jem was her brother-wolf, and she had no fear of him.

"I keep forgetting I'm not the Alpha anymore," Jem whispered. "It's going to take some getting used to. A lot has changed."

"It'll take time, Jem," I sat down next to him, careful not to touch him. His wolf might be asleep by Esme's spell, but I knew just how strong Jem's wolf was and my touching him might be enough to wake him up. "It'll be okay."

Jem shook his head softly. "No, Mai. I don't think it'll ever be okay again."

Maybe he was right. I knew if I lost Ryan, my whole world would disappear. I didn't know how to make this better for Jem.

"Mai, please. Tell me what happened to Hayley. I know she's...I know she's dead. I felt it when she died. But I need to know how it happened."

I swallowed hard, trying to find the words to explain. Ryan leaned back in his chair and placed his hand on the back of my neck. The heat of his hand seeped into my skin, letting me know that he was here, that I didn't have to tell Jem alone.

"We suspect that Hayley was hooked on ripple. It was increasing her paranoia and made her susceptible to the lies that Brock told her."

Jem's eyes widened in surprise. "Ripple? In the Three Rivers?"

Ryan nodded. "Turns out ripple has been here for a while. It's spreading fast, all across the northeast territories."

Jem's shoulders sagged. "There's a lot I didn't know when I was the Alpha."

I hesitated, glancing at Ryan. He gave me a small nod of encouragement, and I turned back to Jem.

"Brock and Hayley had declared themselves as the Alpha couple," I said softly.

Jem closed his eyes, and I could scent his pain rolling off of him in waves.

"Ryan and I went to the Pack Meet where Brock and Hayley were supposed to be announced to all the Packs as the new Alphas of the Three Rivers. We challenged them. There was a fight."

I paused, taking a deep breath before continuing. "Hayley couldn't partially Shift anymore. It's a side-effect of ripple. Wolves who are hooked on it cannot Shift. But I could."

"How was that possible? You weren't the Alphas of the Three Rivers then."

I shrugged. "When Brock and Hayley took over, we went on the run. We formed our own, well, our own renegade Pack. They saw me and Ryan as their Alphas and I was able to use that. It meant I could partially Shift. I'd defeated her. The fight was over, but she came at me again." I could feel tears welling up in my eyes as I forced myself to say the words. "I killed Hayley, Jem. I'm so sorry."

Jem's eyes snapped open, and for a moment, I thought he might lunge at me. His arms shook, and it looked like he was trying desperately not to attack me. Ryan was tense next to me and I knew he was ready to tackle Jem if he showed any signs of moving toward me. Then the moment passed, and Jem slumped back in his chair, his face crumpling as he began to sob.

"I think she wanted to die. At the end. She thought you were dead, Jem. I really do believe that. And I think she wanted forgiveness for what she did."

Jem's weeping filled the room, his shoulders shaking with the force of his grief. Ryan stood up and placed his hand on Jem's shoulder, offering silent comfort to him. I wanted to go and hug my brother, to let him know that he wasn't alone in this, but Ryan shook his head at me. He didn't trust the witch's spell, either.

"I'm so sorry, Jem," I repeated.

Jem swiped his tears away. "It's my fault," he said, his voice hoarse.

"No. It's not your fault. None of this is your fault."

But Jem wasn't listening. "I should have seen it coming. I should have known that Hayley was on drugs, that Brock was poisoning her mind. I failed her. As her mate, I failed her."

He looked shattered and broken, a shadow of the Alpha he had been.

"Do you remember what happened?" Ryan asked gently. "The night you disappeared?"

Jem nodded slowly, his eyes distant. "I remember we had all just gotten home, ready to coordinate against Brock and Tristan's takeover attempt. I remember opening the door and seeing Hayley, and feeling a warning come through our bond. And then...then nothing."

He shuddered, his hands clenching into fists. "I woke up in pain, in the cage room. Brock was there, along with a witch. I was paralyzed, couldn't move. And my bond with Hayley...it was gone. Like it had never been there."

Jem's voice broke, and he buried his face in his hands. "I passed out again after that. I don't remember anything else."

I leaned forward. "Did you see the witch's face? Anything that could help us identify them?"

Jem shook his head. "No, they had a hood on."

I sat back, my mind racing. Could it have been the same witch that I saw when Seth took me? The one who tried to break my bond with the Three Rivers Pack?

I turned to Ryan. "Is it possible? Could a witch have brought Jem back to life?"

He shrugged. "Ever since the Council banned them from practicing here, wolves don't have a lot of contact with witches. We don't keep track anymore; we've no idea what they're capable of these days."

Fuck! We might never know if Jem had really died or not. "What did you mean your bond with Hayley was gone?"

Jem's face crumpled, and for a moment, I thought he might start crying again. But he took a deep, shuddering breath before answering. "It was like she was gone. Like she never existed, and we never mated," he said.

"It might have been something the witch did," Ryan speculated. "Maybe witches have found a way to transfer bonds. It would explain why Hayley thought Brock was her mate. If the witch had somehow transferred your bond to him?"

"If they did, it wasn't permanent. Over the next few days, the bond started to come back. Slowly, like a trickle. They moved me from place to place, but I could start to feel Hayley again. Feel her pain."

Jem closed his eyes. "And then, when Hayley...when she really did die...it wasn't like she was just gone this time. It was a tearing, an explosion of pain. And then...nothing."

He opened his eyes, and I could see the raw agony in them. "I passed out or shut down, I guess, when she died. When I woke up, the bond was gone again. And this time, I knew it was for good."

CHAPTER FORTY

RYAN

Thomas came and helped Jem back to bed. After they were gone, it was finally fucking time to look after my mate. I could still feel her pain through our bond. This hadn't been the happy reunion that Mai had thought it would be.

"Let's go home, baby," I murmured, pressing a kiss to the top of her head. "I'll run you a hot bath and make you something to eat. You need to rest too."

Mai looked up at me, her eyes soft. "Thank you," she whispered. "For everything."

We walked hand in hand to the car, and I opened the passenger door for her, helping her inside before moving around to the driver's side.

Mai was quiet as I pulled out. She leaned her head against the window, her eyes closed, and I didn't need to check our bond to know how exhausted she was.

"You doing okay?"

Mai nodded but didn't open her eyes. "Just tired," she murmured. "It's been a long day."

Mmm. Dwelling on Jem wouldn't do Mai any good. She needed a distraction, something to take her mind off her thoughts.

"You know," I said casually, "We haven't had sex in this car yet."

A faint blush crept into her cheeks. "That's true. Or in any car, for that matter."

I could see the hint of a smile tugging at the corners of her mouth.

"I'm looking forward to exploring all the possibilities."

Mai opened her big brown eyes and looked at me, her black, wavy hair framing her face. I wanted to pull the car over and fuck her right now. It was tempting. So tempting. But she needed food first, especially with what I had in mind for her later.

"I can think of a few myself," she whispered, and my determination to feed her first took a significant hit.

I pulled through the gates at the compound and sped up to the Alpha House.

As soon as I got out of the car, though, I knew something wasn't right. My wolf was instantly on alert.

Mai knew it too. "Something's wrong," she said softly, her eyes scanning the front of the house.

"Stay—"

"Don't even think about it, Ryan. I'm not staying out here."

Knowing Mai, she would follow me inside no matter what I said.

"Stay behind me then."

I moved silently up the steps to the front door. I paused, listening. Nothing. I swung the door open slowly. Nothing looked out of place, but when we stepped inside, the feeling of wrongness intensified. It didn't smell right.

I went right past the bookcases and cleared the living room and kitchen. Nothing seemed out of place, but the feeling of unease grew stronger.

I turned as soon as I felt a tug on our bond, a silent message from Mai. She dipped her head towards the study. I swung open the door. The desk was clear, but there, sitting on the sofa next to a pale and trembling Amara, was Brock. He had one arm draped casually over the back of the sofa, a smile playing on his lips. My eyes zeroed in on the knife Brock had pressed against Amara's side. I could smell her fear from here and saw the way her body trembled against Brock's.

"Well, well, well," said Brock. "Welcome home."

My eyes scanned the room, looking for anyone else there.

"I can't say I particularly like what you've done with the place," Brock's tone was light and conversational, like we were all friends.

"I'm so sorry," Amara whispered, her gaze going to Mai's.

"Hush Amara," Mai replied. "You have nothing to be sorry for."

"Let her go," I growled at Brock.

He laughed. "Oh, I don't think so, Ryan. You see, Amara here is my insurance policy. As long as I have her, you two are going to sit down and listen to what I have to say."

He pressed the knife harder against Amara's side, and she let out a whimper. "Sit," Brock ordered, his eyes gleaming with malice. "Or I'll slit her throat right here and now."

I considered it. Amara was one life compared to the lives of our entire Pack. And this was our opportunity to finally get Brock; we might not get another. As Alphas, we were going to have to make hard decisions like this.

Brock looked between me and Mai and laughed again. "What's the matter?" he taunted. "If it were me, I'd attack. No question. No doubts. What's the loss of someone like Amara to a whole Pack? Nothing. You made that decision with Jem, no? Put the Pack above one life, even if it was your brother's."

His eyes bored into Mai's. "What's the difference? Is it that you're a coward? With Jem, you knew I would have killed him, but you thought I wouldn't have done it right in front of you. But Amara? That's a different story. You're going to have to look her in the eyes, knowing that you are the reason she's about to die. I'm betting you're too much of a coward to make those kinds of decisions. Too weak to do what needs to be done."

How fucking dare he talk to my mate like that. The fury within me swelled like a tidal wave, crashing against the fraying barriers of my self-control. Every fiber of my being demanded that I lunge at Brock and tear him apart, consequences be damned. But I knew I had to rein in the primal urge, to leash the beast within, no matter how it clawed and raged against its confines. I forced myself to breathe through it, to focus on the bigger picture, even as my vision narrowed to a single, crimson point of hatred.

Mai straightened her back and walked forward, her steps measured and calm. She sat down on the sofa, her eyes never leaving Brock's face. "I will never be the kind of leader who sees their people as nothing more than disposable pawns in a game of power. Jem never wanted me to nominate you to the Wolf Council. He wanted me to put the needs of all of us above him. It's what made him a great Alpha, and it's something you never could understand, Brock. It's why you will always be a piss-poor leader."

Pride surged through me at her words. That was my mate, my Alpha. She would never sacrifice her people for her own gain, never see them as anything less than the beating heart of our Pack.

"What do you want, Brock?" I asked.

"I just wanted to chat," Brock smiled. "How was your little family reunion? Was it everything you hoped for, Mai? Or did your 'great Alpha' try and attack you?"

He must have seen the answer on Mai's face because he laughed. "Well, he finally did something right!"

I could feel Mai's anger and guilt pulsing down our bond, but she didn't respond. Just sat there patiently waiting for him to get to the point.

"Tell me, did you kill the witch?" He said it so causally, too causally. The answer was important to him.

I let my rage slip out a little. "You mean the bitch who's been casting spells on your drugs, making Shifters ill? You know the rules, Brock. Any witch caught doing magic here is a dead witch."

Brock nodded, but not before I saw the relief in his eyes. "Well, congratulations. You found your brother. You nominated Sam. You figured out that I run ripple. Clever, clever little wolves."

His smile fell away. "But I don't want you to think that you've won. You've only delayed my plans, not stopped them."

I kept my face blank and uninterested. "Really?"

Brock leaned forward. "Haven't you wondered why I haven't been put down by the Wolf Council yet? They've never needed much evidence in the past to eliminate any threat to the Shifter community or the peace with the humans. And yet, here I am, still breathing."

Brock was right. It didn't make sense. The Wolf Council was notoriously swift and brutal in their justice.

"Quit the games, Brock. If you have something to say, just say it and get the fuck out of my home."

Brock's smile widened, a predator's grin. "I'm trying to connect the dots for you two. In case you really are as stupid as I think. I have powerful friends. Maybe it's Talia. Maybe she hasn't been passing the intel back to the Council. Did you think of that? Then again, maybe it's someone above her, blocking the intel? You don't know who you can trust. I have friends in high places. It's not just me you have to worry about, you two just made some very powerful enemies by crossing me and delaying our plans."

I kept my voice bored. "We already know you have someone on the Council, Brock. This isn't news to us."

Mai showed Brock her teeth. "And we'll handle whatever comes our way. Just like we handled you."

Anger simmered in Brock's eyes, but it was a controlled anger, cold and calculating. "Let's put that to the test, shall we? Two days from now, I will bring my army to the east bank of the Whispering Willow. You bring yours to the west bank, and we'll see who's still standing by sundown."

Mai's eyes narrowed. "Why would we agree to this little plan of yours?"

"Because, Mai, you have two choices. Either you meet me at the river, and we fight it out there, or I'll bring my army onto the streets of Three Rivers. We can battle it out surrounded by children on their way to school, families going about their daily lives. I don't give a fuck either way. How about you?"

I felt another surge of rage at his words, at the casual way he threatened the lives of our people. But I kept my face impassive, refusing to give him the satisfaction of seeing me react.

Brock's gaze shifted to me, his eyes burning with a deep, unrelenting hatred. "I will never forget that you killed my father, Ryan. I want a chance to make you pay for what you did. And when I've finished with you, I'll take over the Council and decimate any remaining members of the Three Rivers Pack."

He stood abruptly, yanking Amara up with him. She let out a cry of pain as the knife dug into her side, but Brock ignored her, his eyes fixed on us as he edged towards the door.

"I'll be expecting you at noon in two days. Don't disappoint me."

With that, he picked Amara up and, like she was a doll, threw her towards us. I surged forward, caught Amara, swung her round, put her on her feet and took off after Brock.

Chapter Forty-One

MAI

It was late afternoon. Tomorrow we were supposed to meet Brock at the Whispering Willow River just outside the boundaries of Three Rivers. Ryan and I were in the Alpha House kitchen, going over our plans for the hundredth time, and I was trying to stay calm. Wally was here, along with the other Shaw brothers, plus Jase. Sylvie had put out food platters in the dining room and they were all attacking it like they hadn't eaten in years. I couldn't; I'd had a lump in my stomach ever since Brock threw Amara at us and ran out of the room. It was a gnawing sense of foreboding. That something was coming and this time, maybe we wouldn't come out of it.

After Brock had done a runner, Ryan had gone after him. I'd established that physically Amara was okay, then knocked on Sylvie's door and told her to stay with Amara. We'd spent the next two hours hunting Brock. Following his scent all over Three Rivers had been easy, but he was always one step ahead. He'd finally crossed the boundary of our territory and neither me nor Ryan wanted to follow him over it in case it was a trap. It would be just like Brock to try to lure us out of Three Rivers so he could double back and attack it.

When we got back, Ryan had demanded answers from our Renegade guards on how Brock had got past them, not once but twice. Raphael had been appalled. We'd done a search and had found two guards unconscious at the east wall of the compound. They were going to be okay, but both had nasty concussions.

This had only cemented my belief that we were doing the right thing in taking down the wall around the compound. If Brock could get in and out when it was there, it was doing fuck all for our security.

Ryan had nodded when I pointed this out to him, his jaw clenched tight. "You're right. We'll find another way to protect the Pack."

Amara was shaken after her ordeal. Brock had grabbed her off the street on the way back from the shops. Seth had kidnapped me from the street, so I knew what that felt like, how helpless it made you feel.

"We've done everything I can think of, but I'm still not happy about this," Ryan sighed, pulling me out of my thoughts. We'd pulled everyone in. Derek, along with Sam and Mason, had used every favor, every one of their contacts to find out that Brock did indeed have an army. As soon as we got some solid intel on it, Derek had gone scouting. He'd returned a few hours later with the news that Brock had at least two hundred Shifters to throw at us tomorrow. With no idea where he'd gotten so many, that's where Sam, Mason, and Waylen came into play. Now that he knew what to look for, Waylen had been able to follow some email trails on a laptop found at the old forestry station. It seemed that someone had been giving Brock a heads up about rogue wolves. Whenever there was a sighting of some Packless wolves making trouble somewhere, Brock would get an email with a location. The emails had gone back years, before Brock had come back to Three Rivers. If Brock had been recruiting an army, it would explain how there had been so many men at the old forestry station guarding Jem, and how he had two hundred to go into battle with. Ryan said the men at the station had been efficient and well-trained. It looked like Brock had managed to mold rogue werewolves into a deadly fighting force. The fact that he'd been building it for years meant that Brock had started planning his takeover of the Council a lot longer ago than we thought.

"You're right. Brock's not going to play by the rules. He'll have something planned, something we're not expecting."

Ryan ran a hand through his hair. "I know. All we can do is prepare as best we can. We have Ronnie and his men coming, the Renegades and all our enforcers. The people from Sam and Mason's PI agency, everyone we could pull in on short notice. We'll leave some enforcers behind to protect Three Rivers, in case it's a ruse and Brock tries to attack here instead. And if the battle goes badly, they'll be in charge of evacuating everyone to Bridgetown. Michael and Camille are preparing, just in case."

"Don't forget me!" Wally called as he walked in, holding a plate of food in one hand.

I looked at Ryan. He shrugged, telling me it was my choice.

"I thought you'd be here, helping with the evacuation if it's needed."

"Oh, hell no! I'll be on the front lines with you. You're going to need every fighter you've got."

"I see. And what does Thomas think about this?" It was a low blow, but I wanted to try everything I could to keep at least some of my family safe.

Wally narrowed his eyes at me. "Thomas will rail against the stupidity of all of us for fighting. He always does. He also knows what will happen if we lose tomorrow. We're fighting not just for the Three Rivers, but all werewolves. Brock will decimate us with his ripple, and if he ever gets to be the Wolf King he so desperately wants to be, we'll all be royally fucked. Probably literally. So, Thomas will support my decision, and I'm asking you to do the same, Alpha."

Alpha? He called me Alpha. Shit.

"I just want—"

"I know what you want. You want to keep us all safe. I do too, that's why I have to fight tomorrow. Alongside my Pack. Where I belong."

Wow, he was really hammering it home.

I sighed, defeated. "Alright, but I'm putting you next to Evelyn. You can watch each other's backs."

Wally grinned at me. "Done." Then he turned and left the kitchen.

"It's not enough," I whispered, stepping into Ryan and wrapping my arms around his waist.

Ryan hugged me back, and I breathed in his scent, knowing I'd do anything, anything, to make sure he survived tomorrow.

"I'll have to get to Brock quickly," he said. "If I can kill him before our side takes too much damage, there's a chance we'll come out of this."

"You think his men will run when Brock falls?"

Ryan nodded. "I do."

I felt his lie through our bond. That was new, but I didn't have time to explore it right now. I doubted Brock's men would run, too. From what Ryan had told me about the men at the forestry station, and what

Derek reported back, these were not the sort to up and run when the leader fell.

"I want to try something. You're not going to like it, so I'm not going to tell you what it is just yet. But I want you to trust me."

Ryan pulled back, his eyes searching my face.

"Mai—"

"I said you weren't going to like it. But this is part of us learning to be the Alpha couple. You have to trust me, Ryan. It's not dangerous. I'll be gone about an hour, maybe two."

"Mai—"

"Please, Ryan. This is important." I would do anything to even the odds, even a little, to give us a chance of getting out alive.

I could see the battle on his face. But this was it; we were both Alphas, and he had to learn to trust me.

I stared into his eyes, willing him to take this leap, his beautiful lashes distracting me for a second. Then he nodded. "Take Jase."

Jase was all up for an adventure. I hoped his puppy-like enthusiasm never got knocked out of him. We pulled up outside a well-maintained warehouse on the outskirts of town. The building was modern, constructed within the last decade, and with its clean lines and sleek design, it screamed of efficiency and functionality.

As Jase and I got out of the car, I spotted Ava and Evelyn standing guard by the door. Ava scowled like someone had stolen her favorite pair of jeans. She'd been at the briefing yesterday and knew what we were up against. She was pissed as hell, though, that Brock had threatened the Pack. Raphael had explained to me that Ava had two teenage sisters in town. They'd be in the firing line if Brock took his army to the streets. Evelyn, on the other hand, smiled as we walked toward them. She was the picture of calm composure. Her long brown hair was tied in a braid down her back and her green eyes were sharp and alert.

"Alpha," Ava greeted me with a sharp nod. "You found it okay?"

I gave her a tight smile. "Yes, the directions you gave me were perfect."

Evelyn stepped forward, her movements fluid and graceful. "We've got them all secured inside, with five Renegades keeping a close eye on them."

I nodded my thanks and took a deep breath, steeling myself. Jase fell into step beside me as Evelyn and Ava led us to the door. Evelyn pulled out a key card from her pocket and swiped it against the electronic lock.

Inside, a concrete floor stretched to fill the space, about half the size of a soccer pitch. The walls were painted a crisp white, reflecting the bright light and making the space feel larger than it was.

Against the far wall, about fifty werewolves in human form sat in neat rows, their wrists bound behind their backs with sturdy plastic zip ties. They looked tired and weary, their clothes rumpled and their hair disheveled, but there was no scent of unwashed bodies or stale sweat. Instead, the air carried a faint hint of disinfectant. I nodded to Evelyn and Ava. I was impressed; the prisoners had been treated well.

The five Renegade guards stood at attention around the perimeter of the room, their stances alert, their eyes watchful. They were each armed with tranquilizer guns and silver-tipped darts.

A few of the rogue werewolves lifted their heads to watch us as we walked in, their gazes a mix of wariness and curiosity. Some looked defiant, their eyes flashing with barely contained anger, while others seemed resigned to their fate, their shoulders slumped in defeat.

I let my gaze sweep over the assembled group. There were young wolves barely out of their teens, and older ones with gray hair and lined faces.

I recognized some of them as the Three Rivers enforcers who had fought for Brock and Hayley at the Pack Meet. Others were the men Korrin had brought into our territory to kill us.

None of them met my eyes.

Good, my wolf chuffed. She was pleased they were acknowledging us as someone to be respected.

These were all wolves without a Pack now, without a purpose. They had fought for Korrin and Brock, and now they were paying the price.

"You sure this is a good idea, Mai?" Jase whispered.

I didn't answer him. Instead, I strode forward, my footsteps echoing on the concrete floor as I made my way to the center of the warehouse..

"Do you know who I am?" I asked, my voice ringing out clear and strong.

One of Korrin's rogues, a burly man with a shaved head, let out a derisive grunt. "Of course we fucking know who you are," he spat. "You're the bitch who defeated us."

I didn't flinch at his words. Instead, I stared at him, letting my wolf peek out through my eyes. He lowered his gaze immediately.

"Yes, I'm the bitch that defeated you. And you are all rogues now. You have no Pack, no place to call home. You each betrayed your own. Some of you chose to follow Korrin and look where it brought you." I paused, sweeping my hand around the room. "For those of you who called yourself Three Rivers people. You let us down. You didn't protect the weak or the innocent. You saw what Brock and Hayley were doing to this Pack, and you let it happen. You betrayed your family, your friends, those you were sworn to protect. You have all been disavowed, and after what you've done, it's unlikely that any Pack will take you in."

A hushed silence met my words. I had their attention. Now I just had to hold It.

"Those of you who were part of the Three Rivers Pack, you will be banished from this territory. You will leave your families, your jobs, everything you've ever known behind. If you return, it will be a death sentence."

A female werewolf with long, dark hair and fierce brown eyes spoke up from the back of the room. "That's not fair! We were just following orders. We shouldn't be punished for that."

I fixed her with a steady gaze. "How can any of us trust you now?"

The woman glared at me, her jaw clenched tight. But she kept her eyes away from mine and said nothing. I let the silence stretch for a moment before I spoke again. "You have all made your choices. You and your families must face the consequences." I tilted my head to one side. "But there may be a chance for you yet."

I paused, letting my words sink in. I could see the confusion on their faces, the uncertainty in their eyes. They had expected judgement, punishment, not an offer of redemption.

"We're going to war tomorrow. Brock and his army want to destroy the Three Rivers. They're going to fight us on the banks of our home, on the banks of the Whispering Willow. If we lose, he will come here to the heart of our land and kill anyone he finds. I'm going to fight for our Pack, for our people. And I'm asking you to join me."

A murmur rippled through the room, a mix of surprise and disbelief.

"Why the fuck would we do that? You're asking us to be cannon fodder for your vendetta against Brock," the burly man said.

I wouldn't lie to them. "We're all going to be cannon fodder. Brock has more than two hundred men in his army. He wants vengeance against me and Ryan. He wants vengeance against this Pack. But there's a chance we'll win, and if we do, any of you who fight beside me will be accepted into the Three Rivers as Pack members."

I could see the wheels turning in their heads, the calculations being made. We were werewolves. The draw of a Pack was strong. We needed to belong, to be part of something bigger than ourselves. It kept us grounded. It kept us stable.

"And why should we trust you?" the burly guy asked, his eyes narrowed. "How do we know you won't just toss us aside when you're done with us?"

I met his gaze steadily. "Because I'm not Brock."

Ten minutes later, Jase and I left the warehouse. Forty-eight of them had agreed to fight for us.

Chapter Forty-Two

MAI

As Jase and I pulled up to the Alpha House, I noticed Thomas waiting for us outside, his face etched with concern. A knot of worry tightened in my stomach as I jumped out of the car.

"Is Jem okay?" I asked, my voice tight with fear.

Thomas held up his hands in a reassuring gesture. "Jem's fine. Well, physically, he's recovering remarkably quickly, faster than I expected. Mentally and emotionally, that's a different matter. It's going to take time."

I nodded, my heart aching for my brother.

Thomas shifted his weight. "But that's not why I'm here. I need to talk to you about Esme."

I frowned, surprised. "Has she been causing problems?"

Thomas shook his head. "No, it's not that. It's just...our house is not the right environment for her. She's struggling to control herself."

My frown deepened. "What do you mean? Did she hurt someone?"

"No, quite the opposite, actually. Even though I've told her to stop, she keeps trying to use her magic to heal my patients. She feels guilty about the damage she caused with the spell on the ripple pills, even though it wasn't her fault."

She was using magic? That was going to be a problem.

"It's taking a lot out of her," Thomas continued, his brow furrowed with concern. "She's exhausting herself, Mai. She needs rest, she needs to look after herself, but no matter what Wally or I say, she keeps pushing herself to the limit, healing patient after patient every time my back is turned."

I sighed, rubbing my temples. I could understand Esme's desire to help, to make amends. But Thomas was right. She needed to take care of herself, too.

"I've been able to keep it quiet for now," Thomas said, his voice low and urgent. "But it's only a matter of time before word gets out that there's a witch at my house, healing people."

"And then we'll have the Wolf Council to contend with."

"Yes," Thomas agreed.

I closed my eyes, feeling the weight of yet another problem settling on my shoulders.

Jase stepped forward. "Esme can stay with me and Sofia."

I raised my eyebrows at him. "Hadn't you better check with your sister first?"

Jase hesitated, then pulled out his phone, his thumb hovering over the screen. Before he could dial, Sofia walked out of the front door, her eyes fixed on her brother.

"Don't bother, Jase," she called out, her voice carrying across the lawn. "I already told Wally that Esme can stay with us."

Jase blinked, lowering his phone. "You did?"

A small smile tugged at the corners of her mouth. "We have the room and she needs to stay hidden until Mai and Ryan work out what to do with her."

Sofia always had my back, no matter what.

"Come on then, girl!" Sofia grinned at me. "We are having a par-tay!"

"A what now?"

"A par-tay!" Wally appeared behind her. "Everyone's been so caught up in doom and gloom lately that we are kicking back and having some fun."

I stared at them both. "The night before the biggest battle we've ever had? The one where we're fighting for the very existence of the Three Rivers? And you want to kick back and have some fun?"

"Oh, tosh!" Wally waved his hand dismissively. "We're always plunging into one emergency or another. It's time we had a break, had some fun."

I raised one eyebrow. "And Ryan agreed to this?"

"I don't think I was given the choice," Ryan said, walking out of the house and scanning me head to toe. Then he was there, scooping me up and holding me close. I breathed in the scent of him and closed my eyes briefly. My wolf chuffed in happiness. She didn't like to be apart from him.

"They railroaded you, huh?" I teased.

"There was no railroading," Sofia called over Ryan's shoulder. "He immediately saw what an awesome idea it was from the Pack's two geniuses."

"Genii," said Wally.

"What?"

"Genius plural, Einstein, is genii," he explained.

I ducked my head around Ryan to see Sofia frown at him.

"No, it isn't!"

"Er, yeah, it is!"

Ryan grinned down at me and whispered. "I figured everyone could use some down time. They've been working hard, and tomorrow..."

"Tomorrow we could all die," I whispered back.

"I heard that!" Wally cried. He came toward us both. "It is par-tay rules, and that means no more death talk!"

I grinned at him as Ryan took my hand and led me inside.

"So, did everything go okay?" he asked, and I knew he was dying to know what I'd been up to.

"Yes. We now have forty-eight more fighters for tomorrow."

Ryan's eyes widened, then narrowed as realization dawned. "Mai, you didn't?"

"I did. We need more fighters on our side. They need a Pack."

Ryan's jaw clenched. "We'll talk about this later," he said, and I knew he didn't want to argue with me in front of everyone.

I stood on my tiptoes and kissed the end of his nose. "It's okay. You can admit that I'm the number one genius in the Pack later."

He opened his mouth to reply, but his brothers walked into the house.

Sam, his usual easygoing grin back in place, slung an arm around Jase's shoulders. "Ready to party?"

Jase grinned back, his eyes sparkling with mischief. "Always."

I noticed Sam was still wincing slightly as he moved, but he was looking and moving a lot better.

"Sam, about the nomination—"

He held up a hand. "You are still my favorite Alpha, Mai. You'd have to really fuck up for Ryan to overtake you on that score. Besides, tonight is for revelry, not reflection."

"Hey!" Ryan said in mock outrage, but Sam just grinned back at him.

Sylvie emerged from the kitchen, wiping her hands on her apron.

"Mai! You're back! That means we can get started. I'm making a feast," she announced, her warm brown eyes surveying the room.

Sam's face lit up. "Sylvie, you're a Goddess among wolves," he declared, placing a hand over his heart. "What would we do without your culinary skills?"

"Starve, probably. I've tasted your cooking, remember?"

The room erupted in laughter, and I felt a warmth spread through my chest. Sam seemed almost back to his usual self.

As the laughter died down, I noticed Mason standing off to the side, a coin dancing across his knuckles as he stared into the distance. He seemed more agitated than usual, his brow furrowed and his jaw clenched.

I sidled up to him, nudging him gently with my elbow. "Everything okay?"

Mason blinked, as if snapping out of a trance. "Yeah, just...thinking."

I raised an eyebrow. "About Shya or the battle?"

He ducked his head. "Am I that obvious?"

"Only to those of us who know you well."

He sighed, pocketing the coin. "Well, enough of that for tonight. Tonight, we celebrate the Three Rivers and the best Alphas we've ever had."

"Alphas?" Ryan said, slipping his arm around my shoulders possessively. He hated any male wolves getting too close to me, even his brothers. "You mean *I'm* at the top of your list of favorite Alphas?" He shot a glare at Sam as he said this.

"Fuck no!" Mason laughed. "Mai will always be number one. You're a far distant second."

Derek and Sofia were standing in a corner, their voices low and tense. Sofia's face was flushed, her hands gesturing animatedly as she spoke. Derek's jaw was clenched, his arms crossed over his chest.

I leaned closer to Ryan. "Do you think those two will ever get out of each other's way and get together?"

"Only the Goddess could get those two together," he said, his eyes twinkling with amusement. "They're both too stubborn for their own good."

I sighed, watching Sofia storm away from Derek, her red curls bouncing with each angry step. "Maybe we should lock them in a room together until they sort it out."

Ryan raised an eyebrow. "It's definitely an idea. They'll either tear each other apart or fuck each other's brains out."

I honestly wasn't sure which one it would be.

As the sun began to set, everyone pitched in to move tables and chairs out to the front lawn. The Renegades opened the gates to the compound, the ones that would soon be torn down, and soon, people from all over the Three Rivers began to arrive, each carrying dishes of food and drinks to share.

Wally and Sofia had sent the message out and our people showed up.

The air was filled with the aroma of grilled meats, fresh bread, and sweet desserts. Laughter and chatter mingled with the clinking of glasses and the scraping of utensils against plates. Children, in human and wolf forms, ran between the tables, their faces smeared with barbecue sauce and ice cream.

I watched as Wally and Thomas sat together, their heads bent close as they whispered to each other, each of them touching the other one every now and again. Soft, little gestures; a hand placed on an arm, a finger tracing a jawline, knees close enough so they nudged. They looked so happy, so in love, and I was glad that they had found that here. In their previous Pack, they couldn't have shown physical affection for each other, not out in the open like this. Here they were safe and loved, and they could finally be who they were.

Ryan's arm slipped around my waist. "Well, what do you think? Is this what you envisioned for our Pack?"

I leaned into him, my heart swelling with love and pride. "Yes," I whispered, my eyes scanning the crowd of smiling faces. "This is exactly what I hoped we could build. This is what we'll be fighting for tomorrow."

Ryan pressed a kiss to my temple, his grip tightening around me. "Then we'll just have to win."

Chapter Forty-Three

MAI

I took Ryan's hand. "Come on, I want to show you something."

I led him down the garden and into the woods. I felt the cool breeze brushing against my skin, carrying with it the tantalizing scent of pine and earth. The moonlight filtered through the thick canopy above, casting a silvery glow over the forest floor as we made our way deeper into the woods.

As we walked, I could feel the tension between us building with each step, a simmering heat that seemed to ignite the very air around us. My skin prickled with anticipation, my heart pounding in my chest.

"You better be bringing me here to ravish me," Ryan teased.

I smiled and pulled off my top, dropping it to the ground as we walked. "You might just get your wish."

"Fuck it. Here, Mai." Ryan pulled me to a stop. "I need you. Now."

I glanced back at the way we'd come. "We're not far enough away yet. They'll hear."

He grinned wickedly at me. "You'll just have to be quiet, then."

Quiet? I was never quiet with Ryan.

"Um…"

"What? Big bad Alpha Mai, can't keep a few groans inside?"

Right. He wanted to play, I'd play.

"You know what? You're on. Think you're good enough to make me scream, Ryan Shaw?"

"Challenge accepted," he growled, as he closed the distance between us, capturing my lips in a searing kiss that spoke of urgent desire and need. His arms pulled me flush against his chest. The forest seemed to hold its breath around us.

He pushed me back until my back met the rough bark of a tree. The sensation sent a thrill through me, the contrast between the solid strength of the tree at my back and the heat of Ryan's lips on mine, driving me wild with need.

With a low growl that seemed to vibrate through my very bones, Ryan whipped my jeans off me and had my bra and panties off before I could blink. He lifted me effortlessly, my legs wrapping around his waist as he pressed me against the tree. I could feel the hardness of his erection through his jeans.

I bucked against him, desperate to feel the friction from his jeans against my clit. With a low groan, Ryan broke the kiss, his eyes dark with lust. "I need you," he whispered hoarsely, his voice thick with desire. "So fucking badly."

I returned his gaze. "Then take me," I dared, my voice barely audible over the wild pounding of my heart.

Ryan's eyes flared with raw desire as he lifted me higher, his lips finding mine once again in a desperate kiss. His hands worked quickly, undoing the buttons on his jeans. He wasn't wearing underwear. His cock, huge and glistening now it was free from the confines of his jeans, brushed against me, sending a new wave of need coursing through me. Impatient, wanting to feel him inside me, I guided him into me, feeling the rush of warmth and fullness as he entered me. I moaned into his mouth, the sound mingling with the rustling of the leaves and the soft hoot of an owl in the distance.

"What was that, Mai? Did you just make a sound? You're gonna have to try harder."

"Fuck you, Ryan Shaw."

He grinned at me. "That's the idea."

He slid out, then bucked into me in one smooth thrust. I could feel his cock everywhere, filling me up, stretching me deliciously. It was a primal, raw connection, and our bond reverberated with his smug satisfaction that he was fucking me. Ryan's hands gripped my butt, his thumbs tracing circles on the soft skin just above my hips. My nails dug into his shoulders as he drove into me again, and I whimpered. With each thrust, Ryan's hips ground against me, his erection hitting a sweet spot inside me that sent shockwaves through my entire body. I arched my back, pulling him deeper into me, wanting him to take me harder, faster. He obliged, his rhythm growing more urgent, our bodies slamming together with a primal abandon. With a low growl, Ryan's teeth nipped at the sensitive skin of my neck. His eyes were dark with desire, and I knew that he was lost in the moment just as much as I was. I could feel the fierce love that he had for me coursing through our bond, and I knew that no matter what happened tomorrow, we would always have this moment. I lifted my hips, meeting his every thrust with eager abandon. I bit my lip, trying to stop myself from crying out. His hips ground against me, the friction sending shivers of pure ecstasy down my spine. I was getting close now, the waves of pleasure crashing over me. I moaned loudly; I couldn't stop myself. What he was doing to me, what he was making me feel, overrode all my defenses. The feel of his thick cock pounding into me again and again had me squirming, desperate for more. I always wanted more of Ryan. I needed to feel his release inside of me. I could feel the tension building inside of me and the desperation in his kiss, the raw need that was tearing him apart. His hips moved faster, driving himself into me deeper. I couldn't take it anymore. I didn't care who heard me. I cried out and Ryan caught my lips once more, swallowing my cries as he continued to thrust into me. The smell of our sweat, the taste of our passion, the feel of his hands gripping my hips; it was all too much. I felt something change within me, my body tensing as the waves of pleasure crashed over me in one powerful storm. With one final, powerful thrust, Ryan let out a low, guttural growl, and I felt him explode inside of me. The sensation was intense, his hot, thick release filling me completely. I gasped, feeling myself shaking uncontrollably as another orgasm hit me. It was an indescribable feeling; knowing that Ryan, my mate, so fucking perfect, so fucking gorgeous, could do these things to me. I was helpless against him; and I knew I'd do anything to feel this way again.

"I won," Ryan panted. Then he grinned wickedly at me. "Round one, anyway."

Round one? *Oh my.*

Chapter Forty-Four

RYAN

A scent on the wind woke me. I didn't recognize it, couldn't place it but my wolf stirred. He wasn't uneasy, just curious. Mai's breaths were soft and even as she slept peacefully beside me. I carefully extricated myself from our bed on the leaves and moss, not wanting to disturb her. As I stood, I felt the familiar tingle beneath my skin, the wolf inside me yearning to be set free.

I stepped away, allowing the shift to overtake me. It started with a prickling sensation along my spine that quickly spread throughout my body. My muscles rippled and reformed, growing larger, more powerful. Fur sprouted from my skin, a thick, dark gray coat that would protect me from the chill of the night. My face elongated into a muzzle, my teeth sharpening into fangs. My senses heightened, the scents and sounds of the forest becoming impossibly clear.

I shook out my fur, loving the strength and power of this form. Then, with a last glance at Mai's sleeping form, I turned and bounded into the trees, my paws carrying me swiftly and silently through the undergrowth.

I followed a path that seemed to call to me, an ancient trail that wound through the heart of the forest. Before long, the crumbling ruins of the Dark Goddess's temple came into view, its weathered stones seeming to whisper secrets long forgotten.

I slowed; ears pricked for any signs of life. Silence. I lowered my nose to the ground, inhaling deeply, sorting through the myriad scents that painted a picture of the temple's recent history. The musty odor of ancient stone was overlaid with the fresher scents of the forest—the earthy aroma of soil, the sharp red of fallen leaves, the acrid tang of animal droppings. There were trails of different creatures—the light, quick-footed scent of rabbits, the deeper odor of a fox, the rich, loamy smell of a deer.

But as I traced these scent trails, I noticed an odd pattern; their paths rarely led them across the temple's boundaries. It was as if some unseen force was gently guiding them away, preventing them from venturing too close to the Dark Goddess's domain.

Intrigued, I padded closer. The scents here were older, more faded, as if few living things, except for those of us who were here the other night, had passed this way in a long time. A sense of anticipation grew within me, a prickling awareness that I was standing on the threshold of something ancient and powerful.

I stepped forward, and a tingling sensation washed over me. A pull on my human form.

Okay, then.

I focused, and the change began. Fur receded into skin, claws retracted into fingers, and my muzzle shortened into a human face. Within moments, I stood on two legs.

I made my way to the altar and brushed away the dead leaves, revealing the ancient stone beneath.

What the fuck did I do now?

How exactly did you go about summoning a Goddess? This hadn't been covered in any school I went to.

Mai's face flickered in my mind, her gentle smile, her kind eyes. She was my everything, and I was nearly bursting out of my skin with the need to protect her. We were facing threats from all sides, and I needed more power if I was going to keep her safe. I scanned the ground. My eyes fell on a sharp rock.

Had to be worth a try.

I picked it up and drew it across my forearm. Blood welled up from the cut, crimson and glistening in the moonlight. I held my arm over the altar, letting the blood drip onto the ancient stone.

For a long moment, nothing happened, the only sound the steady drip of my blood hitting the dusty altar. Then I felt a slight breeze on my naked skin. Leaves scattered across the temple floor. I turned, my blood leaving a dripping trail as I did so.

Nothing.

I felt a soft touch on my shoulder. I spun around, but there was no one there.

Fuck this.

"Enough games," I called out, my voice echoing off the crumbling walls.

A laugh rang out, musical and mocking. "But I love games," a voice purred, "especially with little wolves like you."

I turned back to the altar and found myself face to face with a woman. She was breathtakingly beautiful, with an air of timeless grace that seemed to defy any guess of her age. Her long, golden hair cascaded down her back in gentle waves, catching the moonlight with a glow of otherworldly radiance. Her skin was flawless, smooth and pale as marble, and her features were delicate and finely sculpted, like a masterpiece carved by an artist's hand. She was dressed in sleek black pants that clung to her long, slender legs, and a tight top that hugged her curves, revealing a figure that was both lithe and voluptuous. The fabric seemed to shimmer as she moved, as if woven from the very shadows themselves.

But it was her smile that truly captured my attention. It was mischievous, playful, with a hint of something darker lurking beneath the surface. Her lips were full and sensual, curved into a shape that promised both pleasure and danger.

There was no doubt in my mind who she was. The Dark Goddess. Power radiated from her, an almost tangible force filling the air around us. It was both alluring and intimidating, a reminder of the ancient, primal forces that she embodied.

She looked me up and down, her eyes lingering on my crotch. She raised an eyebrow suggestively. "Well, well," she murmured, "what do we have here?"

I resisted the urge to growl at her. "You're not my type."

"Really? You would say no to a Goddess?"

I held her stare. "I said, enough with the games."

"Pity," she sighed. "I do so love to play. The last one who came to me was much more fun. But, if not for games, then why have you come to my temple, little wolf?"

Okay, I had to get this right. There was no doubt in my mind that she could crush me like a gnat if I got it wrong here. "Your ways have been forgotten here," I swept my arm out, indicating the state of the place. "Your temple abandoned."

Her eyes flashed angrily. "These are things I know already. Are you here, Alpha of the Three Rivers Pack, to make amends? Will you offer yourself as sacrifice for the insults your ancestors gave to me?"

"No. I have come to, respectfully, ask for a gift," I said, my voice steady. "The gift of the True Werewolf form."

She laughed, a sound both beautiful and horrific. I resisted the urge to cover my ears. She circled around me, her fingers trailing across my shoulders. "A bold request," she mused. "And what would you do with such a gift, I wonder?"

I thought of Mai, of the dangers surrounding us, closing in, ready to strike. "Protect my mate," I said simply.

The Goddess came to a stop in front of me, her head tilted to one side. "And would you do anything to achieve this? Be careful of your answer, Alpha. The price of power is often higher than you think."

I met her gaze unflinchingly, my resolve unwavering. I was going with the assumption that the less you said to the Goddess the higher your survival rate.

The Goddess studied me for a long moment, her pale blue eyes searching mine. "I see. I need to hear you say it, my little wolf. You desire a power-upgrade? You wish to become more than you are, to surpass the limits of your kind."

"Yes. I do."

She clapped her hands together, a gleeful expression crossing her face. "Excellent! I do so love a man with ambition. But..." She wagged a finger at me, her tone turning sly, "what will you offer me in return? Your firstborn, perhaps?"

I couldn't stop the laugh that burst from my lips. It was a rough, humorless sound. "If you were truly a Goddess," I said, "you would know that there's no way I would ever agree to that. My children are mine."

The Goddess shrugged. "I am the Dark Goddess. I test my subjects, again and again. You'd be surprised how a little time, a small twist of events, can change someone's answers."

I raised an eyebrow, waiting for her to continue.

"Very well. No firstborn for me. Not yet, anyway," she said, her smile turning shrewd. "Another price then? One that I think you'll find more...palatable." She stepped closer to me, her scent enveloping me, a heady mix of night-blooming flowers and dark spices. "In exchange for the gift of the True Werewolf form, all children born to you will be dedicated to me. They must worship me, and me alone, forsaking all other goddesses."

I frowned, turning her words over in my mind. "I will not enforce this belief on them their whole lives," I said slowly, choosing my words with care. "But until they reach the age of eighteen, I will ensure they come to this temple and learn everything there is to know about you, about the ways of the Dark Goddess. This, I can promise."

The Goddess considered my words, her head tilted to one side. "Twice a week," she said finally. "Your children must come to my temple twice a week until they reach adulthood. Those are my terms."

I took a deep breath, then nodded once. "Agreed," I said, my voice firm.

The Goddess's smile was wide and triumphant. "Then we have a deal, Alpha," she purred.

She raised her hand, and I braced myself, unsure what to expect. Suddenly, an invisible force gripped me, and I felt as if my insides were being rearranged. It started as a deep, wrenching sensation in my gut, like a hand had reached inside me and was pulling everything out.

I doubled over, gasping for breath, as the feeling spread through my body. My bones seemed to liquefy and reform, stretching and elongating in ways that defied nature. My muscles burned as they expanded, growing larger and denser with each passing second. I could feel my skin stretching, straining to accommodate my new size.

The pain was unlike anything I had ever experienced. It felt as if I was being torn apart and put back together, every cell in my body rewritten by the Goddess's power. I wanted to scream, but my vocal cords were changing too, and all that came out was a strangled, inhuman sound.

It seemed to go on forever, an eternity of agony as my body reshaped itself. As suddenly as it had begun, the pain receded. I blinked, shaking my head, trying to clear my vision. Everything seemed different, sharper, more vivid. I could see details I had never noticed before, could hear the rustle of leaves at least a mile from the temple as if they were right next to me. I took a deep breath, and a thousand scents flooded my nostrils, painting a picture of the world around me.

I looked down at myself.

Holy shit!

I was massive, towering over the altar, my head nearly brushing the temple ceiling. Thick, dark fur covered my body, rippling over muscles that bulged with new strength. My claws, when I flexed them, were like daggers, sharp and deadly.

I had done it. I had become a True Werewolf, a being of legend and nightmare. Power thrummed through me, ancient and primal, begging to be unleashed.

Unable to contain myself, I threw back my head and howled, the sound echoing through the night like thunder. It was a sound of challenge, daring our enemies to come for us now.

The Dark Goddess watched me, her smile wide and satisfied. "Go, little wolf," she whispered, her voice seeming to come from everywhere and nowhere at once. "Go and show the world what you have become."

CHAPTER FORTY-FIVE

MAI

I stood beside Ryan at the front of our Pack, the cold wind whipping through my hair as I surveyed the east bank of the Whispering Willow. I glanced over my shoulder at the dense forest stretching out behind us, ancient trees reaching skyward, their branches swaying in the breeze. Between the forest and the river, our forces lined up in the open space, ready for battle.

Everyone in our Pack had shifted to their wolf forms, everyone except for me and Ryan. Wolves had the advantage on this terrain over our human forms. But as Alphas, Ryan and I could partially Shift, and that flexibility was our best weapon here. Brock wasn't an Alpha anymore, if he had ever been one. I still suspected the witch had transferred Jem's bond to Brock and make everyone, including Hayley, think that he was the Three Rivers Alpha.

Jem was here, against every recommendation from Thomas and orders from both me and Ryan. Jem pointed out that technically he was a rogue wolf now; he'd been kicked out as Alpha when me and Ryan took over, and given he had yet to accept us as his Alphas, he could do what the fuck he liked, as he so carefully put it. He was physically weak, his wolf was still asleep, and we couldn't risk attempting to wake him up in case his wolf came after me again. But he was here, he needed to be part of this, to get revenge for Hayley. I hoped, if he survived, if any of us survived, that this would be the first step in his recovery. He needed to feel that he had done something, had tried to get justice.

Our Pack had been divided into units of twenty, each led by one or two Renegades. The Shaw brothers, as our best fighters, would act as roaming agents, going where fighting was fiercest. Sofia and Jase had been added to the unit closest to me and Ryan, their wolves a similar maroon color. As I'd been getting ready this morning, I'd overheard Ryan tell Jase that his only job today was to protect me and watch my back. It rankled; I should be protecting Jase not the other way round, but I knew there was no point arguing with Ryan about this, and if it meant he didn't have to worry so much about me and could concentrate on the fight then it was a small price to pay. We'd discussed bringing in Talia, but it was too big of a risk. We both suspected that Brock had been trying to warn us off Talia by making us suspicious of her. It worked. We didn't know who to trust on the Wolf Council and until we did, we decided not to get Talia involved. We would have to win this one on our own.

Derek's wolf was pacing restlessly, refusing to stray far from Sofia. He kept circling back to her side, his hackles raised, his eyes alert. To our left, Ronnie and his men, about forty of them, stood armed with knives, their faces grim and determined. They had wanted to bring guns, but Ryan had vetoed that idea. In close quarters, the risk of friendly fire was too high.

The rogue wolves I'd recruited had been integrated into our other units, scattered throughout the formation. We couldn't afford to trust them with their own command, not yet.

Across the river, on the east bank, Brock stood at the head of his army. There was a mix of forms—about half in wolf form, half in human. The forest behind them mirrored our own, though their side had younger trees and dense underbrush providing plenty of cover for hidden reserves.

We'd stationed a couple of units in the woods behind us. They were there not just as backups, surprise additional units to charge into the fray if things looked bad for our side; they were there to guard against any from Brock's side trying to sneak up and attack us from behind. Thomas was waiting there too, with Amara, so they could provide medical care. Thomas hated fighting, despaired at all of us for resorting to violence, but he needed to be here, near Wally.

Just as we had forces hidden in the forest behind us, I had no doubt that Brock had extra units lying in wait, ready to strike from the shadows behind him.

I looked out across the river, my eyes locking with Brock's. Even from this distance, I could feel the intensity of his gaze, the raw hatred that seemed to emanate from his every pore.

My stomach churned, and I felt real fear about what was to come. Despite the addition of the rogue wolves to our ranks, we were still vastly outnumbered. I estimated that Brock's forces were at least twice the size of ours.

If he didn't come to us, we would need to cross the river to reach Brock, exposing ourselves to attack as we emerged from the water. The bank opposite would quickly get churned up and muddy, slowing us down. Our Pack would be picked off one by one as they struggled to gain a footing on the opposite bank.

Ryan was beside me, his body tense and coiled like a spring. He looked out over the river, surveying the army opposite. "You know, if you can't handle this, you can head back to town, oversee the evacuation if it's needed. You don't need to get your precious hands dirty in this."

Anger bubbled up, and I slowly turned my head to stare at him.

"You can be a condescending prick sometimes, you know that?"

"That's better," he said, a hint of satisfaction in his voice. "Anger is good. You're going to need it today, along with the fear. Use them both, let them fuel you."

He'd wanted a rise out of me, wanted me to feel the anger so I wouldn't feel so scared. I loved him for it, but still. "Like I said, a condescending prick."

Ryan gave me a grim smile, then turned his attention back to the opposite bank. The wind had picked up, carrying with it the scent of rain and the promise of a storm.

Brock strode forward to the edge of the river, his sandy hair tousled by the breeze. I could see the smug expression on his face, the confidence in his stride, and I felt that familiar urge of wanting to punch it right out of him.

"I'm glad you came," he called out, his voice carrying across the rushing water. "I'm going to enjoy watching you die."

Beside me, Ryan remained silent, his eyes fixed solely on Brock. He was in hunting mode and had got a fix on his prey.

Brock laughed. "So be it, then. I'll make sure your deaths are not easy."

Ryan tilted his head to one side until it cracked. Then he tilted his head to the other side, like he was warming up.

"I forgot to tell you, baby," Ryan winked at me. "I learned a new trick." Then, Ryan's body seemed to explode outward, muscles rippling and bulging beneath his skin as he shot upward, growing taller and broader with each passing instant. A colossal monster burst forth, and in a matter of seconds, Ryan towered above me, standing at least nine feet tall. He was a true werewolf, a massive creature that walked on two legs but was unmistakably beast, with a body covered in thick, dark fur, and the head of an enormous wolf.

Fuck me!

Ryan had learned the true werewolf form. He threw back his head and howled, the sound echoing through the forest and across the river. It was a primal, bone-chilling cry that seemed to shake the very earth beneath our feet. Men on the other side of the river cringed, as did a few on this side. My wolf chuffed in satisfaction inside of me.

Mine, she said.

Yes, ours.

As Ryan's howl faded into the wind, Brock stepped back from the riverbank, a smirk playing across his face. He signaled to his right. I glanced across as a unit of about forty, all in human form, moved. Those on the front line pulled back, letting those behind them come forward. They were carrying something, though. My blood ran cold as I saw what it was. Machine guns. Six of them.

Time slowed down as I realized what was about to happen. There was no way they were not loaded with silver bullets. I had a second to think *We're dead*, and then they opened fire.

Beside me, Ryan moved with lightning speed, throwing himself in front of me. I caught a glimpse of Derek sprinting towards Sofia. I knew it was too late, though. We were all about to die. I had failed them, my family, my friends, my Pack. As Alpha, I had led them here to be slaughtered. I wrapped my arms around Ryan. At least we would die together.

The sound of gunfire was deafening, a relentless barrage that seemed to go on forever. I braced myself for the impact, for the searing pain of bullets tearing through flesh and bone. But it never came.

I lifted my head and peeked round Ryan's chest. The bullets were hitting an invisible barrier a few feet in front of our front line, stopping dead in their tracks and falling harmlessly to the ground. I stared in disbelief, my mind racing to understand what was happening.

Someone had to be doing this. That's when I saw her, Esme, standing rigid on the far left of our formation, her arms outstretched and her face contorted with effort. Sweat poured down her brow. What the hell was she doing here? She was supposed to be back in Three Rivers, safe in Sofia's apartment.

Her strained voice whispered in my mind. "I can't hold it for long."

I didn't have time to think about how she was talking in my head; I just knew that we had to kill the gunners before Esme lost control of the spell.

I didn't hesitate.

"Jase! Guard Esme with your life!" I yelled as I ducked round Ryan and sprinted for the river, my legs pumping faster than they ever had before. Despite the roar of the gunfire, my mind was clear, my vision sharp. I had locked on to the gunners. They were my prey now, and it was us or them.

Ryan must have worked it out too; he overtook me in a blur of motion. I watched as Ryan leaped, his powerful leg muscles propelling him forward with incredible force. He soared over the river, his massive form seeming to hang suspended in the air for an impossibly long moment. The sight of him, a true werewolf in all his fearsome glory, was both terrifying and awe-inspiring.

He landed on the other side of the river, and even the ground on this side shook. He let out a roar that echoed through the forest, a sound that was both a challenge and a declaration of his dominance.

I hit the river a moment later. There was no way I could make that jump; I dove into the water, the icy chill shocking the breath from my lungs. I heard the splash of my Pack following close behind me.

My muscles burned with the effort, but I pushed through the pain. All that mattered was stopping those gunners.

I climbed out of the river, water dripping from my clothes as I scrambled up the bank. Ahead of me, I saw Ryan making a path through Brock's army, his massive form cleaving through their ranks like a hot knife through butter. Bodies flew through the air as he tossed them aside, his claws and teeth ripping into anyone who dared to stand in his way.

It was clear that Brock's army had not been prepared for Ryan's attack, or for the sheer power and ferocity of his werewolf form. They had thought that the guns would be enough to kill us all, and that had given us a small but crucial element of surprise.

I had only a moment to take in the scene before I was charged by ten wolves, their teeth bared. I braced myself for the impact, knowing that in my human form, I stood little chance against them, but I'd fight every last fucking one of them to get to those gunners and protect my Pack.

Just as one of the wolves leaped towards me, a blur of motion intercepted it in midair. Mason, in his wolf form, slammed into the side of the attacker, throwing the two of them to the side, locked in a whirlwind of snapping teeth and slashing claws.

From my left, Derek and Sam flooded past me, interrupting the oncoming wolves.

I sprinted after Ryan, following the path of destruction he had left in his wake. On either side of me, more wolves from our Pack flanked me, Ava and Raphael in the lead.

As we ran, enemy wolves and humans tried to attack us from all sides. But wolves from my Pack veered off each time to intercept them.

I could feel the adrenaline pumping through my veins, the thrill of the fight singing in my blood. Even in my human form, I felt a connection to my wolf, to the primal power and instinct that flowed through us both.

As I reached the gunner station, the scene before me was one of utter carnage. Dead bodies littered the ground. Some of the remaining gunners were still firing their weapons, but the bullets stopped just a few inches from the end of the barrel, falling to the ground. How was she doing this?

As if in answer, Esme's voice whispered in my mind once more.

"Hurry, Mai. The weight is too much, too strong. I won't last long now."

As I watched, one of the gunners swung his machine gun towards Ryan, desperate to take him down. Without thinking, I leaped and swung my arm. Claws erupted from my fingers just as I found the man's throat and I tore it out in a spray of blood.

Out of the corner of my eye, I saw a barrel swing toward me. I took two steps forward, then leaped, spinning in the air above the gunner, and landing on his back. I'd snapped his head before he hit the ground.

I looked round to see the last of the gunners fall under Sam's claws. We'd done it. Ryan was already moving among the fallen weapons, systematically bending and snapping the barrels to make they could never be used against us again.

As I turned to survey the rest of the battlefield, my eyes locked with Brock's across the open space on the west bank. Even from this distance, I could see the fury etched into every line of his face, the hatred that burned in his eyes.

Then Brock Shifted. From one blink to the next, he changed from a human to a massive creature that stood eight feet tall. He was stockier and bulkier than Ryan's werewolf form, a writhing mass of muscles and strength. It was a killing machine, designed for one purpose only: to destroy. His army turned and looked at him, all of them waiting for his signal.

"Fuck!"

In that moment, I realized two things: that Ryan wasn't the only one who'd learned a new trick; and that the army that Brock had brought with him was not just a collection of individual fighters, it was his Pack. He had melded the rogue werewolves he had picked up along the way into a true Pack. With Brock as their Alpha.

With a roar of rage, Brock pointed at Ryan and me, a command his Pack could not ignore.

As one, they turned and charged towards us.

Chapter Forty-Six

Mai

I didn't feel scared anymore. This was it. This was the moment I'd been waiting for, the chance to finally face Brock and make him pay.

Images flashed through my mind—Arabella, rail-thin, strapped to a hospital bed, straining against her bonds; Noreen, her sister, quietly weeping; Jem, a shadow of his former self, sobbing over his lost mate; Brock landing a roundhouse kick on Ryan's head. The pain he'd inflicted on my Pack, on the people I loved most in this world; and his twisted vision for the future of all werewolves, with himself as the Wolf King, ruling over us all.

My body thrummed with anticipation, every muscle coiled and ready to strike. Inside me, my wolf was snarling with a fierce, primal rage. She wanted Brock dead, and so did I. We were in perfect agreement, united in our thirst for vengeance and our determination to protect our mate and our Pack at all costs.

Ryan was at my side, and our bond exploded, a searing, white-hot connection that seemed to set my very soul ablaze. My Pack bonds followed; a web of connections that stretched out from me in every direction, linking me to each and every one of my Pack. I could feel their presence, their strength and their courage, their fears, flowing through me like an electric current. We were one, a single entity bound together by love and loyalty, by the unbreakable ties of family and Pack. It was like nothing I had ever experienced before, a sensation of pure power and unity that left me breathless.

I didn't need to say a word, didn't need to give any commands out loud. Instead, I reached out with my mind, urging my Pack forward with a silent, irresistible call. As one, they responded, each of us taking that first step together. Then another until we were sprinting towards Brock's Pack.

This fight was no longer about us and Brock, about our personal vendettas and the history between us. This was a war between two Packs, a battle for dominance and survival that would determine the fate of us all.

Ryan and I hit the front lines of Brock's army like a hammer, our speed and ferocity catching them off guard. Without a thought, I surrendered to the rage. Adrenaline surged through my body, heightening my awareness of every movement on the battlefield. Beside me, Ryan towered over the battlefield in his true werewolf form, his massive frame rippling with muscle and raw power.

I lost myself in the rhythm of the fight, my body moving on pure instinct as I ducked and weaved, my claws finding flesh and bone with each lightning-fast strike. A coppery taste of blood filled my mouth, and I spat it out, never breaking my stride. The scent of blood and fear hung heavy in the air, mingling with the odor of wet fur and sweat, of Pack, and enemies to slay.

There was no room for mercy or hesitation here—every blow was struck with lethal intent, every move calculated to kill.

To my left, Ryan was a force of nature, his massive claws and teeth rending through the enemy ranks. It was so graceful, almost like a dance, his movements precise and deadly, a blur of speed and power.

I caught a glimpse of Jem through the chaos, standing tall in the sea of battle. He was holding his own, his body a whirlwind as he went for those in Brock's Pack that were still in human form.

I saw a flash of movement to my side and whirled just in time to avoid the snapping jaws of a massive black wolf. It lunged again, but I sidestepped and raked my claws across its flank, feeling the hot spray of blood on my face.

The wolf yelped in pain and fury, its eyes blazing with rage as it circled back for another attack. But before it could strike, Ryan was there, his massive jaws clamping down on the wolf's neck with a sickening crunch.

I had no time to catch my breath, no time to process the carnage around me. The enemy just kept coming, wave after wave of them, each more desperate and ferocious than the last.

Ryan and I fought our way, slowly, one wolf at a time, through the seething mass of enemies, our bond guiding us to work together. I could feel Ryan's presence in my mind, a constant, reassuring thread that kept me focused and centered amidst the chaos.

As a pair of wolves charged towards me, their jaws snapping and their eyes wild with bloodlust, I felt a sudden, urgent tug on our bond. Without thinking, I dropped to the ground, rolling to the side just as Ryan leaped over me, his massive frame slamming into the wolves with bone-crushing force.

I sprang back to my feet, my claws flashing as I slashed at another wolf that had tried to take advantage of my momentary distraction. The wolf howled in pain, staggering back with blood streaming from a deep gash across its muzzle.

The wolves fell before us like wheat before the scythe, their bodies broken and bleeding as we pressed our advantage. Through it all, our bond sang with a fierce, exultant joy, a connection that went beyond mere words or thoughts.

We moved unrelentingly towards our ultimate target—Brock. Time stopped, everything narrowed down to the next punch, the next neck to snap, the next ribs to break. And then, suddenly, there he was—Brock, towering over the battlefield in his true werewolf form, his eyes blazing with a hatred that was matched by mine. Ryan let out a roar of challenge and surged forward. Their bodies collided in a clash of titans, shaking the earth beneath our feet.

For a moment, I could do nothing but watch in awe as the two giants battled, their massive forms rolling and tumbling over the smaller wolves and humans caught in their path. This was a fight that was spoken of only in legends, a primal struggle for dominance and control.

But I didn't have time to gawk. With a feral snarl, I darted in, my claws flashing as I slashed at Brock's flanks and back.

Brock roared in pain and fury, his head whipping around to snap at me, but I was too fast, dancing out of reach and circling back for another strike. Ryan pressed his advantage, his claws raking deep gouges across Brock's chest and belly.

Back and forth we fought, Ryan and I moving in perfect synch, our bond singing with a fierce, savage joy. We were a team, unstoppable and unbeatable, and Brock was starting to falter beneath our relentless assault.

With a roar of pure rage, Brock slammed into Ryan with the force of a freight train. Ryan staggered back, his claws scrabbling for purchase on the blood-slick ground as he tried to regain his balance.

I leaped, landing on Brock's back. He twisted, his jaws clamped down on my shoulder, his fangs sinking deep into my flesh and grazing bone. I screamed in pain, my vision going white as agony lanced through my body.

Dimly, I heard Ryan's roar of fury as he crashed into us. Brock was ready for him, his claws slashing out in a blur of speed and power. I felt a hot flash of pain through our bond, and the scent of Ryan's blood filled the air.

A flicker of fear tickled me, a cold, creeping dread that threatened to extinguish the flames of my rage.

No! My wolf howled inside of me.

I wrenched myself free from Brock's jaws, ignoring the searing pain in my shoulder as I lunged forward, my claws slashing at his eyes and muzzle. Beside me, Ryan surged to his feet, his own claws and fangs flashing as he launched himself at Brock's flank.

Brock roared, twisting and thrashing, as he tried to shake us off. I hung on for a moment, before he reached round, grabbed me and threw me off. I flew to the side, soaring over two wolves scrapping below. They looked as shocked as me to see me fly over them. I landed hard, knocking the air out of me.

Fuck, that hurt!

Up. I had to get up. Pushing myself up on one hand, I saw Ryan's claws rake deep gouges across Brock's chest, but Brock retaliated with a savage swipe that sent Ryan twisting back, blood pouring from a gash above his eye.

I staggered to my feet, ignoring the pain that lanced through my shoulder and the dizziness that threatened to overwhelm me. I had to help Ryan, had to find some way to turn the tide of this battle before it was too late.

Ryan kicked out, his foot smacking into Brock's chest. Brock flew back, rolled and came up snarling. He looked from Ryan to me, and I could see his calculation. I was closer. In this form, I was weaker. With me dead, he could pick Ryan off in his own time. Brock bounded toward me. Out of the corner of my eye, I saw Ryan sprinting for me. He wouldn't get here in time.

That was okay. Brock was owed some time with my fists.

I snarled and ran to meet Brock. Just before he barreled into me, Ryan's arm snaked around my waist, swinging me out of Brock's way. I felt a rush of hot air as Brock's jaws snapped shut inches from my face. Then Jem dashed past me. I caught a glimpse of his face contorted in a mask of pure rage as he rammed into Brock.

I watched in horror as Jem drove Brock to the ground, straddled his chest, his fists slamming into Brock's face with a sickening, meaty thud. Jem grabbed Brock's head and slammed it against the ground again and again, until his skull cracked, and his eyes rolled back in his head. Even then, Jem didn't stop. Just kept smashing Brock's head into the ground until it was unrecognizable, just a pile of meat, brains, and bits of skull.

Beside me, Ryan started to laugh, a deep, booming sound that echoed across the battlefield. I looked at him in shock, but he just grinned at me, his eyes sparkling with a fierce, savage joy.

CHAPTER FORTY-SEVEN

MAI

I watched as Ryan hefted another lifeless body onto the growing pile, his face grim and streaked with blood and sweat. He had Shifted back to his human form. He was topless, but had found some black joggers from somewhere. The stench of death hung over everything, mingling with the acrid tang of smoke from the burning pyres that dotted the battlefield.

Nearby, Thomas kneeled beside Raphael's body, his fingers pressed against the fallen werewolf's neck. After a moment, he shook his head and sat back on his heels, his shoulders slumped in defeat.

My shoulder had stopped bleeding, but it hurt like hell, and I was having difficulty moving my arm. Ryan had picked me up and ran all the way to Thomas when he saw it. I'd have to do a few Shifts to kick-start the healing process, and then we'd see if I would get full movement back. Not yet though. I was too tired to Shift. I felt numb, my mind reeling from the sheer scale of the carnage that surrounded us. So much death, so much senseless slaughter, all because of one man's twisted ambition and lust for power. Fury coiled in my gut like a serpent, hot and venomous. If I could have, I would have brought Brock back to life just to kill him all over again.

Jem had pummeled Brock for at least ten minutes. None of us wanted to stop him. Jem eventually wore himself out and collapsed next to Brock's mangled body. He passed out with a look of satisfaction on his face. After that, the battle had been all but over. The few remaining members of Brock's Pack were rounded up and sat in a huddle next to the tree line. We had won. But the cost had been high. Ava, still in wolf form, stood over Rapheal's body and howled. A haunting sound, full of grief and sadness.

At my current count, we had lost eight Renegades and fifteen werewolves. I had to keep telling myself that it could have been so much worse. Among the survivors, they were some serious injuries, but I was hopeful most would recover in time. We were a resilient species, after all.

I couldn't wait any longer. I pulled on the mate bond. Ryan turned, his eyes homing in on me immediately. I jerked my head and set off, knowing he'd follow.

I went upstream, walking along the river until I knew we'd be out of earshot. There was a large, flat rock ahead, set on an incline, and as soon as Ryan stepped onto it, I spun, kicking out at just the right moment to hit his head. He batted my foot away.

I don't think so, baby.

I snapped my leg up, going for his head once again.

He leaned back, and my foot passed an inch from his nose.

"Mai, what the—"

I drove forward, kicking out again and again.

"Mai!"

I didn't stop; hook kicks, side kicks, axe kicks, I kept going.

A green sheen slid over his eyes, and he stepped into my next kick, grabbed me round my waist and hoisted me up.

"What the actual fuck?" he growled.

I hooked my legs round the back of his neck and threw myself backwards and down. My hands hit the ground, and the momentum flipped Ryan over me. He sailed a good ten feet and, like a ninja, landed in a crouch.

"Mai!"

"What the hell were you thinking?" I shouted. I was so freaking angry with him right now I thought my head would explode. "You made a deal with the Dark Goddess!"

His face went blank and guarded.

"Did you not listen to Camille's story? Nothing good ever comes from making deals with a Goddess!"

"I knew the risks. This was more important."

"What were the terms?" I was so scared right now, I could feel my hair standing on end. What had he given up for this ability? What if we couldn't meet her terms? Would she enact her revenge on him in the same way as she had done with the Lunar Guardians? Was he going to be taken away from me? I knew without a shred of doubt in my body that I would never abandon Ryan, no matter what some Goddess decreed.

"Any children we may have will be dedicated to her. Until they are of age, we will take them to her temple twice a week and teach them about her."

I blinked, turning his words over in my mind. Goddesses never did anything lightly, and never agreed to anything that wasn't in their own interests. Why did she need our children? Was it just about rebuilding her temple and our worship of her? Having the Alpha's children regularly going there would draw other members of the Pack.

"You want children?" I held my breath as I suddenly realized just how much his answer meant to me.

His eyes pinned me in place. The whole world had just disappeared for him and I was the only thing in it.

"Mini-Mai's running around? Fuck, yeah, I want your kids."

I let out the breath as his words sunk into me. Ryan wanted children. Our children. Well, that would be a new fucking adventure.

"Then why? Why would you do this? Explain it to me." I demanded.

He took two steps toward me, but I held up a hand, keeping him back. I wasn't sure I would be able to keep from kicking him again if he got any nearer.

"Why? Why the fuck do you think? I needed a power upgrade. You have a knack for making enemies, Mai."

I recoiled. "Do you really think of me as so feeble and weak that you had to resort to this?"

He strode forward. I backed up, but he didn't touch me. He stopped a foot from me, close enough for me to reach out and smack him if I wanted to.

"It's not you, Mai! Can't you see that?" his voice was low and ragged. "You are magnificent. I wish you could see yourself the way I see you. You're beautiful, strong, a warrior on the field, and you are the best fucking Alpha this Pack has ever had. But I'm an Alpha werewolf. You're mine to protect, and I will do anything to make sure you're safe. This isn't the end of it. Killing Brock didn't change the fact that we're

Alphas now. We might have delayed ripple in the north but it's still here, they'll be looking at ways to pour it into our communities, and then there's the fact that there's someone on the Wolf Council who will be coming after us for fucking with their plans. The thought of losing you scares me shitless, Mai. I've never felt like this. I'm on edge all the time. I need to know that you're safe and I can protect you. With this upgrade, I can do that. Without it, eventually I would have locked you in a marshmallow room. And if I did that, I'd lose you all the same." He slid one arm around my waist, while his hand cupped the back of my head, holding me still. I was trapped. I couldn't move, but right now I didn't want to. I just wanted to understand.

"I can't lose you, Mai. I know you'll leave me if I wrap you in cotton wool, but I can't help it. My wolf and me, we need you to be safe." He stared into my eyes and looked so vulnerable at that moment. Through our bond, I could feel his raw fear, his desperation to do anything to keep from losing me.

"And you think, what? Being able to Shift into the True Werewolf form means I'm somehow safer now?"

"Did you not see the size of me? This form is built to be a killing machine. It'll be easier to protect you when I'm twice the size of anyone else."

"Ryan—"

"I'm not a fool, Mai. I know if the Goddess made this deal with me and Brock, she's just getting started. She had her own agenda and will probably gift this to others. But I have a head start. I'm going to exploit every opportunity I can find. I'll going to mold our Pack into an army that will take down any threats. We'll be able to take on the fucking Wolf Council if we have to."

Oh, the big furry idiot.

"I love you, Ryan Shaw. I'm not going anywhere. It doesn't matter what stupid things you do—and this one is definitely up there with rejecting me in the first place—I'm always going to be here. You lock me in a marshmallow room, I'll kick the door down, and we'll have words, but I'm not ever going to leave you."

His head drew back, and his eyes searched my face. "You're not?"

I gripped his head between my hands, pulling his face closer. "No," I said fiercely. "You're mine, Ryan. All mine. Noone else can have you. Not even the fucking Goddess."

A goofy grin spread across his face. "I'm yours?"

"You really are dense sometimes, you know that? Search our bond, Ryan. I could never leave you. You're my mate, my best friend, you're mine. For now and always."

His lips crashed into mine. They were almost feverishly hot and demanding. I opened my mouth, letting him in, and his tongue igniting a blaze within me. He effortlessly picked me up, my legs wrapping around him, his long, hard length pressing in just the right spot.

"I'm going to fuck you now," he growled. "I'm going to fuck my mate until you can't walk straight, and you still feel me inside for the next week."

Er, yum! Yes, please!

Ryan unbuttoned my jeans with a deft hand, each movement swift and purposeful, as if he couldn't wait one more moment to claim me. He stripped me off without putting me down, his hands roaming my body with a fierce possessiveness that left me both breathless and unafraid. I was naked in his arms, and it was the most powerful I had ever felt. He had claimed me, and I had claimed him, and nothing in this world could ever change that.

Ryan gripped my hips, lifting me higher as he shimmied out of his trousers. Then there was nothing between us. There was no foreplay, no soft caresses. His cock was at my entrance for only a second, then he thrust into me, hard and uncompromising, and I fucking loved it. This was us; raw, desperate, and utterly bonded to each other.

I needed this. I needed him to own me completely. His eyes went dark with intensity and lust. My head fell back, my back arching as he drove deep inside me, each stroke rough and demanding, fueled by our urgent desire. My nails dug into his shoulders as he held me up, rocking into me, his thrusts precise and unrelenting. I was helpless in his arms. He held me in place as he fucked me so thoroughly that I knew his predication was right; I was going to still feel him inside for the next week.

Our bond, already so powerful, seemed to intensify with each surge of his hips. A loop of emotions and feelings bouncing from him to me and back again. This was more than sex; it was a union of two souls, bound together in a way that defied explanation.

My inner walls clenched around him. His eyes blazed with desire, and he drove into me again and again with a fierce urgency that made me cry out. I couldn't take it anymore; I writhed against him, every inch of my body alive with need. Each thrust of his hips was a claim, a promise, a declaration of love and possession. I could feel his cock throbbing inside me, and the friction was so intense and exhilarating that I knew I was going to orgasm soon.

I whimpered softly, my body so close to the edge, the heat building within me. Ryan's hot breath washed over my ear as he spoke. "You're going to scream my name, Mai."

I gasped, the words sending a fiery jolt through my core. His hands gripped my hips tighter, holding me still as he continued to thrust. I could feel him swelling, the anticipation of our release building. Every nerve ending in my body was alight with desire.

Then, just when I thought I couldn't take any more, Ryan's hips drove harder, faster, and I exploded around him.

"Ryan!" I screamed his name, the sound echoing against the rocks as my body shook with the force of my orgasm. He came a second later, his release exploding inside me like a flash flood. My inner muscles clenched around him, milking him, pulling him in deeper.

"Mine," I said, claiming him again. "For now, and always."

His eyes flared with passion, and he looked at me, his expression so fierce, so animalistic, that I couldn't believe he was all mine. Then he smirked, all self-satisfied and cocky.

"No one but you, Mai," he drawled, his voice low and rough. "There is no one but you."

Chapter Forty-Eight

MAI

Ryan and I took our time walking back to the others, but we got there just in time to see a group of newcomers striding towards us, their faces hard and their eyes cold.

At their head was Talia, looking as regal and imperious as ever. She had arrived with impeccable timing with a contingent of Wolf Council enforcers, their clean black uniforms and wolf pins marking them out as the elite force.

I had never seen Council enforcers in action before, but I had heard plenty of stories. They were ruthless, dangerous as hell, and highly secretive. The kind of werewolves you called in when you expected serious trouble, and needed it quashed quickly and brutally.

Talia barely spared me a glance as she strode past, her gaze sweeping over the scene with a calculating intensity. She barked out orders to her enforcers, her voice sharp and commanding.

"Secure any survivors," she snapped. "I want them alive for questioning."

The enforcers nodded and fanned out toward the group from Brock's Pack. I watched them go as Talia turned her attention to me. Her eyes narrowed as she strode over.

"Why wasn't I informed about this?" she demanded.

I felt so fucking tired. I just wanted to bury our dead, go home and curl up in bed with Ryan holding me. I was still covered in blood and mud. My shoulder was a sharp pain stabbing at me in time with my heartbeat, and here was Talia Fucking Johnson, with her perfect hair, and clean suit, demanding answers. I met her gaze unflinchingly. "Brock suggested that you were working for him, keeping his role hidden from the Council. We couldn't be sure whose side you were on."

Talia scoffed, her lip curling in disdain. "And you believed him? Brock was manipulating you, trying to keep me and my enforcers away from him. Did you think of that? That maybe he was scared of what we can do. If you had told me, maybe I could have prevented all this." Her arm swept out, taking in all the carnage before us.

"We considered that possibility. But given your history with us, Talia Johnson, Ryan and I decided it was a risk we couldn't take."

Talia's eyes flashed, and for a moment, I caught a glimpse beneath her usual calm, controlled exterior. Oh, I had pissed her off.

"If we did believe Brock, even for a moment, it's your own damn fault. The way you treat people, the way you manipulate and scheme and lie...can you really blame us for not trusting you?"

"You dare question my loyalty?" I could feel the power radiating off her, the usually contained fury that was leaking out.

But I refused to back down. I had faced far worse than Talia Fucking Johnson in the last month, and I wasn't about to start cowering now.

"You brought this on yourself," I said softly. "You've made enemies of everyone around you, burned every bridge and alienated every ally. You left yourself open to suspicion."

Talia opened her mouth to reply, but before she could say anything, one of her enforcers came running up to us, his face tense with urgency.

"Bethany found something. You need to come quick."

"This conversation is not over," Talia shot me a final glare before turning to follow her enforcer. I went after them; whatever they'd found was unlikely to be good for my Pack. There, at the tree line, two more Council enforcers were standing in front of a familiar figure. Esme.

Shit!

Jase stood between the enforcers and Esme, a determined set to his jaw. Talia strode forward, had a murmured conversation with one of the enforcers, and then turned to Jase.

"Get out of the way," she ordered. It was the tone of voice of someone that knew without a doubt that she would be obeyed.

Jase stood his ground. "No."

Well, fuck me over with a feather! Little Jase Miller just stood up to the fucking Wolf Council. I couldn't decide if he had just morphed into the badass enforcer he always wanted to be or was just insanely stupid. Either way, I had to stop this now.

I could sense Ryan behind me. He didn't say anything, though; he was letting me handle this.

Esme put her hand on Jase's arm and said softly, "It's okay, Jase. I can go with the bird people."

Bird people? What was she talking about now?

I pushed past the enforcers and came to stand beside Jase.

"What's going on?" I demanded.

Talia turned to me. "You brought a witch here, Mai Parker? You let her do magic in these lands?"

I frowned. "I think that's unlikely. We all know the laws about witches."

I was treading a fine line, trying to make sure that I didn't outright lie.

"Mai Parker, this is Bethany Rose," Talia gestured to one of the enforcers standing beside her. I took a closer look and realized that this enforcer was different from the others.

The rest were all the epitome of werewolf warriors—tall, muscular, all radiating an aura of contained aggression. But Bethany...she was something else entirely. Her bone structure was delicate, almost fragile looking, so different to the solid, imposing frames of her fellow enforcers. She radiated a kind of eerie calm. It was unsettling, like the stillness before a storm. I couldn't quite put my finger on it, but there was something about her that made the hairs on the back of my neck stand up.

"Bethany is a very special werewolf," Talia continued. "Her sense of smell is exceptional. She has been trained to scent out witches and magic, and she says that this whole area stinks of it. Especially her." She nodded at Esme.

Damn it. There goes my plan try to bluff our way out of this.

"Yes," Esme whispered. "Yes, I know you, Bethany Rose."

Bethany frowned, her piercing gray eyes focused on Esme. "I have never met you before."

"Yes, not met, but I know you."

I stepped forward, making sure to place myself between Esme and Talia. "Talia Johnson, this is Esme..." I realized I didn't know Esme's surname. That wouldn't do; I had to make Talia see Esme as a person not a witch, and if there was one thing I knew about Talia, it was that she needed two names for everyone. "...Parker."

Did I really just give a witch my surname? My wolf shifted inside of me, suddenly alert, and for a moment everything froze; an unerring sense washed over me that in naming Esme a Parker, I had just changed the future of our Pack.

Shit!

But without Esme, the bullets would have ripped us to shreds.

"Esme Parker," I repeated, and the world turned again, "saved us. We would all be dead if it wasn't for her."

Talia shook her head, her expression hard and unyielding. "That's irrelevant. As the Wolf Council representative, it's my job to kill the witch. Anyone who stands in my way, their lives will be forfeit, too."

I felt a chill run down my spine at her words. Esme had saved Jase at the lab when Talia abandoned him. She had come here, into a battle between two werewolf Packs, and put her life on the line to protect us all.

"You're not touching her," I said, my voice low and dangerous. "I don't care what the Council says. Esme Parker is a member of the Three Rivers Pack," and there it was again, that sense that I had just changed history, "and you nor any of your meat-head bully-boy enforcers are going to lay a finger on her."

Talia recoiled. "A witch? As a member of a Pack? Are you out of your mind?"

"Her name is Esme Parker, not 'witch.'"

"Am I a werewolf now?" Esme asked behind me. "I've always wanted to be a wolf. She will be beautiful, my wolf, and will soar on the winds."

Amidst all this death and carnage, it was such a lovely image and I almost wished it was true and I could see that.

"And then I'll breathe fire on all my enemies until they are tiny flailing pieces of ash, screaming in pain, lost in the horror of their deaths."

I blinked. *Okay then.*

Talia motioned to her enforcers. They were going to take Esme. Brock's words echoed in my mind, *What's the loss of someone like Amara to a whole Pack? Nothing.*

Only this time, it was Esme. And she was a witch, not even a werewolf that I was protecting. If I stopped Talia, it would mean war with the Wolf Council. That was a battle we were unlikely to win. This is what it meant to be an Alpha. To weigh up one person's life against the rest of the Packs'. To make these decisions over and over. I realized then that they would never stop. And when I started, where was the line? Was one person acceptable to lose if it meant the whole Pack was saved? What about two people? What about five? What if they were children?

It wasn't the Alpha I wanted to be. But I was learning that each situation was different, and it was my job to judge. Talia wanted me to stand aside and let her kill Esme. But that wasn't who I was. Not now, not ever. Nothing, not even a war with the Council, would make me cross that line.

I stared at the enforcers. "You touch her, you die."

The heat of Ryan's body radiated into my back, and I knew he was ready to strike. If he could repeat his true werewolf trick, they were going to be in for one hell of a surprise.

"Well, hello there! You must be Talia Johnson," Sam said jauntily, as he sauntered up to our group. It was a ruse. Sam was getting as close to Talia and the enforcers as he could so that he could attack. That was the danger with Sam. He was all fun-loving and easy-going, but he hid a sharp, calculating mind that was just as ruthless and dangerous as any of his brothers.

"I've heard so much about you," he continued, his voice dripping with charm. "I've got to say I sure am looking forward to working with you."

Talia frowned, her eyes narrowing as she studied Sam. "You are Sam Shaw?"

Sam bowed, his grin widening. "The one and only," he said, his voice filled with confidence, and when he stood up, he moved even closer to Talia. He would attack if we couldn't deescalate this now. "I've been reading up on the Council and what you all expect from your representatives."

"The first thing you will need to learn, Sam Shaw, is when it is appropriate to talk. And now is not the time." Talia held up her hand again, about to motion her enforcers on, when Sam continued.

"Actually, I think now is the time for me to make my first decree as the new Wolf Council representative."

"Your first decree?" Talia frowned, not seeing where he was going with this.

"Yes, I pardon Esme Parker for any use of magic she may or may not have used in the defense of her Pack."

"You can't do that, Sam Shaw," Talia snapped. "You need to be sworn in before you can pardon anyone."

Sam's smile never wavered. "True, but I'll be sworn in soon. And during my research, you know what I found? Turns out there are different factions on the Council, all fighting for what they think is best for Shifters. Maxime Ribet finished her rotation a month ago. She went back to her Pack. But she was a neutral member, wasn't she? She didn't vote with one faction, but weighed up each issue and voted as she saw fit. She held the balance. Now, with me, there's a fresh opportunity to recruit me to one faction and give it ultimate power for the next four years." He paused, letting his words sink in. "Wouldn't it be a good move to have me owe you, Talia? On the other hand, do you really think it would be wise to make an enemy of me today?"

Talia's jaw clenched, and I could see the wheels turning in her head. Finally, she let out a long, slow breath.

"I think I'm beginning to understand why Mai Parker nominated you for the job."

She turned to me, her eyes hard and unforgiving. "Very well, then. Esme Parker is pardoned of all magic use up until," she glanced at her watch, "sixteen hundred hours today. Any more magic, though, even to light a candle, and her life is forfeit, along with any who harbor her."

With that, she turned on her heel and stalked away, her enforcers falling into step behind her.

Sam turned to me, his grin still firmly in place, his eyes twinkling with mischief. "You know, being on the Wolf Council might just be fun after all."

Chapter Forty-Nine

MAI

The familiar scent of coffee and aged wood hit me as I stepped into Bottley Bar. Despite the lingering traces of the fight with Korrin, the place was already starting to feel like home again. The shattered windows had been replaced, the broken glass swept away, but the scars of the fight could still be seen in the splintered tables and torn upholstery.

I let my gaze wander over the people here, my family, my Pack, and my heart swelled with a mixture of pride and sorrow. Ryan stood beside me, his arm draped possessively over my uninjured shoulder, holding me close. Me and my wolf felt calmer, felt safe, when he was touching me, and we hadn't stopped touching each other since we left the forest; it was like we needed to be sure that the other one was still there, still alive.

After we burned the dead bodies and loaded our survivors into cars and vans to take them back to Three Rivers, Ryan and I had gone home to meet Talia and give her a debrief. Talia had been all business, but the more we talked, the more unhappy she became, especially when we told her we thought Brock was right, and he did have someone working for him on the Council. We'd left her behind to make a few phone calls, while we came down here to check on everyone.

They were all here. The Shaw brothers: the twins, Derek and Sam, along with their older brother Mason, were huddled together in a corner, their heads bent close as they spoke in hushed tones. They'd come out of the battle with deep cuts and some impressive bruises, but nothing that wouldn't heal in their next Shift. Sofia was passing round drinks, her fiery curls pulled back into a messy ponytail. I could see the purple shadow of a bruise on her throat, and a bandage wrapped round one thigh. She wasn't limping, though.

Ava was standing by the bar, looking pale and drawn, her arm in a sling. I could smell her grief from here; she had been the closest to Raphael. Evelyn hovered protectively nearby, her dark brown hair plaited down her back. She had a nasty gash above her left eye, but her posture was straight and proud.

Jase was sitting at the bar. He'd found some paper and coloring pens, and him and Ben seemed to be drawing themselves playing some sort of soccer match. Amara kept shooting wary glances at Jase. He was in for a bumpy ride if he ever decided he wanted to date Amara again.

"Fuck off, Jase! I'd win with a header right to the middle of the goal!"

"Stop swearing!" both Jase and Amara said at the same time, and I couldn't help but smile.

Wally, alive but with a broken collarbone, stood next to a protective Thomas, deep in conversation with the remaining Renegades. The group looked battered and weary, but there was an undeniable sense of camaraderie among them. We had gone through the fire together and survived.

Jem was slumped in a corner. He hadn't spoken a word since he killed Brock. Thomas said Jem needed rest, but none of us thought leaving Jem alone right now was a good idea. Close by was Esme. She had declared that as Jem was now her brother, she would be looking after him from now on. I didn't know how to respond to that. I wasn't sure what I had done giving Esme our name, but I couldn't worry about that for now. Today, I just wanted to celebrate that we were alive.

I looked up at Ryan and nodded to his brothers. I knew he wanted to go over there, to make sure they were okay. He needed this. He kissed the end of my nose, his arm tightening for a moment, before letting go and heading for his brothers. I made my way over to Sofia. She was absently running her finger along the edge of her glass, her eyes distant.

"The bar's looking good. We'll get it all fixed up, I promise."

Sofia nodded. "Derek's been helping. He sneaks in during the night. I come down every morning and his scent is everywhere, and more things are fixed." She gestured to the bar, where a section of the countertop had been skillfully mended, the new wood blending seamlessly with the old. "He repaired this where it had been split during the fight. And you see those shelves?" She pointed to the wall behind the bar, where the once-shattered shelves now stood straight and sturdy, the bottles and glasses neatly arranged. "He rebuilt them entirely, even added some extra support to make sure they wouldn't collapse again. It's not just the big things, either. He fixed the hinges on the kitchen door, replaced the broken tiles in the bathroom, even patched up the holes in the drywall. It's like he's determined to erase every trace of the damage, to put everything back the way it was."

"He's doing it for you."

Sofia made a face. "But why?"

"You know why," I said softly.

Sofia shook her head vehemently. "Are you kidding, chickie? Derek blew it. There's no way I'm letting him anywhere near my heart again. Knowing him, he'll just stomp all over it again."

I studied her for a moment, taking in the stubborn set of her jaw and the hurt that lingered in her eyes. "Do you know why he did it the first time?"

Sofia kept her gaze fixed on the contents of her glass. "No, and no matter how many shelves he rebuilds, I have no interest in hearing his excuses."

The door swung open, the bell jingling, and Talia strode in. Conversations died down as all eyes turned to her. She looked around, her gaze assessing, ignored everyone else, and marched over to me. Ryan was by my side before she got there.

"Mai Parker, Ryan Shaw, I have finished my report on the events here. You'll be pleased to hear that our sources confirm that with Brock dead and the ripple lab destroyed, the ripple crisis in the northeast has been shut down, for now," she announced, her voice carrying across the room. "You will still need to ferret out some remaining pockets, but for now, things are looking hopeful."

Ryan smiled down at me, relief on his face. "That we can do. We're getting good at ferreting out secrets."

"Very well. I will be taking Brock's surviving Pack members to Adarcan prison for questioning. We need to find out everything they know about the operation and any other players involved. Especially the witches. The Council's top priority now is to track down the witches involved in this. To that end, I request a meeting with your witch, Esme Parker, to ascertain what she knows."

"A meeting or an interrogation?" I asked.

Talia considered me for a moment. "A meeting. You are welcome to be there as well." The words came out from between her clenched teeth, but I appreciated the gesture. Maybe she had learned from how she had dealt with us before and was trying something new.

I smiled. "Good. I'll ask Esme. If she agrees, then we'll set it up."

"Very well then, I'll return in three days to pick up Sam and have this meeting," she nodded her head at me before I could clarify, "if Esme agrees to it."

Then her gaze fell on Sam. "Sam Shaw, be ready. For you, this is just the beginning. Ripple is still spreading in the rest of the continent; the witches are plotting with people on the Council; Shifters are getting addicted to the drug and breaking their bond with the Packs; and we need to put a stop to it all."

Sam grinned his cheeky grin. "I can't wait, Talia."

Talia nodded, then without another word, she turned on her heel and left; the door closing behind her with a decisive click.

I couldn't say I wasn't happy as fuck to see her go, even if she was going to be back in three days.

As the room began to buzz with conversation once more, I noticed Mason slip outside, his phone pressed to his ear.

Ryan's arms snaked around my waist, pulling me close. His warmth seeped into my skin, and I melted into his embrace, the tension of the past few days slowly ebbing away.

"So, Mai Parker, what adventure would you like to go on tomorrow?" he murmured, his lips brushing against my ear.

I turned in his arms, looping my own around his neck. "Honestly? All I want is a week in bed with you. No interruptions, no crisis, just your naked body doing delicious things to me."

A slow, wicked grin spread across Ryan's face. "I think I can arrange that."

Heat bloomed low in my belly, desire coursing through my veins. My skin tingled with anticipation, and I almost had to bite back a moan. We'd have to have the puppy conversation sooner rather than later, but right now I just wanted to enjoy my mate, to have him entirely focused on me and me alone.

"Ryan!" Mason called, his voice strained and full of fury.

We both turned to look at him. Mason's eyes were wild, his chest heaving as if he'd run a long way.

"It's that fuckhead, Tristan," Mason spat, the name like venom on his tongue. "He used the battle as a distraction to attack the Bridgetown Pack."

My blood ran cold, a sense of dread settling in the pit of my stomach. "What happened?" I asked, almost afraid to hear the answer.

Mason's hands clenched into fists at his sides, his knuckles turning white. "Michael's dead. And Tristan...he's taken Shya."

Sign up to my newsletter at www.kiranightingale.com for a free prequel novella about Derek and Sofia's hot and dangerous first date!

Join Kira's Night Pack Readers Group on Facebook for news and updates, sneak peeks of forthcoming books, fabulous giveaways, and fun games!

COME JOIN US IN THE SHIFTER REALM!

Kira Nightingale
Mystically Dark, Wildly Romantic...

Want a free prequel short story about Derek and Sofia's first date? Sign up to my newsletter and sink your claws into Fairground Fling.

As an author, I write paranormal romance books that are mystically dark and wildly romantic. I send out my newsletter every two weeks, and in it you can get exclusive content and snippets from my current work-in-progress, news about what I am up to, and sometimes even photos of my beast of a cat, Scout. You can sign up to my newsletter at www.kiranightingale.com

Fairground Fling, Shifters of the Three Rivers 0.5

No way will I let fate decide my destiny, but Derek Shaw is back and proving impossible to resist

Sofia

All I wanted was to run my coffee shop in peace, avoid my fated mate, and forget about our Shifter bond. Is that too much to ask for?

Apparently it is, because Derek Shaw just walked back into my life, all rippling muscles and piercing eyes. The man sets my blood on fire, but there's no way I'm giving in. I've seen what happens when "fated mates" are torn apart, and I won't let that happen to me.

Derek left to join the military, turning his back on our bond. Now he's back in the Three Rivers Pack, determined to win me over. But I've built walls around my heart that even an Alpha wolf can't break through. At least, that's what I keep telling myself...

Derek

I left Three Rivers to serve my country, but I never forgot Sofia. Every day, her fiery hair and captivating scent haunted my thoughts.

Now I'm back, and the pull towards Sofia is stronger than ever. My wolf won't rest until I claim what's mine. But Sofia's determined to keep her distance. That's okay, though. I'm a Shaw, and we never back down from a challenge.

THE RESCUED MATE

The Rescued Mate – Book 4 in the Shifters of the Three Rivers series.

He might be my fated mate, but torn between duty and desire, I risk losing everything...

Shya

I thought I knew my path—duty to my Pack, an arranged marriage, and a life free from the complications of love. But fate had other plans.

Mason Shaw stormed into my world, claiming to be my fated mate. His touch ignites a fire I can't ignore, but after being betrayed once, how can I trust my heart again?

Just as I start to question the role my parents had set out for me, my world shatters. Kidnapped, caged and brainwashed I'm trapped in a nightmare of dark magic and deadly secrets. Now, I must fight not only for my freedom but for my very soul.

Mason

From the first moment I saw Shya, I knew she was mine. But she's a Pack princess, promised to another, and convincing her we're meant to be together is a battle I'm barely winning.

When she's ripped from me by my enemy, my world turns red. I'll tear through anyone who stands between us, even if it means going to war with her entire Pack.

Time is running out. With every passing moment, my mate slips further away. I've got one shot to prove I'm worthy of her heart—and I'm not about to waste it.

ABOUT KIRA NIGHTINGALE

Kira Nightingale is a Scot living in Canada. She has always wanted to be a writer, and can't believe how lucky she is to finally be able to write romance stories all day long. She lives with her husband, her two children and a massive cat called Scout. Kira loves to drink tea (her favorite is Long Island Iced Tea, but unfortunately she only gets to drink this occasionally) and likes to dunk cookies in it (yes, even the Long Island kind.)

Acknowledgements

First and foremost, I must thank my PAs, The Nerdy Girls Collective. You're not just wonderful and supportive; you're the unsung heroes of this literary adventure. Without you, I'd probably still be lost in a sea of sticky notes and half-formed ideas. Your patience with my overnight panic emails is nothing short of saintly.

A very special shoutout goes to Bianca Ariel Bunners, who coined Mai's phrase "book TBR drowning is occurring." Bianca, you've perfectly captured the plight of bookworms everywhere. I'm pretty sure my own TBR pile has gained sentience and is plotting world domination.

To Jamie Ty and the fantastic team at 100 Covers: you've worked magic with the cover once again. Thank you for your incredible creativity, patience, and support throughout the process.

Any editing mistakes you find are entirely mine. I'd blame my cat Scout for walking across the keyboard, but he'd get grumpy with me if I did and sulk for three weeks.

To my readers: thank you for picking up this book. I hope it brings you joy, laughter, and maybe a few moments where you forget about the craziness that is the world these days or that mountain of laundry waiting for you. (Reading is more important than folding socks, right?)

Lastly, to tea – my faithful companion through late nights and early mornings. You may not be a person, but you deserve a spot in these acknowledgments. Here's to you, and your magical juice.

Thank you all for being part of this journey.

9 781738 283866